The Deluge Deception

By William Stephens

ISBN

Hardcover: 978-1-967616-37-4

Paperback: 978-1-967616-36-7

Table of Contents

"It is a cosmic joke. Preoccupation with survival has set the stage for extinction."
-John Steinbeck

"Immortality is not a gift; immorality is an achievement; and only those who strive mightily shall possess it."
-Edgar Lee Masters

PART I:
THE BEGINNING

Chapter 1

The girl, small for her sixteen years, stirred from the depths of a disquieting dream. A faint droning sound lingered, like the soft purr of a propeller—familiar, comforting, even. Yes, Grandfather often took her flying in one of his private planes, either from his West Virginia estate or the Malibu house.

Still caught in the hazy grip of sleep, she struggled to regain full consciousness. Where was she? The surface beneath her felt hard—a bench? Darkness pressed around her until a sliver of muted moonlight crept through a foggy automobile window, revealing the truth: she was on the floor in the rear of her grandfather's limo. She'd fallen asleep here many times on long drives, lulled by the car's quiet hum.

The buzzing sound that had roused her grew louder, more insistent. Were they switching from the car to a plane? She couldn't remember why she was in the vehicle at all, and that gnawed at her more than the noise.

Pushing herself up onto her knees, she tried to peer outside, but the glass was slick with condensation from her breath and body heat. Frustrated, she rubbed the window with her sleeve, clearing just enough to see. There—a plane. Its single engine idled smoothly, casting faint shadows in the moonlight. Figures moved around it— dark, indistinct shapes. Three of them dragging a fourth.

The one being pulled stumbled, struggling weakly, like someone drugged or dazed. They were too close to the spinning propeller. Couldn't they see it? Panic surged. She rapped on the window, shouted—but of course, the limo was soundproof. No one could hear her.

Moonlight caught on something glinting—metal, maybe— attached to the struggling figure's arm. A briefcase? Or was it something else entirely?

At that moment, the three men gave the fourth a hard shove. His head collided with the spinning propeller, a sickening sound slicing through the night. Blood sprayed in a fine mist, and the metal case—flew high into the air, landing with a dull thud just outside her car window.

A scream pierced the darkness, raw and chilling, the most terrifying sound she had ever heard—until she realized it was coming from her own throat.

The three shadowy figures turned, their heads snapping toward the car. They were coming for her. She could hear the crunch of their footsteps on gravel, growing louder with each step. They're going to kill me. They're going to push me into that propeller next.

Heart racing, she dropped to the floor of the limo, yanking the quilted comforter over her head, cocooning herself in trembling fear. She clenched her eyes shut, waiting for the door to rip open, for rough hands to drag her out, for the nightmare to end in blood and blades.

But instead—movement. The limo lurched forward. She wasn't dead. Not yet.

She couldn't tell who was driving. The privacy partition was raised, sealing off the front seat, leaving her alone in a prison of silence and darkness. The car sped on, the hum of the engine masking the sound of her ragged breathing. Her heart pounded in her chest, loud enough she was sure it could be heard. Her arms wrapped tightly around her knees as her body trembled uncontrollably.

Time blurred. Minutes, hours—she didn't know. Eventually, exhaustion won and blessed unconsciousness crept in, pulling her under like a merciful tide.

When she awoke, warm light filtered through the heavy curtains. She was in her own bed, wrapped in familiar sheets, the faint scent of lavender lingering in the air. Her grandfather sat beside her, his face pale but composed. Kathy, her nurse, hovered nearby, her worried eyes softening with relief.

"Granddad… oh, Granddad—" Sheela burst into sobs, her voice trembling. "It was awful… awful. The poor man… What happened? Why—why?"

Her grandfather and Kathy both stood at once. The old man leaned closer, his hand gently brushing a strand of hair from her face.

"Sheela," he whispered with a heavy sigh, his voice thick with emotion. "It's so good you're back with us. You've been asleep for two days. The doctors were here. You had a seizure."

"Granddad, I was asleep, but I woke up… I heard an airplane. There were men—they threw someone into the spinning propeller! They killed him!" Sheela's voice trembled, her words spilling out in gasps. "I thought they'd kill me next, but instead… I was in the car, on a long—long drive. I don't remember anything after that."

Her grandfather's face froze, stunned for a fleeting moment. Then, slowly, a broad smile stretched across his features—the same warm, reassuring smile that had always made her feel safe since she was a child.

"So that was it," he said softly, releasing a long sigh of relief. "The doctors mentioned you might've had a nightmare that triggered the seizure, leading to temporary confusion."

"No, no—it wasn't a nightmare. It was real. The long car ride…"

"Yes, there was a long ride. In our limo," he interrupted gently. "You remember Hubert, our driver? He was taking us back from Washington after we saw *The Lion King* again for your sixteenth birthday—your favorite musical, remember? You slept the whole way home. But when we arrived, we couldn't wake you. We called the doctor right away. He said the seizure might have been a result of the new insomnia medication he prescribed. Believe me, you won't be taking that again."

"But, Granddad… it was real. I know it was real."

"My little darling Sheela," he whispered, his voice soft with affection. He took her small hand in his, giving it a gentle squeeze, then shook his head sadly. "Look there." He pointed toward the large window beside her bed. "There's the limo we drove to Washington and back. I promise you; we returned promptly because you were sleeping so soundly, we were worried. You must understand—it was just a nightmare, brought on by the medication."

Sheela's gaze drifted to the window. The sight of the familiar black limo parked in the driveway stirred something inside her—a fragile thread of comfort tugging at the edges of her fear. She took a deep breath, the air quivering through her slender frame, sending chills cascading down to her core.

"Really, Granddad?" she whispered, tears still clinging to her lashes as she wiped them from her cheeks.

"Really, Sheela," her grandfather replied with a soft grin. "Now get some more sleep, my darling. The doctor said you might feel like getting up and moving around, but what you actually need is quiet— and plenty of rest."

A wave of relief washed over her, warm and soothing. No one was after her. No one was going to kill or kidnap her, despite the warnings Grandfather often gave about the dangers that careless, wealthy children could face. It had only been a nightmare.

Good old Granddad.

Sheela felt the pull of sleep creeping in again, heavy and irresistible. She snuggled deeper beneath the down comforter, its warmth wrapping around her like a protective.

When she awoke again, her dreams had been restless, fleeting shadows she couldn't quite remember. Silence blanketed the room— thick and absolute. Not a single floorboard creaked in the vast, old mansion, the house she'd known longer than any other. Her earliest memories were carved into these walls. But now, something felt wrong, faint sounds coming from outside.

Moonlight crept in through the tall windows, casting ghostly patterns across the floor. It glinted faintly against the glass, stirring echoes of earlier terror. Sheela froze, her heart quickening.

Then—another sound from outside the house. Faint, but distinct. The muffled slam of a car door—or maybe the trunk—being closed. Sheela's breath hitched. Slowly, she pushed herself up on trembling elbows, straining to see through the glass.

There—moving through the moon lit shadows was Hubert. The family driver. He was walking away from the limo, his steps measured, deliberate. In his hand, glinting under the pale moonlight, was a metal case… with a chain trailing behind it.

Sheela's heart fluttered against her ribs. She grabbed her pillow, shoving it into her mouth to stifle a scream clawing its way up her throat and reducing it to a fragile, trembling whimper.

Chapter 2

Like most LA kids, Hudson Halle thought his childhood was pretty much perfect—except for one thing: his parents had split up when he was too young to remember. For reasons he never quite understood, his grandmother, who raised him, believed it was perfectly "safe" for him to roam the city as long as he was with his friends. Hitching rides to Dodger games, exploring LACMA, wandering through La Brea, and soaking in the chaos of Hollywood's Sunset Strip were some of their favorite adventures. After all, hadn't GG given him a cell phone for his eighteenth birthday? He could always call home if he needed to.

Hud and his crew had recently stumbled upon Rindge Dam, hidden deep in Malibu Canyon on the way to the beach. Rock diving became their latest obsession—a thrill so intense it felt like flying, with the reservoir far below, rushing up so fast. But that rush came with risks. One wrong step could be your last.

And for one of them, it was.

On a clear July afternoon, under a sky too blue to foreshadow tragedy, one of their friends slipped from a forty-foot crag to his death. The fall was quick. The aftermath, unbearable. The next day, without saying much to anyone except his grandmother, Hudson walked into a recruitment office and enlisted in the Air Force. He didn't even bother finishing high school.

Chapter 3

It all began quietly enough on a mid-summer day, beside a winding nature trail in the serene Santa Monica Mountains. Hud had always loved these hills, having hiked their rugged paths countless times. He knew the scent of wild sage and anise carried on spring breezes, the rustle of oak leaves stirred by a gentle wind, and the distant calls of unseen birds hidden in the canopy.

Raccoons, skunks, deer, and coyotes roamed these hills, their tracks etched into dusty trails. Even mountain lions—silent, graceful, and deadly—padded through the chaparral, ghosts among the oaks.

Today, Hud was hunting one of them.

Not with a rifle, though. He wasn't that kind of hunter. His method was a camera, his prize a perfect shot—a frozen moment of wild grace captured for posterity. The California State Parks Bureau considered Hudson one of the best wildlife photographers they had commissioned.

The cougar he tracked was new to the area, a ghost with no name, no collar, and no human record—until today.

Hud had discovered his passion for photography while serving in the U.S. Air Force, two decades after the Berlin Wall crumbled into history. He spent a year in intensive, clandestine photography training—learning the art of capturing images not for esthetics, but for information, for secrets. Eventually, he was stationed in the Middle East, assigned to a reconnaissance unit where his job was to secure, position, and operate high-definition cameras for photo and video intelligence gathering.

Covert camerawork was thrilling, filled with quiet tension and hidden stories. But when his enlistment ended, Hud didn't hesitate to trade espionage for something far more personal. On the very day of their discharge, he and his partner—both in the field and in life—Nicole Richter, were married in a modest chapel on Keesler Air Force Base in Mississippi.

Nicole had a dream: to become a wilderness photographer in the great American West, crafting breathtaking photo albums in the spirit of Ansel Adams. Hud had a dream too—to follow Nicole wherever she went.

Nicole kept her dark hair short and straight, practical for the rugged terrain they explored. She often wore her old Air Force fatigues, finding them perfect for the wild places they roamed—from the icy expanse of Alaska to the tangled wetlands of the Everglades, and nearly every untamed stretch of land in between. She wasn't conventionally beautiful, but her slim build, infectious enthusiasm, and sharp sense of humor made her unforgettable to all who met her. Hud and Nicole laughed together almost every day, their bond woven from shared adventures and quiet moments under open skies.

They worked as contract photographers, taking on any job that paid the bills. No project was too small if it meant earning enough to fund another year chasing their true passion: nature photography. Their contract-work often took them to Las Vegas, installing security cameras in sprawling casinos—a job that paid well but never captured their hearts.

Hud was drawn to wildlife, fascinated by the raw, untamed energy of animals in their natural habitats. Nicole, on the other hand, was enchanted by grand vistas—deep gorges, towering mountains, and lush landscapes brimming with life, from dense rainforests to sun-scorched deserts dotted with resilient cacti.

Together, they built a life stitched together by wanderlust, creativity, and the simple joy of seeing the world through each other's eyes.

Nicole had been born and raised in Long Beach, where the bustling Port of Los Angeles and the Port of Long Beach sit side by side along the edge of San Pedro Bay. Together, they form the largest shipping hub in America—a place of constant motion, industry, and noise. But beneath the economic powerhouse was an invisible threat. The relentless diesel exhaust from cargo ships, trucks, rail yards, and endless freeway traffic seeped into the air, wreaking havoc on Nicole's fragile lungs.

She developed asthma as a child, a secret she guarded fiercely. When it came time for her Air Force enlistment physical, she hid her inhaler tucked inside her bra, determined not to let her condition define her future. But the skies weren't as forgiving. Long photo flights with Hud, breathing recycled airplane air, slowly wore her down.

Nicole passed away on a cold winter's day in a shabby hotel room in the Yukon, her body unable to fight off a relentless COPD attack. Hud was there, the only one there, clutching her fevered hands, his tears falling onto the thin, scratchy blanket that covered her fragile frame. No doctors. No help. Just him—and the unbearable silence that followed her last breath.

When Nicole died, something inside Hud broke too. It wasn't just grief; it was as if the very compass that guided his life had vanished. To numb the ache, he turned to self-medication, seeking refuge in the writings of Carlos Castaneda. Inspired—or perhaps cursed—by those teachings, Hud found solace in the deserts that sprawled south and east of Southern California. There, he harvested Jimson weed and peyote, letting the hallucinogenic substances blur the sharp edges of his grief.

When the darkness grew heavier, when it wrapped around his throat like a noose, he added San Pedro cactus and strains of Godfather OG to the mix. These plants he cultivated in a small backyard plot behind the tiny bungalow his grandmother had left him in the San Fernando Valley.

Homemade brownies became his preferred method of ingestion, Hud made pastries borrowed from internet searches. His latest batch was laced with mushrooms he'd found and dried during a photography trip to the Redwoods National Park. The hallucinogenic fungi, combined with hours of old noir films he watched on a loop, created brief sanctuaries from the crushing weight of Nicole's absence.

In the flickering black-and-white glow of those forgotten films, among long-dead actors reciting lines from a distant past, Hud found the only company that kept him from walking into the ocean, like some tragic character in a story that no one would ever read.

Chapter 4

After setting up motion sensing cameras along rugged trails and fastening them to tree trunks where park rangers had spotted fresh cougar spoor, Hud sank into the familiar weariness of a long day's work. With the equipment packed away and the sun dipping low behind the Santa Monica Mountains, he rewarded himself with a batch of his homemade brownies. The bittersweet taste lingered as he washed it down with stale wine from a battered plastic bottle.

Stretching out on a soft mat of moss, Hud's body relaxed, his mind teetering on the edge of sleep when something flickered at the corner of his vision—a glint, sharp and out of place against the earthy greens and browns of the woodland.

A sliver of gossamer fabric.

His eyes tracked upward, drawn to the ethereal outline of what appeared to be a woman. She stood—or floated—just beyond the trees, her short, dark auburn hair reaching to just below her ears. The color was almost identical to Nicole's, glinting faintly in the waning light. The figure hovered inches above the ground, slowly rotating, with movement unnervingly fluid.

As she turned to face him, the illusion morphed into the surreal. Where he expected to see a face—Nicole's face, it wasn't human at all. Staring back at him were cold, gray-brown eyes, dark and unblinking like polished stones. The woman's features dissolved into something reptilian, scales glinting faintly under the moonlight. A lizard's face, with beady black eyes and flickering, forked tongue that darted in and out, and with a hiss, the creature whispered; "Watch for me."

Hud lay rigid, his breath shallow, heart racing as if gripped by invisible hands. He was there for several minutes after the figure vanished, staring at the canopy above, listening to the distant rustle of leaves.

"I really need to cut back on the psychedelics," he thought, running a shaky hand through his hair. But deep down, he knew it wasn't just the drugs.

Nicole had never really left him. She was stitched into his very existence, the threads woven too tightly to ever be undone. No matter how much he tried to outrun her shadow, it would always there—waiting for him.

Finally, feeling the weight of the moment abate, Hud fumbled for the car key tucked in the pocket of his windbreaker. Climbing into his faded Pathfinder, the familiar rattle of the old engine oddly comforted, as he navigated the winding roads down the mountain.

Still the vision lingered, and the lizard's piercing stare carved into the edges of his mind, its cryptic words echoing louder than the hum of his tires on the asphalt.

"Watch for me."

"It had to be the brownies," Hud thought to himself, gripping the steering wheel tighter, forcing the image to dissolve into the darkness beyond the headlights.

As Hud's worn SUV rumbled into his carport, the neighbor's dogs erupted into a chorus of yips and barks, their enthusiasm piercing the evening air. However, Hud's mood remained heavy, untouched by the familiar sounds. Lethargy weighed down his limbs as he shuffled inside, the stale air of his small bungalow greeting him like an unwelcome guest.

He opened the fridge, staring blankly at its sparse contents, but the thought of food turned his stomach. With a weary sigh, he trudged to the bathroom. The faded mirror above the sink reflected a face he barely recognized—haunted eyes, hollowed cheeks, a shadow of the man he once was. His reflection blurred as tears welled up, spilling over without warning, his body trembling with silent sobs.

Eventually, gathering what little strength he could muster, Hud stumbled into the shower. The warm spray cascaded over him, loosening the tightness in his chest, the steady rhythm of the water lulling him into drowsiness. By the time he turned off the water and toweled off, his legs felt like lead. He barely managed to stagger to his unmade bed before collapsing, and surrendering to a sleep too deep for dreams.

The sharp chime of the doorbell jolted him awake. His heart raced for a brief moment, disoriented by the sudden noise. Stretching out his stiff limbs, he felt the tension in his back and legs ease, replaced by an unexpected sense of renewal. The oppressive weight he'd carried earlier seemed to have lifted completely.

Leaning his head out of the bedroom doorway, he called. "Be there in a couple of minutes."

Pulling on a pair of faded but clean Levi's and a worn Dodgers T-shirt, Hud realized with a sudden pang that he was starving. However, before he could even think about food, the doorbell rang again—this time more insistent, accompanied by another round of barking from the neighbor's dogs. Pausing by the bathroom mirror, Hud ran a quick brush through his rumpled hair before opening the front door wide. He had been expecting a delivery or maybe a neighbor. Instead, he found a woman standing alone on the small concrete porch. She was somewhat frail, but presented herself with the deliberate polish of someone aware of good grooming, and did not seem indifferent to her appearance.

She was attractive, Hud thought, but not in the way that demanded notice. Her eyes caught him first—large, round, and an extraordinary shade of green, framed by long dark lashes that contrasted beautifully with her light blonde hair. It wasn't the bright, artificial blonde of salon treatments, but something more natural, like the pale hair and fair skin of the Circassian women Hud had seen during his time in Turkey and the Levant.

There was something about her—familiar yet foreign—that made Hud forget the heaviness that had been his recent companion. She held a clipboard in one hand and an envelope for donations in the other. Her green jacket, nearly the same shade as her striking eyes, bore a small emblem over her heart, a simple sketch of a whale mid-breach.

Cute, Hud thought absently. She looked to be at least ten years younger than his own age which was approaching forty.

"I'm collecting signatures and donations for the Coast Conservation Corps—the CCC, Mr. Turner," she said, her voice light, with the faintest trace of a Midwestern accent. "We're a tax-deductible nonprofit. The signatures are for a ballot measure our organization is proposing to double the size of the state's marine protected areas. Any donation would help."

Hud blinked, caught off guard. "You must have the wrong house. There's no one named Turner here."

A blush crept across her cheeks as she took a small step back, her finger pointing toward his chest. Hud glanced down—and immediately understood. In his hurry, he'd pulled his Dodgers T-shirt on backwards, with the name "TURNER" now written in bold letters across his chest.

"Oh," he chuckled, shaking his head. "I wish! Justin Turner was a Dodgers third baseman back in the day. Guess I put my shirt on backwards."

Her embarrassment vanished in an instant, replaced by laughter that was light and musical, like wind chimes stirred by a gentle breeze.

Hud had encountered plenty of solicitors before, though these days, they mostly came in the form of texts or emails. He was a sucker for nature causes, sure—but wary when it came to donations. A few years back, he'd been scammed out of five hundred bucks by a fake environmental group, and he'd never forgotten the sting. Since then, he preferred giving cash or signing petitions if the cause felt genuine.

The Coast Conservation Corps was new to him. Still, he wouldn't have minded chatting her up if it weren't for the gnawing hunger in his gut.

"I was just about to head out for some breakfast," Hud hesitated, torn between his empty stomach and curiosity. "But I'd like to hear more. Could you come back?"

She tilted her head slightly, strands of blonde hair falling across her face as she scribbled something on her clipboard. "Well, perhaps. When would be a good time?"

Her smile lingered, warm and unforced, like the sun breaking through a cloudy sky.

Not wanting to miss an opportunity—or put her off—Hud decided to take a chance. She seemed friendly enough.

"Name's Hudson Halle," he blurted, the words tumbling out before he could catch them. "Maybe we could grab a bite together?" He had no idea where the invite had come from—or where it was headed. Stumbling to fill the silence, he added, "There's a little place I like down on Ventura Boulevard. Ci Ci's. Great breakfast. My treat. And I can hear more about your fundraiser and petition."

She hesitated, the clipboard shifting slightly in her hands. "Lillian Baker," she replied after a pause. "Well... I did leave the house without eating. But I'll go—if I can pay my own way. Do they have good coffee?"

"The best," Hud grinned. "Let me just throw on some boots and change my shirt."

After again running a brush through his hair and a quickly rinsing with mouthwash, he was back outside. Lillian stood waiting, her posture relaxed, her earlier hesitation replaced by an easy smile.

As they walked toward his car, she explained, "I'm part of a team canvassing the neighborhood for signatures and donations. I barely made it out of bed this morning—woken up by the car horn of one of the drivers and didn't even have time to grab a couple of crackers." She sighed, shaking her head.

"Take my car?" Hud offered, unlocking the door with a quick flick of his keys.

"Okay, let me just let my team know," she replied, glancing down the street. "Actually, I only live about two miles from here. Think you could drop me off after?"

"Of course."

She jogged across the street, toward an older couple in green jackets matching hers. They were descending the steps of a nearby bungalow. After a brief conversation, punctuated by occasional glances back at Hud, she returned, her smile wide.

"All set," she said, revealing small, even, and startlingly white teeth. "They just wanted to make sure you weren't some kind of creep."

Hud chuckled. "I get it. I'll pull up so they can jot down my license plate if that helps."

She waved it off. "No, it's cool. They've already noticed your house and address. Besides," she added with a playful grin, "I can tell you're not one of the creepy ones."

Hud smiled back, sliding into the driver's seat, feeling lighter than he had in a long time.

As it turned out, they were both famished. What began with a modest order of French toast quickly escalated into plates of scrambled eggs, crispy bacon, and, finally, steaming mugs of coffee accompanied by warm, crumbly muffins. By the time Hud pushed his plate away, and feeling satisfyingly full, Lillian was still diligently mopping up the last bit of egg yolk with a corner of toast.

"I'm sorry," she said, laughing softly and setting her fork down. "It was all so good. I didn't realize how hungry I was." She reached for her purse, fumbling slightly. "How much is my half?"

Hud shook his head, a small grin tugging at the corner of his mouth. "No thanks. This one's on me."

With the urgency of hunger behind them, their conversation settled into an easy rhythm as they lingered over their coffee. They started with small talk—shared frustrations about environmental issues, the absurdity of single-use plastics, and their mutual love for the outdoors. Hud spoke about his most recent contract, explaining how he'd been placing trail cameras to track an elusive cougar deep in the Santa Monica Mountains.

Lillian listened with genuine interest, leaning in slightly as she asked thoughtful questions about his photography background. She shared her own experiences, explaining how she volunteered with

Channel Islands National Park—conducting fish and whale counts, monitoring the delicate ecosystems of kelp forests, and leading both nature and historical hikes. She also served as a docent on whale-watching excursions, her face lighting up as she described spotting a breaching humpback for the first time.

"Have you ever read *Island of the Blue Dolphins*?" she asked, her fingers tracing the rim of her coffee cup.

Hud shook his head. "Can't say I recall."

"It's about a Native American woman stranded on San Nicolas Island—one of the Channel Islands—living alone for years," Lillian explained. "There are a couple of legends about how she ended up there. One version says Spanish soldiers were removing the last of her tribe when a sudden storm forced their ship to leave without her. Another story claims she was already on board when she realized her child had been left behind. She jumped overboard and swam ashore, but by the time she got back, wild dogs had killed him. The ship had sailed without her."

Hud's gaze drifted to the window, the morning light casting soft shadows across the table. The story lingered between them, heavy and haunting, a distant echo of loss. "That's... heartbreaking," he murmured, his mind briefly flickering to Nicole, and the ache that never really faded.

Chapter 5

Lillian paused to take a sip of her coffee, her fingers cradling the warm mug. "Am I boring you?" she asked, a playful glint in her eyes.

"Not a bit. Please, continue," Hud replied, signaling the waitress for another refill. The rich aroma of fresh coffee drifted between them as he settled back into his seat.

As she spoke, Hud remembered having read *Island of the Blue Dolphins* years ago, maybe in Junior High, but he listened to Lillian without interruption, captivated—not just by the story but by the soft cadence of her voice and her expressive face, her brow knitting with emotion as she recounted the woman's lonely struggle for survival. It wasn't just the tale she told; it was the way she told it, with a warmth and depth that drew him in.

Finding himself genuinely impressed, "You've been trained well by the CCC," he said, in sincere admiration. "Your organization keeps you really well-informed."

Lillian smiled modestly. "That's not just CCC knowledge. I'm also a docent on a whale-watching boat twice a month. You wouldn't believe some of the questions people ask. I stay prepared with real stories about the Channel Islands—just in case I get stumped by a tourist's question, like how many years do whales live."

Before Hud could respond, the waiter approached, his polite smile hinting that their time at the table was up. A line had formed near the entrance, where eager patrons waited for an empty table. Hud quickly grabbed the check.

"I've got to go on one of your tours," he promised, standing up and slipping his wallet back into his pocket. "I've learned more in an hour sitting with you than from all my reading and trips to the Channel Islands National Park over the years."

As they strolled back to his Pathfinder, the conversation felt lighter, filled with comfortable pauses that didn't need to be filled.

Hud hesitated for a beat, then asked, "Maybe we could grab coffee again sometime soon?"

"Sure, I'd like that," Lillian replied, her smile genuine, her enthusiasm just the right mix of warmth and ease. They exchanged cell numbers, the simple act feeling oddly significant.

On the drive home, Hud found his thoughts drifting—not to the strange vision of the lizard in the woods, which now felt like a distant fading dream—but to Lillian. The memory of her laughter, and the way her eyes lit up when she spoke about the ocean, lingered in his mind.

For the first time in months, he'd connected with someone real—not a phantom conjured from grief and the haze of psychedelics. Maybe, just maybe, he wouldn't need to chase shadows anymore. Perhaps the prison of loneliness he'd built around himself was starting to crack with the gentle presence of someone new.

Later that day, Hud found himself dialing Lillian's number, more out of curiosity than anything else. He wanted to see if she'd given him her real number—because, let's face it, people had a way of handing out fake phone numbers when they really weren't interested. But before the first ring had even finished, she picked up.

"It's Hud," he said, a little caught off guard. "Just calling to say I had a really nice time."

"Oh, hi! I was just thinking about you," Lillian replied, her voice bright and easy. "Actually, our CCC meeting is tonight. I texted you earlier but hadn't heard back. I'm leaving in about an hour and wondering if you'd like to come along? It's about two hours long, and afterward, maybe we could do something."

Hud grinned, trying to keep his cool. "Sure, I remember—when I met you, it was the… uh, Civilian Coast Corps, right?"

She laughed. "Coast Conservation Corps. That's us. Would you like to come as my guest?"

"Of course. Is it okay if I come by and pick you up?"

"I was going to bum a ride with LJ, but okay—be here by six."

Hud could barely contain his enthusiasm as he hung up. His heart raced with the kind of excitement he hadn't felt in ages. He hopped into the shower, gave himself a clean shave, and topped it off with a couple of sprays of Old Spice, and his favorite Pendleton shirt. He was good to go.

When he arrived at her place, Lillian welcomed him into a small but cozy living room. The furniture was simple, probably from consignment shops, Hud guessed, but arranged with a kind of effortless style. Nature was everywhere—in the fixtures, the colors, the art. Seashell-shaped lamps glowed softly, and a fossilized shark's tooth rested on an antique desk. Pop Art posters brightened the walls, adding a playful, eclectic vibe that seemed uniquely her.

Having arrived a little early, Hud found Lillian in an apron, her hair loosely tied back. She flashed him an easy smile. "Give me a few minutes to change and spruce up," she said, heading toward the hallway. Then she paused, glancing back over her shoulder. "Beer while you wait?"

Why not Hud chuckled, feeling completely at ease. "I'd love one."

Giving a thumb-up, Lillian motioned toward a faded, overstuffed armchair that looked as inviting as it was worn, and then disappeared into a tiny adjoining kitchen. Moments later, she returned, balancing a tray containing a brown bottle of beer and a glass.

Hud examined the bottle, raising it to the light. The label bore the image of a grinning skeleton.

"Poison?" he joked, arching an eyebrow.

"My poison," she chuckled, setting the tray down. "Dead Guy Ale. It's a craft beer from Oregon. Try it—you'll like it."

With that, she breezed out of the room, leaving Hud to himself. The cozy space felt lived-in, filled with little details that hinted at her personality. On the coffee table lay a scattering of CCC newsletters. Hud picked one up, flipping through the pages as he took a sip of the beer.

"Damn good beer," he thought, surprised by the rich, malty flavor.

The newsletters were filled with articles about sea otters, sprawling kelp forests, and efforts to restore fragile abalone beds around the Santa Barbara Channel. Other sections highlighted volunteer opportunities for coastal reclamation projects, urging readers to get involved in preserving Southern California's natural beauty.

Just as Hud was getting lost in an article about kelp restoration, Lillian reemerged—and the transformation was striking.

Her silky blonde hair was now styled with delicate curls that framed her face perfectly. A subtle touch of mascara accentuated her expressive eyes, making their green hue seem even more vivid. She wore dark stockings that complemented a knee-length, gathered skirt, the fabric swaying gently as she moved. The outfit revealed just enough to suggest the graceful lines of a slim, well-rounded figure—elegant without trying too hard.

Hud set the newsletter down, caught somewhere between admiration and awe. "Well," he said, rising to his feet with a grin, "you clean up nice."

Lillian smiled, grabbing her bag. "Glad you think so. Ready?"

Hud nodded, feeling like the evening had just taken a turn for the better.

Chapter 6

The meeting was held in a modest single-family home, one of thousands lining both sides of the streets branching off the Ventura Boulevard corridor, built in the post-World War II boom. Back then, the neighborhoods had a predictable demographic—three kids to every household, owners predominantly white, with a sprinkling of Asian and second or third-generation Hispanic families. Black families had been deliberately excluded through restrictive covenants, a harsh reality of that era's discriminatory housing practices.

But times had changed the neighborhood dramatically. Now, it was more like three kids to an entire block, representing a vibrant mix of cultures and backgrounds. Some of the original homeowners still clung to their aging properties, their houses and patchy lawns standing as the last remnants of their past prosperity. Many elderly residents stretched their social security checks thin, shopping for essentials at 99-Cent stores and local Goodwill retail outlets scattered throughout the Valley.

The media loved to brand California as a "failed state," blaming everything from liberal politicians, high taxes, and gas prices to crime, homelessness, and progressive movements like LGBTQ rights, Black Lives Matter, and Antifa. States like Texas and Florida were hailed as the new promised lands for raising a family, with their media proclaiming the so-called "mass exodus" from the Golden State.

But was that really the whole story? Sure, many middle-class families—teachers, police officers, firefighters, and civil servants—had packed up and left. Yet, California's roots ran deeper than political soundbites. It wasn't built by failed farmers or settlers seeking stability. This was a land shaped by dreamers and risk-takers, from the gold rush to the real estate boom. People didn't come here to settle—they came here to chase something bigger.

The aging, retiring middle class soon realized their modest, well-worn homes were gold mines—worth anywhere from half a million to over a million dollars, depending on the neighborhood. In other states, post-war property appreciation hadn't been nearly as generous. And so, the gold rush reversed itself. Californians packed up, sold their homes, and moved to states where housing was considerably less expensive, armed with enough cash to buy a nicer house in a newer neighborhood, and still have plenty left over for retirement travel and adventure.

Were they welcomed with open arms? Not exactly.

Signs like "Don't Californicate Oregon!" started popping up on state borders, a not-so-subtle message that these new fortune seekers weren't exactly beloved. Their arrival stirred resentment, much like the disdain the old Hispanic rancho owners had felt toward the forty-niners during the original gold rush. History had a funny way of repeating itself—just with new characters.

But Californians adapted, like any determined transplant. They learned to blend in, re-registering their vehicles in their new states even before moving to them, hoping to dodge the hard stares of suspicious neighbors and avoid unnecessary attention from state troopers, who seemed particularly observant of "Californicators, when issuing traffic citations."

When Hud and Lillian pulled up to the house hosting the CCC meeting, it stood out from the other aging homes of the San Fernando Valley. It had a distinct California Spanish design—nothing grand, maybe 1,500 square feet of living space—but it was well cared for. The white stucco exterior was clean, unlike many of the neighboring homes that were begging for a fresh coat of paint. The lawn was a lush, vibrant green, clearly well-watered despite California's relentless droughts.

Lemon trees heavy with bright yellow fruit flanked one side of a neatly bricked driveway, while an eight-foot plumeria with stunning white-and-yellow blossoms stood proudly beside an arched entryway, its fragrance sweet and welcoming.

It wasn't just a house. It was someone's pride, standing resilient in a neighborhood slowly fading around it.

"This is the abode of Jerry Varene, our fearless leader and resident lawyer—just in case we ever need one," Lillian said with a grin as they pulled up to the neatly kept house. "He's single but has a boarder, Kestrel Alan, who's also a CCC member."

Hud, unable to resist asked; "Who names their kid after a small, insect-eating falcon?" The words slipped out louder than he intended.

Lillian burst into laughter. "Kestrel is a real trip. But you'll find that out for yourself soon enough."

She rang the doorbell but didn't wait for an answer, pushing the door open with casual familiarity. Inside, they stepped into a living room that was an eclectic mix of organized chaos. Bookshelves lined the walls, packed mostly with hefty law books, sprinkled with titles about environmental policy and activism. CDs and DVDs were wedged between volumes, held up by quirky bookends shaped like miniature mountain peaks. Random bric-a-brac dotted the shelves— a mix of what Hud mentally labeled bachelor clutter.

Still, it wasn't a man-cave. The space had an air of intentionality. The walls bore framed paintings and prints, alongside neatly hung diplomas and award certificates from environmental groups like the State Parks Bureau, Save the Wild Horses, and bold declarations like "No! To Yucca Mountain." Hud couldn't help but note the contrast to his own more, let's say, relaxed approach to interior design. Jerry Varene was clearly a man who liked things in order—at least more so than Hud did.

The living room opened into a dining area where several people stood gathered around a large oak table. Plates of cookies, clusters of grapes, crackers, olives, and neatly sliced cheeses were spread out like an offering to keep activism fueled. In the corner, coffee and tea steamed gently in pots perched on a white enamel stove. An assortment of vintage mugs—representing both active and lost causes—sat nearby, flanked by an unexpectedly fancy cut-glass cream and sugar set resting on the tiled edge of the sink.

As soon as Lillian and Hud stepped into the room, the conversation lulled for a beat. Heads turned, and a ripple of friendly greetings followed. Men and women, about even in number, waved or nodded, their smiles genuine—activist hospitality at its finest.

A tall, extremely lanky man with pale, thinning hair strolled over, his easy gait matched by a relaxed smile. He gave Lillian a brief, familiar hug before turning his attention to Hud. With long, slim fingers, he grasped Hud's right elbow in a light, almost delicate motion.

"Jerry Varene," he introduced himself, his voice carrying the smooth cadence of someone used to holding attention. Then, with a quick pivot toward the room, he announced, "Everyone, this is Hudson—friend of Lillian." His tone carried an undercurrent of curiosity, as if he was already sizing Hud up for potential recruitment.

Apparently, Lillian had given Jerry a heads-up via text before they arrived, hinting that Hud might be the kind of guy who could be persuaded to join the cause.

Hud did the polite rounds, exchanging obligatory handshakes when offered and enduring a few friendly embraces. Truth be told, he wasn't much for hugging strangers. The whole "let's-clinch-like-we've-known-each-other-for-years" thing wasn't really his style, but he managed to smile through it.

When someone asked about his interest in the group, Hud kept it brief—mentioning his field photography work with the State Parks and the environmental causes he'd supported as a donor. It seemed to strike the right chord because a few members sidled up, eager to swap stories about their own activism. Conversations flowed easily, comparing notes about past projects and shared connections, even if most of the names or events were unfamiliar.

The casual mingling went on for about an hour, filled with snippets of conversation, laughter, and the occasional clink of cups. Eventually, Jerry gave a little tinkle on a glass with a teaspoon, an old-school move to garner attention. Those present began milling toward a cozy adjoining family room, bringing along chairs from the dining area. A scruffy leather sofa sat near a large, well-worn ottoman, surrounded by mismatched seating that gave the room a lived-in charm.

Some people settled into seats while others opted to stand in the back, still clutching plates of snacks or half-empty cups. The room gradually quieted as Jerry strolled to the front, clearing his throat with a mix of authority and ease.

"Looks like most everyone's here tonight," he said, his sharp eyes sweeping the room carried a hint of mischief. "Kestrel's still upstairs but should be joining us soon. Though his usual tardiness is duly noted."

A ripple of laughter followed, the kind that comes from inside jokes and familiar routines. Hud found himself smiling too, feeling less like an outsider and more like someone who might just fit in.

At that moment, a stout young man with broad, muscular shoulders hurried into the room. His coal-black hair was slicked back from a swarthy forehead, and tied into a perfect ponytail that hung halfway down his back. Eyes glued to the cell phone clutched in his hand, he announced confidently, "Precisely on time," which was met with an immediate chorus of playful hisses and scoffs from the group.

Unfazed, he squeezed himself between two women on the scruffy leather sofa. The two were clearly close friends judging from their conversation. They responded to his intrusion with good-natured kidding, one of them even cuddling up to him in mock flirtation.

Jerry cleared his throat and rolling his eyes in exaggerated exasperation. "Will everyone please come to order! And that includes you, Mr. Alan," he added with mock sternness, earning another round of amusement.

The meeting officially kicked off with the reading of the minutes, followed by a brief rundown of old and new business. Hud tried to keep up, though the details were vague and the pace quick. A woman, Lillian identified as Lady Jane stood up next. With an air of practiced efficiency, she read a report detailing the funds and signatures collected during their latest neighborhood fundraising campaign—an impressive haul of around six thousand dollars.

The money, she explained, was earmarked to support Jerry's lawsuit against "unnamed conspirators," a phrase that made Hud's skepticism spike. The more he listened, the more the CCC began to feel like a potential scam. A slick operation run by a charming, fast-talking attorney using passionate environmentalists to line his pockets. Maybe this was just another grift, Hud thought, a way to separate well-meaning Greenies from their savings.

Before he could dwell on the thought, a frail young blonde woman with lime-green hair highlights and a chain dangling from her lower lip chimed in, cutting through the room's hum of chatter. She wore a faded "Greenpeace Rocks!" t-shirt and flimsy teal shorts, her voice carrying a sharp, nasal twang with an accent Hud couldn't quite place. Rural back East? he guessed. Maybe Appalachia.

"I want to know if we're planning to attend another scheduled march on Wall Street," she announced. "Or, if not, what about the concert coming up at Chowchilla? I've can get tickets enough for anyone who wants to go."

Lillian nudged Hud, with a conspiratorial whisper. "That's Sheela. Like in the song," she explained quietly. "She donates big bucks, so Jerry's always super nice to her."

Hud nodded, his curiosity about this eclectic group growing deeper—and not entirely for the better.

As the meeting wound down, people began to shuffle in their seats, stifling yawns and stretching stiff limbs. Kestrel eventually made his way over to Hud, offering a casual handshake. "Hey, man, I'm Kestrel," he said with a grin, then turned to Lillian. "You hungry? A few of us are walking down to Denny's for some pie."

Hud silently crossed his fingers, hoping Lillian would pass on the invite. But instead, she glanced up at him with a smile. "I could use a bite. How about you?"

Hud forced a grin. "Sure, all right—Denny's." He didn't really want to go, but the idea of ending the night with Lillian wasn't exactly appealing either.

The pie posse included Kestrel and the two women he'd cozied up to on the sofa earlier. The first was Sylvia Jamaica, whose Caribbean patois matched the rhythm of her immaculate cornrow braids. She seemed close to Kestrel's age, and her playful body language made it clear she was into him.

The other was Lady Jane Connelly—LJ—the one who'd read the financial report during the meeting. Hud guessed she was a middle Gen-Xer, maybe ten or fifteen years older than him, but with a peppy, captivating charm and a soft southwestern twang that reminded him of old Sons of the Pioneers tunes.

Hud quickly found himself glad he'd tagged along, though—not because of the pie or the company, but because of Lillian. As they made their way down the cracked, uneven sidewalk toward the glow of the main street, she casually slipped her hand into his, giving his heart a little jolt.

At one point, she stumbled slightly on the fractured pavement, and he felt her warmth press against him as she steadied herself. She didn't pull away. Instead, she stayed close, her arm brushing his with every step, her presence sending a warmth through him that had nothing to do with the summer night.

Chapter 7

The group squeezed into a large, brightly upholstered corner booth at Denny's, the vinyl seats squeaking slightly as they settled in. The restaurant was nearly empty, save for an unbelievably upbeat waitress whose sunny demeanor seemed to defy the late hour. Orders were placed quickly—desserts all around, with Lillian going the extra mile by adding an avocado omelet alongside her apple pie à la mode.

Eager to stretch out the evening with Lillian, Hud decided to stir the pot a bit. "So," he began casually, "what's the deal with that lawsuit Jerry mentioned?"

Kestrel leaned back, shaking his head with an exaggerated sigh. "That's Jerry's pipe dream. He wants to be the Clarence Darrow of the green movement—suing the capitalist overlords for wrecking the planet." He shrugged. "Problem is, he's got no solid evidence and even less money."

"What about the fundraising cash?" Hud quired, "Where's all that going?"

"All safely tucked away," Lady Jane chimed in, her tone matter-of-fact. "I'm the treasurer. We've got over $100,000 in the bank—seed money."

"It's nothing!" Kestrel suddenly snapped, slapping the table hard enough to rattle the silverware. His shift from laid-back to fired-up caught Hud's attention. "No one cares. No press, no buzz, no case. I love Jerry, but we need to start thinking about better ways to use that money."

"Oh, Kes, it's not like that," Lillian interjected, her voice soft but firm. Hud found himself liking Kestrel more with each passing minute—not because he agreed with him, but because the guy was at least cutting through the fluff.

Intrigued, Hud asked; "What kind of evidence are we talking about here?"

Kestrel's eyes lit up with a spark of frustration. "Hard evidence. A smoking dress," he said dramatically. "The Kilgallen dossier. The 18 secret treaties with California native tribes. Mary Meyer's diary. All the lost, stolen, and buried documents our government doesn't want us to see. Buffy knows what I am talking about."

"Buffy? Why that?" Hud asked.

"Her name is Sylvia, not Buffy," Lady Jane interjected. "For the record, 'Buffy' is just Kestrel's pet name for Sylvia."

Sylvia grinned punching Kestrel lightly on the arm. "He calls me his 'buffalo soldier.' Claims I'm the toughest woman he's ever met."

"And the prettiest," Kestrel added smoothly, nudging her with a broad shoulder.

Sylvia shot him a mock glare, this time elbowing him in the ribs. "My Indian brave can call me whatever he wants—just not too late for loving," she quipped with a sly grin.

"That'll never happen," Kestrel smirked.

Lillian frowned. "Kes, what were you talking about when you said 18 treaties?"

Kestrel scoffed, like it was common knowledge. "Oh, come on. Everyone knows about the Kennedy assassination conspiracy, but nobody talks about the First Peoples holocaust. The U.S. government forced California's native leaders to sign treaties, 18 of them and then buried the agreements, never ratified them. Left entire tribes homeless, invisible in their own land."

Hud sat back, his slice of pie untouched, the conversation veering into territory far more compelling than dessert. He wasn't sure if he was more intrigued by the topic—or the people unraveling it.

"Everyone knows about your proud Native American heritage," Sylvia cut in, shooting Kestrel a playful glance. "But what about the silver suitcase? The one that supposedly holds all the evidence Jerry needs to take down the polluters?"

Hud's curiosity piqued. "The silver suitcase?" he echoed.

Lady Jane cleared her throat dramatically. "Alright, lovebirds, back to business. Hud asked about the mysterious silver suitcase. Who's going explain?"

Kestrel leaned forward, his tone shifting to something more serious. "Ah, yes. The legend of the silver suitcase. Supposedly packed full of damning evidence collected by a now-dead FBI agent. It's said to prove the Stanley family—owners of Paramount Fossil Fuel Corporation—conspired to accelerate global warming. They're the biggest fossil fuel distributors on the planet, with mines, wells, and investments everywhere."

Hud frowned slightly, intrigued. "What's supposed to be in it that's so important?"

Lady Jane shrugged, "No one really knows. Rumors say it contains recordings from top-secret Senate briefings, photos, videos, thumb drives, even DNA samples and fingerprints on incriminating documents. Supposed proof of politicians colluding with foreign governments and billionaire elites—both domestic and abroad."

Hud folded his arms in his lap. The pie could wait.

"Humongous energy corporations plotting to raise global temperatures intentionally," Kes continued, his voice low but intense. "All to unlock trillions of dollars' worth of resources trapped under sea ice and glaciers in Greenland, the Arctic, and the Antarctic. And who pays the price? Low-lying cities and nations, homes of millions—maybe billions—gone underwater when the ice melts."

Lady Jane nodded solemnly. "Jerry believes if we could get our hands on solid evidence, take it to a nation deeply committed to climate action. Maybe like a member of the European Union—they might submit the evidence to the International Court of Justice in The Hague. Even the publicity could shake the political landscape here and worldwide."

Kes sneered. "The world's had enough of America's hypocrisy. It's people like Julian Assange and Edward Snowden who are the real heroes—the ones risking everything to expose criminals without borders."

Hud was doubtful. "But if this suitcase really exists, where would it be? And who put all this evidence together? For what purpose?"

"That's where things get murky," Lady Jane replied. "The story is, an FBI agent named Jim Reddy went rogue. He was assigned to investigate Stanley Fuel Inc. and some Midwest politicians. Standard conspiracy stuff ordered by a Senate committee. But the deeper Reddy dug, the more he uncovered. Connections stretching globally, implicating big energy companies and political figures across multiple countries."

"Then Reddy got spooked," Kes added with a hiss. "He realized he was being followed. His own supervisors started acting weird—reassigning him to other cases, pulling him away from the Stanley Fuel investigation just when it was getting interesting."

Hud frowned. "So, you think the FBI was in on it too?"

Kes shrugged dramatically. "Who knows? But Reddy thought so. He started making plans to disappear—evidence in hand. Thing is, during his investigation, he'd grown sympathetic to the environmental causes. That's why some folks think he put everything in the suitcase—to make sure the truth didn't die with him."

"Maybe Reddy thought he could use the information as leverage," Lady Jane added, her voice quieter now. "Like insurance. Threaten to leak it if things got too hot."

"A closet tree hugger," Sylvia said with a knowing nod.

Kestrel was clearly relishing the story. "So, Reddy starts planning his escape—on the run, but where to? Not Russia like Snowden. Reddy's evidence supposedly implicated Russia just as much as the U.S. in the push to melt polar ice. Reddy had dirt on everyone. Eventually, he figured he had enough to take to a grand jury—or maybe even the International Criminal Court in The Hague."

"That's the key," Lady Jane chimed in. "Not just exposing it here in the U.S., but getting real international traction, that would frighten the conspirators."

Kes nodded. "Exactly. But Reddy began to believe that staying here in the U.S. was a death sentence. Some believe he was headed for Cuba. So, he packs all his evidence into this large metal suitcase, charters a private plane… and vanishes. Gone. No trace."

"The infamous silver suitcase," Hud muttered, more to himself than anyone else. Heads around the table nodded solemnly.

"But what happened to it?" Hud pressed.

"Disappeared," Kes said with a shrug. "Or maybe it never existed. Hard to say."

Hud wasn't buying it—not yet. "Where's all this information even coming from? The FBI agent's name, the suitcase, the whole Cuba connection? Feels like a made-up campfire story."

Lady Jane began tapping her fingers lightly on the table. "Jerry has a buddy from law school, an environmental attorney up in the Northwest," she interjected. "The guy's made a name for himself winning pollution and conservation cases. Jerry calls him 'Green Throat.' Supposedly, Green Throat had some connection to Reddy. They've been sharing intel, trying to piece the puzzle together. According to Jerry, if Green Throat can locate that suitcase, it could be the smoking gun needed to finally build a solid case."

Kestrel again took over, his expression turning serious. "During a frat reunion weekend in Eugene, Jerry's buddy 'Green Throat' spilled enough details to really pique his interest. According to him, the suitcase might be at Stanley Fuel headquarters in Bluefield, West Virginia."

"Where it's probably been shredded, burned, and buried under six feet of concrete by now," Hud quipped.

Kestrel shook his head. "Jerry doesn't think so. He believes the Stanley Corporation would keep that evidence as leverage— insurance against anyone trying to bring them down. It's their 'get out of jail free' card. As long as they control it, no one's prosecuting them for anything."

Hud chuckled dryly. "So, all we need to do is steal the suitcase, expose the conspirators, and save the world. Easy enough."

For a second, there was stunned silence—then the table erupted in laughter. Even Lillian tried to suppress a grin, failing miserably.

Kestrel slapped the table, his signature bombast returning. "Yeah! We just need the invisible man. He'll waltz into Stanley's fortress—because, of course, they've got a fortress—somewhere in the mountains of West Virginia, slip past a dozen armed guards, crack open a few high-security safes, and stroll out with the Holy Grail."

Sylvia interrupted looking at Kes. "Wait a minute, how do you know all that? The fortress, the security…?"

Kestrel responded with a toothy grin. "Because I've been digging into Stanley Fuel ever since Jerry told us the story. Let's just say… I know things."

Chapter 8

After Denny's, Hud and Lillian left the others and returned to his car.

"Where to now?" he asked, hoping the night wasn't over.

"I saw online that the Art House Cinema on Reseda Boulevard is showing *The Third Man*. It's an Orson Welles film—supposed to be one of his best. Do you like Orson Welles?" Lillian asked.

Hud hesitated for a moment before answering. "I was married once," he admitted, his voice rough. "Nicole, my wife, she loved old movies—especially film noir. We watched a lot of them on Netflix. Since she's been gone, I still do. *The Third Man* was one of her favorites, but for some reason, I never got around to seeing it." He turned to Lillian, his gaze steady. "I'd like to go now and see it."

Lillian blinked. "So, you're divorced?"

Hud swallowed hard. "She's dead," he whispered, barely audible.

"Oh." Lillian's voice softened. "How did it happen?"

His grip on the steering wheel tightened. "I can't talk about her," he admitted, his eyes clouding. "Not yet. Maybe never. It was a lung disease. Maybe one day I'll tell you, but not tonight."

A long pause stretched between them.

"It's okay," Lillian finally said, her voice quiet. "I lost someone, too. A divorce," she added, as if testing the words. "I haven't really talked about it. Not even with the CCC members. Only my mother knows."

She turned toward the window, her fingers toying with the hem of her sleeve. "Why don't you just take me home?" she murmured.

Hud shook his head. "No. I'd really like to see the movie. Maybe it'll help. When I watch an old film, my depression fades." He forced a smile. "See? I'm better already."

Lillian studied him for a moment before nodding. "Okay. Let's go."

After the movie, they both felt lighter. The mix of suspense and unspoken longing in The Third Man resonated with them in different ways. When Hud walked Lillian to her door, he kissed her lightly—hesitant, yet warm.

Over the next few weeks, Hud and Lillian met often—usually for coffee after work. Conversations flowed, the reserve between them softening into something else. Something unspoken but real.

They attended several CCC meetings together, often meeting Kes, Sylvia, and LJ for dessert afterward. On one such night, as Hud drove Lillian home, her small dark house seemed even lonelier than usual when the Pathfinder pulled up to the curb. Neither of them wanted the evening to end.

"It's so lonely," Lillian whispered, peering into the darkness. She shivered slightly. "Maybe you could stay for a while?"

"I know how you feel," Hud replied softly. "I get that way too when I come home after dark."

Inside, Lillian lit a small gas fireplace in the cozy living room. Hud shrugged off his jacket and kicked off his boots, settling in. Even with the warm glow from the hearth, a faint chill lingered. He noticed the heavy comforter spread out on the floor, a clear sign that this was often her retreat from the solitude of living alone.

"A dog might help," Hud thought as he reclined by the fire.

Lillian disappeared for a several minutes. When she returned, she wore a loose red flannel robe trimmed with delicate white lace. Her damp hair, still clinging to her neck, hinted at a quick shower. Tossing a few throw pillows from the worn sofa in his direction, she lay down beside him.

"Someday," she whispered, her voice distant, "I want a big house by the beach."

Hud glanced at her. "It's often chilly and damp by the ocean," he teased gently. "But you smell nice."

"That's why I want a fireplace," Lillian replied, her eyes flickering with the fire's reflection. "I once saw one built by craftsmen during the Great Depression—Job Corps workers, I think.

It was somewhere in the Northwest, maybe Mount Hood. It was so big I could almost stand up in it if I bent down just a little. Later, they lit a roaring fire, and I thought... if I ever have my own house, I'll have a fireplace like that—so I'll never be cold again."

"Well, now you have one," Hud murmured, gesturing toward the flickering fire.

Lillian frowned. "No, this little thing barely gives off any heat. Even when I was a kid in Kansas, I remember always being cold—and I hated it."

Hud moved toward er, his voice low. "I wouldn't mind keeping you warm."

"Then let's snuggle," she whispered, brushing her cool lips against his ear. The shimmer of her smile and wisps of damp hair tickled his cheek in the fire's soft glow.

"Snuggling sounds perfect," he murmured, and together they surrendered to the quiet, primal magic of intimacy. Gentle ripples of tenderness gave way to waves of passion that carried them into a sea of warmth and belonging. When the tide finally brought them back to shore, they lay spent but content, the soft comforter beneath them their only anchor. Sleep came quickly—deep, dreamless, and peaceful.

Morning light streamed into the room, casting soft golden rays over Hud as he stretched, savoring the stillness. His gaze wandered across the simple furnishings, finally settling on Lillian. She looked so young, almost ethereal, her translucent skin glowing in the sunlight. Her breathing, soft and steady, barely stirred the rise and fall of her delicate frame.

Slipping quietly from the bed, Hud turned off the fire and found his way to the bathroom. He removed one of the mismatched but carefully folded towels from a stack next to the sink and ran the water until it was warm. After a quick shower and a rinse with some mouthwash left on the counter, he tiptoed back into the room where Lillian still lay sleeping, he headed for the kitchen to see what might be available for breakfast.

The cupboards were nearly empty. Flour, sugar, and baking powder sat in tin containers on the shelf, with a lone bottle of olive oil beside the stove.

Recalling a mini-mart just a few blocks away, Hud quietly slipped out the door, where he caught sight of large black cat perched on the stoop, gazing up at him with deliberate disdain.

"Hey, kitty. Back in a minute," Hud chuckled as he headed down the street, his voice surprisingly light. He felt good—joyful even—for the first time in ages.

At the market, he grabbed eggs, pork sausage, coffee, and half-and-half, making it back to Lillian's in under twenty minutes.

As Hud opened the door, the cat darted in first, claiming her spot on the kitchen windowsill, which overlooked a wild, unkempt yard dotted with fruit trees begging for a trim. "I could fix that yard up nice," he thought.

Mixing flour, baking powder, an egg, and oil, Hud quickly whipped up biscuit dough and slid it into the oven. After rummaging through cabinets, he found an old percolator, filled it with water, added several generous scoops of coffee, and plugged it in. It gurgled to life—success!

The savory scent of sausage and eggs sizzling on the stove, mingled with the rich aroma of fresh coffee and biscuits, soon lured Lillian from the living room. She beamed, her dressing gown loosely tied, eyes sparkling.

"You're the man," she teased, cheeks glowing. "I'm starved."

"I do what I can," Hud grinned, whistling softly. "Is that your loyal sidekick over there?"

The cat stretched lazily, flashing sharp claws and an even sharper yawn.

"Yep, that's Benny," Lillian said, scratching his thick fur. "But now you might be playing second fiddle."

"Hi-diddle-diddle to Benny," Hud laughed. Lillian giggled, and Benny purred, all three perfectly content.

During breakfast, Hud casually said, "Bet I could get that silver suitcase."

Lillian's face darkened instantly. "Don't go there," she whispered, shaking her head. "Not even as a joke."

"Aw, come on. No faith in my superpowers, like falcon-boy?" he teased.

"Stop it, Hud. It scares me when you talk like that." Her voice trembled.

"I was in the Air Force, Security Service—I learned a few tricks," he grinned.

"No more!" she interrupted, her eyes shimmering with tears. "I'm sorry, Hud, but I've known too many guys with crazy ideas. Benny and I were ready to go it alone. Then you show up. Please, don't ruin this."

Hud reached across the table, gently holding her hand. "I won't hurt you, Lil. I promise. I didn't realize how much I needed someone until you showed up at my door."

Her shoulders relaxed, though her jaw was still tense. "Okay... but no more crazy talk."

"Deal," he whispered, though part of him wondered how she would react if he mentioned the lizard in the mountains.

The scent of coffee filled the room, brightening the mood. Hud suddenly realizing he had plugged in the old percolator.

"I made coffee," he announced with a grin.

"You found that old thing?" Lillian blinked. "I haven't used it in forever. Coffee alone at home... it just makes me sad."

"Yup, found your vintage Mr. Coffee maker way up high, where only giants like me could reach."

He grabbed two matching mugs stamped with "Coast Conservation Corps" and a breaching humpback whale. Handing one to her, he added cream and sugar.

"Looks like these mugs have never seen the light of day," he observed filling two with strong steaming brew.

"They're brand new," she replied, starting to smile. "We had them made this summer." She stirred her coffee, took a sip, and sighed. "Just the way I like it. I hate weak coffee."

"Me too," Hud grinned, feeling the last of his worries lift away.

"I've got a few things to take care of at home this morning," he said, brushing a hand through his hair. "Should I come back this afternoon? Or would tomorrow be better?"

"Call me later," Lillian replied softly. "Tomorrow might be better."

She walked him to the door, and their goodbye kiss lingered— long enough to reassure Hud that everything between them was still good.

"Okay," he whispered, smiling as he stepped outside. "I'll call you later."

PART II:
BRUNO STACH

Chapter 9

Leopold Stach, Bruno's dad, served as an FBI Agent for thirty years. The family—Bruno, his mom, dad, and sister—lived in the same modest frame house in Bladensburg, Maryland, where Leopold himself had grown up. After his parents were moved to elder care, Leo inherited the home, nestled on the Northeast side of Washington D.C., in a quiet suburb many saw as a faded relic of the past.

Bladensburg's infamy traced back to the War of 1812, when Maryland's poorly organized militia crumbled, allowing British forces to sweep through and burn the White House. The town never fully shook off its tarnished legacy, settling into life as a backwater suburb housing mostly lower-middle-class families.

Bruno, however, adored the Southern Maryland landscape. Summers spent crabbing and fishing, autumns duck hunting all with his dad. Evenings were spent gathered around campfires cooking their day's catch as Leopold spun captivating tales of FBI investigations. Bruno's childhood brimmed with adventure.

At sixteen, Bruno's path was set when Leopold secured him a summer job at the Justice Building's basement print shop, where wanted posters were crafted and distributed nationwide. From that moment, Bruno knew his calling.

His FBI career spanned 16 years, but his time ended abruptly after Bruno's investigation into a sexual misconduct allegation uncovered undeniable evidence of the crime—committed by an intern tied to a political appointee. Pressured to stall his inquiry for a behind-the-scenes settlement, Bruno doggedly refused.

Eventually, Bruno was pulled from the high-profile case, and relegated to a dead-end desk job handling inmate grievance filed in federal prisons. Meanwhile, the harassment case vanished under a quiet settlement, and the once-accused intern found herself comfortably reassigned to a Deputy Director's office.

Today marked Bruno's retirement, closing out a two-decade career in federal law enforcement—the final seven years spent at the

Environmental Protection Agency's Office of the Inspector General after his FBI career hit the political wall.

The EPA headquarters, an architectural gem designed by San Francisco's Arthur Brown Jr., stood as a testament to a bygone era. Completed in 1934, the grand building once housed the U.S. Customs Service and the Department of Labor before its transformation into the EPA's home.

Known simply as "Stach" to colleagues, Bruno's hair had turned a distinguished silver at 40, now cropped close in stark white. Thin yet sinewy, he had no use for jogging but could easily spend a day walking the expanse of the nation's capital—a routine that often took him from the National Mall to the Potomac and back during lulls at work. Retirement loomed like a question mark he had no answer for.

"Hey, Stach, got a minute?" Cameron Teller, Bruno's supervisor, breezed into the office just as Bruno was boxing up seven years of accumulated clutter. Teller's cocky grin stretched across his face—a mix of charm and self-satisfaction that was almost too polished.

"Plenty of minutes," Bruno replied, still lost in thoughts of what life beyond the EPA might look like. Despite Cameron's slick exterior, Bruno tolerated him—maybe even liked him a little, which was more than he could say for most people. They both knew the unspoken rules of survival in the federal system, and Cam navigated them with an ease Bruno begrudgingly respected.

Chapter 10

Stach noticed Cam was clutching the arm of a bespectacled, dark-haired man of medium height, wearing ill-fitting, rumpled pinstripes and thick, black-rimmed bifocal glasses.

"This is Kenneth Garrett," Cam introduced. "He's an aide to Senator Drake Roberts, who co-chairs a committee investigating allegations of certain corporate energy companies making illegal extraction deals with U.S. politicians—possibly with foreign co-conspirators."

"Teapot Dome all over again," Bruno snickered. "Good luck with that."

Cam shrugged, flashing his usual smug grin. "They need an investigator with federal experience. I recommended you."

"Did you mention I'm retired? And not exactly a team player?" Bruno raised frowned.

Cam chuckled, revealing his perfect, too-white dentures. "Told them you're the best—unfortunately, just retired—but the Senate Committee is willing to offer you a term appointment. Since you're already off our books, I kindly agreed for you."

"How thoughtful," Bruno muttered. "No need to ask me first."

"Hey, you can always say no and go back to crabbing," Cam teased. Turning to Garrett, he added, "Bruno loves crabbing in the Chesapeake his spare time."

Garrett extended a warm, slightly damp hand. "Senator Roberts would like you to start immediately." His nervous voice was earnest, genuine even, rare qualities in D.C., though often well-feigned.

Bruno waved off the handshake. "When can I meet with the Senator to discuss what his expectations?"

"You're in? Great! I'll set it up and call you." They exchanged phone numbers and email addresses.

As Cam backed out of the office, he shot Bruno a mischievous wink.

"Hey, what about a badge and gun?" Bruno called after him.

"Turned in your EPA stuff yet?" Cam asked.

"Was just about to."

"Keep them," Cam replied. "I'll make sure the paperwork reflects that you're still on our rolls for now."

Bruno leaned back in his chair, letting out a deep sigh. "Always something," he muttered.

On his drive home, Bruno detoured up M Street to pass his ex's townhouse in Georgetown. He slowed as he approached, admiring Denise's azalea bushes—the same struggling sticks he'd planted a decade ago, now blooming in vivid red. The house, a stately red brick with black trim, had stood for nearly two centuries. Worth three million in today's market, Bruno guessed—but she deserved it. They kept in touch, and with the kids grown and the dog gone, their relationship had mellowed into something easier, even amicable.

Denise, his ex, was Chocolate City royalty—but that had not always been the case. Her claim to fame came later, as the sole heir to the rights and royalties of her legendary jazz musician grandfather's compositions.

Bruno still wondered how a stunning black singer like Denise had ever married a no-name civil servant like himself. Sheer luck, he figured—good or bad, depending on your perspective. He had been a young, unattached FBI agent when he first saw her singing at the Gaslight Room, a small club on Georgia Avenue. He'd sat there night after night, hopelessly enchanted, while she paid his longing stares not a bit of attention.

Fate intervened one late night when a towering, drunken Redskins fullback stormed in with his teammates and hauled Denise right off the stage. She screamed. Bruno, slightly buzzed, fired a warning shot into the ceiling with his service revolver, sending the crowd scattering.

After that, Denise fell for him fast and hard. Wasting no time, Bruno proposed. They sped to Elkton, where a bored teenage daughter of a Justice of the Peace served as their wedding witness.

Their whirlwind romance blazed for twelve years, producing two beautiful children before burning out.

They struggled, but the unraveling truly began after Denise inherited her grandfather's royalties and she bought the Georgetown townhouse.

Bruno, meanwhile, clung to their cottage on the Patuxent River in Lower Marlboro—the vegetable garden, the crabbing holes, the seasonal shad runs, and most of all, his rickety duck blind. It was the one place that brought him joy, a tether to the boyhood he had enjoyed when Leo was alive. As for work, each new assignment felt like a slog through the motions.

Two weeks into retirement, Bruno took his skiff downstream to a brackish stretch of the Patuxent River where sweet jimmy crabs waited on his baited trotlines. The calm broke when his phone chimed. A woman's voice greeted him: "Senator Roberts' office for Mr. Stach."

The next morning, Bruno boarded the D.C. Metro at Largo, emerging at Union Station and walking to the Russell Senate Office Building. Ken Garrett met him on the steps, skipping the Senator's office, he led Bruno through a labyrinth of hallways and elevators to a small, unmarked corner room.

"This is where we store evidence," Garrett said, fishing a key from his pocket. "It also doubles as the investigation office."

Inside, Bruno saw a cramped space with metal shelves crammed with binders, portfolios, and dog-eared documents. Two computer stations lined one wall, and a small conference table sat in the center. Garrett held the key up with a grin.

"Now it's your office," he said. "Your letter of authority, signed by the Vice President, is on the table. I made copies for you."

Garrett tossed his suit jacket onto a couple of crushed boxes in the corner and motioned Bruno toward the chairs. Settling in, he began briefing Stach on the investigation.

Despite the cluttered shelves and towering stacks of paper, Ken admitted, the investigation had not produced a single piece of hard evidence.

Chapter 11

"It's all copies of stuff—not even good copies or good stuff," Ken muttered, flipping through some disheveled files. "Most of this junk comes from federal agencies or FOIA requests from state records. A few bits from private energy firms under subpoena, but it's mostly useless. Nothing solid enough for conspiracy charges, much less putting anyone away."

Bruno slumped into a chair. "So, where do we go from here?"

"We don't," Ken replied with a grimace. "Roberts reassigned me to his reelection campaign in Montana. His re-election try is in November, and he wants to keep his environmentally conscious voters happy—by pretending this investigation is a top priority."

"But it's not?" Bruno asked, though he already suspected the answer.

Ken shook his head. "I left Forever Wild—a Montana green group I used to lead—because Roberts promised me real influence on environmental policy. But here? Nothing moves unless the big corporations want it. Then it flies through Congress like it's on roller skates. When I do corner Roberts, I get nods, sympathy, and the classic 'these things take time.'"

"Welcome to the swamp," Bruno quipped. "I take it Roberts won't meet with me either?"

Ken sighed. "I've tried. Requests vanish into the void. Back home, the environmental crowd is losing faith. They wanted this investigation to shake things up, but it's been dragging with no results. Now, a lot of them are thinking of backing Butch Cassidy Bandero."

Bruno laughed. "I read about that guy in The Post. Some cowboy lawyer turned eco-warrior. God is Green, right?"

"That's Butch," Garrett said with a faint grimace. "Temple of the Sixth Day. They pull everything from Genesis—Bandero calls it the 'Big Inning,' like it's some cosmic baseball joke. But most of his followers are dead serious. It's a new, universal faith—no denominations, just 'God's word.' Christians, Jews, Muslims—they all claim it."

Garrett straightened like a schoolkid reciting in class. "God said, 'I give you all plants that bear seed everywhere on earth, and every tree bearing fruit which yields seed: they shall be yours for food. All green plants I give for food to the wild animals, to all the birds of heaven, and to all reptiles on earth, every living creature.' So it was, and God saw all that he had made, and it was VERY GOOD. Evening came, and morning came, a sixth day."

Bruno chuckled. "Not bad. You sound like you're ready to pass the collection plate."

Garrett faltered. "My wife, Connie, was an Oregon State tree-hugger. Met her at a Forever Wild event. The forest was her church back then. But faith... it's in her blood. Her dad was a Four-Square preacher—died a junkie under the Burnside Bridge. After that, Connie found the Sixth Day folks, started going to revivals, and now she's all in."

Bruno asked. "What exactly do they believe?"

"That messing up God's creation is a mortal sin," Garrett replied. "We've got dominion, sure—but no polluting, no abusing, no 'poisoning the land.' Animals? Sacred. Reproductive rights? Sacred too. They're hardcore ZPG—two kids max. But it's the woman's choice. No government interference, ever."

"So, Bandero is just another backwoods kook?" Bruno asked. "But I read somewhere he's also a pretty successful lawyer?"

"Yeah," Garrett nodded. "U of O Law, magna cum something. Sharp as hell—environmental law was his battlefield. Corporate polluter lawyers dreaded him. He snagged massive settlements for his clients. Then one day, he hikes Mount Hood, has some kind of epiphany, and boom—he's 'enlightened.' Swapped his wing-tips for moccasins hand-stitched by Native American women in Warm Springs. These days, he's all bandanas and denim, like Willie Nelson's twin, only he is a lot bigger than Willie was before he died."

"Doesn't sound like Roberts has much to worry about from that quarter," Bruno shrugged.

Garrett sighed. "You'd think. But Connie and her fellow believers say Bandero's raking in donations from every corner of the Montana—probably as much as he made practicing law. And, well... she's still my wife and I Love her to death. But mark my words, Bandero's gunning for Roberts' seat in November, and if he runs— I'm voting for him."

"Come on," Bruno chuckled. "A long-haired eco-warrior winning a Senate race? That's a snowball's chance in hell."

"Maybe," Garrett conceded. "He's brilliant, no doubt—but with his politics and that out-there religion..." He shook his head. "Yeah, I'm with you on this one."

Chapter 12

At the start of any investigation, Bruno always looked for threads, tiny strands that, when followed through all their twists and turns, might eventually lead to paydirt. Or not. If not, he'd start again, hunting for new threads. But in the Roberts investigation, Bruno saw no thread at all. So that became his thread. After years navigating the byzantine world of the federal bureaucracy, he recognized the possibility of a wild goose chase. Garrett's skepticism lingered in his mind. Maybe Roberts wasn't really looking for politically linked corporate conspiracies. Maybe the investigation itself was just for show. The first thread: why?

Roberts represented a state full of committed environmentalists and skeptical ranchers. Sure, there were fossil fuel producers, but wind power was the goldmine of the future. Montana ranked among the top five states in wind energy potential, though profits had not caught up to its promise yet. Roberts had to keep up appearances with young, green-minded voters—or risk losing them entirely.

So, Bruno thought, maybe Roberts started a sham investigation, stacked an office full of useless paperwork, and assigned a loyal guy from back home with solid environmental credentials to oversee it. When Montana's green crowd started grumbling about the lack of results, bring in an over-the-hill retired investigator as window dressing. Give him an office, pay him $150,000 a year to shuffle paper while the whole inquiry quietly fizzles out.

After days of sifting through worthless documents, Bruno realized Garrett was right—this was all worthless junk. He dug out Garrett's business card and dialed. Garrett picked up on the first ring.

"Ken, this is Bruno. I'm planning on doing some traveling. I need a government credit card."

There was a pause before Garrett asked, "Where to?"

"I'm hunting down conspiratorial energy extractors, aren't I? They're not here in D.C. And since you said—and I agree, that the stuff in the office is worthless, I thought I'd head into the field and dig up some real evidence."

"Okay, I'll write up a request and let you know."

The credit card arrived the next day, no strings attached. The travel orders Garrett handed over simply said Senate Office Investigation. Bruno chuckled—someone clearly wanted him far away from Capitol Hill. The card authorized up to $1,000 a day for travel, transport, and living expenses, capped at 90 days without reauthorization. A yellow sticky-note from Garrett read: Keep me posted on your progress and whereabouts in case anyone asks—good luck.

Two days later, Bruno disembarked from a Southwest flight and found himself driving a rental car east from Portland. The Columbia Gorge stretched beside him, the Cascade cones behind him, and the shimmering walls of the Rockies looming ahead. He could have flown straight in, but he'd never seen this part of the country. Besides, if someone in D.C. audited his expenses, the rental car, motel, and meals were cheaper than a direct flight.

Bruno had told Ken not to arrange any meetings with Bandero, just to find out if he was nearby. Surprise visits often got the best answers—people didn't have time to rehearse.

Bruno arrived in Salish, Montana, where Ken Garrett had told him Butch Bandero's campaign office was set up. After checking into the Nighty-Nighty Motel, he quickly found the campaign's phone number online. Sometimes going straight for the jugular worked best.

"Bandero Senatorial Campaign, how can I help you?" a woman's voice answered.

"This is Bruno Stach. I'm working for the U.S. Senate on an authorized investigation into energy companies and government officials. I'd like to speak with Mr. Bandero, if he's available."

A pause. Then a man's voice replied, "This is Butch. You the guy Ken Garrett told me to keep an eye out for?"

Bruno blinked, surprised by his immediate good fortune. "Mr. Bandero, I'm investigating allegations of misconduct involving energy companies and government officials. I'd like to interview you."

"Me? What'd I do?"

"Nothing that I am aware of. Garrett mentioned you as someone who's invested in protecting the environment. I thought you might have insight—or know where I should look."

Butch laughed quietly. "Ken is a hometown boy. Helped start Forever Wild—a group of folks trying to keep Montana's wilderness safe."

"I have my authorization letter with me. I'd appreciate the chance to go over it with you, maybe get your thoughts."

"Am I in trouble here?"

"Not at all. I've heard you know your way around a courtroom though, what counts as evidence, and where it might be hiding. That's all."

"Where are you staying?"

"Nighty-Nighty Motel, here in Salish."

"Meet me at the Black Mesa Café in two hours—unless you've got a court reporter or recording gear. Then it'll have to be the ranch."

"No, this is not a deposition, more of a background interview. I am familiar with your successful career defending the environment and, of course, Senator Roberts' responsibility to look into allegations of fraud, conspiracy, and collusion. I'm also aware of Mr. Garrett's frustration with the progress of the investigation and his belief that Roberts might be stonewalling it. That's about the extent of what I know—I need to learn more."

"Fair enough, then, let's talk at the Black Mesa Cafe. It's on Main Street. Do you need directions?"

Bruno glanced out of his motel window at the scenic vistas. "This town has maybe a couple thousand inhabitants max, the café is on Main Street, my motel is on Main Street—I'm a trained investigator. I think I can find it."

A quiet chuckle came through the phone. "See you in a little while."

The baby back ribs at the Black Mesa were excellent, the local home brew even better. The conversation was cordial and relaxed. Bruno found Butch Bandero easygoing, straight-forward, and engaging. His ruddy complexion and broad shoulders giving him a rugged, approachable air. Must be around six-three, Bruno guessed. With braided reddish-gray hair braided, he did resemble a large version of Willie Nelson, as Garrett had described, though without any of the Native American garb—just well-worn suede boots, Levi's, and a faded bleeding Madras shirt.

Butch Bandero struck Bruno as a man who could and would reinvent himself whenever needed. Bruno's years of experience had sharpened his ability to read people, and Bandero wasn't setting off any alarms. His answers were direct, with no signs of evasion. When asked if Butch Cassidy was his real name, Bandero grinned. "Nah," he replied, "Given, alright—I gave them to myself. My real name's Andrew Bandero. I was small and bowlegged in grade school—kids called me Bandy Andy. Got me into plenty of fights. After a couple years, I started winning some and earned a little respect."

The big man continued, "As I grew in size and strength it started to show on the football field, I became Butch Bandero to the fellows. Then, after seeing Butch Cassidy and the Sundance Kid when I was about twelve or fourteen, my pals started calling me Butch Cassidy—he was a pretty good fighter too. I liked the association, so during law school, I learned a name change was no big deal. I became Butch Cassidy Bandero—legally."

Bruno found himself starting to like the big fellow despite his changing names and wardrobes.

"So, you're a smart man, Bandero," Bruno probed. "Top of your class in law school, brilliant at prosecuting polluters in the courtroom, and now throwing your ten-gallon Stetson into the ring for a Senate seat. It's none of my business, but I understand you're a big supporter of this Sixth Day movement—why all the phony religiosity?"

"Yes, I am!" Butch growled. "First of all, I believe in the Sixth Day Temple's concerns and the proposition that all life is sacred." It was the first time Bandero showed anything other than forthright goodwill. His face darkened, and Bruno found a huge finger pointed inches from his nose, it was attached to a calloused rancher's fist as big and red as a brick.

Butch declared loud enough for anyone sitting nearby to hear, "All this creation"—he waved his free arm toward the large plate glass window, framing the ponderous pines and snowcapped peaks beyond— "the beauty in the world, everything the polluters want to destroy, are destroying every day. Any tax breaks the Temple receives based on people's true beliefs are nothing compared to the billionaire and politician tax breaks."

Bandero paused to gulp down a mouthful of coffee before continuing, "It's not a people's government anymore. There's no governing—just stealing from those with the least, from the middle class, and giving it all to the wealthiest, while all the while destroying and desecrating our God-given world in the process."

Butch quieted a little. Bruno noticed that the spent tirade hadn't startled the waitress in the least. She returned to their table, pouring fresh coffee into their heavy ceramic mugs with a big smile—maybe she was used to it, Bruno figured.

"Listen," Bandero continued turning sideways, "I saw this guy on TV the other day from one of those Middle Eastern countries— his whole city destroyed by bombs. The man had been a taxi driver with nine kids. Nine kids! Living in the desert. It wasn't a desert when his great-great-grandfather lived there, but it is now because of climate change and overpopulation."

"It is nuts," Bruno admitted.

Butch's shoulders eased as he placed both weathered mitts firmly on the table. "My God created a beautiful world and gave me a brain to think, to build, and to protect with. Those energy corporations tearing it apart? They're the real evil." His voice carried a weight that lingered in the air.

Bruno leaned back; "You really believe that?"

"Every word," Butch affirmed without hesitation, his gaze steady. "And I'll fight for it."

Bruno laughed dryly. "Well, I hope that passion holds up when the IRS comes knocking."

Butch's lips curled into a wry grin. "They already have. We're fighting battles in half a dozen states and D.C. Our lawyers are some of the best—and they believe in the cause. What's more, many mainstream faiths—Christians, Jews, Muslims—they're starting to agree with us too. The tide is turning."

Bruno nodded thoughtfully, but his mind was already shifting gears. "That's all well and good, but I've got an investigation to conduct," he said, his tone sharpening. "Is there a conspiracy? I'm not even sure what that word means anymore."

Butch's expression hardened. "There is," he replied, voice low but still resolute. "But proving it? That's the real test."

Chapter 13

Butch Bandero spent the next hour over steaming mugs of coffee with Bruno recounting the haunting tale of Jim Reddy, an FBI agent who had gone rogue while investigating corruption involving Stanley Energy as well as several other energy extraction company's and high-ranking elected officials. His voice, still steady and confident, now carried a more somber tone as he delved into the story. The café's hum faded into the background as Bruno became captivated by Butch's narrative.

The mention of an aluminum suitcase—rumored to be packed with damning evidence—hung in the air like an unsolved riddle. The case, Butch said, was believed to contain a treasure trove of incriminating documents, videos, photos, thumb drives and recordings. But it was Reddy's tragic end, while desperately trying to flee the country with this evidence, that sent a chill down Bruno's spine.

"That's quite a story," Bruno said, his brows furrowed, suspicion and curiosity flickering across his face. "But how did you learn all this?"

Butch's gaze drifted. "I got a call from Reddy's mother," he replied, his deep voice again on track. "An elderly woman living in Gaithersburg, Maryland. Sweet old lady, but sharp as a tack. She told me Jim had grown close to environmental groups in Maryland, Virginia, and West Virginia—people fighting tooth and nail to protect the Appalachian Mountains from being ripped apart by fossil fuel companies."

Bruno nodded, his investigator's instincts kicking in. "And what brought you into the picture?"

Butch leaned back slightly, rubbing his temple as if recalling a painful memory. "Gertrude Reddy—Jim's mom—had heard of me through my legal battles," he explained showing a rare vulnerability. "Jim had admired my work and shared everything with her. She told me about the aluminum case, described it in vivid detail—silver, or

metallic, with a leather handle—she begged me to investigate his
death. She was absolutely convinced that her son had been murdered
and that the case, filled with the evidence he had gathered and
believed could take down both crooked politicians and energy giants,
had been stolen."

Bruno felt the revelation settle over him like a heavy fog. The
room felt a little colder, the coffee a little more bitter. He could
almost see the face of Gertrude Reddy pleading for justice. This was
personal—for her, for her son Jim, and now, somehow, for Bruno
too.

"Do you think she was credible?" Bruno asked, his elbows
rested on the worn wooden table between them.

Butch exhaled slowly. "I asked her— 'Why do you believe Jim
was murdered?'" he recalled. His voice, almost reverent. "She told
me Jim had phoned her; said he was going on a trip and not to expect
him back for a long time—maybe years. But before the week was
up, an FBI agent knocked on her door, telling her Jim had been found
dead, floating in the Potomac River."

Bruno's nodded, he knew Potomac had swallowed many secrets
over the years.

Butch continued, his tone sounding bitter. "Gertrude swore Jim
had warned her. Told her if anything ever happened to him, it would
be thugs hired by private energy extraction companies that he had
tangled with during his investigation that would be culpable. She
was convinced Stanley Energy had blood on its hands."

"What did you do?" Bruno pressed, sensing there was more to
the story.

Butch lifted his hands, palms up, as if surrendering to a past he
couldn't change. "Well, the FBI had already contacted her about
Jim's disappearance. She told them exactly what Jim had said—if he
ended up dead, Stanley Energy employed thugs were responsible.
The FBI Agents promised her they'd reopen the inquiry, but their
official line never changed. Jim's death was ruled an accidental
drowning while kayaking."

The café's faint hum buzzed in Bruno's ears, but all he could focus on was the man across from him, now staring into the depths of his empty cup as if it might hold the answers he had sought.

"I told her straight up—I'm no investigator," Butch admitted, his voice cracking slightly. "Hell, I wasn't even a member of the Maryland Bar. But I poked around. Talked to a few people. Came up empty."

Bruno frowned. "No leads? No loose threads?"

Butch shook his head. "The story never even made the papers. Not a whisper on the internet. Not even an obituary in The Washington Post. It was like Jim Reddy had never existed."

His voice dropped an octave, "I thought about going to a reporter with Gertrude's story, but… I couldn't do it. She was old, fragile. If there were hardball players out there—and I was convinced of the possibility—I didn't want to put a target on her back."

Butch leaned back, his face clouding over with a mixture of frustration and sorrow. "Besides, the whole thing sounded far-fetched even to me. The FBI? Rogue agents? Corporate assassins? It felt like a bad movie plot. And not long after that, Gertrude died too. Alone and of natural causes, with no answers. And that… that was about the end of it for me."

The silence that followed was broken only by the soft clink of a spoon against a saucer as a waitress passed by. Bruno felt the familiar tug of unfinished business, of evidence still hidden. And he knew— this was not over.

"You said about the end of it," Bruno prompted, sensing something else might surface. A thread perhaps?

Butch furrowed his brow, searching his memory. "Well… a few days after the old lady died," he began slowly, "I remember I had just gotten back from a law school reunion in Eugene. That is when I got a call on a confidential cell phone I hardly ever use. Almost nobody has that number—just a few close friends, some clients, and colleagues."

Bruno's interest was renewed "And?"

"The voice on the other end said, 'The silver suitcase is in Bluefield.'" Butch's eyes flickered with the intensity of the moment as he recounted the call.

"What did you say?" Bruno prompted.

"I asked, 'Who is this? What suitcase?'" Butch's fingers tapped the edge of his coffee cup. "The voice replied, 'The guy that was killed with the propeller, the one with the smashed-in head.' I asked again, 'Who is this?' But whoever it was had already hung up."

Bruno's heartbeat quickened. This was the first tangible lead he'd heard. "What did the person sound like?"

"It was a woman," Butch replied, his voice low, almost mimicking the caller's tone. "She was speaking softly, like she was whispering... or scared." He paused. "I looked at my phone, saw the number, and checked the area code—304. Turns out it's in West Virginia, southern part of the state, includes Bluefield."

Bruno stroking his chin thoughtfully. "And then?"

"I called a private investigator I've worked with on some of my environmental cases," Butch explained, rubbing the back of his neck. "He tried to identify the source phone but he hit a dead end. No record of the phone or number."

"A burner, maybe?" Bruno speculated, his instincts kicking in.

"Could be," Butch nodded. "But there was nothing more I could do. I waited, hoping she'd call back, but she never did."

Bruno leaned back in his chair, his mind searching for possibilities. "How could this person have gotten your private number?"

Butch shrugged, "That's the mystery, isn't it? There are no more than a dozen people with that number."

"Mr. Bandero," Bruno requested, "could you make a list for me of everyone you gave that number to? Also, do you still have the number you were called from?"

Butch finally, nodded. "I'm a pretty good judge of character, and you seem like you're on the up and up," he said sincerely. "I want answers as much as you do. Yes, I still have the number—I wrote it down. I'll also make a list of those who have my private line. How do I get it to you?"

"Give me an email address and a phone number where you can be reached," Bruno instructed. "When I get back, Ken Garrett and I will work out a secure method for exchanging information. Do you trust Garrett?"

Butch gave a wry smile. "Ken's as honest and reliable as the day is long. But I'm not sure what he thinks of me... working for Drake Roberts and all."

Bruno smiled. "He told me he might vote for you."

That earned a look of satisfaction from Butch. Bruno rose, extending his hand, and Butch clasped it firmly. "I'll keep in touch," Bruno promised.

Later that night, after touching down at Dulles Airport, weariness weighed his steps. The drive back to Lower Marlboro felt endless but by the time he stumbled through his front door, the quiet hum of his empty home greeted him like an old companion. Stripping off his rumpled clothes, Bruno let a hot shower wash away the clinging fatigue. Once in bed, the day's revelations still swirled in his mind. Exhaustion claimed him quickly though, pulling him into the embrace of dreamless sleep, still his last waking thought lingered on. The whispered words: "The suitcase is in Bluefield."

Chapter 14

The next morning Bruno refreshed, but still groggy, took a slow walk around his Lower Marlboro property. Still getting paid after all, but he couldn't shake the itch that something bigger might be waiting for him just beyond the horizon.

His instinct for investigation once again kicked in and Bruno began calling former FBI colleagues, hoping to dig up more information on Jim Reddy. But the well was almost dry.

The man had existed, certainly, but little else was recalled. Reddy's reputation as a Bureau agent was clear: a loner, the kind who played his cards close to the vest. Bruno discovered that Reddy had been assigned to political cases for years, a quiet but tenacious figure working in the background. Still curious, Bruno took the metro downtown, the familiar rhythm of the train oddly comforting. Leaving the Metro Station in D.C. he made his way to the Justice Building. After showing his badge and letter of authority at the front desk, he maneuvered through the labyrinth of hallways to where he was told Reddy's cubicle had been.

There, Bruno interviewed former coworkers who painted a consistent picture. Reddy was a "quiet guy," one agent shrugged. "Worked hard, but never shared much." Another added, "He listened more than he talked." A female colleague chimed in, "He was a good listener, but he wasn't the type to contribute during conversations." Bruno filed these observations away, noting how they matched the profile of someone who might be keeping explosive secrets.

One story stood out. An agent recounted seeing Reddy kayaking the treacherous Great Falls rapids on the Potomac River. "He was an expert," the agent said, as he recalled the memory. After their chance encounter on the river, they exchanged email addresses, only to discover they both worked for the Bureau. The coworker, eager to improve his kayaking skills, sought advice from Reddy. But Jim had only nodded and said, "If you want to get better, take lessons."

Months later, the agent returned to Reddy's desk with more questions about the rapids, only to be met with grim news: Reddy was dead, a victim of a kayaking accident on the Potomac. Bruno kept digging, but was only hearing similar stories. "Went over the falls," one said. Another recounted, "Smashed his kayak into the rocks." The details blurred together; each account vague. No one had actually seen the accident happen.

Bruno's investigation into Jim Reddy's past grew more perplexing when two former FBI colleagues he spoke with mentioned hearing that Reddy had been cremated. That single detail was odd. If Gertrude Reddy truly believed her son had been murdered, why would she have him cremated?

Without a body—no corpus delicti, reopening the case and proving foul play would be nearly impossible. The contradiction unsettled Bruno, making him wonder if there were more layers to Gertrude's story than he had initially thought.

Determined to learn more, Bruno delved deeper into Agent Reddy's background. He traced his early life to Carmichael, California, a quiet suburb of Sacramento. There, Reddy attended El Camino High School and ran cross-country for the track team. Bruno spent hours searching online archives until he unearthed a digital yearbook photo. Staring back at him was a small, dark-haired teenager with sharp features and an intensity in his brown eyes. Bruno noted that Reddy's appearance hinted at East Indian heritage, adding a dimension to the man he was trying to piece together.

Tracking down former high school teammates from thirty years ago was no easy task. Bruno navigated through several online directories and personal locator services, finally connecting with a handful of Reddy's old running mates. Most barely remembered him. Those who did recalled him as quiet and focused, with few close friends and no memorable romantic relationships. However, two former teammates vividly remembered running cross-country with him. "He wasn't big, but man, was he tenacious," one said. "If you were neck-and-neck with him near the finish line, you could bet he'd push himself to beat you—and he usually did."

After high school, Reddy attended the University of the Pacific in Stockton, later moving on to the McGeorge School of Law in Sacramento. His sharp intellect and dogged determination caught the attention of some FBI recruiters who visited the campus, their efforts led him to Washington, D.C. and an offer from the Bureau. Soon thereafter he relocated with his mother.

As Bruno digested this timeline, he felt a feeling of admiration for the young agent.

Later, Bruno hopped into a cab bound for Capitol Hill, his mind swirling with new information. Once inside the Senate Office Building, he dialed Ken Garrett. "Hey, Ken, how about grabbing a sandwich?" Bruno asked casually, though his mind was already plotting their conversation.

"You're back!" Ken's voice sounded genuinely excited. "Good deal. I got a couple of calls about you from out West. Yeah, let's eat."

Meeting Ken on the front steps, the two headed toward the West Wing Café on New Jersey Avenue. Bruno relished the thought of a warm pastrami sandwich, but more than that, he needed a quiet place to talk—away from the Senate halls. This conversation was not just about lunch; it was about peeling back a layer of the mystery that was Jim Reddy.

"I met with your friend Butch Bandero," Bruno proffered after they had placed their orders.

"Yeah, I know," Ken replied, excited to hear what had transpired during Bruno's visit to Montana.

"News travels fast," Bruno noted with a wry grin.

Ken nodded. "He told me you and I were going to exchange some information back and forth, lists of names and phone numbers?"

"That's right," Bruno confirmed, "but I don't want to work through the Senate offices in case Roberts is a leak. He'll have access to everything because it's his investigation."

Ken's face hardened, weighing what Bruno was suggesting. "Where then?" he asked cautiously.

"Who knows that Bandero contacted you while I was out West?"

"Um, nobody that I know of." Ken replied, "He called me on my cell."

"First off," Bruno began, "I need to be sure I can trust you. I think I can," he admitted. "You suggested right away that you suspected Roberts could be running a phony investigation. You wouldn't have said that about your boss if you were just another shill in the game. Also, Bandero says you are a good man, and I'm pretty sure I can trust his judgement. So, tell me now—do you want to investigate this with me, and only me, until it's over?"

Ken took a deep breath, ad nodded. "To tell you the truth, I like Senator Roberts less today than when I first told you the investigation wasn't going anywhere."

"What's changed?"

Ken lowered his voice. "Butch let me know just yesterday that Roberts was putting pressure on the Governor of our state to use State Troopers to rein in the Black Bloc members. Harass them, arrest them if they are seen on the street or in their cars, unmask them, search them for contraband."

Bruno frowned, He was familiar with the Black Bloc's reputation, and read about the group—demonstrators for controversial causes. Members covered their faces with masks, and often donned dark clothing and hoodies. They were not afraid to get their hands dirty and had even been known for resorting to property damage to make their point. "What does Bandero have to do with them?" he asked, curious about the connection.

Ken sighed, shaking his head. "Butch already defended those guys in federal court—their right to wear hoodies and masks to avoid facial recognition technology. For the most part, they're on our side, college students mainly. Many have ties to strong environmental groups like Greenpeace," he explained bitterly. "And now, seeing how Roberts is handling this, I'm getting ready to hand in my resignation. I believe he's working for the other side."

Bruno could feel the stakes were higher than before he visited Butch. Kenny appeared to be near tears, with frustration bubbling to the surface. "I hate this freakin' town Bruno," he avowed. "After I leave here and go back out West, I swear I will never, ever come back to this zoo."

Bruno responded reassuringly. "Listen, pal," he said, placing a steadying hand on Ken's shoulder. "Don't quit. Not yet. Not till I do. I've got a feeling things might start getting interesting soon." He paused, letting the words sink in before adding, "I have a contact at the EPA—Cameron Teller, remember him?"

Ken nodded, pulling out a handkerchief to wipe perspiration from his brow. "Okay," he sniffed, his voice more even now. "I'll stick it out with you, Bruno. But when you say it's futile, that's it—I'm out of D.C. for good."

"I'll call Cam and tell him you're working with me," Bruno assured him, formulating the plan as he spoke. "We'll say we need some security and a quieter space away from the constant commotion at the Senate Office Building. Cam will buy that—he gets it." Bruno then added. "But listen, we don't tell him about Roberts. I trust Cam, but not with that. He's always looking for the next feather in his cap, and you criticizing Roberts, the guy you're supposed to be working for, might be too tempting for him. We want to keep him thinking this is just about needing a secure place to work, nothing more."

Ken brightened, a spark of hope flickering back. "Okay, I'm in," he said with a determined nod. "So… you really think something's going to happen?"

"We can only hope," Bruno replied, a brief smile tugging at the corner of his mouth as he opened the door to the West Wing Café.

The two men ate their sandwiches in silence, each lost in his own thoughts, their minds contemplating possibilities and uncertainties. On the walk back, Bruno led Ken to Union Station. The bustling crowds providing a backdrop as Bruno made his way to an ATM, withdrawing a wad of cash with deliberate purpose. Without a word, he steered Ken toward a small kiosk that sold prepaid cell phones, the kind often favored for their untraceable nature.

Bruno paid in cash, avoiding the digital trail a credit card would leave behind. Handing one of the phones to Ken, he said, "Here. We'll use these from now on."

Ken furrowed his brow. "Burners?"

Bruno nodded. "Exactly. Harder to trace, especially when bought with cash. Don't let anyone know you have this phone unless I say it's okay. I've loaded up plenty of minutes for both of us, but if you start running low, come back here and top up. And remember—cash only. No cards."

Ken held the phone in his hand, weighing not just the device but the secrecy and risk they were about to undertake. "Got it," he grinned, determination hardening his jaw.

Bruno nodded recognizing, the unspoken agreement between them now clear. The real work could be about to begin.

Bruno paused, running a thought through his mind before speaking. "Here's the deal," he began, "When you need to call me—or anyone else involved in this investigation—use your burner. Especially with me or Butch Bandero. Got it?"

Ken nodded, but Bruno wasn't done. "For everything else—regular business calls to Roberts, Teller, or anyone from the office—stick to your official cell. But if I call you from my burner and you miss it, always, always call me back using your burner. No exceptions."

"Got it, Bruno," Ken replied, with newfound excitement. It was subtle, but Bruno could see it—the thrill of stepping into something that felt real, and perhaps a bit dangerous.

Bruno gave a quick nod of approval. As they parted ways, Bruno shot Ken a playful wink, a silent acknowledgment of the risks they were both taking by circumventing normal communication channels. Ken headed back toward the Senate Offices, shoulders squared, while Bruno made his way to the Metro, eager to get home and plan a next move.

Chapter 15

The next morning, Bruno awoke later than usual, his body still lingering with the fatigue of travel. The warmth of his bed lingering, but his mind already racing through the loose ends of the investigation. Stretching lazily, he shuffled to the kitchen and methodically prepared a pour-over coffee, inhaling the rich aroma filling his small kitchen. The familiar routine grounded him, offering moments of calm. By nine a.m., seated at his worn wooden kitchen table, he dialed Cameron Teller's number, while cradling the steaming mug in one hand.

"Bruno! Long time—what's up?" Cameron's familiar chortle echoed through the line.

"Hey, Cam. I need a favor. Thinking of using some EPA office space—preferably my former office along with a secure phone and email. The Senate office situation is a mess. Admin chaos, you know how it is."

Cameron's reply came effortlessly. "Your old office is still gathering dust. Thanks to the hiring freeze from the big guy upstairs, nobody's moving in anytime soon. It's yours. Use the security measures we had set up back then, they're still active."

"Appreciate it, Cam. Also, remember that kid from the Senate, Ken Garrett? He's working with me now, kind of like a partner. He's got clearance, so let him in when he shows up."

"Got it. Sounds like retirement isn't slowing you down."

Bruno replied. "Honestly, Cam, not much going on. Feels like I'm chasing shadows. But the kid—Garrett—I like him. Got potential. I'm showing him the ropes, letting him handle some security measures. Who knows, when this Senate gig is over, maybe you can hire him as my replacement."

After Bruno finished the call and gave his body a well-deserved stretch, the faint hum of the morning breeze drifting through an open window. His eyes traveled across the river to the marshy reeds on the far shore, dressing quickly, he skipped breakfast and drove to the

Metro subway station at Largo. There, the rhythmic movement of the train lulled him almost back to sleep.

By the time the train reached Union Station, Bruno was wide awake. A dead FBI Agent, Jim Reddy, and his equally deceased mother, Gertrude, had both lived in the same house in Gaithersburg, once a small colonial town but now a burgeoning suburb. Just maybe, someone there knew something—a thread waiting to be followed.

Wandering the now familiar hallways of the Senate offices, Bruno peeked into Garrett's cubbyhole, only to find it empty. The faint hum of a copier caught his attention. In a nearby alcove, a young intern, her hair pulled into a hasty bun, was busy feeding papers into the machine.

"Excuse me, I was looking for Mr. Garrett. I'm working with him here and I need to arrange for a car. Can you help me?"

She greeted him with a polite smile, "You must be...?" she asked, her fingers still resting on the copier buttons.

"Bruno Stach. Has Garrett mentioned me?"

"Yes," she nodded "You're to have anything you want—within reason, of course."

Bruno sighed. "Of course. Now, about the car?"

With the efficiency of someone new enough to still care, she fetched the sign-out sheet and gestured toward the board holding car keys. "Lot 5, spaces 6, 7, and 8. All Chevy Cruzes."

Bruno signed out a key, thanked her, and headed around the beltway to the I-70 corridor towards Gaithersburg, his mind replaying fragments of the investigation. The traffic crawled but an hour later, he found himself on a quiet street lined with post-World War II bungalows. Each house told its own story—some fresh and inviting, others weary with neglect. The Reddy residence sat somewhere in between, its paint faded, the front yard an afterthought, with a weathered 'For Sale' sign tilting on the lawn.

Bruno snapped a few photos with his phone, before cataloging them in his evidence app. Dialing the realtor's number from the sign, he expected the usual spiel. Instead, the voice on the other end turned terse when pressed for details about the house, deflecting Bruno to the Gaithersburg Police Department.

"Call them if you want to know more," the realtor said abruptly before ending the call.

At the Gaithersburg Police Station, Bruno flashed his badge to the desk sergeant and explained his interest in the Reddy residence. The officer silently scrutinized the credentials before disappearing into a back office. Moments later, he returned with a thin file folder and a curt nod toward an empty chair. Bruno leafed through the report; the stale air of the station thick around him. Mrs. Reddy had died alone in her small bungalow, her body discovered days later by a mail carrier who followed the scent of death rather than his usual route.

Heart failure was the coroner's best guess, but the reason was inconclusive. The vague cause of death aroused Bruno's instincts. The desk officer, a man of few words, explained that the realtor's reticence to answer questions over the phone likely stemmed from not wanting to spook potential buyers with the macabre history. The law required disclosure, however a death within had a way of driving down property values.

Bruno closed the file, but the questions in his mind remained. Sitting in the dimly lit station, the worn folder in his hands felt too thin for comfort. His brow furrowed as he leafed through the pages again, mentally cataloging each detail. The cause of Mrs. Reddy's death, inconclusive. Discovered days later by a mail carrier who supposedly caught the scent of the deceased from outside the house.

He pulled out his phone and scrolled to the photos he had taken of the Reddy house. A simple picket fence bordered the front yard, weathered but still standing firm. The mailbox sat perched on a waist-high pole near the sidewalk, a good ten yards from the front door. Bruno wondered about the distance between the mailbox at the curb, and the odor of a decomposing body within the house. Certainly, the odor could travel—but from that distance, through a closed door? It seemed unlikely. Why had the mail carrier approached the house at all with the mailbox at least ten yards away?

Suspicion simmered as Bruno tapped open his map app, pinpointing the nearest post office branch to the Reddy residence. Handing the folder back he thanked the desk officer.

"I copied it for you," the desk cop replied, not bothering to glance up from his paperwork. "It's yours."

"Thanks," Bruno said, before making his way back out to the car.

The post office was a modest building, its exterior as nondescript as any other small town government facility. Bruno approached the counter, showing his badge to the clerk—a young woman who blinked rapidly at the unexpected sight.

"Could I speak with the manager, please?"

Her eyes widened momentarily before she nodded and disappeared through a side door. Moments later, she reemerged and waved him through. Bruno found himself in a cramped back office where rows of mail slots and stacks of parcels created an organized chaos. The manager, a middle-aged woman with tired eyes and a no-nonsense demeanor, stood behind a desk cluttered with paperwork. The wooden nameplate on the desk read Wilma Clark.

Bruno extended his hand, "Bruno Stach, federal investigator. I'm hoping you can help me with a mail delivery question."

Wilma, gestured for him to sit. "Depends on the query," she replied, her tone brisk but not unfriendly. "My clerk said you have a badge?"

Bruno pulled the folded leather badge holder from his jacket pocket, flipping it open as he did so. "I need to know who delivered mail to a specific address on a specific day," Bruno said, hoping his tone conveyed authority but without pressing too hard.

Wilma took the badge from Bruno's hand examining it closely. "So, what interest does the Environmental Protection Agency have in our deliveries?" she asked.

Bruno then produced the letter of authority from his brief case and handed it over. "I am serving on a special assignment for a Senate Investigation," he said. "This letter grants me authority."

Wilma read briefly before smiling up at Bruno. "What address, what house and what day," she asked.

"This house," Bruno said opening the photo he had taken earlier, and handing the phone to the manager.

After glancing at the photo briefly, Wilma nodded, "Okay, I recall the incident well. We have a temp carrier, Jimmy Chin. He went to the house to make a delivery. However, no one responded to his knock. He detected a strong odor coming from the house and wondered if something had happened to the resident. He reported what he found to me and I passed the information along to the Gaithersburg P-D."

"So, my question is," Bruno explained, "why did he go to the door when the mailbox is at the street? Because, as you can see in the photo, the mailbox is at the street not at the door. It seems to me that if the odor was so strong that it reached the street, some ten yards from the door, any passerby could well have noticed it too and reported it."

"I'm beginning to see what you're getting at,"

Bruno offered a tight smile. "Honestly, I'm not even sure what I'm getting at yet. Just fishing for a thread."

"Maybe it's as simple as our mailman delivering a parcel too big for the box," Wilma suggested, her voice thoughtful. "Jimmy's meticulous about protocol. Or, if the delivery needed a signature, he would have gone to the door," she added.

Bruno straightened. "That could explain it. If it was a certified letter or parcel, your mailman would have had no choice but to go to the door for a signature."

"I can give Jimmy a buzz if you like," she offered. "He's off this week but on call. I might be able to clear this up as we speak."

"That would help a lot, thanks."

Wilma punched in a phone number and Bruno listened to the faint rings until someone picked up. Wilma's conversation was brief, her tone warm but businesslike. When she hung up, she turned to Bruno with a slight smile.

"Jimmy said it was a small priority envelope, certified, so it required a signature. That is why he went up to the door, knocked, and noticed the smell."

Bruno's mind ticked through the possibilities, then asked, "So what happened to the envelope?"

Wilma furrowed her brow, as if rewinding her memory. "Now you've got me thinking," she admitted. "What Jimmy should have done is bring it back here. We would've kept it for a period, then tried again on another delivery day. If no one claimed it after that, we would leave a notice in the mailbox, letting the resident know we were holding a certified letter for pickup here at this branch. After 30 days, if no one claimed it, the parcel would have been returned to the sender."

She paused, a flicker of confusion crossing her face. "But that's not what happened either, because once we found out the occupant had passed away, there would've been no second attempt."

Bruno's interest piqued. "So could the parcel still be here?" he asked.

Wilma shook her head slowly. "I would not think so. This was months ago. I am sure it would have been returned to the sender. The sender's name and address are always written or typed on the back of the green certification card."

Bruno let out a quiet sigh, running a hand through his hair. "Yeah, I guess you're right," he conceded. Pulling out his wallet, he fished out an EPA-ID card, scribbling out the old number and jotting down his burner phone digits. "Still, I would appreciate it if you could dig around. See where that letter ended up and give me a call."

Wilma accepted the card with a pleasant smile. "I'll see what I can do, Inspector," she promised. "It's been a while, but I'll track it as far as I can."

As Bruno left the office, the crisp air hit him, stirring a fresh wave of determination. He tucked his hands into his coat pockets and headed back to the Chevy Cruze. Too early to go back to the Senate Office Building—and for what? Endless stacks of paper that led nowhere? No, whatever clues existed were out here somewhere, waiting to be uncovered.

His stomach grumbled, a reminder that his only breakfast had been a lukewarm pour-over coffee at his kitchen table. "Food first," he thought. "If I'm going to chase ghosts, I'll need fuel."

Navigating through winding streets in search of sustenance, Bruno found himself surrounded by the charm of colonial-style architecture, each building a pristine echo of the past. As he spotted the sign for Kentland's Boulevard, a memory surfaced—something he had read about this place. "Faux Georgetown," he recalled. A whole community built from the ground up, a carefully curated replica of D.C.'s historic residential heart.

Then, like fate, a sign caught his eye: Gazebo Café. The open parking spot right out front felt like an invitation.

Bruno pulled in, killed the engine, and took a deep breath. The café's exterior was new but in colonial style, its white trim gleaming against the red-brick façade, the kind of place where the napkins were cloth and the waitstaff probably called the sandwiches "artisanal."

"Bad signs for good pastrami," Bruno muttered under his breath, already picturing a plate of dry rye bread and designer mustard.

But hunger won out for the moment. He pushed open the door, a soft chime announcing his arrival. As stepped into the warmth of the café, Bruno's lips twisted into a grimace as he scanned the menu, realizing most of the items were Korean dishes. Years ago, on an FBI investigation involving stolen government credit cards a single bite of kimchi from a street vendor in the Itaewon had rendered him bedridden for two days, sweating through fevered nightmares. It had been one of those experiences where you're terrified, you will die, then even more terrified you won't. Since then, Korean cuisine had been firmly off-limits.

He pushed back from the table, ready to bolt, but a cheerful Asian waitress intercepted him. "Something to drink?"

"Uh... do you serve pastrami sandwiches?" Bruno asked, certain the answer would be no—a perfect excuse to retreat gracefully.

But the waitress nodded enthusiastically, sealing his fate. "Yes, of course! Have a seat."

"Faux town, faux pastrami," Bruno said under his breath as he sank into a chair, defeated.

"Bread choice?" she asked, pen poised. "Rye, sourdough roll, white, or wheat?"

"Rye," Bruno sighed. "With everything."

Grasping at one last escape route, he asked, "Can you make an Arnold Palmer?"

"Sure thing! One Arnold Palmer and one pastrami on rye coming up."

Bruno resigned himself to culinary purgatory, tapping his fingers on the table. But when the drink arrived, his eyebrows lifted in surprise. The Arnold Palmer was flawless—not too sweet, perfectly blended. And the sandwich? He almost laughed at how wrong he'd been. The pastrami was tender with just the right amount of bite, Swiss cheese melted to perfection, and the Dijon mustard sharp but not overpowering. The coleslaw crunched satisfyingly, a hint of horseradish giving it a welcome kick.

With a deep sigh, he let the unexpected joy of a good meal wash over him, taking in the cozy café's warm lighting and spotless décor. He would have to remember this place—though he doubted Gaithersburg would see much more of him after this investigation.

As he sipped the last of his drink, his mind shifted gears. The Reddy house had looked deserted when he had driven by earlier. Maybe it was worth another quick check. If he found a way inside, he could always claim he was scoping out the property as a potential buyer—no harm, no foul.

The waitress reappeared, smiling. "How was everything?"

"Really good," Bruno admitted with a grin. "I'll be back."

Bruno cruised the quiet streets until the Reddy house once more came into view, sitting forlorn and empty behind the faded "For Sale" sign. He parked out front, drumming his fingers on the steering wheel as he weighed his options. After a moment, he stepped out, the cool afternoon air clearing his head. The mailbox stood empty; it's flag down confirming no recent activity.

Circling to the side of the house, Bruno scanned the doors and windows. It would not take much to get inside. The place had the neglected look of an abandoned property, and if asked, he could play the curious buyer card. However, in reality Bruno wasn't here for a real estate tour. His gut told him something in this house may hold a piece of the puzzle he was trying to solve.

Bruno tugged at the padlocked gate leading to the rear of the property but it did not budge. His eyes scanned the usual hiding spots—a loose brick, a tilted garden gnome, the edge of a worn welcome mat. Then, like a rookie thief's dream come true, he spotted a smooth, out-of-place rock by the fence post. Crouching, he pried it up, revealing a dull brass key nestled beneath. Really? he thought, half-amused. The oldest hiding place in the book.

The key clicked smoothly into the lock, and the gate swung open with a creak. The side and backyard were a jungle of overgrown grass and stubborn weeds. Wild vines strangled the remnants of a once-white garden chair. Bruno noting that even before the Reddy deaths, the yard had likely seen more neglect than care. The air smelled faintly of damp soil and distant asphalt.

The sound of tires crunching on gravel jolted him. A car rolled to a stop out front, followed by the unmistakable sound of sturdy footsteps on concrete. Bruno's gut tightened.

"State your business," came a firm voice. A uniformed officer rounded the corner, hand resting on his utility belt, eyes sharp but calm. Bruno sized him up—a no-nonsense type, maybe mid-30s, with the quiet confidence of a seasoned beat cop. No weapon drawn, but the tension in his stance said he was ready if needed.

Bruno raised his hands slightly. "I'm law enforcement too," he said evenly. "Badge is in my jacket pocket. I'm also armed." He nodded toward the street. "Checked in with Gaithersburg P.D. before heading out. There's a case folder they gave me on the backseat of that Chevy Cruze you saw when you pulled up."

The cop's expression didn't waver. "Slowly," he instructed, "Reach into your pocket, grab your badge, and toss it over."

Bruno was impressed despite himself. Firm but not jumpy. He moved as directed, retrieving the leather badge holder and tossing it gently to the officer, who caught it with practiced ease.

For two long minutes, the officer scrutinized the badge. Bruno waited, hands now relaxed at his sides, reading the man's body language. This was a cop who knew the importance of caution.

Finally, the officer stepped forward, returning the badge. "Officer Stach," he said, the formality evident, "what's the Environmental Protection Agency IG doing poking around a foreclosed property in Gaithersburg?"

Bruno pocketed his badge, offering a half-smile in response. "As I explained back at the station, it's connected to a case I'm looking into. The woman who lived here died recently, but my interest is in her son—James Reddy, a former FBI Agent."

The officer's posture relaxed slightly. "Yeah, we knew of him," he said, a trace of something—respect maybe, lingering in his tone. "Quiet guy, kept to himself. We heard about his accident... some kayaking thing, right?" He hesitated; brows furrowed. "So... is there something new we should be concerned about?"

Bruno knew he had to tread carefully. In D.C., secrets had a short shelf life, and even the faintest whisper about a political investigation could spread like wildfire. He let the silence hang for a moment, considering his words. "I'm on loan to the U.S. Senate," he finally replied, his tone measured. "Agent Reddy was working on a case. Some of the evidence he gathered may have... slipped through the cracks. My job is to poke around, see what I can dig up."

The Officer was not the type to be easily impressed. "So why isn't the FBI looking for its own missing evidence?" he asked. Years on the force had taught him how to read people, and Bruno could feel the cop's instincts probing for more information.

Bruno kept his voice calm, while reading the cops name plate. "Like I said, Officer Kominski? I am with the Senate now. They have a committee looking into corruption. That's about all I can share." He slid a hand into his wallet, pulling out one of Ken Garrett's cards. Handing it over, he added, "If you or anyone at G.P.D. needs more details, call this guy—Ken Garrett."

Kominski nodded, slipping the card into his shirt pocket. "Sure, but if you're thinking of getting inside that house, you are going to need paperwork. A warrant or something official."

Bruno nodded. "Come on, Officer Kominski, you really don't think a federal investigator would try to break into a private residence without the proper documents?" he grinned.

The cop smiled, shaking his head. "Thought never crossed my mind," he replied, sarcasm hanging thick in the air.

As they left the yard, Bruno extended a hand. Kominski accepted it with a firm shake before settling back into his patrol car. But before he drove off, he squinted up at Bruno and added, "By the way, there is an old busybody down the block—Viola McCabe. Lives in that blue house with the aluminum siding." He jerked his thumb toward it. "She's one of our neighborhood watchdogs. Knows everyone's business, reports everything—sometimes too much, if you get my drift."

Bruno thanked Kominski for the tip. "Sounds promising."

Kominski nodded. "Most of the folks around here are older. They trust Viola. She's been here forever. If someone goes to the hospital or takes a trip, Viola's the one picking up newspapers, clearing the stoop of flyers, flipping porch lights on and off to make sure no house looks empty. Some even give her spare keys... you know, just in case they'll be gone awhile. His eyes held Bruno's for a beat longer than necessary, letting the implication settle.

Bruno nodded, storing the information away. Another thread, faint but perhaps worth following. "Thanks again Officer."

"We try to please," Kominski replied, touching the brim of his Pershing hat before easing the patrol car away from the curb. Bruno waved as the cruiser disappear down the street, his mind already turning over the possibilities Viola McCabe might unlock.

Chapter 16

Bruno decided it was as good a time as any to visit Viola McCabe, hoping she was home and willing to talk. Pulling the Cruze up in front of the blue house Officer Kominski had pointed out. The yard was a hodgepodge of garden trolls, potted cacti, and various Plaster of Paris animals cluttered the small front space—squirrels, bunnies, turtles, you name it. The ground, once blanketed in white gravel, now showed signs of neglect, with weeds pushing through the scattered stones, adding contrast to the whimsical ornaments.

As Bruno approached the front door, he pressed the doorbell and heard a chorus of melodic chimes from within. The door swung open almost immediately, confirming his suspicion that Viola had been watching him from a window.

She stood before him, a vivid splash of color in the dull afternoon light. Dressed in a floral-patterned housedress with matching sandals, Viola McCabe appeared every bit the eccentric neighbor Bruno had imagined. Her blue-white hair was teased into a blender-whipped swirl, crowned by a single pink ribbon. Bakelite jewelry adorned her from head to toe—chunky earrings, layered necklaces, oversized buttons, and rings on nearly every finger and even her toes.

"Hello, Ms. McCabe, I'm Inspector Stach," Bruno greeted, displaying his badge with a polite smile.

Viola nodded knowingly. "I saw you talking to that nice young Officer Kominski," she purred, her voice carrying a practiced sweetness. "He's a friend of mine, you know."

"I know. He speaks very highly of you and wonders why you don't drop by the station more often."

Her face lit up preeing at the compliment. "I do my best for the neighborhood watch, and I try to get down to the police station as often as I can to talk to my boys," she boasted. "Are you here about Gertrude, the poor thing?"

Bruno nodded. "Yes, about her—and also her son, Jim. Did you know them both well?"

Viola's expression revealed a trace of genuine sadness. "Yes, her death was so sudden too," she sighed. "I was visiting my sister in Michigan at the time, or I would have found her much sooner than that mailman she sniffed delicately, dabbing her nose with a lace handkerchief pulled from her sleeve. "I visited with her almost daily, you know. We would talk and have tea—some days at my house, some at hers."

Bruno's hesitated, "And I understand you may have a key to her house. Do you?"

"Officer Kominski must have told you that," she replied with a knowing smile.

Bruno lowered his voice and glanced around, with feigned wariness. "In police business, we can't reveal our sources, Mrs. McCabe," he murmured, "but I'm going to ask you an important favor."

Viola pursed her lips tightly to signal that no secret would escape them. She nodded, clearly delighted to be involved in police business.

"I'd like to go through the Reddy house," Bruno continued, "but I need you to come with me. You see Ms. Reddy gave you her key, so she gave you permission to enter. That means you can usher me through as well. You will serve as my assistant."

"Certainly, certainly!" Viola whispered excitedly, already turning to grab a sweater from a hook by the door. She was back in an instant, her eyes sparkling with anticipation. Bruno could tell she was relishing every moment of the unfolding intrigue. This was more than just a neighborhood errand; this was her chance to be part of something significant.

They left Bruno's car behind and walked briskly to the Reddy house, Viola leading the way with a newfound purpose. When she unlocked the front door, Bruno's senses immediately registered the faint, lingering odor of death.

"What are we looking for?" Viola whispered, her voice barely audible.

"Maybe luggage," Bruno replied, scanning the empty room. "A metal suitcase, perhaps. Did you know her son worked for the F.B.I.?"

"Oh yes," Viola nodded earnestly. "I liked Jim very much. Such a shy young man, but he always had a big smile for me." She hesitated, glancing around the barren interior. "But you can see, the furniture and all their possessions have been taken. Auctioned off— right here in Gertrude's own front yard."

Bruno's eyes swept the empty spaces, disappointment settling in as he took in the starkness of the home. It was completely bare. Every trace of the Reddys' lives had been stripped away, leaving nothing but memories embedded in the walls. In one of the small bedrooms, however, something caught his eye—a lone plaque hanging on the wall, bearing an inscription in elegant, foreign calligraphy.

"Is this a religious item?" Bruno asked, tilting his head to study the intricate scrawl.

Viola nodded, "Uh-huh. This was Jim's bedroom," she explained. "Jim's father was from India. Gertrude told me she dated him in college, but when she told him she was pregnant, he skedaddled. Just up and left," she added with a sniff of disapproval. "When Jim was older, before college—he went to India and looked up his father. He was some kind of Hindu... a Jain, I think, Gertrude said. Jim lived with his father's family in India for about a year and became a Jain too. I guess that's where he got that thing," she added, pointing at the plaque on the wall.

The empty house, the lone plaque, painted a poignant picture of Jim Reddy's life. A man caught between two worlds, one of duty and another of heritage, both now forgotten.

"What was Gertrude's reaction to her son's religious conversion?" Bruno wondered.

"She wasn't all that crazy about it," Viola admitted. "But she was just happy to have him back home. All that happened when they still lived in California, before Jim joined the FBI and they both moved here to Maryland."

"After Jim died—or was killed," she added, "Gertrude honored Jim's wishes and notified his temple, or church, whatever it is called. It was terrible what happened next." She shook her head. "The chief monk insisted Jim had to be cremated within twenty-four hours! Gertrude said no way, but Jim had already signed papers with the temple, so she had to let them do it."

"One more answer," Bruno nodded, appreciating her candor and what she had just shared.

Viola perked up, as if eager to offer more. "Gertrude had a niece—Nellie was her name. Closest next of kin they could find. I don't know her last name. This Nellie got the house and everything in it when Gertrude passed. She had all of Gertrude's things auctioned off." Viola said with indignation. "I don't know if Gertrude had any other property."

Bruno considered this new information. "I'm looking into a case where something is missing," he ventured carefully. "A piece of luggage. Did you see any luggage at the auction?"

Viola led him through the small house from room to room, her sharp eyes scanning every empty corner, as if hoping to spot a clue even now. "I thought the auction was in poor taste," she complained. "Selling all their belongings like that right after she passed!" She shook her head in disgust. "I didn't buy anything, but some of the neighbors did." She paused; her brow furrowed in thought. "Luggage? No, I think I would have remembered that. But Nellie had everything that didn't sell hauled away by the Salvation Army. There really wasn't much of value left."

Walking back to his car with Viola, Bruno contemplated the missing suitcase, the auction, and now a connection to a religious group with strict traditions. He glanced at Viola, who was already basking in the glow of having been part of something important.

"Ms. McCabe," he said, turning on his charm, "I understand you also pick up mail for people when they are away. Is that correct?"

Viola started to reply, "I'll bet Officer Kom—"

Bruno raised a finger to his lips, "Police business," he whispered, eliciting a nod from Viola, who pursed her lips tightly once more.

"Did you ever pick up Gertrude's mail?" he asked.

Viola nodded.

Bruno smiled. "It's okay to speak now," he said. "Just don't mention where information comes from. That's the police business."

"Okay, I believe, I now understand," Viola said, nodding again. "Yes, I often picked up her mail—but not at the time she died. I was visiting my sister then."

"Did you ever see a certified letter? One with a green card attached?" Bruno asked.

"Well, yes. That letter. But that came much later. In fact—" She paused, pressing a finger to her temple. "I noticed her mailbox was half open just after the auction. I knew the mailbox had been shut tightly because I pass it almost every day, so I went to take a look. There was a letter with a green card, just like you said."

Bruno's pulse quickened. "Do you know where it is?" He asked calmly.

Viola knitted her brow. "What did I do with that darn thing?" she muttered to herself. Then, snapping her fingers, she declared, "Let me check the box the Post Office gave me to collect mail. I don't think it would still be there, but we'll see."

Bruno followed Viola back into her house. In a corner near the door stood a white canvas box about two feet by three feet, stenciled with 'U.S. Postal Service' in bold black letters on two sides. A jumble of advertisements and catalogs lay crumpled at the bottom.

Viola bent over the box, her jewelry clinking softly as she shuffled through the clutter. Presently she paused, pulling out a small priority envelope partially hidden beneath discarded flyers and notices. The green certified card was still attached.

"Is this what you're looking for?" she asked eagerly, holding it out as if it were a golden ticket.

Bruno struggled to contain his excitement. This could be the break he needed, but HE shrugged nonchalantly. "Maybe yes, maybe no," he replied. "But it should definitely be taken back to the post office. I better drop it off over there on my way out. If you do it, they might ask a bunch of questions about why you had it for so long," Bruno explained. "If you say you forgot about it, they might reconsider letting you pick up mail for folks in the neighborhood."

He shook his head, offering a reassuring smile. "I don't think that would be right. From what I can see, you're doing a fine job. Officer Kominski certainly thinks so, and we don't want anything to get in the way of your eyes being on the street."

Viola gasped, visibly flustered. "Oh, would you return it, please!" she pleaded, clutching at Bruno's arm. She looked rattled, as if she had committed some grave misstep and dreaded being found out.

"Don't worry, I won't mention your name. If I take it in for you, there won't be any questions," Bruno assured her.

"Oh, thank you, thank you," she gushed, "I can't believe I forgot about it."

Bruno shook his head to reassure her. "A small mistake, Viola," he said, retreating out the front door toward his car. Turning back with a wave for a moment, he added, "I promise you—if you don't mention it, you will never hear of the matter again."

Driving back to Washington, Bruno's mind was abuzz with possibilities. The envelope had felt too light to contain documents. Perhaps it was empty?

Upon returning to D.C., he parked the Chevy Cruze in its designated spot and walked briskly to his former office at the Environmental Protection Agency. The familiar scent of stale coffee and government-issued carpet greeted him like an old acquaintance. Settling into a crackled leather chair, Bruno pulled out his burner phone and dialed Wilma Clark at the Gaithersburg Post Office.

She did not answer, so he left a message, careful with his words. "The certified letter we were looking for has been found," he said into the recording. "I will send you an email to that effect so you can have a paper trail regarding what occurred. Since the sender and the addressee are both deceased, I am going to hold on to it for a while. If you have any questions, call me. And thanks again for your assistance. Special Agent Stach."

Hanging up, Bruno next stared at the unopened envelope resting on his desk. Finding a letter opener in the desk drawer he pried it open.

A single small key tumbled out onto the desk's surface. Picking it up, Bruno noticed an engraved number: 608. His brow furrowed. It wasn't an ordinary key—it looked like one used for a security locker or safe deposit box.

"Where the hell is 608?" he wondered, turning the key over in his fingers.

The envelope provided no other clues. The contents were understood by one person and he was dead. However, when he turned over the certified green card there was the senders name and address just as Ms. Clark at the Gaithersburg Post Office had explained. 'James Reddy' was handwritten on both sides of the card with the address of the Reddy house in Gaithersburg. He had mailed the key to himself! rubbing his temples, Bruno pondered possible reasons why. Reddy had been an FBI agent so whatever this key unlocked might still be connected to the Justice Department. But walking into the Justice Building and casually asking about a key without raising suspicions? Impossible.

Bruno's Senate investigation gave him one unspoken authority: the rule of finders, keepers. And Bruno Stach intended to keep key 608 until he could uncover whatever secrets FBI agent Reddy had hidden with it.

PART III:
LILLIAN BLAKE

Chapter 17

Lillian's world was a collision of two vastly different landscapes—the scholarly, book-filled halls of her father's university and the wide-open plains of Kansas. At home, she was surrounded by the accoutrements of academia, yet just beyond the porch, past the barn and the meandering Wakarusa River, lay a simpler, wilder existence.

The Blakes' farmhouse, a sturdy limestone relic from another century, was where her father split his time between grading student essays and tending to his small flock of ducks and chickens. Lillian, meanwhile, poured her energy into raising Chinchilla Rex rabbits, proudly showing them at county fairs. Collecting ribbons and trophies was okay for a small girl, however, as her teen years began that life seemed just a little too small for her growing ambitions.

After the Clinton Dam was built, other professors and deans began moving further from Kansas University, building new pristine homes near the reservoir where Professor Blake and his family resided.

Everything shifted when Lillian turned fourteen. The first stirrings of adolescence brought with it an awareness of the stares and backward glances she was receiving from the opposite sex.

"Precocious," her mother sighed, watching the way Lillian navigated the world. "Charming," her father declared proudly, oblivious to the dangers of that charm. "Trouble," the other girls her age gossiped under their breath, waiting for the day she'd get hers. To the local boys she was something else entirely—thrilling, untouchable, and a game worth playing.

She was courted in cornfields, where older boys fought over a chance to steal a kiss in the front seat of a pickup truck. College guys, fresh from KU's fraternities, tried to impress her with fast cars and cheap beer. And then there was the Shawnee boy, the one who led her down by the river and spoke about his ancestors, pointing to the land where his people had once camped, long before the white settlers arrived.

Her many female friends and "frenemies" held their tongues, waiting to see if Lillian would lose her footing, and fall from grace as other young beauties had before her. But what they didn't understand was that she had no intention of stumbling. Maybe some mothers, except her own, saw her as a girl playing with fire. But Lillian saw something else entirely—a future far beyond the whispered warnings and the Kansas corn and sorghum fields. She was planning on setting the whole world ablaze.

Lillian had always believed she was special. Destined for something greater than the mundane lives of the rural country people she grew up with. When she was with the Shawnee boy, lying in the tall grass by the river, she could almost see it—the life that awaited her, far from Kansas, far from her father's farm, and far from the prairie-town expectations that wanted to pull her into their world.

For all her unspoken ambitions, Lillian was still just a girl in a town where some believed her fate had already decided, a cautionary tale whispered about at slumber parties.

Instead, Lillian left them all behind. For college she chose the University of Southern California, USC was to be her golden ticket, the first step toward the life she had always imagined for herself. Her father had used accumulated academia influence to get her registered as a part time student in the School of Dramatic Arts.

Lillian arrived in Los Angeles with a brand-new Camaro, her confidence as untouchable as the blue California sky. Theatre Arts was her dream, from the moment she set foot on campus, the other sun-kissed, designer-clad girls recognized her as one of their own. The transformation was effortless. Afternoons spent at the beach, singing along with the Phantom Planet as she and her new acquaintances cruised down the 101 in the Camero, the Pacific breezes whipping through their hair. LA was everything she had hoped for, every fantasy she had spun in her head as a girl. She was here now. She had made it.

Then, just like that, the fantasy was fractured. Her father's affair, her parents' divorce, the sudden, brutal realization that money wasn't infinite. The Camaro was sold. Her tuition became an expense her father, now starting a new family, refused to carry. She was left to scrape by on hostess wages and her mother's reluctant support. However, Lillian refused to let it crush her. She eventually finished her degree taking evening classes. She had survived, but survival was not the same as winning, and Los Angeles had its own rules—ones she had not been prepared for.

The film industry was merciless. She signed with an agent who took more than he gave, promising roles that never came. She threw herself into auditions, workshops, and training sessions, all in pursuit of a break that never materialized. And then came the moment every aspiring actress faces at some point—the moment she realized that talent and ambition were never enough. It occurred when a bloated, cigar-scented director made it clear that success had a price. The first time, she swallowed her disgust. She convinced herself it was a necessary evil, a stepping stone. But it was not a one-time deal. The interest on her dreams was compounding, and she was not sure how much more she was willing to pay.

Lillian's former life was unravelling in slow motion, each new disappointment piling on like bricks until she could barely move under the weight of it. Then, like a scene from an old movie, he appeared—the tall, confident guy who entered the coffee shop where she now worked.

He had a solid job, a winning smile, and a way of making her feel like she was still the girl who had once driven down the 101 in a Camaro, singing along with the wind. He took her to places she could no longer afford—steakhouses with white tablecloths, nights at the Pantages Theatre, long, indulgent dinners followed by whispered promises.

When he finally admitted he was married, the revelation barely slowed them down. The wife's a bitch, he told her, and Lillian, desperate to feel wanted, let herself believe that she was different, that she was special. And soon enough, the wife became the ex-wife, and Lillian found herself swept into a whirlwind wedding, with a postcard-perfect honeymoon in Puerto Vallarta. For a moment, she thought she had finally regained stability.

However, her new reality had sharp edges. His drinking started early and always got worse. She met his ex-wife only once, at a weekend custody drop-off. The woman had smiled, shaking her hand like they were old friends, and thanked Lillian for taking him off her hands. His alimony payments to the ex were generous. Still, this meant the money was drained away before it reached Lillian. Soon they were crammed into a North Hollywood flat, his paycheck barely covering the essentials.

Then the drinking turned mean. He lost his job. He lost control, and after two years of abuse, Lillian walked away, signing the divorce papers with a shaking hand. The final blow came not from a judge but from the radio:

"It never rains in California, but girl don't they warn ya? It pours, man, it pours."

And pour it did. But still she refused to drown.

State Parks wasn't Hollywood, but it was a job, a steady one. Writing vacancy announcements and preparing job descriptions. It was not exactly what she had imagined for herself, but at least it paid the bills. She was good at it, too—finding people the right positions, helping others move up even if she sometimes felt stuck herself.

Then, her father died. Lillian returned to Kansas just long enough to say goodbye to her mom. The bitter February wind bit through her coat as she stood by her father's grave, realizing, with certainty, that she no longer belonged there. Her mother had already moved back to Chicago, leaving Kansas behind like an old chapter in a forgotten book. The farm was sold. But with that loss came a gift—a down payment for a bungalow in Tarzana.

It was not a lot, but it was hers. The taxes were no worse than her rent in North Hollywood had been, and for the first time in years, Lillian felt something she had almost forgotten. A sense of relief and wellbeing. She could smile again with new friends.

Settling into a quiet life, one that felt safe, even if it was not the dream she had once imagined, Lillian filled her days with work, her weekends with the Coast Conservation Corps, and her evenings with the soft, comforting presence of Benjamin, the only stray she had kept after her home became overwhelmed with rescued animals.

Then came Hudson, it had started so simply—him answering her knock on his door, an invitation to a CCC meeting, a shared interest in something greater than themselves. Now, she was cooking him dinner. Pot roast, the only dish she knew how to make that did not come prepackaged. It had been years since she had done something like this. The act felt both foreign comforting, as if some long-forgotten part of herself had reemerged.

Hudson fit in easily with the CCC group, especially with Kestrel Alan. The two had become nearly inseparable, their easy camaraderie turning Friday night bowling into a regular thing with Sylvia and Lillian. It should have felt perfect—a small, close-knit circle where she finally belonged—but something about it unsettled her.

Lately, Kestrel and Hud had been talking about West Virginia, about checking out Stanley Energy. About chasing a ghost of a rumor, a silver suitcase that, as far as Lillian was concerned, might as well be a myth. A fool's errand, nothing more. But that was not what worried her the most.

Chapter 18

Later that evening, after the Coast Conservation Corps meeting, a small group of their night owls gathered in their usual booth at Denny's. It had become a ritual—hashing out their discussions over bottomless coffee and late-night food. The piped in music hummed an old Eagles tune, and the clatter of silverware mixed with their quiet chatter.

Lillian was reminiscing about her childhood in Lawrence, Kansas, when Kestrel cut in. "I know that place," he said, leaning forward with interest. "My uncle went to school there. A school for Native Peoples."

"Of course, Haskell," Lillian said, her expression brightening. "Our house in Lawrence was really close to it." She studied Kes for a moment. "What tribe are you from, anyway?"

"Fugawi," he deadpanned, his dark eyes downcast. "The lost tribe."

Lillian grimmaced. "Oh, come on, Kes. I grew up around Indian guys—I've heard that stale old joke a thousand times."

Kestrel shrugged. "Fair enough. Siletz," he acknowledged. "I grew up near a one-horse town on the Oregon Coast, Taft. My people had a name for it long before the settlers showed up, but the whites named it Taft." His fingers drummed absently against the tabletop. "My uncle, Manny—my mom's brother—went to Haskell. Before that, he was at Chemawa Indian School in Salem, Oregon. He was really into being Native, you know? Wanted to reclaim our traditions, our history." He hesitated for a second, then added, "He died at Wounded Knee."

Lillian frowned. "That's the thing with you, Kes. No one can ever tell when you're joking or serious." She said searching his face. "Come on—Wounded Knee? That was the eighteen hundreds."

"No," Kestrel interrupted her. "Like I said, my uncle was deep into his roots. He joined the American Indian Movement—A.I.M. He went with Dennis Banks, Russell Means, Clyde Bellecourt,

Richard Oakes, and the rest of our warriors. They occupied Wounded Knee in the seventies. Pine Ridge, South Dakota." He leaned back against the booth, staring at his reflection in the window. "It was supposed to be a stand for our people's rights. Turned into a war zone. Marshals, FBI, BIA goons—all of them out for blood."

"I thought that was just a standoff," LJ said, stirring her coffee. "I Didn't think people were actually killed."

Kes exhaled sharply. "More than a few died. Official reports say two, but there were a lot more unaccounted for. My uncle included." He glanced at Lillian. "Not a joke, Blondie."

Kestrel's rare seriousness quieted the table. The hum of the music, the clinking of plates, the low murmur of conversations—it all felt distant, like background noise in the wake of something lost in history.

"Several people were shot on both sides," Kestrel went on, his voice carrying an undercurrent of restrained anger. "Some died, some just… disappeared. Uncle Manny was one of them. One day he was fighting, the next day—gone. No body, no closure. As far as my family's concerned, he died at Wounded Knee." Kes added, "His remains were never found, but my mom's family gave him a traditional burial ceremony for tribal elders back home on the Siletz reservation. It is the only way we could let him rest in his native Oregon."

Sylvia Jamaica shifted in her seat. She had known Kestrel's mother was Native American and that his father was white. She also knew Kes had a way of gravitating toward the radical edge of things. It was not just his stance on environmental activism—if a group had an extremist faction, Kes would find it. And if they did not, she had a feeling he would be the one to start it.

Hud cleared his throat, but before anyone else could speak, Kestrel leaned back in the booth and began slapping his palms against the table, a slow, deliberate rhythm. His voice dropped to a low chant, his eyes closing as he sang in a native tongue.

The group sat in stunned silence.

Hud let out a quiet chuckle—half nervous, half unsure of how to react—but Sylvia shot him a glare sharp enough to quiet him.

"It's the A.I.M. Anthem," she announced, her voice reverent. "Kes has been teaching it to me."

Then, without hesitation, she closed her eyes and joined him. Her voice was softer, but it blended beautifully with his, weaving an ancient harmony that sent chills down Lillian's spine. After the song ended for a moment, no one spoke.

LJ finally broke the silence. "It's… beautiful," she said but angry too.

Kestrel nodding once. "It's the A.I.M. Song," he said. "A protest song. A warrior's song sung at Dennis Bankes wake in Minnesota. You can hear it on YouTube." The unspoken message hung in the air—this was not just history to Kestrel. It was unfinished business.

PART IV:

KESTREL ALAN

Chapter 19

Kestrel's father, Scott Alan, worked as an ambulance driver for the Lincoln City Fire Department, serving a stretch of the Oregon coast that spanned seven miles of rugged shoreline. Their home, Taft, was a quiet hamlet nestled along the shores of Siletz Bay, a few miles south of Lincoln City proper. The bay itself bore the name of the coastal tribe that had lived in the region for thousands of years, long before white settlers arrived.

Scott had met his future wife, Mabel, a full-blooded member of the Siletz Tribe, under the most unexpected circumstances. Late one evening, Lincoln City cops had radioed for medical assistance after breaking up a particularly violent barroom brawl. When Scott arrived with his ambulance, he found Mabel lying on the floor in a pool of blood, her dark hair matted with it, a broken bottle having been smashed over her head in the chaos. Though she was barely conscious, her spirit was intact—she had been fighting, not fleeing.

Scott rushed her to the nearest emergency room, staying by her side far beyond what his job required. After that night, he kept in touch, stopping by the hospital to check on her recovery, then later finding reasons to visit her at home. What began as concern soon turned into long talks about life, history, and the land. Less than a year later, they were married in a ceremony that blended Siletz traditions with a modest Western-style wedding. Mabel suffered several pregnancies that ended in loss, but one child—a son—survived. They named him Bobby at birth.

Bobby Alan grew up like many boys in Taft, spending his childhood alongside a mix of white, Native American, and Hispanic kids. They roamed the wild spaces of the Oregon coast, fishing for salmon in the Siletz River, hunting deer and elk in the dense forests, and digging for clams along the muddy flats of the bay. But for Bobby, nothing compared to football. As a linebacker for the Taft Tigers, he became a local legend, not because of his size—he was never the tallest on the field—but because of his raw strength, quick reflexes, and relentless pursuit of whoever on the other team had the football.

Bobby had an uncanny ability to slip through linemen, read plays before they unfolded, and bring down quarterbacks with bone-rattling force. From his sophomore year through graduation, he led the Oregon Coast League in sacks. By his senior year, no player in the state had put more quarterbacks on the turf than Bobby Alan.

Still, Taft was too small for him. He had always known that. Listening to his mother's stories about Uncle Manny—about the American Indian Movement (A.I.M.), about the standoff at Pine Ridge, about the warriors who had fought for their people. A lost world that still pulsed beneath the surface of his own. The injustice Manny had fought against had not disappeared; it had just changed shape. Bobby wanted to be part of something bigger, to stand for something, to fight for his people in a way that still meant something.

There was one thing Uncle Manny had left behind before he vanished, an old Triumph Bonneville motorcycle, wrecked and rusting in the family's garage. For years, it sat there, covered in dust, its chrome dulled, its once well-crafted frame a relic of a life interrupted. But Bobby never saw it as a piece of junk. To him, it was history waiting to be revived.

With the help of his best friend, Luther Fills-The-Pipe, and Luther's father, a skilled shade-tree mechanic who could fix anything with an engine, Bobby worked to bring the Triumph back to life. For months, they tinkered, patched, replaced, and rebuilt, until the old bike finally roared back to its former glory. When Bobby finally swung his leg over the seat and kicked it to life, he knew one thing for sure—wherever he went next, the Triumph would take him there.

Several Siletz tribal elders regularly attended Taft High football games, watching with quiet intensity from the sidelines. They took special notice of the Alan boy, who moved with a speed and precision that seemed almost otherworldly. By the time his senior year was drawing to a close, one of the elders—a respected storyteller and seer—approached him after a game, his deeply lined face and serious voice expressing the traditions of generations of the Siletz people.

"You have been chosen by the spirits of your ancestors," the elder said, gripping Bobby's shoulder with surprising strength. "One day, you will be a leader of your people."

Bobby had heard many things over the years, but nothing quite like that. He listened with respect as the old man continued.

"You play football the way a kestrel hunts," the elder observed. "Fast. Precise. Following your prey like a heat-seeking arrow." His dark face flickered with ancient knowledge. "I have watched kestrels chase bats at dusk—quick, agile, relentless. Bats are unpredictable, darting and twisting in ways that confuse most hunters. But not the kestrel. The kestrel watches. Waits. And when the time is right—it strikes, catching its prey in mid-flight."

The old man spoke of the traditions of the Siletz people, how young men had often renamed themselves upon reaching adulthood, choosing names that reflected their greatest strengths or the traits they had demonstrated in their youth. It was a rite of passage, a way to claim one's true identity, not just the name given at birth.

And so, standing there beneath the stadium lights, sweat still clinging to his skin after the game, Bobby Alan decided to claim his true name.

From that night on, he was no longer Bobby. He was Kestrel.

Chapter 20

Kestrel left a note on his mother's bedside table, weighed down with a small stone to keep it anchored in place. The words were simple: I need to go where I'm needed. I'll be back when I can. Then, without another thought, he wrapped himself in a heavy wool blanket, kicked the Triumph into gear, and rode eastward. The wind bit through his jacket as he rode through the dark highways, feeling the pull of something greater than himself—the pulse of resistance, the call of his ancestors.

Days later, after grueling miles of open road, Kestrel arrived at Standing Rock Reservation, at a place called Cannon Ball. The sky was thick with smoke, the glow of fires flickering against the dark horizon like distant spirits dancing. He parked the Triumph near a cluster of makeshift tents and ran toward the commotion, heart pounding, instincts sharp. Like a linebacker reading the field, he charged forward, always toward the center of the action.

Backwater Bridge was a war zone. Protesters, many wrapped in traditional shawls, raised their voices in defiance as law enforcement stood in a tight phalanx, shields up, gas canisters hissing. The Blackfoot Confederacy, the Great Sioux Nation, and Ponca tribal leaders had already signed a declaration against further pipeline construction on sacred land, ratified in a ceremony meant to invoke the power of their ancestors. But paper and prayers were not strong enough to stand against trained officers in riot gear.

Morton County law enforcement, backed by federal observers, responded with force. Rubber bullets cracked through the air, slamming into bodies, breaking skin, and bones. High-pressure hoses fired torrents of ice-cold water into the crowd. It was 28 degrees, and the water turned to ice almost instantly, forming crystalline shells over beards, parkas, and shawls. Protesters staggered, some screaming, some too cold to do anything but shiver, their limbs going numb as hypothermia set in.

Kestrel pressed forward, dodging through the throng, his breath ragged in the freezing air. Flames from two burning vehicles sent plumes of smoke curling into the sky, turning the bridge into a hellscape of flickering light and shadow. He had no time to detect the rubber-coated steel projectile before it struck him. The shot hit square in his jaw with the force of a hammer, sending him sprawling to the pavement. He tasted blood, his head spun, and then a freezing blast from the hoses soaked him to the bone, the shock stealing the breath from his lungs.

Hours later, he awoke wrapped in warmth, the first thing he saw was a woman—her skin the deep, rich brown of her ancestors, her features sharp and proud and framed by long dark braids. Her hazel eyes, filled with quiet strength, met his own. A healer. Her hands, warm and steady, pressed against his. He reached for her instinctively, fingers curling around hers, seeking comfort, connection. She did not pull away.

Kestrel had come looking for purpose. In that moment, he realized he had found something more. She came to his bedside daily to bring food and change bandages and he learned her name was Sylvia, at her last visit they exchanged cell numbers and he promised to call.

Kestrel recovered quickly among the Sioux and Blackfoot, immersed in the unwavering determination of the activists around him. These were not just people fighting for a cause—they were warriors, bound by blood, history, and an unshakable belief that they were standing on the front lines of something far greater than themselves. The air at Standing Rock was thick with both resilience and sorrow, as though the land itself understood the cost of battle.

Some of the younger men and women he had met were planning to head to Los Angeles, where they had heard of a growing movement—a coalition of Native Americans, environmentalists, and activists determined to raise awareness and stop construction of the pipeline project. The fight would not end in the Dakotas; it would spread, forcing the entire country to take notice. Kestrel did not hesitate when they offered him a place among them.

The next morning, they set out in two battered pickup trucks, crammed together with their belongings stuffed into duffel bags. They took turns riding Uncle Manny's restored Triumph, its engine purring along the endless stretch of highway. But before Kestrel left Standing Rock, he phoned Sylvia. When she did not pick up, he left a message, "Some of us are headed for LA, call me when you get a chance."

Once in Los Angeles, reality bit. The men from Dakota found work at the downtown Farmers' Market, hauling crates of produce, busing tables, and stacking pallets. It was hard work, but it paid just enough to rent squalid rooms in the downtown area of the city. Most of their food came from leftovers at the market, or traded among workers like a secret economy. The work days were long, sun-up to sun-down, but the city had an electric energy, something wild seemed to always be humming beneath its surface.

Despite the adrenalin rush the City of Angels provided, Kestrel's mind remained elsewhere. No matter how many faces he saw, or how many voices he heard, Sylvia was there, lingering in the back of his thoughts. He asked the men from Standing Rock if they knew anything more about her.

"Her name's Sylvia," one of them recalled while leaning against a wall and passing a cigarette during a work break. "She came to Standing Rock as an emergency med-tech intern. She was studying to obtain her EMT certificate."

"Where's she from?" Kestrel asked, pressing for anything more.

The man shrugged. "She's got an accent, but no one could place it. "Not tribal," he said, "maybe French Canadian."

In the evenings, the Dakota men met in Pershing Square Park, gathering in tight circles, sharing whatever food and smokes they had scrounged from the market. It wasn't just a place to relax—it became a meeting ground, a nerve center for many locals. Every night, more young activists arrived, drawn together by chat rooms and other online contact methods, talking about an organized resistance. As the conversations grew bolder, they were not just talking about the pipeline anymore; they were talking about the bigger picture—the corporations, and the government, the system itself and how it had to change.

Then, one day a wiry, pale-skinned techy guy showed up. He was jittery, but he had something the rest of them did not—connections and a shrill speaking voice.

"I can get this out," he said, tapping furiously on an iPad at the edge of their group. "I can get people here. Real people. People who care. Give me a few days."

No one expected much. But when the day of the protest arrived, the Dakota men were impressed. The streets were filled. Not just with activists but with veterans' groups, biker clubs, eco-warriors, anarchists in black hoodies, members of Black Bloc and Antifa. Some carried homemade banners painted on sheets. Others had megaphones, chanting slogans that echoed off nearby buildings.

Kestrel stood in the middle of it all, his pulse pounding. He had never seen anything like this—not in Oregon, not in the Dakotas, not anywhere.

"This isn't just a march," he heard himself yell to some of the other Dakota men, his voice carrying over the crowd. "This is the start of a movement! This is like A.I.M.!

A small stage had been set up at the heart of the rally, its aluminum framing barely elevated above the crowd. Loudspeakers flanked each side, crackling slightly as they amplified the chants that had become a rhythmic pulse through the throng.

"What do we want?"

"Environmental Justice!"

"When do we want it?"

"Now!"

Signs scrawled on sheets and cardboard waved above the heads of the protesters, others professionally printed, with stark warnings about corporate greed, climate destruction, and indigenous land rights.

Then, a figure emerged from the side of the scaffolding, and stepping up to a hastily erected podium. The same tall, slender young man who had first put out notices of the rally. His receding hairline doing nothing to diminish the confidence of his presence. His long, clean-shaven face was drawn with purpose, wire-rimmed glasses perched on the bridge of a thin nose. He wore western boots, well-worn Levi's, and a green t-shirt emblazoned with bold letters: CCC. A small whale decal adorned the upper left pocket.

He tapped the microphone twice, a dull thump-thump vibrating through the speakers. The murmuring crowd gradually quieted as he looked out over them, his easy manner contrasting with the restless energy in the air.

"There are people here from all walks of life, different backgrounds, different causes," he began, his voice clear but thin, carried effortlessly by the sound system. "We come from cities and reservations, from farms and factories, from the streets and the universities. But we are all here, one way or another, to stand against the latest assault on our planet. We are here to fight against another pipeline, another violation of the land, another corporate stronghold that values profit over life itself."

A ripple of applause moved through the crowd, scattered at first, then swelling as people turned toward one another in agreement.

"This pipeline is not just bad for the environment," he continued, his voice growing stronger. "It is bad for the people. For the land. For the rivers, for the air, for the very future of this planet! And today, we recognize those who have already put their bodies on the line to stop it."

He turned toward a small group of men standing together near the front, their rugged faces unmistakable.

"The Dakota warriors are here today," he announced, "men and women who stood on the front lines, who faced rubber bullets, tear gas, fire hoses and freezing temperatures. They fought not just for their people but for all people everywhere."

A wave of cheers erupted. The Dakota men stiffened slightly, caught off guard by his acknowledgment of their presence as the applause rolled over them. Other protesters turned to clap in their direction, raising fists in solidarity.

"There is only one reason this poison pipeline is being built," he said, his voice measured, deliberate. "And it is not for energy. We know that better alternatives exist—wind, solar, tidal. We know these sources are safer, cleaner, limitless. We know they do not defile our air, our water, our land."

The silence that followed was telling. He had them now. The restless shifting, the side conversations—gone. The crowd was listening with rapt attention.

"And yet, the fossil fuel companies, the energy extractors, tell us climate change is a lie," he continued, his voice gaining urgency. "They call it false science. They say that the earth has warmed and cooled before, and that humans had no part in it."

"Well, what if they're right?"

The crowd stirred, uncertain.

"What if every credible scientist in the world is wrong?" he asked, pausing, letting the tension build. "What if man's activities are not changing the climate?"

He continued, "This is still happening!" he shouted, his voice ringing out over the sea of people. "This is a fact! 200,000 Americans die every year from poor air quality related diseases. In California alone, over 600,000 children suffer from asthma! Some will never see adulthood. Some will die before they have a chance to fight back. And globally?"

He spread his arms wide, his voice like steel now.

"More than seven million people will achieve an early death each year, suffocated by the poison we allow into our skies."

"And yet." The speaker raised a hand, and the crowd, once again fell silent.

"And yet the cynical billionaires continue their murderous business, and their paid-for politicians not only allow it but legislate on behalf of it!" His voice rising again. "For what reason?" He let the question hang in the air, heavy and accusatory, before answering it himself. "Greed! To fill their already overflowing coffers. To control the wealth of the world!"

A murmur rippled through the crowd, as waves of understanding and fury collided.

The speaker paused, reaching into his back pocket and pulling out a well-worn Western-style bandana. He wiped his mouth, slow and deliberate, letting the moment breathe, letting the tension thicken like smoke in the air before continuing.

"A generation ago," he began again. "A generation ago, our forefathers fought a terrible and just war against a tyrant who sought to erase an entire population from all of Europe and almost succeeded. Secretly sending men, women, and children to their deaths, to chambers where poison gas was the instrument of execution."

The silence deepened. A few people inhaled sharply, trying to recall stories they had heard as children.

"Today's monsters wear different masks," he declared, scanning the sea of faces. "But make no mistake, they are at work again."

He continued, "They tamper with the very air we breathe. They alter the monitoring systems of automobile engines to hide the truth vehicle engine emissions secretly pumping five times the legal limit of toxic diesel fumes into our atmosphere. Five times! Our grandparents called those tyrants of our grandparents generation what they were—" his voice rose, "MURDERERS. Rightfully so! CRIMINALS AGAINST HUMANITY. Rightfully so!"

"And yet," he continued, "those who knowingly, secretly, illegally pump poison into the lungs of our children are called 'Captains of Industry.'" The phrase dripped with disgust. "They are fined when they are caught red-handed, but even then, they continue—creating more toxic pollution, feeding the gears of an industry built on destruction, suffocating us one breath at a time."

The crowd was no longer silent.

"Which are the worse criminals? Those of our grandparents' time… or those of today?"

And then—one voice, then another, then ten, then fifty—a chant began. At first, a murmur. Then a rising wave.

"We know who is responsible. We know who is responsible. WE KNOW WHO IS RESPONSIBLE!"

When the speaker began for the last time, the chanting stopped. "People need jobs, the corporate powers and politicians argue, extraction of fossil fuel and manufacturing combustion engines creates jobs around the world so the people can feed their families. But I ask you, do you know people named Smith, Chandler, Waggoner? Are they shoeing horses? Making candles? Building wagons? NO! The government needs to lead the way. There can be many more jobs in clean energy than in dirty energy. Are there not more jobs now than there were in the days of the horse and buggy economy?"

The speaker spread his arms wide, "Manufacturing jobs, high paying jobs, jobs in the business of creating wind power, solar power, tidal power, and power sources not yet imagined. There will be people building new types of vehicles for new generations of buyers. And at the same time jobs healing the land, healing the oceans, removing the plastics, healing the rivers and the air devastated by corporate greed."

"One last important thing," the speaker said lowering his voice. "And yes, I said 'the businesses of creating clean energy and reversing the pollution.' Because we are not communists! We are not socialists! We believe that American industry, when focused and incentivized by government, can rebuild our energy infrastructure in a few short years not decades or centuries. By that time, it will be too late. Our grandparents destroyed the killers in World War Two in four years by pulling together as a nation, we must do no less."

Wiping his flushed face, his voice now hoarse, the balding man called out, "In a couple of years our fathers transformed an industry building cars and refrigerators to one building weapons to destroy the enemy."

"World War Three should not be a nuclear war or even a war with guns and bombs but a war against climate change, against, pulmonary diseases, and against those who are cynically destroying our planet so they can remain the one percent."

"I say bring down the one percent! Together we can build a cleaner greener world for our children and grandchildren! We will all be so much better off, we will all be richer for it, working in a higher paying clean energy world. If we fail, if the glaciers melt, and sea levels rise 70 meters, and our great cities flood and forests burn. Then we have lost – the world as we know it is lost!"

Kestrel looked around at the people standing nearby. Some had tears, he had tears. "Who is this guy?" someone asked. "Who was that guy speaking?" one of the Dakota men asked. "He is good!"

"His name is Jerry Varene." A voice responded. "An environmental attorney. I met him at a meeting at his house. He runs an organization called Coast Conservation Corps."

PART V:
JERRY VARENE

Chapter 21

Morgan and Constance Varene, husband and wife, were both educators at Sparks High School in Sparks, Nevada. Morgan a science teacher, Constance a geometry instructor. Their love story had unfolded years earlier at the University of Nevada, Reno, where they met as students, their shared curiosity about the world pulling them together. It was a whirlwind romance; one impulsive Friday during their senior year, they exchanged vows in one of Reno's famous wedding chapels, only to be back in class by Monday morning as if nothing had changed. But everything had.

More than anything, the Varenes loved to travel. Before their son was born, they spent their summers exploring the world, their adventures fueled by a well-thumbed copy of Europe on $30 a Day. They wandered through narrow cobblestone streets, hiked in the Alps, and slept in hostels, making the most of their modest teacher salaries. These experiences shaped their worldview—an awareness of different cultures, the fragility of historic landscapes, and the realization that even the most seemingly eternal places could change, or vanish, in the face of modernization.

Then along came Jerome—Jerry to everyone who knew him. Their pride, their joy, their little knight in shining armor. From the start, Jerry was precocious. By four, he was devouring books; by five, his fingers danced over piano keys with surprising finesse; by six, he was already throwing fastballs on the baseball field. His sharp intellect made him stand out in school, but it was his thoughtful nature, his quiet observation of the world, that made his parents believe he was destined for something bigger.

When Jerry enrolled at the University of Nevada, Reno, it was no surprise that he chose to study political science. His early travels had given him a unique perspective—unlike many of his peers, he had seen firsthand the impact of human expansion on the environment. He understood, even as a teenager, that untouched landscapes could be gone within a generation. His growing awareness of climate change and environmental policy became more than just an academic interest; it became a calling.

That passion led him to law school at the University of Oregon, home to one of the nation's most respected environmental and natural resources law programs. It was there, in the heart of Eugene, that Jerry met an instructor—a larger-than-life cowboy from Montana named Butch Cassidy Bandero.

Butch was everything Jerry was not—older by fifteen years, rugged, and deeply charismatic. He had enlisted straight out of high school and served as a Navy SEAL, fighting in both Gulf Wars. His stories were harrowing, but his insights were even sharper. "The Blackwater contractors should never have been used in Iraq," he told Jerry one night, his voice tinged with quiet anger. "After the first Falluja battle, they were hanging like so much charred meat from the Euphrates River Bridge." There was no bravado in the way he spoke about combat—just an unflinching honesty, the kind that came from having seen too much.

After completing his legal studies and passing the Nevada bar exam, Jerry headed straight to Carson City, eager to make a difference. He landed an internship with the Nevada State Department of Environmental and Natural Resources, hoping to be on the frontlines of environmental policy. He got more than he bargained for.

At the time, Nevada was at war—not against another state, but against the federal government. The issue? Yucca Mountain. The U.S. Congress had chosen the site, located a hundred miles north of Las Vegas on a former Nevada Nuclear Test Site, as the nation's final dumping ground for nuclear waste. The decision, formalized in 1987, became infamously known among Nevadans as the Screw Nevada Bill—a backroom deal that assumed the state had neither the political will nor the clout to resist.

Inside the Nevada Capitol, Jerry heard the whispers. Washington elites scoffed at Nevada's outrage. One senator was overheard joking, "What do Nevadans care? All they do is gamble, party, and visit brothels—not necessarily in that order." Another, less discreet, sneered in a cloakroom, "We thought they might enjoy an atomic cornhole!"

Jerry learned quickly that in politics, condescension could be a powerful motivator. Nevada's leadership, long underestimated, was furious. And while most politicians hesitated to take on the federal government, one unlikely Senate warrior stepped forward. His words echoed through the halls of Congress: "Not up Nevada's hole, you don't."

The fight was on.

Jerry, fresh-faced and determined, was assigned to lead a research team tasked with exposing the flaws in the Yucca Mountain plan. It was a daunting challenge. The Department of Energy (DOE) had poured billions into the project, and their reports framed Yucca as the perfect storage site. But Jerry's team dug deeper—literally.

Their findings were damning. Beneath the proposed storage site, the volcanic rock of Yucca Mountain was riddled with fractures, allowing groundwater to flow freely through a vast aquifer. Worse, earthquake faults ran directly through the area, connecting the planned storage zone to the water table, which lay just 600 to 1,500 feet below the surface. If radioactive waste leaked, as history suggested it eventually would, it could contaminate Nevada's limited water supply—possibly for thousands of years.

Yet, the most absurd claim from the DOE was not geological— it was temporal. They insisted the waste would remain secure for a compliance period of 10,000 years.

Ten. Thousand. Years!

Jerry's team had a field day with that one. Ten thousand years ago, woolly mammoths roamed Nevada. Glaciers covered the mountains. The Great Pyramid of Giza would not be built for another 6,500 years. How, they asked, could anyone predict what would happen to nuclear waste so far into the future?

Public sentiment shifted. What had once been seen as a bureaucratic decision became a fight for Nevada's sovereignty, its future. The state's residents—miners, casino workers, ranchers, and politicians alike—stood together. No one wanted their home to become America's radioactive toilet.

The battle was long and brutal, but Jerry's team delivered the final blow. Their report, backed by independent scientific analysis, dismantled the DOE's claims and provided lawmakers the ammunition needed to shut the project down. Billions had already been spent, but no amount of federal funding could outweigh the overwhelming opposition.

Yucca Mountain was dead.

Today, the 38-billion-dollar hole remains—a ghost of a bad idea, sitting alone in the Nevada desert. There are no nuclear waste shipments, no high-tech storage bunkers. Just empty tunnels carved into stone, surrounded by desert landscapes and the occasional howl of a lonely coyote.

The Yucca Mountain battle seemingly won; Jerry found himself riding a wave of political goodwill. His work had not gone unnoticed, and a grateful Nevada senator pulled some strings to secure him a position as an advisor at the Department of Energy in Washington, D.C. On paper, it was a prestigious role—an insider's seat at the table where energy policies were shaped. In reality it was an exercise in frustration.

Nothing meaningful ever crossed his desk. Reports piled up, meetings droned on, and every memo seemed to be written in a language designed to say nothing at all. His official title sounded important, but the work itself was empty, a never-ending loop of bureaucracy that kept real change at arm's length.

Within months, disillusionment came calling. Jerry had spent years fighting for something real, something tangible, only to land in a world where decisions were made behind closed doors, shaped by corporate interests rather than scientific evidence or public good. The same industry giants he had battled in Nevada had deep roots in Washington, their influence stretching through congressional offices and government agencies alike.

One evening, sitting in his cramped D.C. apartment with the hum of the city outside his window, Jerry picked up the phone and called the senator who had helped him land the job. "Can you get me out of here?"

The answer came a week later in the form of a new opportunity—not in government, but in activism. A Los Angeles-based non-profit, dedicated to preventing the expansion of nuclear power plants in California, needed someone with experience in environmental law and policy. The pay was not great, but Jerry didn't care. He had learned the hard way that real change did not happen in marble-floored offices under fluorescent lights. It happened on the ground, in communities, in the trenches.

Within a month, he had packed up and left Washington for good.

Back on the West Coast, Jerry used a loan from his parents to buy a modest house in Tarzana. It was not glamorous, but it was his—his first real home since leaving Nevada. The non-profit work kept him engaged, but something still felt missing. He wanted to do more, something beyond reports and board meetings.

So, he started gathering like-minded people—scientists, activists, lawyers, students, and ordinary citizens who cared about the land, the water, the air. What began as informal discussions over coffee turned into structured meetings. Before long, The Coast Conservation Corps was born.

PART VI:
SYLVIA JAMAICA

Chapter 22

Sylvia was born in Jamaica but raised on the streets of St. Croix in the Virgin Islands, where survival often meant resilience. Her family's oral traditions wove a powerful narrative of their lineage, tracing back to her great-great-grandfather, Horace Johnson—a Buffalo Soldier who fought alongside Teddy Roosevelt in the Battle of San Juan during the Spanish-American War. The Buffalo Soldiers, as the legend went, earned their name from Native American warriors who likened their fierce determination, dark skin, and coiled hair to the American Bison.

Horace had enlisted in the Tenth Cavalry at eighteen, back in 1880, joining one of the all-African American regiments deployed in the receding Indian Wars across the upper Midwest. During these years, he met and married Winona, a Sioux woman whose ancestors had lived on the land long before the U.S. Army arrived. His final assignment in the American West came in the early 1890s when the U.S. Cavalry was tasked with rounding up the last of the free-roaming Cree tribe living in Montana and forcing them onto reservations. Though history called it a peaceful settlement, the truth was more complex.

By the time war broke out with Spain in 1898, Horace was nearing retirement, but duty called him to battle once more. The Tenth Cavalry played a pivotal role in the charge up San Juan Hill, a conflict that would later be glorified in Teddy Roosevelt's war stories. When the war ended in December, with the Treaty of Paris securing Cuba's independence and transferring Guam, Puerto Rico, and the Philippines to the U.S., Horace made a decision that would shape his family's future.

Rather than return to the harsh winters of the northern territories, he chose to retire in Jamaica, where the warm Caribbean air suited him far better than the bitter cold of the plains. Soon after, he sent for Winona and their two children, settling into a life of quiet stability, supported by his Army pension.

By 1917, at the age of 55, Horace received an unexpected proposition from an old comrade, Pete Hamilton, a fellow Buffalo Soldier from the Tenth Cav. Pete had retired to his hometown of St. Croix, one of the islands the United States had just purchased from Denmark, forming what would become the U.S. Virgin Islands. He had an idea—to open a bar—and he wanted Horace as his business partner.

For Horace, the timing was perfect. After nearly two decades in Jamaica, he had grown restless, eager to take on something new so the Johnson family packed up their lives and relocated to St. Croix, where they quickly became known as the "Jamaica family." The nickname stuck, as did the bar, which remained in the family for three generations. Sylvia would be one of the last in the Caribbean to carry its legacy.

She loved hearing the family's history, passed down like sacred—fables. Stories of her great-great-grandfather, the Buffalo Soldier who fought alongside Teddy Roosevelt and fell in love with a Sioux woman. A story of resilience, adventure, and identity, one that shaped her sense of self.

After high school, Sylvia returned to Jamaica to attend the University of Technology, or UTech as it was known. She had no desire to spend her life behind a desk, so she pursued Emergency Medical Technician (EMT) training instead. A natural in the field, she graduated at the top of her class, earning her certification with distinction.

Restless once again, she found herself searching for the first step in her new career. One night, scrolling through job listings at the Utech library, she spotted an ad for a federal internship with the Bureau of Indian Affairs. The position was open to recent EMT graduates, offering work at the Standing Rock Reservation. Her heart skipped a beat. *This is meant for me,* she thought. *My great-great-grandmother was Sioux.*

Now with her internship at Standing Rock behind her, Sylvia was eager for a new beginning. She scoured job listings and quickly discovered that Los Angeles was a goldmine for EMT opportunities.

Not only was the demand high, but California also offered the best salaries in the country. The decision practically made itself.

She packed her bags, booked a one-way flight, and stepped off the plane at LAX, where Kestrel was already waiting. His face lit up when he saw her, and for a moment, she felt the warmth of familiarity in the overwhelming sprawl of the city.

"You should move in with me," he urged, in boyish eagerness.

"Not now Kestrel," she replied. We barely know each other. "I'm glad we reconnected though so if you help with my suitcase I will buy lunch. I am famished! Do you have wheels or should I call an UBER?"

"Forget the UBER, Kes shrugged, "I borrowed the community pickup truck."

Sylvia had learned the value of guarding her independence.

"I think I'll get my own place for now," she said, softening the rejection with a smile.

The transition was smoother than she expected. The hospital in Winnetka, just a few miles from Kestrel's place in the San Fernando Valley, welcomed her with open arms. Within days, she secured a comfortable three-bedroom apartment with two other women from the hospital staff. It was not glamorous, but it was clean and convenient. She felt like she was exactly where she was meant to be.

Chapter 23

Hudson and Kestrel had committed to their plan to travel to Bluefield in pursuit of Jim Reddy's elusive suitcase and driven by Hud's belief in the possibility that it might hold evidence of a grand conspiracy to expand the oceans of the earth, and not in a good way. The purpose, to fulfill the greed and profit dreams of the super-rich without regard for the millions of people who would be displaced or killed in worldwide floods.

They had set their departure for five days away, the morning after their next CCC meeting. So far, they had kept the plan to themselves. Hudson was not ready to face Lillian's inevitable tears, and more than that, his instincts from his time in Air Force security were flashing warning signals. Someone had already killed an FBI agent over this alleged suitcase, which meant the game they were about to enter could be quite dangerous.

Lillian's soft heart and sentimental soul, cried at sad movies and songs. Stray animals were fed and cared for. She had taken in more than she could count. Once, she even rescued a gopher that had been hit by a car, cradling the tiny creature which bit into her hand. She took it to a veterinarian, who promptly euthanized the animal and charged her $200 for the effort.

As she left the clinic, still gripping the plastic bag containing the gopher's remains, she glanced down at her bleeding finger. When she showed it to the vet, hoping for some medication, she got nothing but a clinical response. "I don't treat humans," the vet said. "You might want to get that looked at for infections or rabies." But Lillian never made it to a doctor. By then, she was flat broke.

Later, when she told Hudson the story, he had laughed, shaking his head. "So, you spent your last dime on a gopher's vet bill, but you wouldn't spend it on yourself?"

"I didn't think of it that way," she argued. "It just happened, one step at a time. By the time I left the vet's office, my bank account was empty."

Hudson smiled wryly. "You do realize your employer, the Park Service provides health insurance, right?"

"Yeah, but it comes with a $500 deductible," she sighed. "And a $100 co-pay."

The biggest obstacle standing between Hudson and Kestrel's trip to West Virginia was money. They barely had enough funds to cover the journey, let alone any unexpected expenses. To make matters worse, they had no choice but to drive. The Pathfinder was essential for transporting Hud's extensive camera gear, which might prove invaluable. But the vehicle was aging, and Hud was not convinced it was up to the task.

Desperate for a solution, Hud recalled a junk mail envelope he had tossed in the wastebasket—a pre-approved credit card offer he had never activated. He avoided credit cards as a rule, preferring to deposit his photography contract checks directly into his bank account and withdraw cash as needed. But now, with limited options, he retrieved the discarded application, dialed the number on the flyer, and followed the automated prompts. A recorded voice directed him to complete the process online. Within minutes of submitting his details, an email notification flashed on his screen: **Approved**.

But with the approval came hesitation. The more Hud thought about using the credit card, the more it unsettled him. His military training had ingrained a deep awareness of operational security. During his Air Force assignments in the Middle East, he was always provided local currency to avoid leaving any digital footprints. He knew firsthand how easy it was to trail someone through their transactions. If this hunt for the Reddy suitcase was as dangerous as it could be, credit card use could lead to bad consequences.

Caution nudged Hud in another direction. He would need cash and lots of it. He drove to the bank where he always cashed the checks, he received from his photography work and he even kept a small savings account. Skipping the ATM, he headed straight to a teller window with no customers, smiling as he approached a familiar face.

"Hi, Linda," he greeted, sliding over his ID and bank account cards. "I need cash for a long-awaited vacation."

He hesitated only a moment before producing the brand-new credit card. "How much of a loan do you suppose I can get?"

The clerk took his information with a professional nod. "I'll be back in just a couple of minutes," she said before disappearing behind the counter.

When she returned, she was all smiles. "Mr. Halle, for a long-time customer like you—with an impeccable credit rating—my manager has approved a $25,000 cash withdrawal, available immediately."

Hud nodded, "Can I get a loan on my house, too?"

"I'll need to check with my manager," she replied stepping once again through the door behind her.

This time, she returned with the manager in tow. A small woman in a sharp pants suit extended her hand with a practiced smile. "Mr. Halle, I'm Ms. Coletti. I hear you're interested in taking out a loan using your residence as collateral. Do you own the property free and clear?"

"Yes," Hud confirmed. "My parents left it to me—it was one of their rental properties before they passed away. It's fully paid off and in my name."

"Bring in a copy of the deed, and our real estate people will conduct an assessment."

"Understood." Hud shifted his weight slightly. "If everything checks out—and I'm sure it will—when can I get the cash? And how much are we talking?"

"If all is in order, you'll have the funds in five days at the earliest," The manager explained. "As for the amount, we'll need to conduct an appraisal before I can provide specifics."

Hud thought about five days, and he needed that time to prepare. "Sounds good. I will be back with the deed. And in the meantime, hold onto that $25,000—I'll pick it all up at once. Cash only, in nothing bigger than hundred-dollar bills."

Four days later, Ms. Coletti called Hud's phone. "Bring a copy of the deed to your house," the clerk said, "and something to carry a large amount of cash in."

When Hud arrived back at the bank, he was carrying one of his larger backpacks—the kind he usually used for hauling camera equipment. Ms. Coletti was waiting for him; flanked by two men in dark suits, both flashing professional smiles.

"This way, Mr. Halle," the manager said, leading him to a desk where three Styrofoam cups of steaming coffee sat waiting.

Hud didn't bother sitting. "How much?" he asked, cutting straight to the point.

One of the suits nodded toward the papers stacked on the desk. "Once you sign everything, we have $150,000 for you."

Hud let out a low whistle. "More than I expected. Guess the old place appreciated more than I thought."

"The San Fernando Valley real estate market is heating up again," the other man chimed in. "You do understand the risks? If you default on payments, there are penalties—a potential foreclosure. Are you absolutely sure you want to proceed?"

Hud's grin didn't falter. "I'm good, thanks."

The process was not quick. Bank policy required that the money be counted in his presence. Then came the paperwork—pages of legalese and carefully worded terms. By the time he stepped outside, two hours had passed, but his backpack was considerably heavier.

He adjusted the straps and exhaled. "Well," he murmured to himself, "I'm all in now."

Chapter 24

As soon as Hud got home, he picked up the phone and called Kes.

"You still up for heading to West Virginia as soon as possible?" he asked.

"Well, yeah," Kes replied. "My motivation is strong, but my pocketbook is weak. You?"

Hud said. "Got a brand-new credit card—we'll be fine." He knew Kes would not accept a handout, so he added a little misdirection. "Actually, I landed a contract with the State Park Service to set up some cougar cameras up in Topanga Canyon. It's a lot of climbing through brush and over rocks. If you tag along as my assistant, I can make it worth your while. Besides, I'm thinking we might need cameras in Bluefield, so this could be good OJT before we go."

"Great!" Kes yipped, leaping at the offer. "I was feeling bored and dejected, but you just made my day. Hell, my whole month."

Hud laughed ending the call.

Before heading home, he stopped by the Topanga Mall, picking up new clothes with his credit card—not his cash. He was saving that for the trip. Across the promenade from REI, a high-end men's boutique caught his eye, reminding him of the expensive suede jacket he had once splurged on there when he and Nicole were headed to Vegas on a job. Just beyond the clothing store was a sleek men's hair salon.

Why the hell not? he thought. I'll surprise Lillian.

Service was quick, and less than an hour later, he stepped back out into the mall, freshly cut hair, a shave, and looking sharp in a new sports jacket. He laid the new sports jacket along with a new pair of slacks, all carefully wrapped in a thick plastic bag on the back seat of the pathfinder.

That afternoon, he took the Pathfinder to a trusted mechanic in West Hills. It was farther than the local shops, but Gus's place was the best—and he and his team knew Hud's Pathfinder inside and out.

"Hey, Gus," Hud greeted the Argentine shop owner. "I'm taking her cross-country and back. Need you to check everything that could be a problem, I will be leaving in a few days."

Gus let out a low whistle. "Big order, Hud. My bays are full, and I'm short a mechanic." He rubbed his chin for several moments. "You remember Memo?"

"Yeah, sure. He's good. Think he can handle it?"

"I'll give him a call. Memo opened his own shop in Canoga Park. Last I heard, he was looking for business." Gus pulled out his phone, made a quick call, and nodded. "Yeah, Hud, he's hot to trot. Said to bring it over now."

At the Canoga Park shop, Hud greeted Memo with a firm handshake. "I need everything done and out the door in two or three days," he said. "Anything needed for the engine, new tires, new brakes—the works. Also, she's starting to show some rust. Think you can re-primer it or something?"

Memo crouched down, running a hand over the lower frame. "More than a little rust," he frowned, pointing at spots where the metal was almost eaten through. "I'll try to stop it from spreading, not just cosmetic." He straightened and gave Hud a serious look. "Listen, man, this shop is new, and I've got bills piling up. I'll need some cash when I'm done—not the full amount, but maybe half?" Hud grinned. "Cash isn't a problem. Just don't hold back. And don't call me—I'll be busy the next couple of days. If you see anything that even looks like it needs fixing, do it, and do it right. I'll pay in full when I pick it up."

Memo squinted at him. "You rob a bank or something Hud?"

"Nope. Vegas," Hud lied easily. "Got a lot of photo work out there. I am going to be driving back and forth—hard driving for the old heap."

"You sure you mean everything? Transmission, alignment, the whole ball of wax?"

"Spare no expense. It needs to run perfectly, and for a long time."

Memo nodded, already making a mental checklist. "Alright, let me get started."

Hud hesitated. "You think you will need to order parts? I can't afford delays."

Memo chuckled. "This is L.A., Hud. I could rebuild this whole rig from scratch with parts I can get today. You need a ride home?"

Hud considered, then pulled out his phone and called Kes. The line barely rang before Kes answered.

"Hey, Hud, what's up?"

"I'm out in Canoga Park, getting the Pathfinder ready. Can you swing by on your bike and pick me up?"

"Of course. Where at?"

Kes pulled up to the auto shop in under thirty minutes. The moment Memo spotted the Triumph, he let out a low whistle.

"Whoa, baby. My grandpa used to race one of these in Mexico, back in the day. 'Sixty-eight Bonneville, right?"

"You know your bikes," Kes confirmed.

Memo grinned, nostalgia lighting up his face. "I was just a Niño, maybe six or seven, when I saw *mi abuelo* race in the Baja 1000. My *pop* would take *abuelo*, me and a sixty-eight or 'sixty-nine Triumph Bonneville, just like this one. I remember sitting on *pop's* shoulders, scarfing down churros while the dust and noise swallowed everything. Man, those were the days. His bike was already twenty-five years old by then, but he kept it *perfect*—just like you keep this one." He shook his head. "He won a lot too… until the Honda 750s came along. That's what got me hooked on engines."

Hud pocketed a couple of Memo's business cards before climbing onto the back of the Triumph behind Kes.

"I'll pass these around." He said, "I might get you some new customers."

"Appreciate it, Hud," Memo said. "And don't worry—I'll get everything taken care of."

As Kes pulled out onto the road, Hud dialed Lillian at work.

"Hey, kid. How about dinner?"

"Oh, sure, Hud!" She sounded surprised, then playful. "Can you swing by my office in about an hour?"

"I can, and I will."

She was still giggling when the call ended.

Back home, Hud wasted no time. He showered, shaved, and dressed in his new clothes, smoothing a much shorter haircut in the mirror. He was not sure what he wanted to tell Lillian tonight—*or* if he should tell her anything at all. The fewer people who knew his plans, the safer.

Walking quickly to an Enterprise car rental office located five blocks from his house he picked out an almost new Audi A3. He then drove up Ventura Boulevard stopping at an upscale confectionery and florist shop, where he purchased up a box of fine chocolates and a dozen roses. Then, he drove to the State Park Service office at the Warner Center, where Lillian worked.

When he walked through the doors, she caught sight of him immediately, "I didn't recognize you in those clothes," she gasped. "Where on earth..." but the words trailed off, lost somewhere between shock and delight.

Hud noticed heads turning and popping up from between partitions. Lillian set the roses and chocolates aside before throwing her arms around him. Looking up into his eyes, she mouthed, *I love you.*

"Me too," he said aloud.

Smiling, she carried the box of chocolates to a nearby table and flipped open the lid. "Alright, everyone—dig in! My dude and I are heading out for lunch, and we *may* not be back."

The offer was like a beacon, drawing Lillian's coworkers out of their cubicles. A few of the women shot appreciative glances at Hud, while exchanging amused smiles with each other.

"Only look, ladies," Lillian teased. "He's all mine."

Out on the sidewalk, she was still shaking her head, staring at him like he was a stranger. "Okay… *what* is going on with the fancy clothes and the jazzy haircut? What happened to my woodsy Hudson?"

"Woodsy is still in here," he grinned, patting his chest. "Just figured I'd mix things up. Do you like it?"

"I mean… yeah, sure," she admitted. "It's a nice change. But what's the occasion?"

Hud's expression turned serious. "I have something to tell you—but not to worry."

She did not miss a beat. "You and Kes are going to West Virginia."

Hud blinked. "How did you—? Wait. Did Kes blab?"

Lillian smiled. "Hud, I can *read* you like a book. You've mentioned it before, and I've seen you whispering to Kes at meetings."

"We weren't whispering."

"Oh, it was *conspiratorial* whispering." She shook her head, her expression softening. "Look, I've already said my piece, but I'm not going to stand in your way. I will be wishing you luck… and praying nothing happens to you two. You both mean a lot to me. To all of us."

She exhaled, arms crossing. "I still don't know what you hope to accomplish. Honestly, I'm beginning to think this whole *silver suitcase* story is just a ridiculous myth. But I know you feel like you *must* try, and I respect that. Just… promise me you'll take care of yourself. And *please* keep an eye on Kes. He's reckless, impulsive— we all worry he's going to get himself into real trouble one day."

Hud pulled her into his arms, kissing her with feeling. "I appreciate that," he murmured against her hair. "We'll be fine. I'll call you every day that I can with a progress report—just don't mention it to the others yet. Kes and I need to decide what we want to say."

He pulled back slightly, giving her a knowing look. "Remember, I *was* in military intelligence. *Loose lips sink ships*, and all that."

They lingered at Ruth's Chris for two hours, and Lillian never made it back to the office that day.

On the drive to her house, she eyed him curiously. "So… what's with all the spending? Fancy clothes, chocolates, flowers, steak dinners? I had no idea you were so well-fixed."

Hud grinned. "Got another cougar contract up in Topanga, Hud lied, I'm bringing Kes this time as my assistant—want to teach him the ropes. Photography, video, camera setup… the whole deal. These next two days in the woods will be good practice."

"And after that?"

"We leave for West Virginia. Saturday morning, right after the CCC meeting."

"Driving?"

"Yeah. The good old Pathfinder."

"Ouch."

"I know," he admitted. "But I need the space for all our gear. We might even camp along the way."

When they reached her place, Hud settled at the dining table and scribbled a list of equipment he'd need. Then, he pulled out his phone and dialed a familiar number—a wholesale camera supply house in New York City.

"This is Pete."

"Hey, Pete, it's Hudson."

A pause. Then the voice filled with recognition. "Hud'son! *Long* time, man. What have you been up to?"

"Actually, a lot. Got a new gig and need some supplies."

Pete hesitated. "Hud, we all heard about Nicole. We feel really bad."

Hud exhaled. "Yeah, me too. Thanks for mentioning her. But listen, I've got a new partner, a new job, and a long list of gear to get through. Let me read it off to you."

"Go for it."

Hud rattled off his list. When he finished, Pete let out a low whistle. "Wow, that's quite an order. We've got most of it in stock, or I can grab it from the warehouse, but a few things might need to be sourced from outside CONUS. When do you need it?"

"I'll be stopping by your place in about a week, maybe ten days. I don't want to order online and get stuck in L.A. waiting for shipments. Rush anything you don't have—I'll pay for it when I get there."

"Hudson, coming to the Apple, huh? We'll be looking forward to seeing you."

"Me too. See you then." Hud ended the call.

That night, curled up in front of the fire, was bliss—physically and mentally.

Hud awoke first and nudged Lillian gently. "Hey, kiddo. Time for me to get moving. I'm heading home to shower, change into my outdoor gear, and pick up Kes for our new contract work. I'll be back in a couple of days; I will call you Saturday before the CCC meeting."

She yawned, stretched, and kissed him goodbye at the door. Then, just as he reached the sidewalk, she called after him.

"Wait! You forgot your new jacket."

Hud waved her off with a grin. "No worries—I'll grab it when I get back."

Chapter 25

That day in the woods, Hud walked Kes through the finer points of camera placement—how to hide them for the best shots, the use of motion sensors, infrared triggers, and stills. He demonstrated how the video and sound equipment worked, explaining the best camera mounts, memory cards, and setups for various conditions.

Kes was a quick study. Agile and sharp-eyed, he moved through the dense undergrowth with ease, scaling rocks and slipping through spaces Hud would not have even attempted. Watching him, Hud realized that Kestrel had a natural talent—he would be a real asset in the photo reconnaissance business.

By the time they climbed back up the trail to the Pathfinder, the sun was sinking below the treetops.

"Tomorrow, we'll collect the cameras and check the memory cards," Hud told Kes. "Much easier day than today. Then, after the CCC meeting, we hit the road."

Kes laughed. "It's going to be a hell of an adventure. I was getting bored here—actually thought about heading back to Oregon. But this photo business? It's a real hoot."

That same day, over lunch with a few members of the State Park staff, Lillian casually mentioned that her boyfriend was working on a new cougar photography contract in Topanga Canyon State Park.

A man from the contracting department frowned. "No way, Lillian. We haven't put out any contracts up there in a while. No budget for it."

She hesitated, then shrugged. "He must've meant Santa Monica Mountains Recreation Area. That whole region overlaps."

The contract supervisor shook his head. "SMMNRA always coordinates with us when it comes to photo work. We both want to make sure we don't trip over each other's equipment or duplicate work we have. I'd be surprised if they put out a contract without us knowing. But I can check if you want."

"No," Lillian said quickly. "I'll talk to Hudson."

That evening, as she tidied up around the house, she picked up Hud's new jacket from where he'd tossed it over the back of a chair. Smoothing it out, she felt something crinkle inside the upper vest pocket.

She pulled it out—a receipt from an exclusive men's shop. Over two thousand dollars spent on clothing! Also, some cards from a Canoga Park Auto Garage.

As Lillian folded clothes and straightened up, her mind kept circling back to the receipt and business cards. Then she remembered—the large camera equipment order Hud had placed from her dining room table.

Has he been lying to me?

Hud had never spent money like this before. Not on himself. Not like this. And fixing up the Pathfinder? Even a legitimate photo contract in the mountains wouldn't justify these kinds of expenses.

On impulse, she picked up her phone and dialed the number on the auto repair card.

"Memo's. Canoga Park," came the immediate response.

The voice caught her off guard. She hesitated, then forced herself to speak. "Hi, this is Lillian. I'm a friend of Hudson Halle. Is he there?"

"Nope," Memo replied easily. "Left a while ago. Should be back in a couple of days to pick up his SUV." There was a slight pause before he added, "You the one who brought our man all that luck in Vegas?"

A sharp breath left her lips. Her fingers clenched around the phone.

Without another word, she hung up.

Her pulse pounded in her ears. *When something seems too good to be true, it usually is.*

Her thoughts spiraled—back to the other men in her past. The phony agent who had fed her empty promises. The lecherous producer who saw her as nothing more than a sex object. The alcoholic husband who drained every ounce of love from her.

She walked to the bathroom and met her own reflection in the mirror. Tears burned in her reddened eyes.

"I hate liars," she moaned.

A sob hitched in her throat.

"I hate tears."

Her fingers curled into fists.

"I hate guys. I hate my life."

Chapter 26

To make trip preparations easier, Kes moved into Hud's place for the last couple of days before their departure. As they sorted through their gear, Hud handed him an envelope thick with cash.

Kes flipped through the bills, his brows furrowing. "What's this for?"

"For your work on the cougar photo contract."

Kes scoffed. "Two thousand dollars? You've got to be kidding."

"I'm not. The Park Service paid me five grand." Hud was getting used to lying—too used to it. Each time, it felt easier. "That's your share."

Kes shook his head. "No way. I can't take this. Climbing around on rocks all day? That's what I *do* for fun."

"Same here," Hud admitted. "But you weren't just some tagalong—you got into spots I couldn't. That made you valuable." He patted the envelope. "Take it."

Kes hesitated before tucking the envelope into his pocket.

That evening, they washed their clothes, bundling underwear and socks into pillowcases for the trip. As they worked, Kes glanced over.

"Hud, what are we telling the CCC members tomorrow night? About, y'know… what we're *actually* doing?"

Hud paused. "Good question." He hesitated. "Lillian already knows."

"What? You *told* her?"

"Not exactly. She figured it out."

Kes's face tightened. "Damn, Hud."

"She saw us talking. Called it 'conspiratorial whispering'—said we were planning to head to West Virginia to look for the silver suitcase. I didn't deny it, but I asked her not to tell anyone."

"She said she wouldn't?"

"Yeah."

Kes mulled it over. "Maybe we should just tell the whole group, then. They might have good ideas—avenues for us to pursue."

Hud eyed him carefully. "So, you *haven't* mentioned it to Sylvia either?"

"I told her I've been bored around here, not doing much of anything," Kes said. "Told her I was excited about taking wildlife photos with you. That's about it."

Hud took a moment to think. "If word gets back to Bluefield that some snoops are coming to plant cameras, our cover's blown. The only thing we'll get out of this trip is a couple of cracked skulls."

"At least if *anyone* back there finds out what we're up to, we'll know exactly who spilled the beans," Kes reasoned. "It would have to be Lillian."

Hud shook his head, "She'd never do that. Lillian wouldn't put us in harm's way. *Especially* not you." He shot Kes a sideways look. "Sometimes I think she likes you more than me. You know what she said before we left? 'Take care of our falcon.' She's worried you'll go off half-cocked."

Kes smiled, hitching up his jeans. "Not to worry—I always go *fully* cocked. Ask Buffy if you don't believe me."

Hud let out a dry laugh. "Let's stick to *fully prepared*, okay?" His expression turned serious again. "We'll say we got a photo contract from the National Park Service in the Dakotas. That shouldn't raise any suspicions."

And with that, it was settled. But as much as Hud tried to justify the lies, they began to gnaw at him. He couldn't shake the words of Walter Scott—*Oh, what a tangled web we weave…*

Hud phoned Lillian to let her know he was on his way to pick her up for dinner. She did not pick up. No call back, no message.

Maybe she really is pissed about West Virginia, he thought.

The next morning, he checked in with Memo about the Pathfinder.

"She's pretty much ready, Hud," Memo reported. "Some of the primer paint isn't completely dry, but otherwise, you're looking at a *brand new* 1999 Pathfinder."

Hud grinned. "Can I come by and get her now?"

Memo chuckled. "Yeah, I suppose so. I'll hit the primer with a blow-dryer if it's still a little tacky."

Later that morning, Hud and Kes rolled into Memo's shop on the Triumph. The Pathfinder sat gleaming in the sun, polished and shining like a new penny.

Memo was kneeling by the side panel, blow-dryer in hand, putting on the finishing touches.

Kes parked the bike, and Hud climbed off the back, running a hand along the freshly restored body of the SUV.

"Here she is," Memo said, spreading his arms toward the SUV like a showman. "Took her for a spin this morning—purring like a kitten."

Hud slid into the driver's seat, started the engine, and shifted into gear. He took it around the block, testing the brakes, the transmission, the handling. Everything was tight. Smooth. It *did* feel brand new.

"How much?" he asked as he pulled back into the lot.

"You don't have to pay it all at once," Memo said, handing him a clipboard with the bill.

Hud glanced at the total: **$5,280.**

Without hesitation, he unzipped his camera bag, pulled out a thick stack of bills, and peeled off **$5,300.**

Memo let out a low whistle. "Damn, Hud. Next time you hit Vegas, take me with you."

Hud just grinned and pocketed the receipt.

Following Kes on the Triumph, they rode back to Hud's Tarzana house and stored the bike in the garage. Without wasting time, they headed back up Topanga Canyon to retrieve the cameras they had set up the day before.

They could not believe their luck. Two cameras had captured cougars. One image showed a large male, taken from the rear. The other? A female with a six-month-old kit.

Kes's eyes widened. "No way. We *did it!*" he whooped. "We actually got cougars on camera!"

Hud studied the images, his excitement tempered by concern. "Yeah… but this might not be good."

Kes frowned. "What do you mean?"

Hud tapped the screen. "That big tom could be *stalking* the female. If that's the case, he might try to kill the kit—to push her back into estrus."

Kes's enthusiasm faltered. "Shit. Really?"

Hud checked the timestamps. "The photos were taken about two hours apart. If she knows he's trailing her, she might be trying to put some distance between them. That's her best shot at keeping the kit safe."

Kes exhaled. "Nature's brutal."

"Yeah," Hud agreed. "But it's also smart."

After retrieving the rest of the cameras, they drove back to Hud's place, cleaned up, and changed for the CCC meeting at Jerry's that evening.

"I'm calling Lillian," Hud told Kes. "We'll stop by her place on the way and pick her up I promised her dinner tonight."

Lillian's usual first-ring pickup did not happen. No response at all.

Hud frowned and left a message at the tone. "Hey, Lil, just checking in. Give me a call when you get a chance."

He told himself she was probably in the shower and decided to stop by her house on the way to the meeting anyway.

But when they pulled up, the place was dark. No lights, no movement. Even Benny—her ever-watchful cat—was missing from his usual perch on the window ledge.

Hud exhaled, rubbing a hand over his jaw. "There could be a dozen reasons for this," he pondered, but unease crept in.

At Jerry's, he scanned the room. No sign of her. He asked around.

"Gee, Hud, I thought you'd be the *first* to know," Lady Jane said, looking surprised. "Lillian put a notice on the CCC webpage—she left for Chicago to visit her mother."

Hud froze. His mind jumped to the worst—her mom must be sick. Maybe she had to leave in a rush.

But why hadn't she told *him*?

If she had, he would not have hesitated to delay the trip and go with her.

Pulling out his phone, he quickly navigated to the CCC webpage, a site he barely ever checked. And there it was:

"Won't be at the meeting tonight. Left for Chicago to visit Mom. I'll keep you posted. —Lil"

His stomach tightened. No text. No email. Nothing.

Kes wandered over. "What's up, Hud? Still no Lillian?"

Hud stared at his screen. "She's gone." His voice was quiet, strained. "Chicago. To visit her mom."

Kes studied him for a beat. "Are you going to Chicago to look for her?"

"I don't know what to do yet," Hud admitted. "But we're still leaving in the morning—just like we planned. If we decide to take a side trip to Chicago... we'll see. Maybe she'll send more information. Maybe it *is* an emergency, and she had to drop everything. I just don't want to show up uninvited."

That night, at the CCC meeting, Hud and Kes shared their cougar photos with the group. Hud explained his theory about the male possibly stalking the female and the potential danger to her kit. Then, shifting the conversation, he casually mentioned that a *possible* National Park photo contract in the Dakotas had caught their interest. He and Kes were thinking about driving up to check it out.

After the meeting, they packed at Hud's house. Kes cast a longing glance at the Triumph, but there was no way it would fit in the Pathfinder. Instead, Hud secured his off-road bicycle to the roof rack with bungee cords.

They left before dawn, stopping at a late-night coffee shop before jumping onto I-210, then heading north until they merged onto I-40. As the first streaks of daylight broke across the horizon, Barstow's neon signs flickered in the distance.

I-40 would take them straight east. At some point in the Midwest, they would have to decide whether to veer north toward Chicago. Hud still was not sure. Either way, they needed to hit New York to pick up their camera supplies before turning south toward West Virginia.

Sipping coffee and munching scones, they barely spoke. Each man was lost in his own thoughts.

Lillian's sudden disappearance cast a shadow over the trip—for both of them.

They drove in shifts, pushing forward relentlessly, only stopping at motels when exhaustion forced them off the road. Finally, in the early hours of a cold, drizzly morning, they reached the Staten Island Ferry landing.

Hud stared out at the gray water, hands gripping the steering wheel.

Chicago would have taken time. *Too* much time. Hopefully, Lillian would call. He'd keep trying to reach her.

They left the Pathfinder in a ferry parking lot and walked up to the terminal entrance, purchasing round-trip tickets. After crossing the water, they grabbed coffee and breakfast on the Manhattan side.

Hud studied a subway map, tracing routes with his finger. "Looks like this'll get us there the fastest," he murmured.

A short ride later, they arrived at the camera shop just as the metal gate was rolling up.

Pete stepped out, grinning as he hoisted a big box onto the counter. "Been waiting for you, Hud. How was the drive?"

"Not bad," Hud said, shaking Pete's hand. "This is my new partner, Kestrel. We're heading down to West Virginia today to test out this new gear."

Pete nodded at Kes. "Good to meet you." Then he patted the box. "It's all here. You want to go through it now?"

Hud glanced at the clock. "Nah. We're in a hurry—hoping to get out of town by the end of the day."

He skimmed the invoice, counted out the cash, and handed it over.

Pete tucked the bills into the register. "You guys on some kind of mission?"

Hudson just smiled. "Something like that."

Chapter 27

After saying goodbye to Pete, they retraced their route to the ferry landing, picked up the Pathfinder, and hit **I-95 South**. It was just past noon.

By the time they rolled into Bluefield, exhaustion had set in. Hungry and drained, they pulled into what looked like a decent roadside motel on the outskirts of town.

Bluefield had a certain *quaintness* to it—if you were feeling generous. Otherwise, it just looked run-down.

The early fall morning was cold and damp, the streets lined with ruts, the atmosphere swallowed by a damp fog. Maybe it was just their mood, but even the food tasted off. Diner breakfasts, fast food burgers, fried potatoes—hell, even the coffee—all of it felt stale, like their taste buds had checked out.

To make things worse, both men had developed nagging coughs.

But the miserable weather was not the real problem. It was the lack of a plan.

Finding the **Stanley estate**—or *Stanley family compound*, as some locals called it—was proving impossible. Every time they worked up the nerve to ask questions, they hit a wall. Either the people they talked to did not *want* to be helpful, or the conversation felt like they were speaking entirely different languages.

"Stan Lee?" one man repeated, scratching his head in confusion. "Nope. Don't know any Stan Lee."

Kes muttered under his breath, just loud enough for Hud to hear, "Not *Stan Lee* the comic book artist, you dope. *Stanley*—as in *Steamer the Carpet Cleaner*."

Hud stifled a laugh, but it slipped out anyway. The man they were questioning stiffened, his face clouding with offense.

The conversation was over.

Without another word, the man turned on his heel and stalked off, shaking his head.

"Damn it, Kes," Hud sighed. "I *swear* I was getting somewhere with that guy."

The language barrier did not remain an obstacle for long. A good-natured service station attendant—who had spent time in the Army and could understand Yankee—tipped them off.

"The Stanley property? Starts off a private road about seven miles north of town," he said.

Following his directions, they drove seven miles out, then another five miles down a private road before reaching a high chain-link fence topped with layers of concertina wire.

Hud and Kes parked the Pathfinder in a secluded glade and continued on foot, trekking a mile through dense forest. From a hilltop, Hud raised his binoculars.

A gated entrance stood below.

They kept watch for a while as vehicles approached. Some drivers offered ID or stated their business and were allowed in. Others were turned away without discussion.

"This is locked up tight," Kes said quietly.

Hud nodded. "Let's see if there's another way in."

They spent the rest of the day scouting, but no luck. North of the compound, paved roads were scarce. GPS was useless—just vast green spaces on the screen.

The next morning, they changed tactics.

Instead of approaching from the front, they'd hike in from the back of the property.

Driving over rocky forested ground to where they guessed the rear of the compound might be, Hud hid the Pathfinder deep in the woods, and he and Kes began trekking southward. The terrain was unforgiving—steep inclines, rocky paths, thick brush.

After a grueling few miles, they came across a well-worn trail, running in the same direction they were headed.

Hud's instincts kicked in.

A trail like this? Could mean surveillance cameras.

He signaled Kes to take cover behind a cluster of boulders while he scanned the area with binoculars while lying prone.

Bingo.

Not well hidden, Hud spotted their motion-sensing cameras covering the trail from tree stands hidden in the branches.

Hud motioned for Kes to stay off the path, and they continued south, sticking to the undergrowth.

Eventually, they hit a fence line, stretching as far as the eye could see in both directions.

On the other side? More of the same. Trees, brush, rocky slopes—no sign of human habitation.

Hud raised his binoculars again, scanning the fence line.

Every 100 yards or so, a security camera stood watch. Coverage was solid. Crossing unnoticed would be nearly impossible.

They followed the fence for miles, staying out of sight of the cameras.

Finally, they reached the same guarded gate they had seen the day before. Retracing their steps to where they had first approached the fence from the north, they continued following it until they once again reached the guarded gate.

By the time they made it back to the Pathfinder, they were exhausted, wet, cold, and starving. The sky had turned pitch black, but despite their misery, there was a sense of accomplishment. They now had a full picture of the Stanley compound—and it was massive.

Instead of heading back toward Bluefield, they took I-81 north. Thirty minutes later, they found themselves in the village of Wytheville, Virginia. The sun had long since set, replaced by a hint of autumn in the night air. Spotting a roadhouse advertising *Best Steaks in Town*, they pulled in without hesitation.

Hud and Kes ordered prime rib—thick cuts, served with potatoes, brown gravy, and creamed spinach. The food was excellent, the best they had had since leaving California. Over slices of apple pie and coffee they discussed what they had experienced so far in Bluefield. Hud leaned back in his chair, his mind considering what might follow.

"Well, Kes," Hud mused, "Stanley Energy security is probably aware of us by now."

Kes cleared his throat, "Yeah, you think so?"

Hud nodded. "More than likely back on that first drive up their private road. We know they rely on motion sensor cameras—and are probably taping our movements too. I'd bet anything they recorded our Pathfinder's movements on our first approach to the Stanley compound."

Kes agreed, "Our California plates alone would've raised a big red flag and with all those trees around everywhere, cameras could have tracked our whole drive."

Kes set down his coffee. "So, we're on their radar."

"No doubt."

They agreed—extra caution was necessary for the rest of their stay in West Virginia.

That night, neither of them slept well. The compound, the security, the sheer forbidding presence of the place lingered in their dreams, causing their sleep to be brief and confusing.

Almost three weeks into their time in Bluefield, Hud finally located the Mercer County Craft Memorial Library, where he discovered the Eastern Regional Coal Archives—a trove of history and records that could hold useful information whatever that turned out to be. In the AIR Force it was called flying blind.

Meanwhile, Kes was growing more restless by the hour.

"Hud, we need to get out there and set up cameras," he insisted, impatience creeping into his voice.

Hudson understood. The waiting was getting to both of them. At least, they had charted the layout of the Stanley family compound but that was all they had accomplished.

"Look, Kes," Hud said, "let's split up our efforts so we do not have to spend too much more time in this place. Do you think you can take the cameras I trained you on and set some up around the Stanley property? See what kind of pics and videos we can get near the property with maybe our telephoto lens getting a peek inside."

Kes's face lit up. "Nothing I'd like more. Where do you think I should start?"

"You'll have to be careful," Hud warned. "Get as close to the house as you can, but we want you back in one piece."

"I'm your guy," Kes said, practically buzzing with excitement. "I've been itching to find out what's really going on over there."

"Okay, you've got free rein, but you'll be working solo," Hud instructed. "Leave in the evening, find a spot to stash the SUV, and camp out for a night or two if needed. You've been in the field long enough to know how this works. Try to get as close to the fence as possible at night to avoid their surveillance cameras spotting you." He continued, "Always have an escape route plan. If things go south, leave the cameras behind."

Kes nodded, already mentally running through his experience so far and how he might approach the photo work.

That same day, Kes stocked up on supplies he thought he might need, while Hud finalized his own plan. They agreed to check in every evening with each other by cell phone, no exceptions, while they were working separately.

The next morning, Kes drove off in the Pathfinder, after Hud had unloaded his trail bike. As he pedaled the couple of miles to the library, Hud was not sure exactly what he was looking for—whatever it was though he knew he would not find it on Google.

He needed something tangible, something about the Stanley family West Virginia estate that might provide clues, details about the compound that would be out of the ordinary. Or, how people, workmen perhaps, obtained access.

Flipping through a thick book on local history, he came across something unexpected—the dark, violent history of the West Virginia coal wars. Fascinating and frightening. Hudson kept reading.

PART VII:

BEUFORD STANLEY

Chapter 28

The coal deposits in and around Bluefield were among the richest in the world. The Pocahontas coal seams, stretching along the Virginia–West Virginia border, ran for nearly fifty miles, with coal beds measuring an astonishing eight to ten feet thick. Though these vast reserves had been known as far back as Thomas Jefferson's time, they remained largely untouched, waiting for the Industrial Revolution to transform them into an economic powerhouse. It was not until after the Civil War that the booming northern economies helped reshape America—and coal became the lifeblood of industry.

Between 1912 and 1921, a brutal conflict erupted between mine owners and union organizers—one of the longest labor wars in U.S. history. It began in May 1912 when coal companies hired a gang of mercenaries known as Baldwin-Felts detective agents to harass and intimidate miners, preventing them from joining the United Mine Workers union. In response, the union began arming its members, supplying miners with weapons and ammunition to defend themselves.

By September of that year, the conflict escalated. Six thousand union miners crossed the Kanawha River—the largest waterway in West Virginia—to support their non-union counterparts on the other side. Among them was a tough young Welshman named Bleddyn Stanley. His fellow miners called him Wolf, a translation of his given name. But unlike the others, Wolf Stanley was not just looking to fight for labor rights—he was looking for a way out of the darkness of the mines. His escape came when he joined the very forces working against the miners, by becoming an investigator for the Baldwin-Felts Agency.

During these turbulent times, Mother Jones, an outspoken union activist and former schoolteacher—became a symbol of the miners' struggle. She was arrested and tried in a military court for inciting a riot after attempting to read the Declaration of Independence at a Union rally.

The labor war raged on for years, culminating in the deadly Matewan Massacre of 1921. Ten men lost their lives in the shootout, including Matewan's mayor, Cabell Testerman, two miners, and seven Baldwin-Felts agents—among them, Albert and Lee Felts. The violence only escalated.

Sheriff Sid Hatfield and his deputy, Ed Chambers, became heroes among the miners after surviving the massacre, but their fame was short-lived. Soon after surviving, Baldwin-Felts agents lured them to McClure County under false pretenses, then ambushed and gunned them down on the steps of the McDowell County Courthouse.

By then, Wolf Stanley had become a seasoned killer, reveling in his work with Baldwin-Felts thugs.

In response to the growing violence, thousands of miners— some estimates claim as many as 20,000—gathered at Lens Creek, preparing to march for their rights. However, the U.S. government intervened with brute force. Federal troops deployed aircraft to drop bombs on the miners, crushing the uprising in what became known as the Battle of Blair Mountain—the largest insurrection on U.S. soil since the Civil War. The crackdown was swift and merciless. More than 550 miners were arrested and charged with murder, insurrection, and treason.

After the dust settled, Wolf Stanley and two fellow Baldwin-Felts agents from Oklahoma saw an opportunity. They had been miners but had no desire to return to the tunnels. However, they had no intention of leaving the coal business behind either. The Oklahomans introduced an idea that would change the industry forever. Instead of sending hundreds of men underground to mine coal, they proposed a simpler, cheaper method: use dynamite to blow the tops off mountains, exposing coal seams for easy extraction.

Wolf Stanley, soon became a very wealthy man, and married mountain girl named Molly Smith. They had two sons, Maurice and Joseph, who grew up alongside their father, learning the family trade—blowing up mountains to extract the precious Black Gold.

Together with the Oklahoma men, Moury and Joe expanded their fathers mining empire, but tragedy/or fortune, depending on one's point of view, struck when the two Oklahomans died in an explosion. Some locals whispered that the incident was suspicious, yet no one dared investigate a man as powerful as Wolf Stanley in West Virginia. With no other obstacles in their way, Wolf and his sons grew richer, expanding their influence across the state.

After World War II, the underground mines were being sealed, their tunnels left to collapse with equipment and machinery buried deep within. The frenzy over coal mining had faded, but the Stanleys had no intention of ceasing energy extraction. They began leveling entire mountains, using surface mining techniques—some of which were highly illegal, but no one cared or dared enough to stop them. Locals had dollars in their pockets now and most knew Stanley enterprises had helped put them there.

During the war, Joe Stanley served in a demolition unit, reducing Nazi infrastructure to rubble as the American Army pushed through Germany. One night, in a Heidelberg beer hall, he had a fling with a dark-haired waitress named Trudy. Not long after, he wrecked an Army jeep while crossing the Neckar River Bridge. The crash cost him a leg, but Trudy walked away with little more than bruises.

As Joe recovered in a Heidelberg military hospital, Trudy visited him daily. When he was well enough to travel, Wolf arranged for his son to be flown home. Much to Wolf's displeasure, Joe refused to return alone. He sent for Trudy, and the two eloped. A few years later, they had a son, Beuford.

After the war had ended, Stanley Energy continued to expand at a relentless pace. Wolf Stanley died in 1950, leaving the family empire in the hands of Moury and Joe. Trudy, never fond of West Virginia, returned to Germany, and when Beuford was old enough, he was sent to elite private schools in Pennsylvania, and later attended a prestigious Law school and obtained a pilot's license. He returned home—only to find his father and uncle locked in a bitter feud that threatened to topple the entire Stanley fortune.

State regulations on surface and strip mining were tightening. Money was beginning to matter more than brute force.

Digging through family records, Beuford discovered that he would be the sole heir to the Stanley businesses once his dad died because Uncle Maurice had never had children. But before he could act, fate intervened. Maurice and Joe died in a plane crash while scouting for new mountains to destroy.

With the family empire now fully in his hands, Beuford set out to build a dynasty all his own. He married a glamorous Oscar-winning actress half fifteen years is junior, but she had no interest in children—at least, not then. A decade passed before she finally gave birth to a son. Beuford, overjoyed, named the boy Joseph. By seventeen, Joseph was a wealthy Hollywood playboy, surrounded by girlfriends, indulging in excess, and showing little interest in carrying on the family legacy.

In 2010, Joseph Stanley died in a crash on the Mulholland Highway. His toxicology report revealed multiple illegal substances in his blood.

Beuford mourned deeply, but his grief took an unexpected turn when one of Joseph's former lovers arrived at his doorstep—holding a baby. A DNA test confirmed it. The child was Joseph's.

A granddaughter!

Beuford named her Sheela and adored her from the moment he first held her. She became the center of his world, his legacy reborn. The two moved into the Stanley Malibu mansion, but Beuford frequently flew his private jet to Bluefield, running his ever-expanding energy empire from the heart of coal country.

Chapter 29

Finding nothing useful in the library, Hud shut the old volumes with a sigh. He approached the front desk, where a young woman looked up expectantly.

"Anywhere good to grab lunch?" he asked.

She pointed toward a small café just outside the library doors. "You can get a prepared sandwich and a bottled drink there," she replied.

Minutes later, Hudson sat at a café table, chewing on a stale ham sandwich, his appetite diminishing with each bite. He pushed the food aside and reached for a local newspaper left behind by another patron. A feature article caught his eye.

Copper bandits, as they were called, had begun raiding long-abandoned mines, breaking through sealed tunnels in search of scrap metal. These were not petty thieves; they were desperate men and women—many of them former miners—risking everything to carve a living from the remains of an industry that had left them behind. The subterranean maze of collapsed shafts and forgotten passageways had become a battleground for survival.

And as it turned out, there was treasure to be found. Copper, the most valuable of the salvaged metals, fetched high prices, but steel and iron could also be sold by the pound.

The dangers, however, were as severe as ever. Many who ventured down in search of scrap metal never made it back to the surface. Lack of breathable air was the greatest hazard. Isolated pockets of oxygen still existed deep underground, but they posed a deadly risk—one spark from a headlamp or torch could ignite coal dust and set off catastrophic explosions.

Yet the gleaners, as they preferred to call themselves, were undeterred. For them, the earth had always yielded both sustenance and a final resting place.

Finding the right shafts to scavenge required knowledge— secrets buried along with the men who had once worked in the tunnels. To unearth forgotten locations, gleaners often turned to a last remaining resource, old miners still living. Now, mostly confined to nursing homes, or living with family members, their memories had often dissolved into TV vegetation. Others however, were still sharp, with vivid recollections of what lay beneath the rocky West Virginia landscape.

Chapter 30

Bobby Felts led a group of gleaners, men who had turned desperation into an enterprise. Striding into the Happy Valley Nursing Home in Bluefield, he flashed a grin and a handshake to a passing nurse.

"Going to visit old Steve. That buzzard still in the same room?"

The nurse gave a curt nod before continued down the linoleum hallway.

Inside, Bobby pulled up a metal chair beside the bed of a man who had once been lean and powerful but was now withering under the slow suffocation of black lung disease. Bobby gave the frail figure a nod.

"How's tricks, Steve?"

Steve

Pruitt's head turned toward the voice. His breath rattling in his chest. "That you, Bobby?"

"Sure enough."

Steve's lips curled into a shadow of a smile. "Tricks could be better." A miner never admitted to suffering—not from the first smack of the midwife's hand to the last breath of coal dust clogging his lungs.

"Got anything for me today, Bobby?"

Felts shifted back in his chair, balancing it precariously on two legs. Even with the extra weight of his beer gut, the chair held steady without so much as a creak. His eyes flicked left, then right, scanning for prying eyes or ears. Satisfied they were alone, he reached into his inside jacket pocket and pulled out a pint of bourbon whiskey, cradling it close like a winning poker hand.

One more eyeball sweep of the room convinced him they were alone so he unscrewed the cap and offered the bottle to Steve's cracked lips. The old man sucked at it greedily, throat working as he gulped down the fiery liquid. Bobby let him drink for several long seconds before yanking the bottle free with a wet pop. He pulled a

Kleenex from the nightstand and dabbed the corners of Steve's mouth.

"Easy, old-timer."

The whiskey did its job. Steve sat up a little straighter, a flicker of brightness returning to his watery blue eyes.

"Mighty fine, Bobby. Thank you for that."

Felts' voice dropped to a husky whisper. "The gleaners think there might be valuables out by the Parrot's Beak, Steve. What say you?"

Steve shivered, as if recalling a frightening experience. "Company left a lot of stuff down there when she blew."

"Copper?"

A pause. Then a slow nod. "Tons."

"Tons? You sure?"

"Bobby, they left two electric mine locomotives down there—almost a full load of copper coils in each one. Not to mention rolls of wire for vent fans, generators, transformers, pumps… yards and yards of communication cable."

Felts let out a low whistle. "Retrievable?"

Steve's fingers trembled against the thin hospital blanket. "My grandson, Otis… he needs one of those spina bifida operations, Bobby."

Bobby didn't hesitate. He pulled the bottle from his pocket again—this time, tucking it beneath Steve's pillow. "The gleaners know about Otis, Steve. We voted you a full share if you can get us some workable maps. Can you do that?"

Steve exhaled slowly. "I'll do my best. I'll need paper, pencils… and a visitor now and then to take notes so I can explain myself."

Bobby stood, almost tipping over the chair as he pushed off it. He grinned, revealing uneven, yellowed teeth.

"We'll be in touch, old-timer. Soon."

Chapter 31

That evening, back in the library, Hudson stumbled across a thin, dog-eared binder tucked between thick, dust-covered tomes. The title, handwritten in faded ink, read: "Maps of the Mines – Bluefield, West Virginia, 1979." Below it, another name had been scrawled in shaky script: Steve Pruitt.

Hudson flipped it open. If these were maps, they were unlike any he had ever seen—dozens of pages filled with chaotic networks of intersecting lines, overlays, and erasures. The names of long-abandoned mines were scribbled in the margins, some barely legible. But what caught his attention most was a fascinating detail; much of the overlapping maze of tunnels appeared to stretch well inside the boundaries of what he now knew to be the Stanley family compound.

Just in case there was still some official record, Hud cross-referenced Steve Pruitt in a miner's database on the library's computer. Two columns appeared—one titled Living, the other Deceased. There, under Living, he found it,

Steve Pruitt – Happy Valley Nursing Home.

Hud quickly Googled the home and dialed the number.

"Yes, we have a Mr. Pruitt," a polite voice on the other end confirmed. "Who is calling?"

"A friend. When are visiting hours?"

"Every day until 9:30 p.m. If guests plan to stay for dinner, we need to know by 6:30 p.m."

Hud glanced at his phone—2:00 p.m. Plenty of time.

"Thanks," he said, ending the call. Maybe his luck was just beginning. Who knew? So far, he and Kestrel had accomplished nothing since arriving in West Virginia—aside from confirming the vast reaches of the Stanley Compound. Maybe a meeting with this Pruitt guy would be the break they had been searching for... or maybe this entire trip was shaping up to be a colossal waste of time.

Hud took out his phone and meticulously photographed each page of Pruitt's binder before slipping the binder deep into the stacks, out of sight.

Leaving the library, he hopped on his bike and pedaled toward the nursing home, his mind considering possible approaches. If he and Kes had learned anything, it was to stay cautious when talking to the locals.

The ride to Happy Valley Nursing Home was an easy mile and a half. Fifteen minutes later, Hud pulled his bike up outside and stepped through the entrance. Approaching the front desk, he noticed a young receptionist already smiling in his direction, "Can I visit with a person living here, Steve Pruitt?" Hud asked.

She glanced at a roster. "Mr. Pruitt's room is 311, but he's been spending a lot of time in the day room lately," she said with an open smile. "He likes to draw maps there. Try the day room first—just down the hall to your left. If he's not there, he'll be resting in his room, but first, I'll need you to sign in and show a photo ID."

Hud pulled out his driver's license and signed the guest book, scrawling the date beside his name.

"So, California, Mr. Halle," the receptionist said, her smile widening. "We don't get many visitors from out that way." She tilted her head, studying him. "How are you enjoying our West Virginia?"

Hudson smiled politely. "Why, it's wonderful."

"Really?" She looked both surprised and a little disappointed. "I've always wanted to visit Hollywood. Have you been to Hollywood?"

Sensing this could turn into an extended conversation, Hudson steered it back on track. "I'm doing research for a college course on the United Mine Workers union. I need to interview some old-time miners. I found Mr. Pruitt's name at Craft Memorial Library."

"Oh! Sorry," she blushed, tucking a loose strand of hair behind her ear. "I won't keep you. Be sure to sign out when you leave, bunks in room 341, if he is not in the day room." As an afterthought, she added, if you want to stay for dinner, just let me know by 6:30. You can pay at the cafeteria."

Hudson thanked her and moved on, quickly locating the day room.

Only one person was inside. An old man, possibly in his mid-seventies, but worn by time in a way that made him seem older. Thin strands of white hair clung to his skull clearly visible beneath fragile skin. His frame was more a collection of bones draped in cloth than a living body. He sat hunched over a large sheet of butcher paper spread across a work table. Scattered around him were colored markers, their caps removed and tossed aside.

"Mr. Pruitt?" Hudson called out.

No response.

The old man leaned closer to his work, gripping a marker tightly in his left fist. His tongue pressed between empty, purple gums, a look of fierce concentration on his face.

Hudson stepped forward. "Mr. Pruitt?" he repeated, this time louder. "Could I have a word with you?"

Slowly, the wrinkled face lifted from the paper. Two watery, alert eyes blinked at Hudson, squinting as if trying to bring him into focus.

"My name is Hudson Halle, Mr. Pruitt," Hud said, speaking carefully. "I'm working on a college paper about old-time miners. I found your name on a list at the Craft Library. I also found some maps you made of old mine shafts in this area."

As the old man shifted, his movements made a sound—like a bag of potato chips being crushed.

Hud swallowed and moved across the room, lowering himself into a chair directly in front of the man.

"Who be you, boy?"

The words were clear, Hud was relieved. Communication was possible.

"Mr. Pruitt, is that your name?"

The old man's watery stare did not waver. "Who be you?" he repeated, the question firmer this time.

Hudson reached into his pocket and carefully pulled out his driver's license, laying it on the table between them.

Steve Pruitt's glance flicked downward—just for a second—before snapping back and studying Hudson with a wary glance.

"I'm working on a graduate degree back in California," Hudson forged ahead. "A paper I'm writing is important it's called a thesis. I have some grant money—I can pay you for anything you tell me that I can use."

A long silence stretched between them.

"Pay me?"

"Not a lot," Hudson stuttered, "but maybe twenty dollars an hour for the time I spend interviewing you."

Pruitt's gaze returned to the driver's license. With broken, yellowed nails, he scraped it from the table and held it inches from his nose.

"Californee?"

"Yes, sir. All the way from Los Angeles," Hud replied. "I came just for this meeting. I've seen pictures of some of your maps."

"Pichers?"

"Yes, sir. I'm a graduate student at UCLA—a big university out in Los Angeles. I study geology, specifically coal mines." The lie was not fully formed even in Hud's own mind, so he spoke carefully, choosing his words with deliberation.

"In the university library, I came across some old photos of maps you made. Here, take a look."

Hud pulled his phone from his jacket pocket and tapped the screen, bringing up the title page of the map book, Steve Pruitt's name scribbled across it in faded ink. Using his thumb and forefinger, he zoomed in, making the name larger, then held the phone up close for the old man to see.

Pruitt's shaking fingers gently took the phone. His watery eyes stared at the screen in silence. A full two minutes passed.

Then his hands trembled, tilting the phone. The page slipped sideways.

Confusion took hold. His fingers shook harder, fumbling to steady the image. "What happened—where is it?" he cried, panic in his voice.

Hud reached over and gently took the phone back, righting the image. "Here, let me fix it." He swiped to another photo, this one showing a chaotic mess of interwoven lines depicting shafts and tunnels. "Hold it steady like this," he demonstrated before returning the device to the old man's grasp.

Pruitt squinted at the screen again, his expression filled with amazement, but after a few moments, he shook his head. "It's too small. I can't make it out."

Hud moved around the table, taking a seat beside him. Carefully, he enlarged the photo again, using his thumb and forefinger. The examination stretched on for over an hour as Pruitt studied the maps one by one.

Finally, the old man leaned back, but his expression remained one of awe. "These maps disappeared from me years ago… How in the hell did they get all the way out to Californee?"

Hud blinked. He hadn't expected that. "I haven't a clue," he said, surprised that lying came so easily now. "And the collection isn't complete. There might be more pictures I can find. If you'd like a copy of the original manuscript, maybe I can help you get it."

He dangled the offer like a carrot on a stick, but Pruitt didn't seem to hear.

Instead, lost in thought, he murmured just loud enough for Hud to catch, "I was a mapper for years. Every crew had one, but I was the best in the Pocahontas. Best in the whole damn state. That is why the union had me make that picture book you got a holt of."

His voice drifted, brittle with the memory.

"They gave it to me after I broke my hip. I Could not go down no more after that."

Chapter 32

"I really need to find out if there's a way to get into one of these old tunnels," Hud interrupted, sensing that the conversation was slipping and that the old man might lose his train of thought altogether.

Pruitt let out a derisive grunt, clearly annoyed at being sidetracked. "Them tunnels is all sealed." His gaze narrowed. "Besides, why the hell would you want to go in there? Ain't nobody been down there in years—legally, that is."

Hud kept his voice steady. "Mr. Pruitt, my project would be tremendously enhanced if I could take photos or even film inside some of these tunnels. Especially this area." He pointed to a section on the map where he believed the center of the Stanley compound might be located.

Pruitt's bushy brows knitted together. "Them's old shafts, boy," he said, shaking his head. "Why there?"

Hud's mind fumbled to find something to say that made sense. "Old is exactly what my whole thesis is about—the 1930s, '40s, '50s. The time of the old union wars."

Pruitt gave him a doubtful look. "I thought you said you studied geology?" A note of suspicion creeping into his voice.

The old man was sharper than Hud had anticipated. He quickly adjusted. "I do—I mean, I did—but my degree also covers the social aspects of the mining process. That is a big part of it. How the miners lived. How they worked. The big picture, as my professors call it. Any photos or videos I could get of those old shafts would be invaluable to my project."

Pruitt shifted his body, eyeing Hud carefully. "Boy, you can't just go wandering around down in them shafts with a damn camera. Even if you could breathe down there—which you probably couldn't—you would need vehicles to get around in. Those tunnels go on for miles. One wrong turn, and it's Katy bar the door. You're lost forever." He exhaled sharply. "We have had seasoned gleaners—men who mined all their lives—get lost down there looking for copper, metal, anything worth a damn. Some never come back."

Hud did not flinch. "How much?"

"Huh?"

"How much to get a crew together? The vehicles, the whole bit?"

Pruitt shook his head. "Boy, you ain't listening. Something like that? It'd cost you. Twenty-five grand, at least." He let the words settle. "Not to mention—it's illegal as hell."

Hud barely hesitated. "I'm eligible for a grant. I can get the money. And think about it, Mr. Pruitt—what this would mean for your legacy. You have made all these maps, spent years putting this together. My project could get you some notoriety, maybe even some royalties down the line."

Pruitt let out a harsh laugh. "Notoriety? Hell, son, that would get me five to ten up at Moundsville." His mood darkening. "And if I take you where you want to go, it might even earn me a seat on Old Sparky."

Hud swallowed. He had read enough West Virginia history regarding the union wars to know exactly what 'Old Sparky' had been back in the day. The Moundsville Prison Electric Chair now no longer in use.

"Of course, we'd want to keep it hush-hush—" Hud started, but Pruitt cut him off, waving a bony hand as if dismissing a pesky fly.

"Royalties," the old man mused, as if savoring the word. "Got a nice ring to it." He sat up, lowering his voice. "Listen here, boy. I've been workin' on a separate project for some gleaners. They're lookin' for treasure down there—same as you. But here's the deal. This don't get out. Your project stays secret. Just like my maps. Until it's all over."

Hud hesitated. "Well… I have another student working with me. Can I tell him?"

Pruitt's eyes narrowed. "He from Californee, too?"

"Yeah, he came with me."

After a long pause, Pruitt nodded. "Alright. When can you get started?"

"I'll need a day or two to get the grant money."

"Cash money."

Hud nodded. "Sure. Cash money, of course."

Pruitt gave a slow, knowing grin. "My boys can be ready in three, maybe four days. And you want to know something else?" He tapped a bony finger against the map. "That place you want to go? It's under the Stanley compound."

Hud tensed. "I… I don't know of any Stanley compound."

Pruitt's grin widened. His voice was low, almost amused.

"Boy, you ain't a very good liar." He chuckled darkly. "And you've told me some whoppers just now, but that's the biggest one yet."

Hudson could feel his face burning, but he didn't move or speak. What could he say?

Pruitt studied him for a moment, "Listen," he said, "I don't give a damn what your business with the Stanleys is. The folks I'll be working with? They don't like no Stanleys either. Never have. Those bastards ruined this country. Ruined the mines when they started blowing up the mountains years ago. Most mining jobs disappeared. Now, the only ones left open are the open pits, and the only miners are the damn bulldozers."

Pruitt moved slightly, his voice low and measured. "Once we are underground, it's every man for his-self. My crew knows what they're after. They know how to get in and get out." He gave Hud a knowing look. "You, on the other hand? You won't know shit."

Hud swallowed. "All I ask is that you take us where we want to go and bring us back—if possible."

Pruitt nodded. "You'll need two-way radios to stay in touch with my crew. Get some at the miner supply warehouse, along with anything else you think you'll need. Every man brings his own provisions."

He paused, tapping a bony finger against the table before adding, "And I'll need that map of the Parrot's Beak."

Hud hesitated. "Which one is that?"

Pruitt motioned impatiently. "Show me them photos again."

Hud scrolled through his album of the mine photos until the old man's cloudy eyes lit up. "There. That's the one."

Holding up the image, Hud watched as Pruitt grabbed a marker and began sketching jagged lines onto his butcher paper. His hand trembled, and he cursed under his breath, before finally shooting Hud a glance.

"Could use a shot of whiskey to steady my hand. Don't suppose you got any?"

Hud shook his head.

Pruitt sighed. "Didn't think so."

With a grunt, he tore a corner off the butcher paper, scribbling out rough lines and words before shoving it into Hud's hand.

"Today's Monday. Friday, you meet me at the time and place written on that there note. You and your buddy come with your own provisions—and don't forget the $25,000 cash money." His voice dropped into a warning. "And don't tell a soul except that other boy, or there won't be no getting into them shafts—for either of us. Ever."

Hud stared at him. "Meet you?" he repeated, dumbfounded. "You're planning to go down there, into the abandoned mines—at your age?"

"You think you got a better chance than me of coming back out?" he asked.

Hud hesitated. "Well… not really. I just figured it'd be rough going. Maybe I'm wrong."

"No." He answered, "You ain't wrong. But every man has a job. And if you don't pay close attention to what I tell you, you won't last long down there."

Hud nodded. "Okay. I get it."

"Listen, Bub," he said, his tone shifting. "I lay around in that home, day after day, week after week and year after year. I watch the other old-timers waste away, sitting around, watching TV, playing cards, waiting for someone to visit. And one by one, they die off." His voice grew quiet. "You know what the worst part is?"

Hud shook his head.

"It's the damn doctors on TV—the ones on the Public Channel. I only watch the Public Channel, because the advertisers on the other stations drive me nuts. One pill for diabetes. One so you don't feel pain. One to thin your blood and on and on. Well, I want to feel my pain." His fingers tapped against his thin chest. "Because it reminds me where I got it. Somewhere down under the ground."

Pruitt continued. "I like the explorer shows on the public stations. But the doctor shows—they're the worst. Always got some new secret to living to be ninety, a hundred, a hundred and ten—hell, a hundred and twenty! No fat, eat fat, no sugar, no dessert, no whiskey." He scoffed. "And don't forget, practice yogi every morning."

He shook his head in disgust. "Let me tell you something, boy. If someone promised me twenty more years of life—guaranteed—as long as I ate kale salad, did that damn yogi every morning, and visited the doctor once a week, you know what I'd say?"

Hud shook his head.

"Shove it."

Hud let out a quiet chuckle, but Pruitt wasn't done.

"If someone offered me a fancy cruise to the Bahamas to give up this little caper with you and the boys down in them mine tunnels," he exhaled, shaking his head, "I'd say shove that, too."

Hud replied. "That sounds like a no-brainer to me—twenty extra years of life and a Caribbean cruise in exchange for a single day in some old, abandoned mine shafts?"

Pruitt's laugh was rough and dry. "Boy, I'd give up the twenty years and the damn boat every time. I'd rather die with a smile on my face, living and toiling with men, than sit here, rotting, or taking a boat ride with a bunch of fat stragers." His voice hardened, "That ain't living, existing maybe. Being kept alive in that home by a bunch of shysters making money off my sorry hide for another twenty years!"

His voice softened, but his manner didn't fade.

"Back when this country had farms instead of industry, old seniors had a reason to live. Teaching boys how to hunt, fish, and plow. Teaching girls how to gather food and medicine, sew, cook, and bake."

He raised an index finger as if imparting something vital.

"Remember this, boy—if you ain't being of help to your kin, or someone else, you ain't living. No matter how much kale you eat, yogi you do, or cruise boats you ride."

Chapter 33

After pedaling back to the motel, Hud spotted the Pathfinder already parked outside. Stooping next to it, Kestrel wiped muddy water from the frame, a rag in his hand.

"Hey, Hud," Kes greeted him. "Just cleaning off the car. It got pretty dirty today out in the boondocks."

Hud swung a leg off his bike and let it rest against the curb. "How did it go? I thought you might be out another day or two."

Kes grinned. "We'll find out tomorrow. I placed all the cameras, got inside under the fence."

Hud was amazed. "Under the fence, how did you pull that off? It looked to me like the fencing went straight into the ground."

"It did at first," Kes acknowledged, tossing the wiping rag into the back of the Pathfinder. "But I kept following the fence line from the back side of the compound where we were the other day. I railed it down the east side a couple miles, and found a spot where the ground surface was pretty much solid rock. They had to bore holes into the rock to set the posts, which meant the base of the chain-link wasn't anchored in concrete like the rest."

Hud nodded. "And so?"

Kes continued again, "I scouted for their surveillance cameras and found a blind spot. I then cut through the base of the fence with the wire cutters, pulled the fencing up enough to crawl under through the brush. I was on the other side! Dragging the camera duffel through behind me. I lay prone for several minutes, but when no alarms went off, I surveyed the entire area with my field glasses." Kes shook his head as if amazed by his accomplishment.

Hud let out a low whistle. "Good work. Then what?"

"I was still maybe two miles from the big house, surrounded by trees and boulders. I worked my way closer to the Stanley mansion, and began planting cameras everywhere I thought people might be coming and going."

Wow, Hud said wiping his hands on his jeans. "We'll head back tomorrow, grab the cameras, and see what you were able to capture." Hud patted Kestrel's back, "Think there was any chance you were spotted?"

"Not likely." Kes replied, "I've been crawling through the woods since I was three years old." He chuckled, "You taught me good about wildlife photography and avoiding being observed by critters or people. Once I knew where to look, I avoided every one of their surveillance cameras. What's more there were nowhere near as many of their cameras inside the fence as there were outside. They must believe the cameras focused towards the woods are sufficient to secure the compound."

Hud asked, "what about guards? you must have seen a bunch of them.

"There were only a few security guards inside, Kes replied shaking his head. Mostly standing around—smoking and shooting the breeze. Occasionally, one would check in somewhere on a walkie-talkie, but overall?" He grinned. "Easy pickings."

Hud smiled. "Damn good job, Kes." Then his expression grew serious. "But getting the cameras back out may be harder than it was getting them in."

Hud grabbed Kestrels' arm, "But listen—on Friday, we're going *under* the compound."

Kestrel gasped, "Under?"

Hud nodded. "I came across an old atlas of maps at the library. There are abandoned shafts running directly beneath the Stanley mansion." He hesitated, "I've been talking to a man who knows people who can take us down inside them. So at least we're getting a toe-hold."

Kestrel contemplated the remark for a long moment giving Hud time to continue, "You don't have to come, Kes." His voice was quiet. "They say there could be poison air down there."

Kestrel let out a sharp whistle, then grinned, rubbing his hands with the drying cloth.

"Hooray! Something's finally happening. Wow!"

They bumped knuckles, and Kes added, "And there's no way in hell you're going down there without me."

Back in their motel room, both men drifted into restless sleep—but deep, relaxing REM sleep never came. Both men tossed and turned, bombarded by nightmare—visions of being shot at, chased, and lost in tunnels deep within the earth.

At first light Wednesday morning, they set out for the remote glen where Kestrel had previously parked behind the Stanley Compound.

Once inside, Hud followed Kestrel's lead, moving with slow, deliberate steps. As they approached, he was amazed at just how close the cameras had been placed to the Stanley mansion.

The nearness forced them to creep in silence, boots sinking into damp leaves, careful not to snap a twig or rustle a branch. So close, they came to the mansion that thru the large plate glass windows, they could see human silhouettes moving behind the muted glass.

Once inside the fence it took them an entire day to retrieve all their cameras before scooting back under the fence once more, just before finding their way back to the Pathfinder as dusk settled over the woods. By the time they reached the car, they were filthy, drained of energy, and starving but pleased by their seemingly unobserved escapade.

Back at the motel, after quick showers and changing out of their worn clothing, they decided against driving into town in search of a hot meal, settling instead for whatever bland food they could find nearby.

Just before closing time, they stumbled upon Patty Joe's, a small-town cafe that, to their surprise, turned out to serve the best meal they'd had in Bluefield to date.

They shoveled food down in great gulps, only pausing to breathe and guzzle hot coffee. The large, jovial waitress chuckled at their appetites. "Looks like you boys had a long day. You ought to try the key lime pie."

They did.

It arrived in thick slabs, topped with whipped cream, and after devouring it, they finally felt sated for the first time in a while.

"One more day before our Friday meeting," Kestrel said, wiping crumbs and cream from his face with a cloth napkin. "Tomorrow morning, we need to double-check our gear before heading into the mines."

"True," Hud agreed. "But when we get back tonight, I want to go over some of your photos and videos you got from within the compound. It's incredible how close you got to the big house—and the positions you placed each camera were spot on."

Kestrel replied. "To tell you the truth, I'm surprised I found all the cameras again. But having both of us there made it a hell of a lot easier than when I was out there scattering them around."

Lying in their bunks that night, they examined the photo footage, one clip after another.

The motion sensors had done their job; however, most scenes were of little of interest. Mostly, the wildlife had taken center stage—squirrels, possums, raccoons, and foxes darting through the underbrush. A mother black bear, fat and ready for hibernation, ambled past with her two cubs frolicking behind her.

Then came the humans. Several clips showed people moving in and out of the mansion—security guards mostly, but also a few men with briefcases. One clip even captured two sheriff's deputies walking toward a patrol vehicle.

Hud paused the footage he had been scanning and scrolled back. "Look at this one," he grimaced, "It's really ugly."

Kestrel took the camera and squinted at the screen.

In the grainy night vision, two men were holding back a large black Doberman straining at its collar.

A third man stood about thirty yards away, next to a metal cage. One of the men holding the dog waved to the man by the cage—who promptly tipped it over.

A large, fat raccoon tumbled out, landing awkwardly in the dirt. For a split second, the startled animal froze, looking around in confusion—before bolting toward a nearby grove of trees but the raccoon never had a chance.

The Doberman lunged, closing the distance in a few long, bounding leaps. The rest was too brutal for words. The grainy video captured the moment the dog tore into its prey, ripping the helpless creature to shreds. Blood spattered the dirt. The raccoon let out one final shriek, then fell silent.

The men watching from the sidelines erupted into applause, and cheering in morbid glee.

Kestrel's face paled. "Sickening, isn't it?" he muttered. "The way some people find pleasure in suffering?"

Hud did not respond.

Instead, Kestrel heard a low whistle.

Turning toward the sound, he saw Hudson squinting into another video, while hitting the replay button and watching the same scene over and over.

"What is it, Hud?"

Hud looked up, refocusing his eyes, then shoved the camera toward Kestrel. "Look for yourself."

Kestrel took the camera, his gaze narrowing as he watched the grainy footage. A large black limousine pulled into a circular driveway, rolling to a slow stop. A chauffeur emerged from the driver's side, walked around the car, and opened a rear door. A thin young woman, late teens maybe, stepped out, a backpack slung over one shoulder.

She wore a pleated tartan skirt, and a white blouse, with a white yoke collar. But the detail that stood out most was her short blond hair highlighted with pale green streaks.

Kestrel frowned. "Hard to make out, but she looks familiar." He squinted at the image. "Looks like a girl that came to one of our Coast Conservation Corps meetings not too long ago."

Hud nodded. "She came in a limo, too?"

"Yeah," Kestrel exclaimed. "I remember it now. A lot like the one in this video. Jerry said she's some rich kid from Malibu, ga-ga over the environment in a naïve way. She spends summers with her grandparents somewhere on the Southern California Coast, according to Jerry."

He furrowed his brows, thinking back. "She said she picked up one of our flyers asking for donations—left in some Malibu coffee house. Her grandfather later called Jerry from the number on the flyer. The old man donated a couple thousand bucks so his granddaughter could 'see what real conservationists do.'"

Kestrel went on, "Jerry thought she was a funny kid. Showed up in the limo for a few meetings, then I guess she got bored and stopped coming."

Hud scratched his head. "I vaguely remember the green hair… and the short shorts."

"That's her," Kestrel nodded, "always wearing something skimpy. She even raised the eyebrows of Buffy and LJ," Kes smiled, "but Lillian thought it was hilarious and cute. She said she had dressed the same way at USC—but without the limo."

Hud knew that enlarging the image would only make it blurrier, so he backed it down to a smaller size and reached for his supply pack. Pulling out a magnifying glass, he handed it to Kestrel along with the camera.

"See if looking at a smaller but magnified image makes her features any clearer."

Kestrel stared at the screen for several long moments, then sighed, "Looks like her," he agreed handing the camera and magnifying glass back, "but I can't be certain."

Hud took another look, the girl's face was clearer, but he realized he had never really observed her closely enough to be certain either, but the green hair highlights-that, he remembered. "What's her name? Do you know?" Hud asked.

Kestrel thought for a moment. "Sheena… Sheela… something like that."

Chapter 34

The next morning, Hud and Kes returned to Patty Joe's for breakfast where the same stout, smiling waitress greeted them as they slid into a booth. After ordering ham, eggs, and another slice of pie, they headed out, driving to a large miner supply outlet they had found online: Miner's Warehouse. The store was massive, with open floor space packed with everything a person would need to go underground.

Pushing a cart through the wide aisles they selected Steel helmets with attached headlamps and full-body jumpsuits. Waterproof high-strobe flashlights, Hammers with hooks hanging from the handles, and over-the-shoulder utility belts to attach everything to. Remembering Pruitt's instructions, they grabbed a set of two-way radios as well.

At the checkout counter, they tossed in snack packs—which, conveniently, also had belt hooks. The balding clerk rang up their gear, eyeing them with mild curiosity.

"Spelunkers?" he asked with a knowing nod.

Hud grinned. "How'd you guess?"

"Well, you ain't miners, that's for sure." The man chuckled. "Only folks who buy this kind of gear are miners or explorers. You look like the second kind."

"A lot of cave exploring happen around here?" Hud asked casually.

"Oh yeah," the clerk nodded. "Couple groups get lost every year. Some never found. Very dangerous spelunking in these hills— mining is dangerous too."

He leaned on the counter, lowering his voice slightly. "Sometimes," he said, giving a knowing look, "caves lead into old mine shafts. Poison air in those holes. People suffocate."

He gave a pointed look, and continued; "Folks from around here are too smart to go in 'em."

The clerk looked over their selected merchandise. "You boys taking oxygen tanks?"

Hud shook his head. "Nah, we're going into a cave we've been in before. Not too far in. Just getting ready for next summer exploring."

The clerk frowned, eyeing the pile of brand-new gear stacked on the counter.

"Most experienced people already got their own stuff." His gaze drifted over their haul. "Everyone who goes spelunking takes strong nylon cord. Lightweight—twenty-yard packs go for fifteen bucks."

Hud hesitated.

"Trust me," the clerk continued. "It's worth your while."

Hud exchanged a glance with Kes. "Sounds good Kes shrugged, "where do you keep it?"

The clerk tapped the shelf behind him. "Right here. One of those items people forget—I always remind 'em."

Kes snatched up a pack of rope, tossing it onto the counter. "Yeah, ring it up. We're planning to be more adventurous this summer. New rope is always good."

The clerk nodded ringing up all their new provisions. "Very dangerous," he repeated as he handed them their shopping bags filled with supplies.

Back at the Pathfinder, Kes threw the gear into the back.

"Nosy cuss," he remarked, shutting the hatch.

Hud nodded in agreement. "Say, Kes—I want to find the place we're meeting Pruitt's people tomorrow morning."

"Smart." Kes agreed, "better to get lost looking for it today than getting lost tomorrow morning."

Hud pulled the scrap of paper from his pocket—the one Pruitt had scribbled directions and a rough map and handed it to Kes.

"You navigate. Let's see how good Pruitt is at giving directions."

Pruitt's map was spot on. Using landmarks such as filling stations and creek crossings, it led them deep into the nearby hills. Soon, the paved road gave way to mud and Hud needed to shift into four-wheel drive to maintain a steady pace as the road climbed and dipped.

Several miles in, the road sloped downward—steeply. The dirt surface thinned, exposing worn rock underneath, "Here goes nothing," Hud thought, gripping the wheel as they descended into the ravine. Sifting into low gear, he let the tires crawl over the rocky surface to maintain traction.

At the bottom of the ravine, the road jogged sharply to the left. However, Hud's experienced hands took the turn slow and steady. Suddenly—Kes called out "wait, pointing out the passenger window with one hand, and a finger resting on a red circle on Pruitt's map. "There. That must be the place!"

Hud glanced to the right, narrowing his eyes as he took in an old shotgun-style clapboard house.

The original paint was faded and peeling, except for a few patched areas where it had been worn or washed away. The ram shackled structure appeared abandoned. Weeds and fallen branches choked the yard and the roof sagged. Broken eaves were clogged with debris from the surrounding forest. The interior appeared dark—black as a tomb.

Scrubby woodland stretched in every direction, with no other structures in sight. "Want to park and take a look inside?" Kestrel asked.

Hud shook his head. "No, Kes. The place might be watched, and whoever we're meeting tomorrow might not like us poking around early."

Kestrel let out a low whistle. "I'll tell you what though—if this is a trap, I couldn't think of a better place to set it."

"Let's turn around and get back to the motel, and try on all our new gear." Hud said with a forced a grin. "If it's a trap, it's a chance we have to take, I guess."

The drive back was uneventful, as they retraced the route easily—now confident they would be able to find the rendezvous spot in the morning.

At the motel, they removed the tags from their new equipment and pulled on their jumpsuits, helmets, and utility belts. The hammers and flashlights were clipped onto the belts. Thus-dressed they stood back, grinning at each other, while striking a few ridiculous poses and taking several selfies.

Afterwards, Hud sat on the edge of the bed, counting out $25,000 in hundred-dollar bills from the cash stash and tucked the money into a pocket of his jumpsuit. The rest of it, he hid in a battered toolbox in the back of the Pathfinder, tossing a few old tools on top for good measure.

"That about does it," he assured Kes.

After a dinner of liver and onions—with, of course, more pie—they returned to the motel, fully aware that sleep would not come easy. For the second night in a row, both men tossed and turned, occasionally grumbling about how uncomfortable the beds were but they both knew—it was not the mattresses keeping them awake.

At some point, Hud heard Kestrel's quiet snore. Staring at the ceiling he wondered what tomorrow would bring?

The plan—or rather, the fuzzy half-baked scenario he had concocted now seemed stupid. He replayed the idea in his head.

Step one; get inside the Stanley compound. Steve Pruitt had assured Hud that older mine shafts in that area came extremely close to the surface and even recalled one or two tunnels with openings inside the property. "That's from thirty, forty years ago," Steve had warned. "No telling whether they've been blocked off since."

Step two; once inside, get into the main house—by any means necessary and find a safe hiding spot. Wait until dark and the house is silent. Figure out where old man Stanley slept. Enter his room, gag him into silence, scare him, maybe threaten his granddaughter. Finally force him to reveal the location of the suitcase and its contents. Lastly bind and gag Stanley and get out of Bluefield like bats out of hell.

In retrospect, Step One seemed possible—but the rest was the kind of half-baked plot that belonged in one of those cheap 1950s film noir movies Nicole had dragged him to. Hud had never intimidated or threatened anyone in his life.

As the first light of morning seeped through the motel curtains, Hud zipped up his jumpsuit and adjusted the straps on his utility belt. "Listen, Kes," he said "If we get separated today, you have to stay with Pruitt at all costs."

Kestrel paused, glancing up from fastening his own belt clips.

"Then listen for me—on your radio and your phone," Hud continued. "If you don't stay with him, neither of us has a snowball's chance in hell of getting out of that compound."

Kes nodded slowly, "I don't know what you're planning, Hud, but it sounds like you get to do all the fun stuff."

Hud snorted. "Yeah. Real fun."

After suiting up, they sat in silence, watching the clock as the hours crawled by, they went over what might happen, what could go wrong, and what they would do if it did. They agreed on one thing— they would not eat out this morning. Too risky. The locals were too damn curious—and two guys in headlamps, jumpsuits, and utility belts would stick out like a flare in the dark.

They did not need anyone asking questions, and they sure as hell did not need the word getting out about suspicious strangers to any local authorities, or worse, the Stanley goon squad.

Chapter 35

It was still early when Hud and Kestrel retraced their route back into the hills, towards the run-down house they had driven past the day before. This time, a pale-yellow light seeped from behind the worn window shades.

As Hud pulled the Pathfinder into the weed-choked driveway, he caught sight of two pickup trucks parked behind the house. They climbed out of the Pathfinder, boots crunching against gravel, and mounted the rickety steps. Just as Hud was about to knock, the door swung open. Old Pruitt's grizzled head appeared, his pinched face floating in a dim pool of light, surrounded by a murky cloud of gloom and tobacco smoke.

"That you, Hudson?"

"It is."

"Come on in, then, and meet your cohorts in crime."

Hudson and Kestrel stepped inside, met by four men, all dressed in dark coveralls.

One of them, a large man with narrow shoulders, and sagging gut, stepped forward, extending a gnarled hand.

"Bobby," he introduced himself, his voice like dry gravel grinding inside a hand-operated cement mixer.

Hud took his calloused grip and nodded.

Bobby stood about the same height as Hud, but his black jumpsuit was deeply stained, and unbuttoned at the throat.

Bobby jerked a thumb toward the corner. "You know Steve."

Old Pruitt flashed a wide grin, revealing a full set of almost white dentures.

"This here's Otis—Steve's kin," Bobby continued, motioning with his jaw toward a small, stout figure lingering at the back of the room.

Otis was a stout gnome of a man. His damp, stringy black hair merged into a full scraggly beard, and his expression was surly and angry.

The moment Bobby announced his name, Otis did not step forward but instead, scuttled sideways, crab-like, as if trying to get a better view of the newcomers from the back of the room. As he moved, Hud noticed a decided limp, like one leg was either shorter or deformed. His hips sagged under the weight of a holstered revolver; the worn leather belt cinched tight around his waist.

When Hud and Kes gave him a small wave, Otis did not respond with a nod or a greeting—he just tilted his chin up an inch. It was the same half-nod, half-dismissal, that Hud noticed Steve Pruitt give back at the nursing home. No doubt Otis was related to Steve.

The last man was introduced as Chuck, unlike the others, Chuck looked to be around Hud's age. His red coveralls were streaked with dirt, as if he had been digging in them recently. The name 'Chuck' was embroidered over the upper left chest. He wore a miner's helmet with a flashlight attachment, which he nudged up with his thumb when introduced. Chuck smiled—but without showing teeth.

Bobby turned back to the group. "Boys, this here's Hud and…" He hesitated.

"Kes," Kestrel announced.

Bobby nodded slowly, "Before we get started, you're supposed to have something for me."

Hud did not answer Bobby. Instead, he turned to Steve. "My deal is with Steve. Isn't that right, Mr. Pruitt?"

Steve spryly stepped forward, "Sure enough, Hud," he yelped. "You keep our bargain?"

Hud reached into the breast pocket of his jumpsuit and pulled out a thick wad of hundred-dollar bills.

Immediately, the men moved in, bodies tensing.

Kestrel reacted instantly—stepping forward, arms out, blocking their approach.

"Let's go over there," he said evenly, nodding toward a small, battered oak table and chair. The table was cluttered with used Styrofoam cups and a large pink donut box, its contents half-eaten.

Hud took a seat, while the others carelessly brushed the mess aside. As he counted out hundred-dollar bills, the room fell silent. Eyes bulged. Adam's apples bobbed involuntarily.

When he finished, Hud reached up and shook Steve Pruitt's right hand, placing the thick bundle of cash into his left.

"A deal's a deal," Hud said, shooting a glance at Otis.

The gnome-like man had been rigid, but as Hud acknowledged the transaction as Pruitt's, Otis seemed to relax ever so slightly.

Hud's intuition told him that for the whole expedition to work, he and Kes would need allies—and Otis and old Pruitt would be the most important ones.

Hud spoke to the group. "My deal with Mr. Pruitt is simple. He takes Kes and me to a location we marked on one of his maps. We explore for a while, and when we radio in, he is either waiting for us or comes back to get us." He turned back to Pruitt.

"That's right, isn't it, Steve?"

Pruitt grinned. "Yup."

"Let's divide her up now," Otis announced.

The others nodded vigorously—Bobby begrudgingly.

With shaking fingers, Steve Pruitt counted out $6,000 into four stacks handing one each to Bobby, Otis, and Chuck, from the remaining $1,000, each man got an extra $100. The old man hesitated, then handed another $300 to Bobby and pocketed $400.

"Bobby had the idea, and I had the maps," Pruitt declared.

"Now it's all even."

He let out a giggle. "Even Steven. That's me."

Then, in a more serious tone, he added, "Before I drop off these two," he nodded at Hud and Kes, "we head for the shaft where I reckon the copper wire and wrecked engines are."

He looked around the room. "Each man gets an even share of whatever we glean—agreed?"

Every man appeared pleased, gripping more cash in his hands than he'd likely ever held before.

Every man—except Bobby. He still looked miffed, as if he had expected more control over the split. But he did not argue. Instead, he turned sharply and led the way toward the pickup trucks parked out back, where each man unloaded a backpack and a utility belt, securing their gear.

At the same time, Hud and Kes retrieved their own equipment from the Pathfinder. When all were ready, Bobby walked toward a large padlocked garage at the edge of the property and unlocked it, while the men swung the doors open wide.

Two heavy duty ATVs were parked inside. Chuck and Otis clambered behind the wheels and started the engines, the growl of the motors filling the air. When they drove out into the backyard, Hud noted that each ATV had a flatbed trailer attached to the rear. The trailers each carried six oxygen tanks, all secured with cables. Shovels, picks, and large coils of rope were bungeed down tight as well.

Hud exchanged a glance with Kestrel. It was time. They followed Bobby once more, this time on foot, toward a brush pile at the edge of the woods. Bobby and Otis rolled the brush aside, revealing deep tire tracks leading into the forest. The ATVs were then driven through the hidden opening.

Once the vehicles were clear, the men moved the brush piles back into place, concealing the track once again and the journey resumed.

Bobby and Steve rode in the front seats of the two ATVs, while Kestrel and Hud took the rear bench seats. Once buckled in, Chuck followed by Otis drove slowly down a narrow track, winding toward a rocky out-cropping looming less than a mile away.

Steve, kept his headlamp trained on his lap, where a bundle of maps lay spread across his knees.

Seeing that the money was now out of his reach, Bobby called out, loud enough for both vehicles to hear. "The bill for the rent on these here vehicles will also be divided up when we get back." His gravelly voice carried through the trees.

A few amused sniggers came from the crew of the following vehicle. Hud glanced at Kestrel, who returned a knowing look. Bobby was not about to let go of the fact that others now had control of the money.

The party soon arrived at the base of the out-crop, where a massive concrete block wall stood in their path. A tangle of concertina wire lay spread across the ground in front of it.

Mounted on the wall, seven feet off the ground, a sign loomed over them.

DANGER! NO TRESPASSING!

Violators Will Be Prosecuted to The Full Extent of the Law!

Once again, the crew dismounted, moving with workman-like efficiency as they tackled the barrier ahead. With gloved hands, they hauled the rusted wire aside. Then, using pry bars wedged under the bottom edge of the concrete wall, winches were attached to the bars, and in a coordinated effort, two adjoining sections of the wall were pulled backward simultaneously.

A gap now yawned before them—just wide enough for an ATV pulling a trailer to pass through. One by one, the vehicles rumbled through the narrow breach in single file.

When the entire party was inside, all six men climbed down from the ATVs and immediately got to work. Brush was cut and stacked strategically to mask the opening, while the displaced concrete blocks were camouflaged.

Despite their skepticism about the Californians, Bobby's men found themselves impressed as Hud and Kes kept up with the work, effortlessly moving with speed and skill. To Hud and Kes, this was just another job. They had both cut trail before, cleared barbed wire, and covered their tracks to return the environment to a natural state.

Within minutes, their entry point was invisible to any casual observer.

Bobby gave a final inspection, stepping back and nodding, satisfied. "Looks good," he remarked.

The men reboarded the ATVs Steve Pruitt stood up, balancing beside Otis in the lead vehicle. Clearing his throat, he raised his voice above the rumble of motors. "Listen up!" he wheezed. "We all want to come out alive and kicking, right?"

Heads nodded.

Pruitt continued, "These ATVs Bobby rented? They're each equipped with an MSA ALTAIR 4X monitoring device. I made sure of that." He let the words sink in before adding, "These devices tell us if there's methane, carbon monoxide, or not enough oxygen."

His eyes scanned the group, making sure everyone was listening.

"Any one of those three things will knock you out in seconds and kill you in minutes."

The men shifted uneasily.

"Any questions?"

Silence.

Pruitt nodded and pressed on. "The ALTAIR will sound an alarm if a lethal gas or oxygen drop is detected. But don't wait for the alarm. Watch the monitor."

"If oxygen drops below 19 percent, grab an air tank—and don't put it down until the reading climbs back above 19." Then he added: "If it keeps dropping, you turn the hell around and run—lickety-split."

Pruitt wiped his brow with a blue bandana, then continued, his voice rasping. "When we was mining here, the upper shafts always had enough air to breathe. Bosses said it seeped in naturally. When we dug deeper, we had blowers moving the air around. But when the explosion hit? That shut us down. So, watch your ALTAIR, because if you catch the blackdamp—" His voice dropped to a whisper. "You're a dead man."

The weight of the words settled over the group. Hud exhaled, gripping the edge of his seat. This old boy had seen a lot in his time, and still knew a hell of a lot.

As the ATVs' continued thru the passageway LED headlamps cut through the darkness, illuminating the tunnel ahead. The visibility was phenomenal.

After fifty yards, the trail merged into what must have been the mine's original main shaft. Beneath thick layers of dust and rubble, narrow-gauge track marks lined the floor—though much of the metal had been cut away and carted off. The air was cooler here. Hud swallowed, eyes flicking to the ALTAIR monitor.

As the ATVs rumbled deeper, old Pruitt seemed to come alive. It was as if years had peeled away, his gnarled frame now buoyed by the thrill of exploration. He nodded to himself, eyes flicking over the rock walls, seeming to recognize familiar features from long ago.

Finally, he turned to Hud and Kes, his voice laced with pride. "Pocahontas bituminous coal fueled the steamer ships of the navies of the world," he declared. "Stoked steel mills, powered plants— kept everything running."

Hud nodded absently, watching the roadway slope downward in a steady, manageable descent. Not too steep—maybe ten degrees, at most.

They traveled along for miles—the roadway mostly straight, though jarring at times.

Then the tunnel changed. Up ahead, the passage bore deep scars from a violent explosion. Steel tracks on the floor were twisted beyond recognition.

The walls and ceiling, once neatly chiseled, now bore gaping wounds, where massive chunks of rock had been ripped away.

The ATVs slowed to a crawl.

Men peered out, eyes wide with awe and unease.

Several times, they had to stop completely, using muscle and winches to drag large boulders or other debris aside as they wound through the wreckage of a past catastrophe.

Finally, they emerged into a vast chamber—an oversized open room, its walls scarred with blackened blast marks. Near the center, a wrecked elevator shaft yawned like a mouth of an abyss. Chuck pulled his ATV to a stop in front of it, and Otis did the same. The helmet lamps gleamed, casting long shadows against the cavern walls. The headlamps of the ATVs burned brightly, illuminating the entire space like a late-night baseball game.

Pruitt set his maps aside and climbed down.

"This here's where one of the really huge blasts happened," he said, his voice almost reverent, almost distant. He scuffed the ground with his boot, revealing melted iron, steel, and copper fused into the floor.

"Gleaners before us already stripped a lot of the metal," he continued, gesturing toward jagged cuttings along the chamber walls. "Mostly steel. There was only copper wire for lighting here—not much else."

The men listened in silence. Here, underground, old Pruitt was the expert and they were hanging on his every word.

"If we can get a man winched down about fifty, sixty feet," he said, motioning toward the elevator shaft, "a big side tunnel—goes off to the right." He pointed to the far wall. Pruitt squinted into the darkness, his mind digging back, retracing the tunnels by memory.

"I recall there being a small engine down that side shaft," he murmured. "Two, maybe three spools of copper wire on it." He nodded to himself, as if confirming a long-forgotten memory.

"And those spools were full, too—lighting cables hadn't been laid yet."

His gaze next flickered toward the collapsed remains of the passage. "We found a real nice seam of coal down that way."

"We were fixing to start a major dig—long as she was yielding."

He exhaled sharply, shaking his head in amazement. "Bosses pressed us too fast, though." His voice dropped, "Coal dust built up. She exploded." A long pause. "Miners died. Scuttled the whole deal."

Hud absorbed the words, but his mind wandered elsewhere to ancient Egyptian tombs. Raiders moving through the darkness, prying open sealed chambers, scavenging whatever had been left behind. Gleaners of another age. Not so different from the crew he was with now. For as long as there was treasure to be found—desperate men would seek it out.

Hud studied the men around him. Rough, hardened, driven. They were no different from the fortune hunters who had come before. Since the dawn of human history, men had followed the same path—drawn by the promise of something hidden just out of reach.

Chapter 36

Steve Pruitt motioned for everyone to gather around. "I'm going to direct Otis to the place the *Californee* boys showed me where they'd like to be taken—for *college research*, you understand?" He leered, and the gleaners snorted with laughter. Hud felt his face redden, but Kes just laughed along with the others.

"We should be back in a couple of hours," Pruitt continued, "but we'll stay in touch using the radios to keep you posted on our progress."

He turned to Bobby Felts next. "Bobby, first thing—before you lower Chuck down that elevator shaft—make sure you send the portable ALTAIR down with him. Don't go yourself; you ain't in good enough shape." His tone was sharp, but Bobby just crossed his arms and listened. "I've been checking the detector on my ATV, and the breathable air's getting thin in some places, but no sign of gas yet. There would have been a lot of carbon monoxide at the time of the explosion, but that's all gone now."

Placing a firm hand on Chuck's shoulder, Pruitt warned, "If you notice the air's thinner than 19 percent, or you get a gas reading, quick as a cat you call Bobby to send down one of the small oxygen tanks. And Chuck—*make sure you use it*."

"When you're down about fifty feet, start looking for that side tunnel," he went on. "It should not be hard to find. Swing in there once you see it and take a look around. You can bring back up whatever is easy, but don't get greedy. If there is as much down there as I think there is, we can take all month getting it out."

"Hope so," Bobby grinned. "This shaft's going to make us rich men."

"If we're careful, we can more than double what we got from the *Californee* boys just from that one hole," Pruitt boasted. "And I know of others in this pit too."

By the time Otis started driving off, guided by Steve's ever-watchful eye, the *giddy thrill of discovery* had infected them all. Hud and Kestrel were squeezed together in the small rear seat of the ATV, while Otis drove and Steve Pruitt sat beside him, maps spread across his lap, and pointing out directions.

Before climbing in, Pruitt had taken two oxygen tanks from the flatbed and laid them across Hud and Kes's feet. "Hold on tight," he advised, craning his neck to look back at them. "Some of the track ahead might be pretty rough, and there might not be time to grab an air tank from the trailer. We are headed for some very old tunnels."

As they journeyed deeper, Steve constantly directed Otis, his attention split between the ALTAIR and his maps. As far as Hud could tell, they were now *climbing* slightly instead of descending as before. The tunnels around them looked *older*, the walls rougher, their structure different from the others they had passed. He leaned toward Steve Pruitt.

"These shafts look different," Hud noted.

"They *are* different," Steve agreed. "These were dug way back. Built in my forefathers' time, when mule teams pulled the coal cars in and out of the mines."

Hud took cell phone photos constantly, throwing in the occasional video clip to maintain the illusion that he and Kes were genuinely working on a documentary film. Pruitt had been skeptical at first, but Hud figured the more footage he took, the harder it would be to question their cover.

About an hour into the ride, Steve suddenly gasped for air. He grabbed at his chest and barked, "Stop! Grab an air tank—now!"

Otis slammed the brakes, and all three of them fumbled for their oxygen masks. Hud's pulse jumped as he checked the ALTAIR Oxygen: 18 percent.

"This damn dead spot's been here since my granddaddy's day," Pruitt spoke between gulps of air from a tank. "Three-mile stretch where there's almost no air. Nobody ever figured out why."

They all sat still for a moment, pulling deep breaths of oxygen from their tanks. Steve kept a watchful eye on the oxygen gauge now, checking it every few seconds. After what felt like an eternity, he gave a curt nod. "Readings are back over nineteen percent. Shut off the tanks. Never know when we'll need more air."

Kestrel removed his mask, exhaling sharply. "I don't get it," he said. "How does air get down here in the first place? No plants, no photosynthesis. What's keeping this place from suffocating?"

"Several ways, maybe," Steve replied, brushing coal dust from the sleeves of his coveralls. "Some folks say it seeps in from the surface. Up in Pennsylvania, fires have been burning nonstop in abandoned mines since the nineteen-sixties, never going out. Can't have fire without oxygen, so it's got to be coming from somewhere."

He leaned forward, staring into the dark ahead. "My daddy's friends used to say some of this air's been trapped underground since these hills were first formed a million years ago."

Steve's fingers suddenly gripped the dash of the ATV. Otis noticed too, frowning. "What's the matter now?"

"Hush, boy," Steve hissed. His voice had dropped to a low whisper. "We're almost to the spot."

The ATV's pace slowed to a crawl. At Steve's command, Otis dimmed the headlights, plunging them into a murky semi-darkness. The beams now barely pushed through the thick shadows, illuminating only a few yards ahead. Hud squinted into the black, seeing nothing but darkness.

Then Kestrel said barely above a whisper. "There's light ahead," he said. "I can feel it."

"You got a keen sense," old Pruitt hissed. "You part Injun?"

"Yeah," Kes whispered back. "What is it?"

"I can't see it yet myself," Steve admitted, his voice low. "But from what I'm looking at on this map, it's probably coming from real near the Stanley mansion—just above us." He cast a glance at Kes. "Miners with Injun blood always said they noticed light before other men. Some even claimed they could smell it."

As the track dipped downward, the walls around them closed in. Then, just ahead, a solid rock barrier emerged, cutting off the tunnel. Coming through between the rocks, thin slivers of light glowed dimly, threading through hairline fractures in the stone.

"This is as far as Otis and I go," Steve announced under his breath. "The place you wanted to get to? It's right here, above us."

Hud turned toward Steve's profile in the inky darkness. "I want to try digging through," he said. "See where the light's coming from. If it's open air, Kes and I can get out here, and our bargain's over. But if there's no way out…" he hesitated. "I guess we go back with you."

Pruitt was silent for a moment, considering. Then, with a slow nod, he said, "Otis and I'll stand by for an hour—no more. If we don't hear from you over your radio by then, we head back to the others. With or without you."

"Deal," Hud said. "Got anything to dig with?"

Steve climbed gingerly out of the ATV and retrieved two pick and shovel from the trailer. Hud and Kes took the tools, and went straight to work, swinging the picks at the brightest slivers of light.

The glow seeped through the cracks just above a boulder, about shoulder height.

. "Not there," Steve hissed sharply. "Dig there, and you'll bring the whole damn ceiling down on us."

He dimmed his helmet light and shuffled closer, hands running along the obstruction's base. After a moment, he reached for the shovel. Bending low, he dug into the loose gravel where the barrier met the side wall, the debris came away faster now.

With each passing moment, the cracks widened, the light grew stronger. "Looks like electric light," Steve muttered, shaking his head. "Not the sun."

He handed the shovel back to Hud, his voice laced with curiosity. "We must be just beneath a house… or an outbuilding of some kind."

"Just a little more time," Hud said, his voice tight with determination. He stepped down into the newly dug hole, shoveling dirt and debris away. "Our hour's just begun," he said to Steve.

Kestrel worked beside him, scraping away loose dirt, clearing Hud's path. The digging was easy at first, but before long their way was blocked by a large boulder stuck between the walls of the passage. No way past it—not without serious effort.

Hud backed out, gasping for breath, coughing hard. Sweat dripped down his face, streaking the coal dust on his skin. "I can't get through," he choked out, defeated. "It's too tight."

Kes snatched the pick. "I'll give it a try."

The hole was barely wide enough, but Kes forced himself in, wriggling his shoulders forward, pressing himself into the dirt.

When he reached the boulder he braced his feet, twisting his torso for leverage. Then, gritting his teeth, he shoved upward with all his strength. For a moment—nothing. Then, he felt a slight shift. The smaller rocks on the left of the boulder moved, just barely. Kes froze, realizing the risk. He was wedged tightly between two massive stones. One wrong move, and he could trap himself completely—or bring the whole slope down on top of him.

He did not hesitate. "What the hell," he said and shoved again as hard as he could, straining every muscle I his body. This time— his shoulders popped free, sliding through an opening above like a cork from a bottle. The rest was easy.

Once he squeezed his whole body through, Kes found himself peering into a large room, roughly twenty feet square. The space was dimly lit by subdued halogen fixtures, their bulbs protected by wire cages. Kes crouched low, Hud's warning about cameras flashing in his mind. His eyes swept the room, taking in the walls lined with bins, floor-to-ceiling, and a row of filing cabinets.

Then his gaze landed on the third wall where a massive metal vault door loomed before him. Whoever built this place had cut it directly into solid rock, probably the basement of a building or maybe even a cliffside.

The builders had no idea how close they'd come to breaking through to an old mine shaft. "An almost perfect impregnable storage facility," Kes thought, rising to his feet. His flashlight swept across the space, scanning the bins, the cabinets, and the corners cloaked in shadow.

Then—something glinting high up on a shelf caught his eye.

A quick flash of shiny metal?

Kes once more swept the beam along the tops of the bins. Slowly, he traced the beam back, moving it inch by inch. There—a metal container. His heart hammered. "Holy shit!" he breathed.

The container sat about twelve feet off the ground—out of reach. The bins beneath it were too flimsy to climb, and nearby wooden crates looked too weak to hold his weight.

Kes scanned the room, searching for something to extend his reach. Near a back corner, he noticed several leftover strips of aluminum bin scaffolding, like an erector set. Each strip was only about three feet long, not long enough. He estimated he needed at least five feet to reach the container and knock it loose.

The scaffolding was designed to be adjustable, with pre-drilled holes for nuts and bolts—but none of the extra pieces had extra screws attached. Cursing under his breath, Kes felt along the constructed bins, pressing his fingers against the screws, checking for any that might be loose. Finally, he found a loose one with a lug-nut attached.

He unscrewed the loose lug and then worked the screw free by hand. The structure of the bin wobbled a little—but nothing collapsed. He kept searching and felt a second loose lug, he was able to unscrew this one and remove the screw by hand. Two screws would have to do. Kes fastened two of the extra scaffolding strips together with the screws attaching the lugs, fashioning a crude pole over five feet long.

He angled it carefully aloft, toward where the metal case sat and began nudging it inch by inch toward the edge of the bin. One more prod—and it would drop but a loud noise caused by the fall could lead to disaster. For all he knew, a security guard could be standing right on the other side of the vault door. Kes took a slow breath, then positioned himself beneath the shelf.

If he timed it right, he could catch the container before it hit the concrete floor. He gave it one final push. It fell, but he was too slow to catch it. The container crashed against the floor with a sharp metallic clang.

Kes listened intently but no noise or alarms went off. He exhaled. Squatting over the fallen container, he noticed the locks had already been forced—the lid slightly bent.

He flipped it open, shining his flashlight over the contents. Inside—a neat bundle of documents, appeared all taped together tightly in plastic wrap. Beneath them—several thumb drives and videotapes were also wrapped tightly in the plastic wrap all forming a single tightly wrapped bundle. An embossed, official-looking label was sealed across the top of the entire package.

Kes did not stop to examine it further. He pulled the bundle free, then opened the buttons of his jumpsuit. Underneath, he wore sweatpants. Quickly, he shoved the package into the waistband of the sweats letting it settle beneath the loose fabric and his bare skin. The jumpsuit was baggy enough so that the hidden cargo barely made a bulge.

Shoving the empty container under one of the bins, out of sight, he glanced around realizing he had left tracks all over the dusty floor, Kes brushed the tracks away with his hands, doing his best to cover his entry. It was not perfect, but it would have to do.

He glanced at the wooden crates he had tested earlier for climbing on. They were stacked on a lower shelf, flimsy but still useful. He needed something to cover the hole through which he would hopefully return. Anything was better than leaving it wide open. Kes grabbed one of the crates, but as soon as he lifted it, his breath caught. He noticed inside were stacks of individually wrapped packets of paper currency.

He hesitated for only a second before dragging the box over to the hole, and positioning it just above the opening. Then, backing himself into the tunnel, he pulled the crate into place over the gaping hole. It would have to do.

Descending headfirst seemed like the easiest way out. Using his hands like a mole's front paws, Kes pushed dirt and debris out of his way as he wiggled forward. When he reached the blocking boulder, he twisted his shoulders while bracing his feet against the wall above. By pushing hard with his legs and angling his body like a corkscrew he was able to maneuver around the boulder again.

With one final shove, he slid through the hole headfirst, landing right at Hud's feet. "Is that you, Kestrel?" Hud whispered. "You are one filthy customer."

Kes coughed, spitting out dust. "It's me. But let's go. I got it. We better hurry."

"Got what?" Hud asked while helping brush the dirt off Kes.

"What we came for." Kes sucked in a breath. "I'll explain later. We need to move."

Before they could move further, Pruitt and Otis appeared in the ATV. "What did you find?" Pruitt asked, his eyes sharp in the dim light. "Anything?"

"Yeah," Kes wheezed, still recovering from the dust in his lungs. "It was just in some kind of vault. That's where the light was coming from, I took a few photos and then left it like I found it" Turning to Steve he said "You were right, it's not sunlight."

He quickly described the storage room, the walls lined with bins, the filing cabinets, and most importantly, the massive steel vault door, and the dim light bulbs.

"Looked like the vault door was mounted straight into the rock. No windows, no alternate exits. Whoever built it never realized how close they were to these tunnels. It was designed so that the only way in or out is through the vault door."

"Any alarms go off?" Otis asked, his voice sharp.

"Not that I heard," Kes replied. "But who knows what's happening on the other side of that door? That's why I turned around and got the hell out."

Hud glanced at him. "Did you see any security cameras?"

Kes shook his head. "Not a single one."

Otis frowned. "Anything in there look valuable?"

"I don't know," Kes said, thinking fast. "I pulled a crate over the hole I came in through to cover my tracks—could've been money inside."

Otis perked up. "Cash money?"

"Yeah, that's what it looked like."

"How much?"

Kes hesitated, but before he could answer, Pruitt cut in sharply.

"You didn't take anything from that vault, did you, boy?"

Kes held up his hands. "Nothing," he said, shaking his head.

"Like I told you—I got the hell out before anyone showed up."

"Okay then," Steve Pruitt said, rubbing the stubble on his chin. "Because we aren't thieving, we're a-gleaning. Rule among the miners—what's found is yours, but taking someone else's stash is stealing. And we do not do that."

The remark felt more like a warning to Otis than a reminder for the Californians.

Pruitt looked at Kes again. "You could be right, though, there could be an alarm you didn't hear, and someone might already be looking around in that vault." He spat to the side. "Won't matter. We will be long gone." He pointed down the tunnel. "They won't follow us for long, either. Not in these shafts, I guarantee that."

"Let's skedaddle. Pronto. Steve said." So, without another word, they piled back into the ATV. Otis gunned the engine, speeding off, with no one looking back.

Even so, Hud and Kes could tell that Pruitt was dead right. The tunnels were a maze. They had just come through these passages less than an hour ago, yet Steve still had to guide Otis from taking a wrong turn—again and again.

By the time they reached the large chamber with the elevator shaft, they found Bobby and Chuck stacking copper wire onto their flatbed trailer. The pile was already huge, the entire trailer nearly full—bundles tied down tight.

"Easy pickin's!" Bobby whooped, walking up to Steve. "This one's pretty much ready to go!" Steve nodded. "Looking' good," he said.

Then, his voice lowered as he explained how Hud and Kes had found the vault. "Could be Stanley property," he explained. "So, we left it straight away. Won't be long before they notice someone has been inside and start pokin' around. No one took anything, though.

So maybe they won't be too worried. Might just seal up the back wall."

"Anything of value in there?" Bobby asked, eyeing them with interest.

"Cash money," Otis blurted.

"I can't be sure about that," Kestrel cut in fast, shaking his head. "I was in such a hurry, I don't know what it was."

Otis glowered at him. "You said cash money before."

Before Kes could answer, Pruitt broke in, sharp as a whip.

"DON'T MATTER what it was." His voice rang out in the cavern. "Cash. Gold bars. Diamonds. Makes no difference. I told them, and I am telling you—we ain't thieves, we're gleaners."

His gaze swept over the crew. "We got no right to anything in that vault or any other private property."

Chuck who had been edging closer to better hear the conversation let out a low whistle. "Solid gold bars, huh?" he said. "Wow."

"Now, now, calm down, y'all," Bobby said, rubbing his jaw, eyes flicking between them. "Steve's right. We came here gleaning. That's all we're doing."

He jerked his chin toward the trailer. "Now let's get the rest of this copper loaded up—and get home."

Chapter 37

After both trailers were piled high with copper wire, Otis was still fuming. He jabbed a finger in Hud's face.

"Well, you two ain't coming back. That's for damn sure. Next time, it'll cost you fifty thousand, not twenty-five. College project my ass."

Hud brushed past him and climbed into the ATV. "You couldn't pay me enough to come back down into this hole again. Not for all the tea in China," he shot back. "I don't know how you guys do it."

Chuck laughed, breaking the tension. "Gotta do something," he shrugged. "Anyway, we're all loaded, so let's beat it."

The drive out went without a hitch. When they passed the rock barrier and emerged into the evening sun, both Kes and Hud breathed deep sighs of relief.

Blue sky. Birds singing. Fresh air. Hud shook his head. "Nope. Caves are not for me. I felt claustrophobic in there."

The team worked for another hour, moving the concrete blocks back into the wall, replacing the barbed wire, and covering their tracks. By the time they were done, even an experienced woodsman like Hud could barely tell anyone had been there.

Back at the old house, Hud and Kes shook hands all around, thanking Steve Pruitt for taking them to their destination.

Steve smiled. "You young bucks will be alright. I still don't know what you two were after in that tunnel, but I hope you learned a lesson. Got your pictures, at least. No place for city fellers down in those mines."

Once they were back on the road, Kes turned to Hud, his voice tight. "We need to pack up and leave as soon as we get back." He patted his belly. "I think I found the suitcase you and Jerry have been looking for. And I have the contents right here."

Hud slammed on the brakes.

"Slow down, Kes! You mean you found the silver suitcase?"

Kes exhaled. "I found a metal container with a broken lock, yeah. The lock had been forced. I took out the contents—neatly packed, plastic-wrapped, with an official-looking government seal."

Hud stared at him.

"I unbuttoned my coveralls and stuffed the package down my pants," Kes continued. "But listen—what's important now is that the Stanleys may already know it's missing."

"They'll walk in and see the empty suitcase, Hud. See the dirt I tracked in. They'll know nothing else was touched. No money, no valuables.

"They'll know whoever broke in came for one reason."

The alarm in Kes's voice snapped everything into focus.

Hud didn't hesitate. "You're right. We have to hit the road. Now."

They rushed back to the motel, showered fast, ditched the coveralls, and threw everything into the Pathfinder.

Within minutes, they paid their motel bill and hit the road out of town.

Twilight was settling in when the turned north on I-77, but as soon as he saw an exit Hud veered onto Highway 33 West.

"Interstates are too obvious," he said clutching the steering wheel.

They drove on, contemplating the enormity of what had just occurred in the mine, what they had retrieved from it, and the magnitude of their current dilemma.

Chapter 38

Chaos reigned at the Bluefield Stanley mansion. Two days had passed since the vault breach, and the situation had only worsened. The security team had captured three men who had quite literally popped out of the ground near the rear of the house, picks and shovels in hand. After some canine persuasion, it was revealed that they had been attempting to enter a hidden vault through an abandoned mine shaft below the mansion.

They claimed to have been tipped off that bins of money were stored there. They insisted, that to the best of their knowledge, nothing had been taken during the foray into the vault, Moreover, they claimed that none of them were ever previously in the vault or in the mine. The man who told them he had the entered the vault and described its contents, said he was from California.

A closer examination of the vault proved otherwise. Its most valuable contents were missing. Under more aggressive interrogation, the Stanley security team extracted more crucial pieces of information—the group had in fact previously entered the mine, included two men from California. One had gone by the name "Kes," while the other had been referred to as "Hud."

According to one of their captives, it was Kes who had entered the vault while Hud had remained outside. However, neither appeared to be carrying anything when they emerged from the vault some forty minutes later.

When even more extreme interrogation methods were applied, the captives finally admitted they knew little else about the California men except that they drove a Pathfinder with California plates. A name surfaced—Steve Pruitt, a former mine mapper now living in a Bluefield nursing home. If anyone knew more, it would be him.

Once it became clear that no further useful information could be extracted, the three captives were sent back the way they came—into the tunnels. Their ATVs were disabled, and their lamps, shovels, and ropes confiscated. Despite their frantic pleas and tearful cries, Stanley security assured them they would eventually find their way out—if they were lucky. To make sure they did not return to the Stanley compound, large boulders were bulldozed over the opening from which they had emerged.

The next stop was Steve Pruitt himself. However, upon being questioned, the old man became so agitated that the nursing home staff ordered the Stanley security men to leave the premises immediately.

At the mansion, Buford Stanley was seething. His rage was barely contained as he barked orders at his security detail. "Get my Malibu team on the line! Tell those idiots to stop sitting on their hands and track down that gang of tree-hugging fools my granddaughter hangs around with. Their leader is named Jerry—something. My secretary in Malibu has his number and address. Find out who these 'Hud' and 'Kes' characters are and keep them in sight every second. I want my property back!"

The head of security team hesitated. "Should we have them brought to the Malibu compound, sir?"

"Not yet," Stanley snapped. "Not until we know exactly where my property is. But use every means necessary to find the two thieves and hold onto them. I want back what was stolen. I want it in my hands! He paused, breathing heavily, then narrowed his eyes. "Where's Sheela?"

"She flew back to Malibu on a commercial flight two days ago. You approved it yourself, sir," the security chief reported.

Bueford Stanley's fury was barely contained. "Then have her picked up and taken to the Malibu compound. I want Nurse Kathy watching her day and night until I get there. And tell the nurse to bring plenty of sodium pentothal—I want to know everything my granddaughter has in that foolish little head of hers."

Chapter 39

Hud and Kes arrived near Columbus, Ohio, five hours after leaving Bluefield. By the time they pulled into town, it was pitch dark. A Motel 6 just off the highway in Worthington, Ohio, caught their eye. After checking in and parking in the back, they asked the desk clerk if any restaurants were still open. She pointed them towards a nearby Denny's.

Too exhausted to eat, they both opted for showers and collapsed into bed. At dawn, Hud woke to the sound of Kestrel's soft snoring. Slipping out of bed, he gathered their dirty clothes and took them to the motel's laundry room, waiting as they washed and dried. When he returned, Kes was awake, sitting up amid crumpled sheets, clutching the plastic-wrapped package from the vault.

"We have to get rid of the Pathfinder," he said.

"I've been thinking the same thing," Hud acknowledged. "We should find another car first, then ditch the Pathfinder at a different dealership. Make it harder to track us."

They drove around Worthington, scouting for used car dealerships, and eventually spotted a lot with a weathered sign that read "Buy – Sell – Trade." Hud parked the Pathfinder two blocks away in an alley. Pulling up their hoodies and slipping on sunglasses, they walked back toward the dealership.

A salesman was just unlocking the chain across the lot's entrance.

"We're looking for a set of wheels," Hud said.

The man gave a curt nod. "Wheels, we got. What's your price range?"

"Trying to keep it under three grand," Hud replied. "We're students, just need something to get us home to Florida."

The salesman motioned toward a row of older models. Kes zeroed in on a Toyota Camry with $2,500 scrawled across the windshield in bold red paint.

"Camry's a solid car," he murmured to Hud.

"You know more about cars than I do," Hud replied. "Your call."

Popping the hood, Kes checked the fluids and inspected the engine. After a quick test drive, they noted the car pulled slightly to the right but they did not detect any engine knock.

"Let's get this one," Kes decided. "It needs new tires, an oil change, and a transmission fluid change, and some brake fluid. Probably needs a wheel alignment too, but the bones are good—only 150,000 miles, which isn't too much for a Camry."

Hud paid cash for the car. Inside the cramped office, the salesman filled out the paperwork and handed them a temporary title.

"Good luck," he said. "Enjoy your drive to Florida."

Before heading out, Kes asked, "Know a good spot to get tires and an oil change?"

"Smitty's Garage, just a few blocks down," the man replied. "He's good, fast, and honest."

At Smitty's, they were the first morning customers. The grizzled mechanic seemed pleased to see them.

Kes rattled off what needed fixing, and without hesitation, two men in coveralls stepped from the shadows and got to work. Smitty quoted them a reasonable price for four new tires and even threw in an alignment for an extra fifty bucks.

"Give us a couple of hours," he said, wiping grease from his hands.

Hud and Kes stepped out into the morning air, relieved but still uneasy. The clock was ticking.

They retraced their steps to the Pathfinder.

"What now?" Kes asked.

Hud considered their options. "We take what we need—pack up the cameras, anything valuable, and remove the plates, registration, insurance cards, anything that links the Pathfinder back to me. Then we ditch it. If we try to sell it, even to a dealer, it'll leave a trail. And we don't have time for a private sale."

Kes nodded but sighed. "Shame, though. Just when you got it all fixed up. I was starting to like her." He glanced at the roof. "What about your bike?"

Hud frowned. "We take it off. Leaving it on top is a dead giveaway if someone's looking for us."

They drove back to the Denny's near their motel and fueled up on Grand Slams while discussing their route west. Afterward, they parked the Pathfinder three blocks away and walked to Smitty's Garage to pick up their newly serviced Camry. Hud paid in cash before testing the car out. It ran smoothly now, and the pulling to one side was gone.

Satisfied with the car, they returned to the Pathfinder for the last time. Carefully, they transferred everything of value into the Camry, stuffing gear snugly into the back seat and trunk. The package from the vault was placed directly under the front passenger seat.

To dispose of the Pathfinder, they followed a plan Kes had mapped out using Google. Heading into an older Columbus neighborhood called Milo-Grogan, Hud led the way in the Pathfinder, searching for the right place. A dimly lit side street off 5th Avenue looked promisingly rundown, quiet, and unlikely to attract attention.

Once parked, they did a final sweep of the vehicle—checking the glovebox, under the seats, making sure no personal traces remained.

"Can't do anything about the VIN," Kes muttered, "but at least it won't be obvious right away."

He wiped down the most frequently touched surfaces with an old towel while Hud climbed onto the roof, unfastened the bungee cords, and wheeled the bike to a nearby sidewalk, leaning it against a rusted fence.

Meanwhile, Kes unscrewed the license plates and stuffed them under the Camry's front seat.

With the Pathfinder left unlocked, windows down, and keys dangling in the ignition, they walked away without looking back.

Feeling lighter but still cautious, they grabbed two large dark-roast coffees from a Starbucks and pulled onto I-80 West. The road stretched endlessly ahead. They drove all day, stopping only for bathroom breaks, switching drivers, and inhaling Big Macs and shakes along the way.

By the time they reached Lincoln, Nebraska, late that night, exhaustion had once again set in. Another Motel 6 just off the freeway became their refuge for the night.

Over breakfast the next morning, Kes took a sip of bad motel coffee and said, "I think we need to call Jerry. Tell him everything—about the mine, the vault, what I found. And the girl in the photo."

Hud did not comment.

"You know," Kes continued, "the one with the green hair. I swear she's that rich girl from Malibu who showed up at a few of our CCC meetings."

Hud nodded slowly. "If she is, then this mess is about to get a whole lot bigger."

Kes sighed. "Maybe not, but we can't assume we have shaken them either. If they know we are connected to CCC and Jerry, they might be watching anyone associated with us. They'll figure we will make contact sooner or later."

Hud leaned back on the bed, rubbing his temples while dialing Jerry Varene's home number. The call was answered immediately.

"Jerry, this is Hud, we are heading west. Has anyone been asking about us?"

Jerry hesitated. "I can't say for sure, but there have been a lot of black limos cruising around my neighborhood, the CCC members are worried so I canceled meetings for the time being, anything going on I should know about?"

Hud hesitated for a long moment thinking of what he should say over the phone, when Jerry's voice interrupted. "Listen friend," Jerry's tone had changed ever so slightly. "I'm not hearing you very well. Go to Walmart and buy a new phone."

"What," Hud asked in surprise, "did you say buy a new phone?"

Jerry repeated, "Go to Walmart and buy a new phone."

Hud started to reply but the call was disconnected. Puzzled he turned to Kes, "I don't get it, Jerry just told me to go to Walmart and buy a new phone, then we were disconnected."

Kes thought for a moment, "Doesn't make sense to me," Kes replied. "But you're the big security expert, maybe he thinks the call was bugged."

"Of course that's it!" Hud exclaimed. "Kes, you're a genius!"

"Call Buffy and tell her, she might be impressed."

Hud laughed, "Look on your phone and find the nearest Walmart, we both need some cheap burner phones."

Kes searched his phone and found a Walmart in the small town of Seward, Nebraska. "Actually, it's not far out of our way. When we leave there, we can still head due west on a highway that is not interstate."

They followed the directions on the phone and easily located the Walmart Supercenter in the small town. After purchasing new phones, they were once again heading west, this time on Highway 34. While Hud read the directions about setting up the new phones Kes drove. "So, what do we do with our old phones?" Kes asked.

"Let's think it thru before we do anything," Hud advised. After another half hour of driving Kes' phone rang, it was Sylvia.

"Sylvia!" Kes said so loud it caused Hud to pay attention. "God, I've missed you girl!"

"Me, too" Sylvia said, "but this is a business call, we can talk more later."

"Sure, what sort of business, babe?" Kes said his voice still elated.

"Do you have your new phone?"

"Wow the CCC network is on the job! Yes, as a matter-of-fact I do. Hud and I just bought us each one."

"Okay then listen carefully, remember what Hud said about loose lips. It goes for tongues too. The less you say the better."

"I'm all ears, babe."

Sylvia began slowly saying short single syllable words in a language foreign to Kes, but also strangely familiar. "I don't get it Sylvia," Kes cried out in frustration. "You know I don't speak any native tongues."

"I will repeat it once more slowly, but get something to write with, just spell what you hear phonetically. It's your native tongue."

"You mean..." He started to say, but she hushed him immediately. NO! Don't say anything that identifies either of us in any way. Just write what you hear as best you can. I will repeat slowly and then I am going to hang up. Do not call me back until you understand. Are you ready?

"Uh okay go ahead I guess," Kes replied clutching a short pencil and a sandwich wrapper.

Once again Sylvia began repeating the strangely familiar words. When she was finished in about two minutes and then the call disconnected.

"What was that all about?" Hud asked.

Sylvia gave me some k*ind of cry*ptic message which I totally do not understand."

"So, who understands women?" Hud laughed, "You know what I've been going through with Lillian."

After using a computer at a small-town Nebraska library, it didn't take long for Kes to realize that the words Sylvia had spoken were the numbers one thru ten in the Siletz language. "Why numbers?" Kes said, turning to look at Hud who was standing behind him.

"Well, you can make a very simple code using numbers. It's called the letter-number code, kids use it all the time." Hud replied, "as a smile began tugging at the side of his mouth, "You substitute numbers for letters, A equals the number one, B equals two, and so on."

"Oh great," Kes said raising up his hands in despair, "So, we have a code any second grader can flush out in five minutes, what good is that?"

"Only if the second grader speaks Siletz," Hud laughed.

Kes pondered for a second. "Of course! Kes yelped, you are a genius, Sylvia's a genius, I'm a dunce."

The code spread among the CCC members like Covid through a nursing home. Now all CCC members were armed with burner phones for security calls. "You know," Kes laughed. "Now we are all Code Talkers, like the U.S. Military Native Americans of World War Two!"

Jerry still feared for the safety of CCC members. "They are not just going to let this go," Jerry told Hud and Kes. "You two showing up here could bring the whole damn swarm of Stanley security thugs down on us."

Kes's dander was way up; "So, what's our play? We can't run and hide forever."

Jerry thought for a moment. "Lay low a few more days. Let me see if I can get a read on how deep this goes. I'll talk to LJ and Sylvia, see if we can figure out who all else is being followed. So, you guys... stay off the radar. No credit cards, no social media, no traceable phone calls, in the meanwhile I'm going to call a guy I know in Montana, not that far from where you are right now. Maybe he can put you up for a few days."

Hud exhaled, staring out the window as the Nebraska landscape blurred past. "Everything is risky at this point. But we can't just keep running with no plan. Let's have Jerry make the call. If his guy agrees to take us in, we head to Montana."

Kes nodded. "Alright. But if we notice anything is off when we get there, I'm out. No second-guessing."

Hud pulled out his phone and sent a quick text to Jerry: "Call the friend. If he says okay, we're on our way."

Now all they could do was continue driving, wait for Jerry's call, and hope they weren't walking into a trap.

Chapter 40

Kes wanted to head straight for California to make sure Sylvia was not in harm's way. However, Hud considered Jerry's advice to be the wiser choice.

"Listen, Kes, wouldn't it be smarter to have Buffy meet us in Montana? Maybe LJ could come with her. That way, we could figure out a plan for them to slip out of L.A. unnoticed."

Kes rubbing his chin. "Yeah, okay, Hud. You and Jerry are probably right. We could protect the girls better out here in the West than in L.A. I'm a country boy at heart—my instincts are sharper in open spaces."

With the decision made, they left the highway at Grand Island and took State Highway 2 north, stopping for lunch in the town of Broken Bow, simply because Kes liked the sound of it. They were not disappointed. Parking across from the town plaza, they stepped into a diner called City Café, where they ordered hot roast beef sandwiches with mashed potatoes and gravy. The meal was perfect.

After refilling their Starbucks cups with fresh diner coffee at the counter, they grabbed a dozen homemade donuts for the road. The donuts were so good that the bag was empty before they had driven a hundred miles.

Kes scrolled through his map's app and suggested Hud take Highway 250 north, leading them toward the Pine Ridge and Rosebud Reservations in the South Dakota Badlands.

"Let's stop at a reservation Kes pleaded, "It's still on the way to Montana," Kes assured Hud. "Wounded Knee is on the Pine Ridge Reservation where Uncle Manny disappeared back in the seventies. There's a monument there for the men, women, and children massacred by the 7th Cavalry—revenge for Custer's defeat. They're all buried in a mass grave at the site."

Hud agreed to the stopover. As they drove, he reminisced about how he and Nicole had camped in Badlands National Park twice. They had stayed for weeks, capturing photos and videos of black-footed ferrets—the most endangered land mammal in North America. A nature magazine had paid them well for the article, and Nicole's photos had gained recognition. Their documentary had even aired on a PBS nature channel.

By late evening, they pulled into The Nebraskaland Motel in Rushville, just south of the South Dakota border. At the desk clerk's recommendation, they grabbed dinner at The Twisted Turtle Pub, where they shared a wood-fired pizza and sampled a local brew. It hit the spot, and soon after returning to their room, they were both out cold.

At first light, they were back on the road, following Highway 87 north to Pine Ridge, arriving in less than an hour. Breakfast was quick—wraps and coffee at Subway—before they continued to the Wounded Knee Memorial.

The monument was striking, standing solemnly over the land where Kes's uncle had vanished. Kes fell silent, taking in the bitter history around him. An elderly Native American sat nearby, selling handmade dreamcatchers. Kes struck up a conversation, and the man shared that he had been around during the skirmishes of the 1970s. "It was 1973, I was fifteen years old," the old man recalled, "just a boy, but I carried water for the AIM warriors. I met Dennis Banks, Russell Means, the Bellecourt brothers—all of them."

Kes nodded, absorbing the old man's tale. The past still echoed in this place.

The old man shook his head, his weathered face thoughtful. "I don't recall hardly anything from back then, a warrior from Oregon? maybe my dad would know but he is long gone. He did tell me when I got older that many men came from tribes all over the U.S. and Canada. More died than were ever reported."

His gaze drifted, lost in memory. "Dad said it was late February or early March—still bitter cold at night. Protesters slept on the bare ground with nothing but thin blankets." His scowl deepened. "Dad said the cold could kill just as fast as a bullet. Some men wandered off in the dark just to take a piss, got turned around, and never made it back. Those without family to claim them… well, they were laid to rest in hand-dug graves, not far from the mass grave of the original massacre."

The old man shook his head, I later learned more of what occurred from our oral history. "The tribal leader at the time was half Sioux, half white. He made a fortune leasing tribal grasslands to white ranchers for a fraction of what they were worth. Meanwhile, babies were dying of malnutrition on the reservation, men had no work. Whiskey—illegal whiskey was everywhere." He exhaled, eyes glistening. "Diabetes was eating us alive too. A man was lucky to see fifty."

He paused letting out a deep sigh. "The tribal leader had an enforcer group called the goon squad. 'Guardians of Oglala Nation,' called goons for short."

Kestrel frowned. "Couldn't the AIM men do anything to help?"

The old man's face darkened. "Our chief hated AIM. Any man who supported them was marked. A lot of folks went missing— before, during, and after the AIM occupation. The goons even tried to kill the Bellecourt's in their own home. Clyde Bellecourt was shot and had to be rushed to the hospital. AIM guarded his door so the goons couldn't finish the job."

The old man's voice was grim. "Of course, no one ever investigated the Native deaths. The marshals and federal law enforcement, the judges and especially the local cops—they were all on the side of the white ranchers and our so-called tribal leader."

Kes listened, absorbed by the old man's words. When the story of the siege at Wounded Knee ended, he quietly purchased dreamcatcher necklaces and earrings for his mother and Sylvia, along with a rawhide-strapped amulet for himself. "These were made by Wade Standing Bear," the old man explained. "Son of a chief. He knows the prayers to say while crafting them."

Kes nodded, then bought one more. "For Uncle Manny."

The old man then led him to the unmarked graves of those lost warriors from the seventies. Kes knelt, finding a stone about the size of a football, he placed Manny's dreamcatcher over it with quiet reverence. Then, slipping his own amulet around his neck, he stood for a long moment in silence before turning to rejoin Hud.

Afterwards, they drove northwest, taking I-90 before switching to Highway 212 at Belle Fourche. Hours later, after crossing into Montana, they pulled into a tiny gas station in Hammond.

Hud and Kes high-fived. "Montana at last."

PART VIII:

MONTANA

Chapter 41

It was another four-hour drive to Salish, the town where Jerry had arranged for them to meet a larger-than-life cowboy named Butch Cassidy Bandero. A rancher turned U.S. Senate candidate, Bandero was running against the incumbent, Drake Roberts.

During the drive, Kes got a call from Jerry. "Bandero's rep is expecting you," Jerry said. "His name's Kenny Garrett. He'll meet you at the Black Mesa Café on Main Street when you get to Salish." Jerry rattled off a phone number before adding, "And don't be late— Butch doesn't like waiting around."

Approaching Salish from the south, Hud and Kes found it to be the quintessential one-horse town. Main Street was lined with a handful of old brick buildings, a feed store, and a gas station. They pulled up in front of the Black Mesa Café, a rustic diner with a hand-painted sign swinging lazily in the breeze.

Inside, they immediately spotted a paunchy young man perched on a stool at the counter. As soon as they entered, he stood and grinned. "You must be Hudson Halle and Kestrel Alan."

"That's us," Hud replied. "You must be Kenny Garrett?"

"Absolutely," Garrett confirmed. "Butch sent me to make sure you get some of the best ribs and coleslaw in Montana before heading out to the ranch."

The food lived up to the hype, and after polishing off their plates, Hud and Kes followed Ken outside. Instead of heading to the parking lot, Ken gestured toward a small airstrip behind the café, where a sleek twin-engine Piper sat waiting.

"It's about a two-hour drive to the ranch," Ken explained, glancing at their Camry. "Roads aren't the best, but you should make it okay. We have had some early fall freshets, but things have mostly dried out. I'll be flying the Piper and keeping an eye on your progress from the air."

Following Ken's directions, they took a narrow highway at the edge of town, weaving north through breathtaking countryside.

"I've been to Montana a few times," Hud told Kes, gripping the wheel as they climbed into the hills. "Mostly around Yellowstone and the Grand Tetons. Nicole loved Glacier National Park too. But I have to say, this stretch of the state might give even those places a run for their money."

The scenery was truly spectacular. Rolling grasslands, freshly green from late-summer rains, stretched toward the horizon. Their road wound between two towering ranges—the Big Snowy Mountains on the left and the Little Snowy Mountains on the right. Higher up, they could see ancient stands of Douglas fir and Ponderosa pine clinging to the slopes, interspersed with bright yellow birch trees, already donning their autumn colors. Above it all, the endless Montana sky unfolded in every shade of blue.

"Now I get why they call it 'Big Sky Country,'" Kes murmured, awestruck.

Hud, however, was less enamored with the drive itself when the Camry bounced violently over yet another pothole.

"I'm pretty sure I'll need new shocks," he complained.

Kes laughed. "If we didn't before we started down this road, we will by the time we get off it."

Because there had been rain—but not too much—the road was neither dusty nor muddy, making their journey pleasant aside from the occasional bumps in the road. Time passed quickly as they drove, the vast Montana landscape stretching endlessly before them. Then, the hum of a propeller broke the silence.

A plane buzzed by low overhead, just fifty feet above the ground. Hud and Kes watched as Ken Garrett pointed the nose toward a spread of low buildings off to their left, banking smoothly in the direction of the Bandero property.

Two miles later, they pulled up in front of a ranch-style house, where a tall man leaned casually against a porch post. His salt-and-pepper hair, streaked with red and gray, was pulled back into a ponytail just brushing his broad shoulders. A wide-brimmed fedora sat pushed back on his head, it's snakeskin band still bearing the rattles.

He wore faded Levi's, scuffed leather roper boots, and a plaid Pendleton woolen trail shirt, its cuffs rolled twice and the top two buttons undone, revealing a sun-reddened chest. In his hands, he whittled the handle of a walking stick with a small clasp knife, the shavings curling onto the wooden porch.

"Looks like something out of a Larry McMurtry novel," Hud said to Kes. "Think maybe he's got you beat in the shoulder department?"

Kes gave the man a quick once-over before responding, "No, I don't believe he does—but I'll grant you, it's close." He said, "I never read McMurtry. I was thinking more of Willy Nelson meets Indiana Jones."

The man tilted his head skyward, watching as the plane made a graceful landing in a field behind the house.

After handshakes all around, Kes and Hud were invited inside the main ranch house. Their host introduced himself simply as Butch, leading them to rooms where they could stow their gear and freshen up. By the time Ken Garrett arrived from the airstrip, the three men were seated in overstuffed leather chairs around a large tiger maple coffee table in a cozy nook just off the kitchen. Ken, rotund and studious, sat down next to the towering Butch Bandero, while the road-weary Kes and Hud sprawled across from them in overstuffed chairs, the cushions covered in a bright geometric native American motif.

A heavyset woman appeared wearing a simple prairie-style dress reaching to the tops of her cowboy boots, her flaxen hair braided around her head. She entered with a steaming pot of dark roast coffee which she poured into ceramic mugs. She left the room, returning in a moment with a platter of fresh cornbread and lemon muffins. The warm, homey scent filled the room.

"Thank you, Rosa," Butch said, nodding at the woman before turning to his guests.

"So, you boys have been doing quite a bit of traveling," he said, his blue eyes twinkling. "My old law school buddy Jerry Varene briefed me—said you went all the way to West Virginia in search of environmentalism's Holy Grail. Something about a silver suitcase?"

Kes and Hud stared at each other in surprise. The mention of the suitcase caught them completely off guard. Jerry had been explicit about keeping their discovery under wraps.

Hud stared at Butch, stunned. "Silver suitcase?" he repeated carefully.

Butch chuckled. "Don't act so surprised. I was the one who first heard whispers about it—and I'm the one who first told Jerry about it."

"You're Green Throat?" Hud asked.

Butch let out a hearty guffaw. "Is that what Jerry's calling me? Good for him. I always told him to keep his cards close to his vest."

Kes looked directly at his host, his expression serious. "What exactly did Jerry tell you?"

"Let me start at the beginning," Butch said resting an arm over the back of his chair. "A while back, I got a phone call from a woman—said her name was Gertrude. She told me she was the mother of an FBI agent, James Reddy. Said she'd read about me in The Washington Post—something about my work on environmental cases and the legal battles I've won against wealthy corporations."

He set down his coffee mug. "Her son, James, had been investigating politicians with shady, maybe even illegal, dealings with energy companies. One of the major players?" Stanley Fuel, based in Bluefield, West Virginia."

Bandero broke off another bite of muffin before continuing. "Gertrude—Ms. Reddy, noticed that her son was preparing for a trip but wouldn't tell her where to. Only that it was too dangerous for her to know. When he left the house for the last time, he had a large backpack and a metallic suitcase.

His body was found days later at the base of a cliff in Great Falls, Maryland. He had been in the water for some time," Butch paused, his expression puzzled, "But neither the backpack nor the suitcase he left his house with were ever recovered."

"The FBI must have conducted a thorough investigation, right?" Hud asked.

Butch exhaled shaking his head. "You would think so. But according to Gertrude, after calling the Bureau multiple times, she was finally told Jim's death had been ruled accidental. The report—what little there was of it—stated that he was an experienced outdoorsman who often kayaked hazardous stretches of the Potomac. They found one of his wrecked kayaks washed up a mile and a half downstream from where his body was discovered. That was enough for them to close the case."

His ruddy hands tightened around his coffee mug. "But Gertrude wasn't convinced. She reached out to me because the suitcase and backpack were never recovered. And because Jim had warned her—his own mother—that knowing where he was going was too dangerous."

"So, you shared Reddy's mother's story with Jerry," Kes said.

"I did," Bandero confirmed. "Jerry and I were at a fraternity reunion in Eugene, Oregon. We were tight back in law school—both in the environmental law program at the University of Oregon. Both of us felt an urgency for the government to take serious action to save our air, our climate, and our planet."

"What was Jerry's reaction to the suitcase story?" Kes asked.

"Excited. More than I was, to be honest." Butch leaned back in his chair. "For me, it was an interesting story, but my focus had always been on individual cases against polluters—big corporations, city water and power companies. I represented farmers, ranchers, people suffering from cancer—folks whose lives had been devastated by environmental destruction."

He took a sip of coffee, then shrugged. "I won a lot of damages for clients. Got some good settlements. But as for the suitcase? I could not wrap my head around what I could actually do about it. If there was evidence out there, somewhere back East, what would be my next move, I worked individual cases one at a time?"

Kes and Hud exchanged quick glances. Both wanted to tell Butch the truth—that they believed they now had the very contents of the suitcase Jim Reddy had died for. But they held back.

Unaware of their inner doubts, Butch buttered another piece of muffin before continuing. "Jerry, though—he saw it differently. After law school, he went back to Nevada, where he worked for the state government. He was involved in one of the biggest environmental battles in history: stopping the Yucca Mountain nuclear waste facility from being built in his home state. Jerry had worked for Billy Bronson in the Nevada Environmental and Natural Resources Department. The federal government and the energy industry didn't see Nevada coming. But they sure as hell noticed when the state voted to shut the project down."

"Wait," Hud said, straightening in his chair, "Jerry was involved in the Yucca Mountain closure? I did not know that."

Butch nodded. "After that, he went to Washington, D.C., to work for the Department of Energy, which gave him a whole new perspective. He realized real change could not happen without political pressure. That was when he started shifting toward grassroots activism. And where better to start than California?"

Hud studied Butch. "Seems like you're shifting too. From an attorney to an activist."

Butch chuckled, running a hand thru his ponytail. "Yeah, I guess Jerry and I ended up in the same place—just took different paths to get here. After years of winning lawsuits, I started realizing I was not actually solving the root problems. I was just making a lot of money while corporations kept right on polluting. So, I started getting involved with local movements here in Montana."

He smiled at Ken. "Ken introduced me to the Sixth Day movement. Then I found my way to the Black Bloc and Antifa while defending some of their... let's just say, more controversial activities."

Hud and Kes exchanged a glance, the pieces falling into place as they listened to Butch's narrative. It was clear that what they had just learned about Jerry fit into a much larger picture. Butch did not seem to notice their silent exchange.

"I told someone else about the suitcase too," he added, pausing to reflect.

"A little while ago, when I first decided to run against Drake Roberts for his Senate seat, I was visited by a federal investigator named Bruno Stach. He was working for a Senate committee looking into collusion between large energy companies and government officials."

"That's where I come in," Ken Garrett spoke up for the first time. "Senator Roberts oversaw that committee, the one supposedly investigating ties between public officials and big energy. But let's be real—he had no interest in exposing corruption. Those same energy companies were some of his biggest campaign donors."

Ken's frustration was evident. "Thing is, a lot of Montanans are well aware of the damage being done to our land. Our environmental movement is growing stronger by the day." His voice carried conviction, underscoring just how much he was proud of his home state.

"The State Constitution, ratified back in the 1970s, is the only one in the country that guarantees a clean and healthful environment. In fact," he added, "it lists environmental protection before it even mentions freedom of speech, religion, or assembly."

Butch nodded, "The people here wanted real results from Roberts' committee, Butch nodded, "So Roberts needed to make it look like he was doing something. That is when he brought Ken to Washington—to show he was taking the inquiry seriously."

Ken grimaced, "Yeah, hiring me had the intended effect at first. Everyone in Montana—whether they agree with me or not—knows I don't take kick-backs or bribes, and I don't back down. I have spent over a decade fighting to keep our big sky blue and to stop corporations from exploiting this land. And, to be fair, we've had some wins. But after months in D.C., I was completely frustrated. Nothing was getting done. Roberts kept tossing softballs and brushing me off whenever I pushed to locate real witnesses for the hearings. Then Bruno showed up."

"Bruno?" Hud and Kes asked in unison.

"Bruno Stach," Butch clarified. "The investigator for Roberts' committee. He paid me a visit too."

"Yeah," Ken interjected, "when Roberts saw I was fed up, he got nervous. I told him straight up—I wasn't going to be his puppet. If he did not start taking action, I would resign and tell the folks back home exactly why I quit. That rattled him a little. So, in a last-ditch effort to stall me, he suddenly claimed he was bringing in an FBI investigator to 'assist' the committee. As it turned out, Bruno was not FBI—at least, not when he started working for the Senate Committee."

"So, not a real Investigator?" Hud asked.

Ken explained. "When we first met, I did not expect much, but I've come to respect Bruno. "He is sharp and knows what he's doing. He was with the Environmental Protection Agency, Office of the Inspector General when he came in with us. But he was an FBI Agent for many years prior."

Resting his elbows on his knees, Ken Garrett proffered. "Not too long ago, I told Bruno Stach I was going to quit the whole sham of a Senate inquiry and ready to walk away. But he asked me to hold off, said he was working on something. So, I agreed to stick it out a little longer. That is why I have not resigned yet."

Hud frowned. "So, if you're still working for Senator Roberts, what are you doing here with the opposition?"

"Officially, I'm out here rallying environmental groups to support Roberts in the election. In reality? I want Butch to win. It's that simple. I have no loyalty to Roberts—if I ever did—and I am pretty sure he knows that by now."

Ken's expression became more serious. "My loyalty is to the Montana Constitution, which guarantees the people a clean and healthful environment. Butch is the one who will actually fight to uphold that. Roberts? He's in the pockets of agribusiness, mining, and land developers."

Kestrel crossed his arms. "But surely you can't openly support Butch while you're still on Roberts' staff?"

"True," Ken sighed. "But Roberts doesn't care what I do out here. He is just relieved to have me out of Washington. He probably figured that if I stuck around D.C. too long, my complaints about a phony Senate probe might end up in The Washington Post or on NPR—right before the election. That's why all the Re-elect Roberts offices across the state are staffed by paid consultants, while the Bandero campaign is made up entirely of Montana volunteers. We have donated office space in most major towns, and an old high school buddy of mine owns a print shop—that makes all our flyers, campaign posters, and yard signs for free."

Butch interjected, "Of course, Ken can't exactly be seen slapping one of my 'Butch is Better' stickers on his truck," Butch added with a grin. "But dropping by my ranch to chat? That flies under the radar."

He turned to Hud and Kes, his expression thoughtful. "I believe this Bruno Stach guy is legit. He came all the way out here to see me—not by plane, either. He flew to Portland and drove the rest of the way. Said he wanted to see this part of the country because he had never been out here before. And said that he doesn't care much for flying anymore."

Butch had finally given up on trying to get one last sip from his empty coffee mug. "I told Mr. Stach about Reddy, the conversation I had with his mother, and her theory that he was killed for a suitcase full of evidence he had gathered while working for the FBI. Just as Stach was leaving the Black Mesa, I remembered another interesting phone call I had received from a young lady about the suitcase and told him about that, too."

"What was her call about?" Hud queried.

"Her voice sounded more like a girl than a woman," Butch recalled. "She said, 'The suitcase is in Bluefield.' When I asked, 'What suitcase?' she responded, 'The one taken from the guy with the smashed head,' or something to that effect. Then she added, 'Killed by an airplane propeller,' and hung up.

"What made it even stranger was that the call came in on a number I only use for personal business. That number isn't even on my business card."

Kes looked up, "So, that's where Jerry heard about a man killed by an airplane propeller? Because he told our CCC group about it."

"I told both Stach and Jerry about the call. They were definitely interested," Butch confirmed. "Stach asked if I still had the number she called from, and I did—it was still in my call log. So, I gave it to him. Then he asked for a list of everyone I had ever given my personal number to. I wrote it all down for him."

Ken Garrett spoke up, his voice carrying a note of excitement. "That's when Bruno Stach and I bought burner phones. He did not want any information we were collecting for the Senate hearings to be compromised." Ken added, "I called Butch on mine and asked him to mail the list of names to Bruno Stach. But instead of having it sent to my office; I gave him the address of a P.O. box I set up near my apartment in D.C. Now, both Bruno and I have the list—and the number the girl called from."

Kestrel frowned. "I don't get it. Is this investigator working for Roberts or for Bandero?"

Butch chuckled. "That remains to be seen, his position is with the Environmental Protection Agency. But I'm trusting my instincts—and Ken's—that Bruno Stach will not take sides. He actually seems to be working for the American people. Imagine that."

The mention of a federal investigator being involved reassured Hud somewhat. If an agent officially assigned to a Senate investigation was looking for the same thing they had possibly uncovered, then maybe he and Kes weren't fugitives after all. Maybe, instead of being on the run like common criminals, they would be called as witnesses in the Senate's collusion probe.

Hud's mind drifted back to the contents of the suitcase. How should they be handled he wondered? "Jerry will know." So, until he and Kestrel had another conversation with Jerry, they would not breathe a word about the suitcase or its contents to anyone.

Chapter 42

After the morning gathering, Butch invited Kestrel and Hud on a tour of the ranch. Both accepted at once. After the long drive from West Virginia and the growing anxiety over their friends in LA being followed, the chance to explore the open countryside was too good to pass up. The landscapes they had glimpsed from the Camry windows had been breathtaking, but experiencing them up close was another thing entirely.

They were given the option of riding horse back or taking an ATV. Both men chose horses—Hudson with a touch of caution, Kestrel with eager confidence. When a wrangler at the corral asked for their preferences, Kes walked around, inspecting the animals before making his own selection. Hud, on the other hand, smiled and asked for one that was "not overly spirited." Once their horses were saddled, Butch led the tour himself.

The ride started smoothly, the three men chatting and laughing as they adjusted to their mounts. They began at a slow walk, then picked up to a trot before finally breaking into a full gallop across the rolling terrain. Butch explained that his ranch exclusively raised American bison—"the bovine most suited to these prairies," he declared.

The thrill of spotting a massive herd of bison as they crested a chaparral-covered hill was electrifying.

"Does this remind you of your native heritage?" Hud called over to Kestrel as they galloped side by side.

Kes grinned. "My ancestors were salmon eaters," he shot back. "But I could get used to this real quick!"

On the way back, Butch pointed out landmarks of interest, naming distant mountain ranges and identifying various native plants and grasses. He seemed impressed by Hud's knowledge of local flora and fauna.

"My wife and I used to photograph and document plants and animals all over the West," Hud explained. "We did an NPR show on the Black Footed Ferret."

Back at the ranch house, they were shown to separate but adjoining rooms, each with its own bathroom. Their clothing had been washed, dried, and neatly laid out for them. After showering and changing into fresh clothes, they were summoned to the dining area, where a hearty meal of bison sirloin steak with dumplings, brown gravy, and creamed spinach awaited.

"I prefer dumplings to potatoes," Butch said as they ate. "My grandmother on my mom's side was Polish. She made the best dumplings—Rosa's are close, but nothing beats grandmother's cooking."

After dinner, Butch pulled Hud and Kes aside. "I wanted to talk to you both about helping with my Senate campaign," he said. "There's a lot of work to do in these final weeks before the election, and we could use all the hands we can get."

Hud hesitated. "I don't know about Kes," he admitted. "But I'm not sure I can stay on."

Montana was incredible, but Hud's mind had wondered elsewhere. He needed to find Lillian, to know where they stood. More importantly, he needed to ensure that the other CCC members were not in danger because of what he and Kes had uncovered in West Virginia.

"I'd like to stay and help," Kestrel agreed without hesitation. "I love it here. But I have a girl in LA—I would like to ask her to join me. Maybe her friend Lady Jane can come too. She writes our CCC newsletter and could be a real asset to a political campaign." He paused, then added, "I want to check in with Jerry first though, see if there's anything he needs me for. If I stay on, where would you want me to work from, and what would I be doing?"

Butch nodded. "You and your lady can stay in the room you have now. If her friend comes, we'll find space for her in the bunkhouse—or if Hudson leaves, she can have his room. We can't pay you, but room and board are on the house." He gestured for them to follow him into an office and led them to a table covered in computer printouts. "As for work, it will be mostly phone canvassing. We make multiple calls to registered party members to keep them engaged and make sure they submit their ballots—either by mail or in person."

He pointed at a separate stack of papers. "After that, we reach out to as many independents as we can. They are the swing voters in Montana, and there are a lot of them. People here like to think of themselves as independent-minded, so they cross party lines all the time. We also try to connect with environmentally conscious voters from the other side when we hear about them."

Butch studied Kes for a moment before speaking again. "There's something else I'd like to run by you."

"Yeah?" Kes prompted.

"Out on the range, I heard Hudson say something that made me think you might be Native American."

"That's true," Kes replied. "Is there a problem?"

"No problem—maybe an advantage," Butch said. "We have a lot of—"

"It's all right to say Indians," Kes remarked. "Native Americans or First Peoples is okay too."

Butch chuckled. "Okay then. Montana has a large Native American population, but voter turnout on the reservations is extremely low. There are a lot of reasons for that. Historically, both political parties discouraged tribal communities from voting. Some areas do not even have polling stations anymore—residents are expected to vote by mail. But the nearest mailbox might be a hundred miles away. Then there is the ID issue—many Native Americans don't have one, and some don't even have mailing addresses. And for some, the language barrier makes the process even harder."

Kes nodded, taking it all in. "I was mostly a townie. My dad was white, but I spent a lot of time with my relatives on the reservation. Ours was small—only about five square miles. We had voting booths, post offices, and decent schools. Everyone spoke English because our traditional language has pretty much faded away, although some tribal members are now working to bring it back."

"No such luck here," Butch said, shaking his head. "Montana has seven reservations, most of them massive, covering hundreds of square miles. Native Americans make up nearly eight percent of our population. If we could get those who support us on the voter rolls and ensure their ballots make it in on time, it could make a huge difference in the election."

Butch added, "It's almost too late to register any new voters—Montana requires registration at least 28 days before an election, and we're right up against that deadline. Fortunately, folks have been working for years to get Native Americans in Montana registered. Now, we just need to make sure they actually cast their votes by helping them understand the differences between me and my opponent, Roberts."

He turned to Kestrel, squinting slightly. "Would you be willing to travel to the reservations? I can send someone ahead to schedule a time and place for you to speak—give a pitch for me, our party, and our platform."

"What exactly is your platform?" Kes asked.

"Making sure everyone gets a fair shake," Butch replied, It's that simple. "The environment is a major priority, of course, but we are also focused on keeping ranchers on their land and helping them turn a profit. Civil rights for Native Americans, healthcare, and support for women and children's issues are all key. We talk about jobs and the economy—especially how clean energy, like wind and solar, can create better-paying, more sustainable jobs than fossil fuels. That shift is already happening, and Montana needs to get ahead of the curve."

Kes considered and then asked, "Is it a good or bad thing that I was at Pine Ridge, protesting the Keystone pipeline? That's what got me into the whole green movement in the first place. Later, I met Jerry and his people at a big 'Stop the Pipeline' rally in LA."

"That's perfect!" Butch said enthusiastically. "Talk about that. Just like you're telling me now. I can hear the passion in your voice—so will they. They will love you, I promise."

"I've never done any public speaking before," Kes admitted.

"No problem," Butch assured him. "You come off as sincere and honest—that's exactly what we need. I'll introduce you to our volunteer PR person, Margaret. She'll listen to your story, help you refine it, and guide you on what to emphasize or leave out. She will also work with you on timing and delivery."

Kes liked the idea. He had always enjoyed visiting the Siletz reservation and observing the native culture. Speaking to his native peoples about the environment and his personal journey as a Native son had a certain appeal.

After wrapping up with Butch, Kes settled into the front porch swing and called Sylvia. Her phone rang several times. Just before it went to voicemail, she finally picked up.

Sylvia answered, slightly out of breath. "I was going to let it ring at first—most of my calls have been dropping lately. But then I had this feeling it might finally be you. I ran to grab it, and it was!

"I've been on the run as you know," Kestrel admitted. "But I do not want to get into that now that we are all code talkers. No matter what those cell-phone ads say, there are still a lot of dead zones out here in the Montana. We've also been hearing about some weird stuff happening in LA—people getting followed, and you flipping off a limo."

"Oh, that?" Sylvia laughed. "Yeah, I'm not worried. Just jerks in big black cars."

"There might be more to it than that," Kestrel cautioned. "But we'll talk about it later. Listen, how would you and LJ like to come to Montana and help out with a Senate campaign?

"You mean that guy Jerry knows?"

"Yep. It's crunch time, and he's still trailing in the polls. Butch wants me to visit some Native American reservations, but there is plenty of other work to do, too. You would have a place to stay here with me, the food's all home-cooked and really tasty, and we can ride horses into the sunset every evening—all courtesy of the campaign."

"I think I'll pass on the horses, but the rest sounds pretty great," Sylvia said. Then, hesitating, she added, "And... don't forget, I'm part Native American, too. I worked on a reservation when I met you remember? Maybe I could help out at the reservations there."

"Good point," Kestrel said, pleased by the idea.

"I don't think LJ will come, though," Sylvia continued. "And... I probably shouldn't be telling you this, but Lillian's back. She's staying at LJ's for now."

Kestrel stiffened. "Lillian's still upset with Hud?"

"No, I wouldn't say upset. I just do not think she feels the same way about him that he does about her." She hesitated again. "And... there might be someone new."

"Damn," Kes said. "Hud's going to take that hard."

"Yeah... I figured. I wanted to give you a heads-up."

"He really has it bad for her. And he's been struggling—on and off, you know?"

"I know."

"Think I should talk to him?"

"I'll leave that up to you. You know him better than I do."

Kestrel sighed. "I love the guy to death, but sometimes I feel like none of us really understand him. There is a lot he keeps locked away."

Sylvia let the silence settle before changing the subject. "So, I'll watch for an email from the campaign?"

"Yeah. It will have all the details about travel and transportation." Kestrel grinned. "I can't wait to see you."

"Me too. Feels like you have been gone forever." She paused, then softly added, "I love you."

Kestrel's grin widened. "Me too."

Sylvia laughed. "What do you mean, 'me too?' You mean you love yourself too?"

"No," Kestrel said. "You know I love you, Buffy."

"That's better." She hesitated again. "Do you think Hud can handle bad news about Lillian?"

Kestrel's smile faded. "I'm starting to worry about him," he admitted. "He seemed happy when we first got to the ranch, and damn, he can actually ride a horse pretty well. But then he starts thinking about Lillian again… He gets into these dark moods, and no amount of my goofing around can snap him out of it."

At that moment, Hud stepped onto the porch.

"Gotta run," Kestrel said quickly. "Keep an eye out for that email."

Hud's voice was low and urgent. "You have got to see this," he said, thrusting his laptop toward Kestrel. His expression was tense, his eyes focused on the screen.

Kes glanced up at him, then down at the screen.

The headline was from the Bluefield Daily Telegraph. "Three men are missing and feared lost in an abandoned mine in the Parrot's Beak area of the Pocahontas coal field. The former miners, often referring to themselves as 'gleaners,' were reportedly searching for scrap metal. Still missing are Robert 'Bobby' Felts, 65; Otis Pruitt, 24; and Charles 'Chuck' Hatfield Jr., 30. The three were reported missing yesterday by Steve Pruitt, Otis Pruitt's grandfather. Mr. Pruitt stated that he believed the men had returned to the mine after first breaking into it the day before. He said he had tried to talk his grandson out of going, but his grandson's sister later called the Sheriff's office, reporting that he never returned home.

"A search party, composed of former miners including Steve Pruitt, scoured the area for two days. Though they confirmed signs of a forced entry into the mine, no trace of the missing men was found.

"The following morning, Steve Pruitt was discovered dead in his nursing home room. The facility's doctor attributed his death to complications from black lung disease, which he had suffered from for years."

Kestrel let out a groan. "Oh, hell no. Those crazy idiots."

Hud shook his head grimly. "It's possible they got taken out by Stanley's thugs. Or maybe they are being held somewhere. If that's the case, they know our names. And that we're from California."

"Yeah," Kes agreed, his voice tight. "And they know the car we were driving." He exhaled sharply, "It's a good thing we got rid of the Pathfinder. We need to call Jerry and fill him in on this latest news."

Hud nodded. "Yeah, let's do it as soon as possible." He hesitated, running a hand through his hair. "I'm leaving, Kestrel. The CCC crew might be in danger because of me, and if something happens to Lillian or the others, I'll never forgive myself."

Kes studied his friend's face. "I figured you'd say something like that," he admitted. "You've been down lately. But this isn't on you. If any of us are in danger, we're all responsible, one way or another." Kes paused. "I talked to Buffy. She's coming up here to help with the campaign. She also told me that Lillian's back in LA—staying with Lady Jane." He left the part about her meeting someone else, if there was someone else, Hud would find out soon enough.

Hud's expression flickered—hopeful, but wary. "You should stay here and help with the campaign," he said after a moment. "Both of us going back won't change anything. But I need to know now if she still cares about me."

Chapter 43

Kes took his assignment to assist with the Tribal Nations' voter turnout very seriously. He researched Montana's tribes and was astounded by the vast amount of land dedicated to reservations—far more than in his home state of Oregon. He also discovered that Montana was home to nearly 80,000 Native Americans, yet their voter turnout lagged significantly behind that of non-natives. This disparity was largely attributed to several barriers; the lack of ballots printed in Native languages, the extreme remoteness of many communities, and the difficulty of accessing ballot drop-off locations or nearby post offices for mail-in voting. Political apathy was also a major factor. Kes knew from his own reservation experience, that many Native Americans had no interest in the politics of the people that had taken their land, and broken all their treaties.

When Sylvia arrived in Montana soon after their phone conversation, she and Kes set a goal; to reach all seven of the largest reservations in, or boarding on, Montana—Blackfeet, Flathead, Chippewa Cree, Crow, Fort Belknap, and Northern Cheyenne. Sylvia felt a strong connection to the Sioux, as her family had always claimed an ancestral link to the Sioux people.

Kestrel, on the other hand, felt kinship with the Confederated Salish and Kootenai tribes of the Flathead Reservation. "These people have an established fishing tradition," he explained to Sylvia. "Before they dammed the Columbia and Snake Rivers, spawning salmon almost reached their backyards! Back in the day, traders, settlers, and Native Americans in the Pacific Northwest used a pidgin trade language called Chinook Jargon. My mom told me her grandparents used it all the time when trading—it was spoken by both Whites and native peoples alike."

To carry out their mission, Kes and Sylvia traveled across the reservations in a Jeep loaned to them by Butch. They distributed voter guides in both English and Native languages, along with mail-in ballots. Kes's easygoing nature, boundless energy, and "I'm one of you" attitude made him a favorite among the tribespeople. His storytelling skills—particularly his tales about Uncle Manny, and the AIM movement enthralled his listeners.

During their visits, Kes learned that several Montana tribes had joined the protests at the Keystone Pipeline and were already deeply invested in environmental causes. As election day neared, he had a new idea—one that he immediately discussed with Ken Garrett and Sylvia. "What if we collect mail-in ballots from remote communities and fly them directly to the state capitol in Helena for counting?" he proposed.

Chapter 44

Bruno Stach sat in his cluttered office at the U.S. Senate Building, rifling through the box of meager evidence and witness statements that had been gathered thus far. It felt lonelier without Kenny Garrett around to bounce ideas off. He picked up the small key from the envelope found in Gaithersburg, Maryland—in Viola McCabe's delivery box. Still the most puzzling item in his possession. It might be of paramount importance or nothing at all.

The certified envelope that had contained the key still had the green address card attached, carefully taped down by a diligent postal clerk. Bruno suspected the key had been manufactured under contract—possibly for the FBI, or maybe one of the many other intelligence agencies scattered across Washington. It looked familiar but was not an exact match for any Bureau-issued key he had seen during his time there. Then again, he had not worked at the Bureau for years. Security measures frequently changed in Washington.

The real problem was figuring out what the key unlocked. He and Ken had discussed ways to obtain that information from the Bureau, but every scenario they considered raised red flags. How would an investigator from a Senate hearing come into possession of what appeared to be a federal security key without knowing what it opened? And if they did not know, why would that person be given access to whatever was behind the locked door?

Bruno grimaced. The situation could easily escalate to the Attorney General's office for clarification, and that was a level he wanted to avoid. His instincts told him that the only way to get into whatever the key unlocked—without triggering a bureaucratic firestorm—was to have something in hand proving it was directly relevant to the continuing Senate hearings on political collusion and energy extraction.

He shook his head and sighed. This was one of the most convoluted investigations he had ever been a part of. "Bunch of kooks," he muttered under his breath.

Adding to his frustration were the looming time constraints. National elections were just around the corner. Could Roberts lose his seat? Probably not. Bruno, liked Butch Bandero when he met him at the café in Montana, but based on everything he was reading online and in The Washington Post, Bandero's chances ranged somewhere between slim and none.

If the political tides shifted after the elections, the entire investigation could be scrapped. Senate committee inquiries were notoriously fickle, often driven by public interest rather than real substance. All it would take was one bored reporter—or an independent blogger looking for a scoop—to file a Freedom of Information Act (FOIA) request, asking for an update on the committee's findings and expenditures. If that information went public, it could put an end the entire probe.

Bruno refocused on his current task; cold-calling the people on the list of individuals who had Butch Bandero's private phone number. He had worked his way through most of the names with little success. Cold calls were always a tough sell. Most of the people he reached wanted to check with Butch before answering any of his questions, which he understood. He assured them that was fine but urged them to follow up as soon as possible. So far, none had called back.

The probability that close acquaintances of the Senate candidates, would consider Bruno's calls some kind of political dodge and simply ignore them.

Ken Garrett was using his burner phone almost exclusively whenever anything related to the investigation was discussed.

Butch Bandero, on the other hand, kept his personal phone always within reach so that when it chimed, he could assure callers that Inspector Bruno Stach was who he claimed to be—and that anyone called by him should cooperate, fully and truthfully.

To lend further legitimacy to their outreach, Ken had set up a basic website detailing the scope of the Senator Roberts' committee investigation. These steps helped sanction their witness contacts, and slowly, Bruno began securing interviews. However, the process remained cumbersome and time-consuming. Worse yet, it was largely unproductive.

No one had ever heard of a metal suitcase, or a missing FBI Agent. Bruno had worked methodically through the alphabetized list of names he got from Butch Bandero, striking out repeatedly. But when he finally reached the letter V, he hit pay dirt.

"This is Jerry Varene." The voice on the other end was bright and direct. "Oh, Mr. Stach, how are you? Yes, of course, I know Butch Bandero. He was my best friend in law school. Butch told me about your investigation and that you might be contacting me."

Bruno got straight to the point. "Mr. Varene, are you aware of any reference to a silver suitcase or a metal container? A briefcase, perhaps—possibly containing evidence compiled by an FBI agent?"

"I certainly am." Jerry's voice shifted slightly, as if memories were being dusted off. "Butch told me about it at a law school reunion in Eugene, Oregon. He said an FBI agent…" He hesitated for a moment, searching his recollection. "I can't recall the agent's name. I'm not sure Butch ever mentioned it."

"Reddy?" Bruno offered.

Jerry's voice lit up. "That's it! Now I remember—Jim Reddy. That was the name. I think Butch said the agent's mother had contacted him. That's how he found out Reddy was an FBI agent and that he had gathered evidence, storing it in a suitcase. It's all coming back now. The mother believed her son was trying to leave the country with some evidence, but instead, he turned up dead."

Bruno pressed on. "And did you ever tell anyone else this story?"

"Yes, as a matter of fact, I did." Jerry took a breath. "I am the founder of an environmental activist group here in Los Angeles— The Coast Conservation Corps. We are officially registered as a Political Action Committee in the State of California. Our focus is primarily on the marine environment. Ocean acidification is a major concern. We lobby for everything from expanding marine protected areas to safeguard whales, fish, kelp, and sea otters, that sort of thing. We've also been raising money to join a larger lawsuit—along with other concerned groups—against major energy extractors for knowingly contributing to environmental damage."

"What's the status of that lawsuit?" Bruno asked.

"It's a critical issue among marine scientists right now. Acidification is destroying coral reefs, which are vital to ocean health. But we need far more concrete evidence before we can take it to court. Climate change and CO_2 fluctuations have been occurring forever, and pinning direct responsibility on powerful carbon energy producers is a monumental challenge."

"So, what did you tell your group about the alleged metallic suitcase?"

"Oh yeah—sorry, I got sidetracked. I told them pretty much what Butch Bandero told me. But I didn't mention his name. I just called him 'Green Throat.' You know, like 'Deep Throat' from Watergate?"

"Yeah, I get it. Please go on."

"Well," Jerry continued, "I'm an attorney, so I know how to handle privileged information. I wasn't trying to spread classified details—I just wanted to fire up our group. I wanted them to feel like they were part of something bigger. You have to understand—going door to door with petitions for donations is not exciting and our young recruits lose interest quickly. I figured telling them about potential evidence that might be out there could help keep them motivated."

Bruno moved forward. "Did you ever mention West Virginia as a possible location of the suitcase?"

The pause on the line was long-too long.

"Mr. Varene?" Bruno repeated.

A sigh. "Yeah, I'm still here. And yes, I did unfortunately."

"Why unfortunately?"

"Well, I don't know what else Butch Bandero may have told you," Jerry admitted. "But two guys from our group went to West Virginia to see if they could find the damn suitcase. Dumbest thing I ever heard. I mean, how could two guys from Los Angeles think they could just waltz into Appalachia, locate a suitcase full of incriminating evidence—possibly in the possession of corrupt billionaires—steal it, and bring it back to California? It boggles the mind."

"But they did go?" Bruno pressed.

"That's why I said 'unfortunately."

Bruno asked Jerry for more details about the trip. There was a pause. "I haven't heard from them for a while... do you know anything?" Jerry asked in return.

Bruno sensed prevarication—perhaps even evasion—but he chose not to press the issue just yet. The safest course of action, he decided, would be to check in with Ken Garrett and see what he could dig up about the two men who had gone to West Virginia.

His reply to Jerry Varene was deliberately vague. "Not a lot. But thank you for the information—we'll add it to the file." Then, recalling something, he added, "By the way, I'd like to interview some of your conservation corps members. How many do you have?"

"They come and go, but there's a small committed core—maybe eight to ten, including me."

"Would you mind emailing me their names and phone numbers? Feel free to give them a heads-up that I'll be calling."

"Not a problem."

"If anything, else comes to mind that might be helpful, please reach out to me or Ken Garrett right away." Bruno gave Jerry his burner phone number and a secure email address before ending the call.

Bruno reflected on the conversation, his instincts told him it was time to go out to Los Angeles and interview the Coast Conservation Corps members in person. Something told him that this small cadre of environmentalists might have stumbled into something far bigger than they realized.

He had been granted premier per diem, so he might as well use it for a trip west. As he considered his next steps, a line from Robert

Penn Warren's novel *All the King's Men* drifted into his thoughts, "West is where you go when you look down at the blade in your hand and blood is on it."

Bruno pulled out his phone and called Ken. "I'm heading to LA."

Ken had no objections, so Bruno packed what sparse evidence he had collected into a spare briefcase and booked a flight using his government credit card. That evening, he took an Uber to Dulles Airport, planning to grab a scone and a Starbucks coffee before departure.

During the red-eye flight Bruno was restless. He drifted in and out of sleep, occasionally waking to read and re-read his interview notes. Finally, frustrated, he shoved the briefcase back under the seat in front of him and closed his eyes. However, his subconscious refused to let go. His mind kept circling back to his conversation in Gaithersburg with Viola McCabe—her nosy eyes on the street—and the certified letter she had given him holding the mysterious key.

What was he missing? Viola had said that the letter had shown up in Gertrude Reddy's mailbox much later than the local Post Office manager recalled delivering it. According to the manager, a certified letter like that would have remained in the recipient's mailbox for a set period before being returned to the Post Office, where it would sit for another designated period before final disposition.

Something about that timeline didn't add up.

Bruno shifted in his seat; eyes still closed while his mind kept struggling. A sliver beneath his fingernail—that's what it felt like.

What was he overlooking? A note would have been left in the mailbox informing Gertrude Reddy that the certified letter was waiting for her at the Post Office. If it remained unclaimed for the designated period, it would have been returned to the sender.

But who was the sender? Bruno struggled to recall seeing a return address on the envelope. If there hadn't been one, how had it ended up back at the Reddy residence?

Suddenly, his subconscious clicked the pieces together. Jim Reddy had mailed the letter to himself. Bruno pulled his briefcase from under his seat and rummaged through it until his fingers found the envelope. He examined it closely, finally flipping the attached green address card over.

There it was—the same address on both sides of the card, both in Jim Reddy's familiar scrawl.

That explained something but not what was most important. The letter had been delivered twice—once when Jim first sent it and a second time after it had been returned by the Post Office, arriving in Gertrude Reddy's mailbox not too long after her son's death. Viola McCabe had retrieved it during that second delivery after which she had forgotten about it.

Bruno stared at the envelope in his hands. One more thread, he mused, and this one may have hooked something.

Chapter 45

Even though the sun had yet to rise, Bruno was wide awake as his plane touched down at Los Angeles International Airport. Solving the mystery of the envelopes circuitous trip had reignited his determination to track down the evidence Jim Reddy had uncovered—and perhaps lost his life over. Yet, despite this breakthrough, a larger puzzle piece was still missing; the key. What did it unlock, and what secrets still lay hidden?

Bruno knew that LA drivers were notoriously aggressive, especially in heavy traffic, so he opted for an SUV rental, unconcerned about any travel clerk scrutinizing his expenses later. Let Ken Garrett deal with that headache.

As he navigated Century Boulevard toward the I-405 freeway, he spotted a 24-hour IHOP near the on-ramp and pulled into the parking lot. Switching his phone off airplane mode, it immediately lit up with a flood of undelivered emails and text messages. Scanning them quickly, he found one from Jerry Varene. Opening it, he was pleased to see a list of names, addresses, and phone numbers of the Coast Conservation Corps members.

Cross-referencing their addresses with his map app, Bruno noted that all residences were located in the San Fernando Valley. He then searched for a hotel there and booked a room at the Hilton in the Warner Center, an area known for its business park and shopping mall.

Driving was smooth in the early hours—an anomaly for LA's notoriously clogged freeways. Merging onto the 101 northbound, he reached the Warner Center without incident, appreciating how efficient the LA freeway system could be when not gridlocked. Once checked in to his hotel, he took a hot shower, then lay down, knowing sleep would be difficult after the three-hour time change.

Morning sunlight streamed into Bruno's room when he finally stirred. Sitting on the edge of the bed, he grabbed his phone and perused Varene's list of CCC members. He jotted down their locations, names, and numbers in his notebook—a habit from years before smartphones took over. Technology was useful, but habit trumped it.

Bruno was hungry, however, not in the mood for overpriced hotel food. He found a nearby breakfast spot called The Corner Bakery, but it was not open yet. Eager to get started, he decided to make his first call. Scrolling through the list, he dialed the number for Lady Jane Connelly, her address was closest to his present location. When she picked up, he introduced himself as an investigator and let her know that Jerry Varene had given him her name as a key member of the Coast Conservation Corps.

"Jerry told me to expect your call." The voice on the other end was clear and sweet, tinged with a slight Western lilt—Texas or Oklahoma, Bruno guessed. "We've all been pretty worried about those two crazy boys."

Bruno immediately recognized that Jerry had prepped his group, hinting that Bruno's inquiry related to missing evidence from an FBI investigation. "Yes," he said, keeping his tone neutral. "Have you heard from them?"

"We've had calls from both Hud and Kestrel—mostly Hud. He's worried about Lillian, but he doesn't need to be."

Bruno skimmed his notes. She was referring to Hudson Halle and Kestrel Alan. Lillian had to be Lillian Blake. "So, Mr. Halle and Mr. Alan haven't returned from West Virginia yet?" he asked, seeking confirmation of information Jerry Varene had provided.

"That's correct. Kestrel's in Montana helping with a political campaign. His girl, Sylvia, just left to be with him. She is also a member of the Coast Conservation Corps. Hud's back, but all he cares about is talking to Lillian Blake. Poor guy."

Bruno liked it when people he interviewed volunteered information he didn't yet have. "It was Mr. Alan and Mr. Halle who went to Bluefield, West Virginia, looking for evidence—ostensibly regarding a metal suitcase. Is that your understanding?"

"That's my understanding, yes."

"It's also my understanding that Lillian Blake is in Los Angeles?" Bruno kept fishing while the waters were productive.

"Yes. She's been staying with me—mostly avoiding Hud. But she's out today with her new friend, apartment hunting. I'm not sure when she will be back."

"Lillian and Hudson were close, right?" Bruno pressed.

"For a while, yeah. It seemed like true love at first, but later she felt like Hud was not being truthful with her. Lillian's been through a lot in her life. She has had several bad experiences with men. You should probably ask her about that yourself though."

"Thanks, I will if it becomes relevant. What have you heard about Mr. Alan's and Mr. Halle's trip to West Virginia?"

"Have you spoken to Jerry Varene yet?" Her sudden hesitation mirrored Jerry's at the same point in their conversation. Bruno's antenna went up.

"Yes, we had a full discussion. I'm just looking for corroboration—filling in any blanks."

"Okay… so, he told you they found what they were looking for."

Bruno took a wild stab in the dark. "The metal suitcase."

A long pause. Followed by an almost inaudible, "Yes. Jerry's trying to negotiate its return. The owners claim it was stolen, and Jerry's doing what he can to keep Kestrel and Hud out of trouble."

Bruno cleared his throat audibly, buying himself a moment to process what she had just attested to. "Ms. Connelly," he said carefully, "before we go any further, I would like to meet with you in person. I am an investigator for a Senate Committee Hearing, as I'm sure Mr. Varene must have explained. My call today was just to outline our inquiry, but this conversation is moving into an area that could be material to the investigation."

Letting that sink in for a moment, Bruno continued, "At this point, meeting in person is necessary so you can review my authorization and see my badge. You understand that any information I obtain must be given voluntarily and with full disclosure. Do you follow?"

"But I thought you said Jerry already told you everything?" Bruno could hear confusion creeping into her voice again.

"That doesn't matter, Ms. Connelly." He adjusted his tone to a more formal one—what he called his legalese. "Everyone we interview must provide their information independently. Otherwise, it could be considered hearsay, or even appear contrived to fit a specific narrative. As I said, I have spoken with Mr. Varene, and you can verify that with him if you'd like before meeting me. He provided us with the names and phone numbers of the most active members of the Coast Conservation Corps. Yours was one of the first on the list."

"Well, I guess we can meet. When and where do you want to get together? Of course, I do want to run it by Jerry first."

"Very well, Ms. Connelly. I see your address here—it looks to be about a twenty-minute drive from my hotel, the Hilton at Warner Center. My office is in the Senate Office Building in Washington, so let me check with the front desk to arrange a room for our discussion."

"Well, is it okay if we just meet here at my home?" she asked. "I have a very needy puppy, and Lillian and her friend might be stopping by later. We have plans to go shopping if they get tired of apartment hunting. If you can come by soon, we'll have a couple of hours to talk before they get back."

Bruno found himself enjoying her voice—not the harsher, nasal twang common in modern country music, but something warmer, carrying the honest inflections of an earlier time. "Meeting at your place is fine. Should I bring coffee and maybe a pastry?"

Her laugh was soft and musical, like whispering bells. "I made scones last night," she said. "Still fresh and warm. But a cappuccino would be nice."

"Two cappuccinos coming up. I should be there in less than an hour—that includes the Starbucks stop. One more thing about contacting Mr. Varene—please don't go into details about our conversation so far. As I mentioned, all interviews need to be conducted independently. There cannot be any suggestion that Mr. Varene or I influenced your responses in any way. It's a standard procedure for all witnesses, and it is very important. Do you have any questions?"

She now sounded much more relaxed. "No, I understand now. Thanks for explaining. One other thing—could you get the cappuccinos from the little independent coffee shop at the end of my street? It's just before you turn off Reseda Boulevard. Lucy's—you can't miss it. I really like the way she makes them."

"Lucy's it is. See you soon."

Bruno quickly located an ironing board and iron in the hotel closet. He set it up and plugged in the iron before jumping in the shower. As he ran an electric shaver over his chin and jaw, he caught himself looking forward to meeting Lady Jane Connelly. Fully aware, of course, that an agreeable demeanor and a drop-dead voice didn't necessarily indicate an equally pleasing countenance.

After running the lukewarm iron over his rumpled suit jacket and trousers, he stood before the bathroom mirror, smoothing down a few unruly strands of white hair.

"It'll have to do," he breathed, grabbing his briefcase on the way out the door.

Chapter 46

Twenty minutes later, Bruno stood in front of a charming cottage on a quiet street, holding a cardboard carrier containing two cappuccinos. After he pressed the doorbell, a high-pitched yipping could be heard from inside.

The door opened at the first chime, and Bruno was not disappointed. Lady Jane stood in the doorway; one delicate foot stretched out to block a miniature white dog from escaping. "Ginger!" she hissed. "Keep still."

She was slim, neat, and pretty in a wholesome way. Her loose-fitting white blouse revealed just a hint of cleavage, while dark slacks and simple sandals completed the effortless yet polished look. Not that much younger than me Bruno, guessed.

"Hurry," she added, slightly out of breath. "She doesn't have all her shots yet and can't be outside off the leash."

Lady Jane led the way to a kitchen table, where Bruno placed the coffee container beside a tray of freshly baked scones. A small vase of freshly cut white roses sat on the windowsill. Bruno's investigator's eye took in the details—she had prepared for this meeting, just as he had.

"Ms. Connelly—" he began.

"Call me LJ," she interrupted with an easy smile. "Everyone does. My parents were stationed at an Army base in Alabama before my dad was sent to Afghanistan. My mom stayed in a boarding house owned by a woman named Lady Jane. I was born there. Daddy went fugazi in that crazy war, and for some reason, Mom liked the boarding housekeeper and her name. So here I am." She lifted one hand in a playful ta-da pose.

Bruno grinned. The anecdote had immediately put him at ease—perhaps a little too much. Not an ideal mindset to begin a serious interview, but he could not help himself.

"Sounds like you've told that story a lot," he noted.

"Hundreds of times," she admitted. "When I was little, I wanted everyone to call me Ginger. My mom and I used to watch old musicals on TV, and my favorite was Ginger Rogers—you know, the dancer with Fred Astaire? Instead, I got stuck with LJ, so I named my puppy Ginger instead."

Bruno recognized the term fugazi—G.I. slang for fucked up, got ambushed, zipped in—a grim reference to dead soldiers in body bags. "I'm sorry about your dad," he said quietly.

"I guess I missed him," she replied, her tone getting softer. "At least his picture, which I kept by my bedside." Then, shaking it off, she added, "But I've been over it for a long time—stupid war."

The ice now completely broken, they pulled out chairs and sat across from each other, sipping cappuccinos and munching on surprisingly delicious scones.

"You made these?" Bruno asked, nodding in approval. "They're really good—I'm tasting walnuts, and something tart in the filling, but I can't quite place it."

"Kumquat preserves!" LJ grinned. "I make it myself. There's a beautiful little tree in the backyard, and every year, it produces hundreds of kumquats."

Bruno set his cup down on the table and retrieved a notebook from his briefcase. "Ms. Connelly—LJ," he corrected, "tell me, in your own words, exactly what you know about Mr. Alan and Mr. Halle's trip to West Virginia, and how you came to know it." He flipped open the notebook. "I don't record conversations, just jot down a few notes as we go."

LJ paused, considering where to begin. "They left Southern California more than a month ago. In Hudson's Pathfinder." She brushed a wisp of hair from her forehead. "Hudson told Lillian where they were going, and later, she told the rest of us."

"How much later?" Bruno asked.

"That, I don't know," she admitted. "We noticed after they did not show up for one of our meetings. But Lillian said she told Hudson going back east to search for something was a harebrained idea, though she would not try to stop him."

She sipped her coffee and took another bite of scone. "Hudson was a bit of a strange duck," she added. "But then again, most of us who are committed to saving the world are a little daft by most people's standards."

"Strange how?" Bruno prompted.

"Okay, so a bunch of us went to Denny's for a snack after Hudson's first CCC meeting. Lillian had brought him along—she met him while canvassing for signatures and donations. The conversation turned to how the money we were collecting was being used, and someone—maybe me—brought up Jerry's involvement in organizing a lawsuit against big polluters over ocean acidification and climate change."

Bruno jotted down a few words while she continued.

"Jerry Varene is—was—the club president. He's a lawyer. Worked in Washington for a government agency for a while but got disillusioned and moved back west, his home state is Nevada. According to Jerry, we needed hard evidence to support the lawsuit. That's when the whole silver suitcase story came up."

Lady Jane gave a feeble smile. "We started talking about the 'silver suitcase.' Jerry had told us about it maybe a month before. He was excited—he'd just gotten back from a law school reunion in Oregon. A big-shot environmental lawyer, who Jerry jokingly called Green Throat, had told him about a suitcase chock-full of evidence that could stop the carbon energy lobby in its tracks. It had purportedly been stolen from a dead FBI agent. I forget the agent's name, but Jerry thought the suitcase might be in Bluefield, West Virginia, the headquarters of Stanley Energy, one of the largest energy companies."

Bruno made a note. "What about Mr. Halle being a 'strange duck'?"

"Okay, I'm getting to that." LJ shifted further back in her chair. "We were all crammed into a booth at Denny's when Hud suddenly says something like, 'Why don't we go to West Virginia and steal the suitcase back?' I mean, it cracked everybody up—it just sounded so ridiculous. I could see Lillian was embarrassed."

Bruno nodded. "Why do you think Mr. Alan went along with such a cockamamie scheme?"

"Hud hinted that he had certain… skills. Things he picked up in Air Force Security Service. But honestly? I think Kes was just restless. He met Sylvia at a protest in the Midwest—over the Keystone Pipeline, I think—and they hooked up again after they both moved to LA. They are still really close, but Kes has this adventurous streak. He was always embracing his Native American heritage, always testing himself. He was the youngest male in our group, and maybe a cross-country odyssey appealed to that side of him."

Bruno made another note. "Is Mr. Halle considerably older than Mr. Alan?"

"Oh, yeah. Hud's in his forties, while Kes is mid-to-late twenties." LJ hesitated, then added, "But don't get me wrong—Hud is talented. Lillian found out he's an expert in nature photography—vistas, animals, plants, that kind of thing. She used to work for the State Parks and knew the people who hired photographers for wildlife documentation. Hud was at the top of the list for motion-sensitive photography and videos. One of his documentaries—about black-footed ferrets—was even shown on PBS."

LJ cleared her throat. "Hud was also an expert in tracking rare species like cougars and condors—animals the State Parks wanted counted, or sometimes collared and tagged."

Bruno scribbled another note. "You mentioned that Mr. Halle claimed to have 'certain powers.' Can you tell me more about that?"

"Nothing specific," she said with a shrug. "But what really ended things for Lillian was the day Hud showed up at her workplace with a huge bouquet of flowers, all dressed up in expensive-looking clothes—new haircut, the whole bit. He told her he got the money from a new photography contract."

Bruno raised his eyebrows. "And Ms. Blake found that suspicious?"

LJ hesitated, choosing her words carefully. "When he first came around, Hud was the scruffy, woodsy type—old Levi's, flannel shirts, worn desert boots, and definitely in need of a haircut. I figured he might be into soft drugs—pot, maybe peyote. So yeah, Lillian was really floored when, out of nowhere, he shows up looking like he just walked out of a fashion catalog."

She lifted a finger, emphasizing her next point. "But that wasn't all. He left a jacket at Lillian's place, and when she found a receipt in the pocket, it showed he had spent as excessive amount of money on new clothes. That would not be weird on its own, except he bought it at a time he claimed to be out in the field on a photo contract. When she casually mentioned it at her work, she found out the State Park Service hadn't issued any new photography contracts at all!"

Bruno said. "And that was the last straw?"

LJ nodded. "Pretty much. Then she heard from a mechanic—some guy who had worked on Hud's car—that Hud had hit it big in Las Vegas. That is when Lillian cut ties for good."

Bruno let that sink in, then finally he closed his notebook and set down his pen. "Interesting," he murmured.

Their conversation had stretched well into lunchtime, so they decided to lunch together and walk to a taco and burrito place about a mile away—one that LJ swore was the best in town.

PART IX:

CANYON CHASE

Chapter 47

Hudson drove over the Grapevine and into the Los Angeles basin just as the first rays of sunlight crept over the horizon. The sprawling city stretched before him, a sea of lights dimming in the growing daylight, yet despite its vastness, a sense of solitude pressed in around him.

When he pulled into the driveway, his bungalow felt abandoned, as if it had been waiting for something—or someone—that would never return. He sat for a moment, gripping the steering wheel, unwilling to step inside. The house had always felt different without Nicole, but after weeks away, the emptiness seemed even stranger.

Finally, Hud reached under the seat retrieving the packet of documents Kes had taken from the mine. He carried it into his garage, where a few old paint cans gathered dust in the corner, and a single workbench sat undisturbed. He found an empty rigid plastic container, placed the packet inside, and snapped the lid shut.

Walking around the house to the side yard, Hud stopped near his pot and cactus garden where a garden spade stood leaning against the house. The familiar scents of fertile earth and pungent Jimsonweed lingered in the air. He took up the spade, and began digging in the loose fertile soil until he had a hole large enough, and then placed the plastic container inside.

At the back fence, a pile of heavy flagstones sat among the weeds—leftovers from a walkway he and Nicole had once considered but never built. He pulled a large stone from the top of the stack, its weight straining his tired muscles, and carried it to the freshly dug hole. Lowering it unto the disturbed soil, he then stood upon the stone's surface, ensuring it was secure.

Driving the final 200 miles through California's Central Valley and over the Grapevine hills had been relentless, each mile dragging by more tedious than the last. When he finally entered his small bungalow, he found the fridge was bare, as expected. However, in the freezer, he found a plate of his baked homemade brownies—

same as the ones he had consumed when Nicole's death had still felt like an open wound and the dull ache required relief.

Too drained to consider anything else, he placed the entire plate in the microwave and set the timer for one minute. While the brownies thawed, he searched the cupboard and found a mostly full bottle of burgundy. He poured a tall glass, watching the deep red swirl in the dim light. When the timer beeped, he retrieved the warm brownies and settled down on a stool standing at the kitchen counter and ate the entire batch, washing them down with the stale wine.

The air inside his house was thick and musty. He pushed at a stubborn window, its frame stiff from lack of use, until finally it creaked open several inches and a cool breeze drifted in from the backyard, however, the relief was minimal.

Barely managing to strip off his clothes, he stepped under the shower, letting the lukewarm water wash away the exhaustion of the road. Standing under the soothing spray for at least ten minutes, eyes closed, muscles loosening, while the rhythmic sound of the water lulled him into something close to peace.

When Hud finally collapsed into bed, naked and drained, he plugged in his phone to charge while he slept. He did not stir for nearly twenty-four hours.

When Hud awoke, the sun was already high, blazing through the window he had forced open. He reached for his phone, blinking against the brightness of the screen. It was an hour before noon. He had lost an entire day.

As he sat up, stretching, Hud's body felt strangely light, his mind also seemed clearer than it had in weeks. The house, however, was still stifling, the air thick despite the open window. His cell phone weather app confirmed what he already sensed—ninety degrees outside.

Through the window glass, he could see a haze of smoke had settled over the valley, the telltale sign of Southern California's fire season. The sky had taken on an ugly yellow tint, the distant hills barely visible through the smog. Yet for the first time in a long while, he felt good. Clear-headed and strong.

A hour later, when he stepped outside to unload the Camry, something caught his eye. A long black car sat idling across the street, sleek and unmoving. Hud thought, so, this must be one of the stalkers he had heard about.

Without hesitation, he reached back inside the doorway and picked up a heavy walking stick from the corner—one he often used to chase off coyotes when he was in the woods. Holding it casually at his side, as he crossed the street toward the vehicle. The windows were tinted so dark he could not see a thing inside so rapped the driver's side window with the stick.

A few seconds passed before the window lowered—just six inches. From the dim interior, two hostile, ice-cold eyes stared back. No words. Just a glare, sharp as glass. Hud met the gaze head-on. "Can I help you? Are you lost?" His voice was flat, edged with menace. The eyes did not blink.

Hud's grip tightened on the heavy stick in his hand. "Guess I'll call the cops, then," he said. "Neighborhood watch said to report any weirdos hanging around, and you fit the bill."

Walking back up his driveway, Hud began unloading the Camry, keeping one eye on the black car across the street still sitting silently.

Back inside, he dumped everything from the Camry into a pile on the living room floor, before stripping off his clothes, and pulling on a pair of swim trunks and a t-shirt and an old pair of sneakers. But still the heat pressed in like a thick wall, the kind of dry suffocating atmosphere that made the thought of a long ocean dip essential. Hot enough for a swim at the beach, he decided. Hud was not going to let anything ruin the good feeling he had woken up with.

Stepping outside, Hud slid into the Camry, but before pulling out, he made one more stop. Lowering the driver side window, he pulled up next to the black car still idling at the curb, aligning the driver side window with that of the black car he reached out touching his middle finger against the tinted glass. "I called the cops," he shouted. It was a lie, of course. The last thing he wanted was to deal with the police right now.

Revving the Camry's engine, he peeled out of the driveway, tires screeching as he shot down the street, heading for Topanga Canyon and the Pacific Coast Highway. A glance in the rearview mirror confirmed it. The black car was following. Hud grinned, this should be fun. No one knew the canyon roads between the valley and the beach better than he did.

Making a sharp turn onto Old Topanga Canyon Road, he picked up speed—but not too much. He wanted the following driver to keep up. "I've got a surprise waiting for you, pal," he sneered, gripping the wheel.

The Camry weaved over the winding road, its tires hugging the curves, but he slowed at the hairpin turn just before the Mulholland intersection, making sure the larger car stayed on his tail. When he reached Cold Canyon Road, he deliberately signaled before taking the turn, giving the following car a clear view of his direction.

"Now the fun begins," he said through clenched teeth.

Two miles down, the narrow road curved sharply to the left-into a section that had been blocked by a rockslide for over a year. Hud did not take the turn. Instead, he veered sharply onto an almost invisible old forest road, an unpaved trail so overgrown it didn't appear on maps or GPS, it traveled straight up at a 70-degree angle.

Almost three hundred yards in, he brought the Camry to a stop. From here, he had the perfect vantage point to observe the road below. Peering down through the trees, he had a clear, unobstructed view of Cold Canyon Road and the spot just beyond the slide where he saw the black car approach the washed-out road way too fast, the over confident driver ignored the warning sign, barreling straight toward a missing section of pavement.

"Oh, brother," Hud grinned, gripping the wheel. "That fool's going to go right over the edge." He eased the Camry forward just enough to get a better view. The moment the driver realized his mistake it was already too late.

The car skidded hard, tires screeching as the brakes locked up, and momentum carried it forward. The front end dipped, the vehicle tilting dangerously before sliding down the steep embankment. A cloud of dust and gravel kicked up around it as it came to a shuddering stop against a massive boulder.

Hud watched as both front doors flung open wide. A second later, a rear door creaked open. Three men in dark suits and hats climbed out, dusting themselves off, their movements stiff and cautious. They stood for a moment, surveying the hopelessness of their situation.

Hud smiled, scooping up a few large rocks from the ground. With a flick of his wrist, he tossed them tumbling down the slope sending the men below diving for cover, hats flying as they hit the dirt. Satisfied, Hud put the Camry into gear and eased back onto an upper dirt trail, eventually turning onto Malibu Canyon Road toward the beach. He let out a quiet chuckle. "And there's no cell phone connectivity for at least two miles from where they're stuck."

Just ahead, the entrance to the Malibu Canyon tunnel loomed, its dark, narrow mouth cut into the hillside. After passing thru the tunnel, Hud slowed pulling the Camry to the side of the road. An idea was taking shape in his mind.

If those men were after him—and possibly other members of the Coast Conservation Corps—this first chase might have been just a dress rehearsal. Next time, they could come back with more men, armed men with deadlier intentions.

Hud sat in the driver's seat for a long moment. Mulling over a plan that was still taking root, a reckless one, but one built on his deep familiarity with the area.

Finally, he grabbed his towel and stepped out of the car, locking it behind him he jogged toward an old familiar trail, knowing exactly where it would lead.

The path was hot rocky and narrow. Over the years, divers heading for Rindge Dam had been sideswiped by cars before they even reached the true death trap. Hud had not been diving there in years, since the fateful day years ago when he saw the boy slip and fall to his death.

He was still intimately familiar with this part of the trail system having spent plenty of time cutting brush and placing cameras in

Malibu Canyon he knew precisely how to reach the reservoir. After a short descent, Hud reached the canyon rim and peered down into a pool of water far below. Seven months without rain had taken its toll—the water level was noticeably lower than he remembered.

Moving cautiously along, he crept another thirty yards down through the tangle of brush and boulders, searching for a better vantage point. From where he now stood, the pool looked larger, the drop, still somewhat dangerous, but considerably less daunting. With the pool now less than sixty feet below, an unobstructed launch into the reservoir would be easy for someone familiar with the uneven footing.

Hud dropped his towel, sneakers, t-shirt, and sweatpants. Now standing at the rim in his swim trunks, with the hot summer wind scorching his bare shoulders, he took a running start and hurled himself into the open air.

For a split second, he was weightless, the world silent around him. The sky stretched a wide, pale blue, while the dark pool below rushed toward him.

The water was icy cold, a sharp contrast to the scorching canyon air. It engulfed him, clear and deep, waking every nerve in his body. As he surfaced, he let out his breath and floated for a moment, feeling renewed, as if a fountain of youth had washed everything away. Then he recalled again the boy who had died here. Pushing the thought aside, Hud paddled slowly to shore and pulled himself onto the warm rocks.

Climbing back out of the canyon was no easy feat. His muscles ached as he made his way back up the steep incline. When he finally reached the spot where he had jumped, he gathered his clothes and scanned the area, searching for anything useful to mark the trail.

Discarded beer cans littered the brush. Perfect.

He picked up three and placed them in a pyramid directly at the edge of the leaping spot. Another, three he positioned at the vantage point where he had first spotted the pool below. At the top of the trail—where it would be visible from the road—he arranged three more cans in a triangle, balancing a rock on top.

Satisfied, he could easily see the first marker from Malibu Canyon Road, he turned and hiked back to the Camry.

As he pulled onto the road, the thought of food finally caught up with him. He recalled Jimmy's Changas, a small Mexican joint he used to hit after long days working for the State Parks. Turning back toward the 101 freeway he took a familiar side road up Las Virgenes Canyon, before pulling into Jimmy's parking lot with the hunger of a man who had spent the morning outwitting a tail, diving off a cliff, and plotting his next move.

Hud was now in the small but extremely wealthy town of Calabasas, a place known for being home to the Kardashians—but they were not alone among its glitterati. The town was a haven for Southern California's elite; including movie stars, television moguls, rap-artists, pro-athletes, and business tycoons who dwelt in sprawling mansions tucked behind guarded security gates.

Hud pulled into the parking lot of Jimmy's Changas, a small but popular Mexican joint he had visited often over the years. The place was packed, both inside and out, the late lunch crowd spilling over onto the patio. Deciding to avoid the chaos, he ordered takeout.

When his name was called that his food was ready, he took his meal to a grassy lawn near the edge of a pavilion. The afternoon breeze carried the scent of grilled meat and fresh tortillas, mingling with the lingering heat from the pavement. As he ate, he watched small lizards dart through the grass, their thin bodies quick and agile as they darted about.

Just as he was finishing his meal, his phone chimed.

Lillian! Hud's breath caught in his throat as he scrambled to answer.

"Lil," he said, exhaling. "I've been missing you so bad. You don't know how much. I think I know what went wrong—"

His words tumbled out in a rush, but she cut him off. "Hud, I called you, remember? So let me talk, okay?"

He blinked. "Yeah… yeah, of course. I'm sorry. Go ahead."

She took a breath. "It was good while it lasted, Hud. But it's over. I've moved on."

His chest tightened. He felt something rising inside him—something raw, something that wanted to claw its way out—but he swallowed it down.

She continued talking, her voice steady. "Hopefully, we can still be friends in the CCC, but if not, I'll quit so you won't have to."

Hud opened his mouth, but words failed him. Finally, all he could manage was, "Lillian, I can change."

She sighed, soft but firm. "It's no use, Hud. I've met someone… and I've never been this happy."

His fingers curled around the phone. "I don't understand," he said, his voice almost a whisper. "When did you meet this guy?"

She was quiet for a heartbeat. Then, gently, she said, "First of all, honey… it's not a guy."

Her words confused him. What was her meaning, It's not a guy?

"I've discovered who I really am," she continued. "Who I really want to be. And I have come to realize that I have never been happier with anyone like I am with her."

He felt like the ground beneath him had shifted. He tried to grasp onto something, anything, but all that came out was, "I… I hope you are happy."

"I am," she said, and there was a certainty in her voice that made it clear she was not just saying it—she meant it.

He exhaled, forcing his voice to steady. "No need to quit CCC," he mumbled. "The only reason I went was because of you anyway… and later, Kestrel, of course." His voice turned hoarse, barely a whisper now.

"Good luck with your new life, kiddo. Your happiness is what is most important to me… and I really mean it."

"Thanks for that," she replied softly, and then she was gone.

Hudson Halle stood like a statue, staring at the dead cell phone in his hand. His face was blank, his gaze distant, as if staring through the shades of time and memory. A buzzing in his head started as a faint hum but quickly grew into a crescendo. He climbed into the Camry and started to drive, gripped the steering wheel so tight his knuckles were white. In the rearview mirror, a face flickered—Lillian? No. Nicole!

He sucked in a sharp breath and after several miles turned onto his street. His house loomed ahead, but he couldn't go inside. Not yet.

Bitter dreams waited for him in there, and he was out of dream-killer pastry. Instead, he kept driving, past familiar intersections, through dimly-lit streets, until he reached a familiar old haunt. Shorty's Place.

It sat tucked in the corner of a rundown shopping center off of Victory Boulevard, a small, down-on-its-heels sports bar that had seen better days. Hud had spent plenty of nights there, watching Lakers and Dodgers games, escaping the silence of his house. During the worst of it, Shorty's had saved his life.

He parked in the back, same as always, and slipped through the rear entrance—a door reserved for regulars, the ones who weren't there for small talk, just a drink or watch a ballgame and take a break from the outside world.

"Hud! Long time, no see!" Shorty whooped the moment he stepped inside.

The bartender-owner, Shorty, dubbed himself the Chief Cook and Bottle Washer, although nothing was ever cooked at Shorty's. He had an infectious grin and a talent for making even Darth Vader feel welcome.

Hud slid onto a barstool. "Hey, Shorty. I will be having Dead Pigs tonight—if you still serve them."

Shorty's smile faltered for the briefest second. "Aw, hell," he muttered, shaking his head. "I thought you was over her for sure this time."

Hud knew exactly who he meant. "I will be after tonight," he said.

He pulled a hundred-dollar bill from his wallet and set it on the bar. "Let me know when that's gone. I think I got a couple more left. Can I sit in a back booth—won't bother nobody."

"No worries, Hud," Shorty said, pocketing the bill. "Not much of a crowd tonight, anyway. Take that booth back there." He motioned toward a darker corner of the bar. "And yeah, I still got your Dead Pigs, Shorty said getting out a bottle of Whistle Pig Rye whiskey and a glass of Dead Guy Ale from a keg. You were the only one who ever ordered that combination, our invention!" He grinned, pleased with himself.

Hud nodded. "Appreciate it."

Shorty wiped the counter with a rag and pointed toward a newly mounted flat-screen TV. "You can see my new TV from that booth—it's sixty inches, Hud. And the Lakers are on tonight."

Shorty beamed. "Lakers coming all the way back this year, Hud."

"You bet, Shorty."

Chapter 48

Hudson Halle didn't remember how many Dead Pigs he had consumed that night, but judging by the way his head pounded, the answer was way too many.

When he finally cracked his eyes open, he realized he was still in the booth where Shorty had served them up. The bar was eerily quiet, the only sound coming from the muted hum of the television. Morning sunlight filtered through the dingy windows, casting long streaks of dust lingering in the air.

With effort, Hud pulled himself upright, his muscles stiff from a night spent in the cramped booth. A blanket had been draped over him at some point. He ran a hand across the fabric smiling, "Good old Shorty."

On the table in front of him, a note and a key sat beside an empty glass. He picked up the note first.

"Hud, had to run home for a bit – Left the TV on for you. Lock up when you leave. Hang the key on the hook and pull the door closed—it will stay locked. Thanks, Shorty."

Dragging himself to his feet, Hud stretched and rolled his shoulders, feeling the stiffness settle into his bones.

The large TV mounted on the wall was still on, playing some morning news feed about the upcoming national elections. He instinctively looked around for the remote, wanting to turn it off, but could not spot it anywhere.

Just as he gave up searching, the commentator's voice pulled his attention back. "After a word from our sponsors, the Montana Senatorial race will be next when we come back."

Hud frowned, rubbing his temples trying to recall. Montana - Bandero - the ranch. Hud dropped back into the booth, rubbing his hands over his bleary face before focusing on the screen.

When the commercials ended, Ken Garrett, now a political analyst for the Montana election, was seated with a panel of talking heads, breaking down the race.

"I think Drake Roberts will pull it off again," Ken was saying, his tone measured, but Hud could hear no enthusiasm in it.

"Roberts is still a couple of points ahead of Bandero in the polls."

"Butch Bandero has made up some surprising ground, though," the moderator countered. "He's really making this a close race."

"Close, but no cigar," a conservative commentator chimed in. "Roberts always runs a lackluster campaign, but then pulls ahead of the pack on election day."

"He's never run up against a maverick like Bandero, though," Ken Garrett interjected. "A rancher as handsome as Reagan, fighting lawsuits for the little guy. This state is known for its independent voters, and I don't think his environmental agenda will hurt him as much as some people think. Montanans love mavericks—four-legged and two-legged."

"His lawsuit supporting that 'church group' will hurt him, though," another talking head responded. "Evangelicals in this state don't like the Sixth Day folks, I can tell you that."

Ken cut in, "You may be right about the Sixth Day movement," he said, "but our polling shows that even mainstream churches are beginning to have concerns about the environment. That is one reason Senator Roberts brought me to Washington—to work on a committee investigating whether politicians and polluters have, in some cases, become illegally conjoined."

Hud barely heard the rest. He pulled out his phone and punched in Kes's number.

"Kestrel, this is Hud. I'm coming up there to Montana right away. How many days until voting starts?"

There was a pause before Kes responded. "Where are you, Hud? We thought you were headed for Chicago… or back to LA."

"I am in LA, but I lost track of time. When do the polls open?"

"It's already started—mail-in ballots are coming in as we speak."

"What about in-person voting? When do the polls open?"

Kes sighed. "Well, today's Thursday. Voting starts on Tuesday. You do the math."

Hud calculated quickly. "Okay, so if I leave now and drive straight through, then get up early Friday and push all day, I can be in Montana by late Friday or early Saturday… assuming the Camry holds up."

"But why, Hud?" Kes asked. "There is nothing you can do up here now except sit around with Butch and the boys and watch TV as the returns come in. In fact, Sylvia left on a plane for LA this morning, and I'm heading back to the southland as soon as this thing wraps up. I already called an Uber to pick up Buffy at Burbank Airport."

Hud ran a hand through his hair, glancing at the exit. "It's not that simple, Kes. It's getting dangerous here."

"How dangerous?"

Hud's jaw tightened. "I was followed yesterday. A car full of thugs. They know where I live, so I'm not even stopping at my house. They want their suitcase back."

Kes went quiet for a beat, then said. "So, you need to lay low."

"Yeah," Hud admitted.

"Does Jerry know what's going on?" Kes asked.

"Not the whole story. But some."

As soon as the call with Kes ended, Hud's phone chimed again. Jerry Varene.

Hud frowned. "Jerry, I was just about to call you."

"Hud, this is urgent," Jerry said, his voice brisk. "I've been dealing with some representatives from Stanley Energy on behalf of you and Kestrel. They are serious about getting that suitcase back. They know you have it."

Hud's grip on the phone tightened.

Jerry hesitated, then continued, "They're being reasonable, Hud. They've agreed to endow CCC with several million dollars for the safe and speedy return of their property."

Hud's jaw clenched. "Kestrel and I went to West Virginia to get evidence for your lawsuit, remember?"

"No!" Jerry exclaimed. "Hud, in a sense, this is the lawsuit. A settlement, out of court. Stanley Coal gets its documents back, and we get the kind of funding that could turn CCC into a legitimate, nationally recognized environmental organization. It's far more than we could have won, even if I took them to court."

"I thought we were trying to put criminals in jail, Jerry."

"Hud, sending people to jail was never my goal." Jerry's tone grew more impatient. "My mission has always been to work within the system to improve the environment and fight the acidification of the oceans, global warming and slowing glacier melting, I thought you knew all that. Civil disobedience is one thing grand theft is something else entirely."

"So, what are you saying? They are threatening legal action?"

Jerry lowered his voice. "More than that. Stanley Energy is willing to waive criminal charges against you and Kestrel—if the documents are returned immediately and intact. They have taken inventory. They know exactly what was in that suitcase. If they don't get it back soon you and Kestrel could spend years behind bars."

"Sorry, Jerry." Hud said, "I'm heading to Montana to help Kes with the election. You remember Butch—your old friend? In any case, what Stanley Energy wants is still up in Montana. When Kes and I decide what to do with it, we will let you know."

Jerry's voice turned cold. "Hud, I'm warning you."

"That so?"

"If you set foot in Montana, you'll be arrested the moment you step off the plane."

Hud smiled. "If that happens, the contents of that suitcase will go public. And neither you nor I will be able to stop it."

Nothing but silence from the other end but Hud could hear muffled voices in the background. He pictured Jerry sitting in an office, flanked by lawyers or maybe even Stanley Energy reps, scrambling for leverage.

Then Jerry spoke again, his voice carefully measured.

"Wednesday," he said. "The day after the election. I've secured confirmation that if you're here in LA by noon on Thursday—at a location I'll provide—and return everything in its original, unopened form, you and Kestrel will not be prosecuted."

Hud let that sink in.

"What about your millions, Jerry?"

"CCC will still get its settlement. No strings attached."

Hud tapped his fingers on the steering wheel, thinking.

"Hope to see you on Thursday after the election, Jerry," he said, and ended the call.

Hud knew one thing for certain—he would not be flying to Montana.

First and foremost, whoever was working with Jerry was likely watching the flights. If Stanley Energy had their claws in the deal, his name would already be flagged.

As he wandered the dim interior of Shorty's Bar, still turning over his conversations with Kes and Jerry in his mind, Hud's gaze drifted toward the street outside. Through the grimy front window, he spotted a newer-model black Mercedes cruising by at an unnervingly slow pace.

A chill prickled down his spine.

This wasn't the kind of neighborhood where luxury cars blended in. Tracking the Camry would not have been difficult. Hell, for all he knew, it already had a GPS tracker planted on it.

Hud turned on his heel and walked through the bar toward the back. Shorty's ancient Chevy van sat parked under a cluster of trees on the hillside, about thirty yards away. It was an eyesore of a vehicle, dented and rust-streaked, but also could make the perfect getaway car—nobody would suspect that hunk of junk.

Retracing his steps, Hud scanned the bar until his eyes landed on a row of hooks near the register. If Shorty still had a spare key to the van, it would be there.

There was only one of the hanging keys that was for a car, Hud took it from its hook.

Moving quickly, he slipped through Shorty's back door and crouched low as he made his way to the Camry. He yanked open the front seat passenger door, reaching beneath the seat for the paperwork envelope from the Ohio dealership. Then, leaning into the backseat, he fished around until his fingers brushed against the plastic bag containing what he and Kes referred to as their stash bag.

Ever since they left West Virginia, this bag had been their piggy bank, a mix of loose cash and rolled bills, carelessly shoved inside it with one of Hud's old gray hoodies.

He glanced around outside the bar once more. The parking lot was still empty.

Slipping back inside, he dropped into the booth where he had crashed the night before. He emptied his pockets and the bag onto the table, carefully sorting through what remained of their cash. Fifteen hundred dollars and change. Not much left of the Halle estate.

Without hesitation, Hud slipped the hoodie over his head before pulling out one thousand dollars and tucking it inside the Camry's dealership envelope. Then digging out the pink slip, he scrawled his signature across it, signing the car over to Shorty.

The last five hundred dollars he stuffed into the pocket of the hoodie. Then, grabbing a pen lying next to the cash register, he flipped the envelope over and scribbled a note:

Shorty — Thanks for everything. On the lam. I bought your van, so don't call the cops on me. A down payment and the pink slip for the Camry parked in back are in this packet, along with a set of keys. I'll make up the rest of what I owe you sometime next week. Will call you when I get back. Thanks, Hudson Halle

Chapter 49

Hud returned to the parking lot behind the bar, keeping his head low as he made his way to Shorty's van. He slid into the driver's seat, inserted the key, and turned the ignition. The engine rumbled to life on the first try.

Backing the van up to the Camry, he quickly transferred everything from the back seat and trunk into the van. Without hesitation, he pulled out onto the road, driving slow and steady, keeping his exit from the parking lot as unremarkable as possible.

He didn't need maps or directions—he was heading north on I-15 to Vegas. From there, due north to Montana. Shorty's old van surprised him. It ran smooth, better than he expected for a vehicle that had clearly seen its share of hard miles. The odometer read just over one hundred thousand, and the fuel tank was half full.

By the time he reached Vegas, if he reached it, he figured he'd know if the van had what it took to make the full trip all the way north to Montana.

The old beast chugged along, mile after mile, carrying him across the desert, past neon skylines, and into the vast, open stretch of Utah.

By the time Hud reached St. George, both he and the van needed a break—with full tank of gas and a hot meal, and shower.

Just as he pulled into a 24-hour diner, his phone chimed. It was Kestrel. The moment Hud answered, he could tell Kes was agitated. "Hud! Glad I caught you in time," Kes blurted. "Just got a call from Varene, and he's hopping mad. Apparently, he's made some kind of big deal with Stanley Energy, and now he's afraid you're going to fuck it up."

"Interesting," he said, his tone flat. "Anything else?"

"Yeah," Kes exhaled. "Jerry's threatening legal action. Says if we do not get the suitcase back to him immediately, we are going to be prosecuted to the full extent of the law."

Hud scoffed. "Did he tell you that his deal with Stanley is to sell him back the package?"

A moment of silence. Then "Yeah," Kes said. "He thinks it is good for CCC. Says he really nailed a fantastic settlement."

Hud shook his head. "And he's 'worried about me-huh?"

"That's what he says."

Hud leaned against the van's door, staring at the neon glow of the diner's sign. This was bigger than just Jerry looking for an easy way out.

"What do you think of Jerry's deal, Kes?"

After a pause Kes said, "Sylvia's fine with it, she doesn't want me going to jail."

"And you?"

There was an edge in Hud's voice now.

Kes hesitated, "We worked hard, Hud. Risked our lives—more than once—for that package." His voice was filled with frustration. "If you want to hold onto it, maybe wait until after the election and get it to Butch, I'll back you one hundred percent." "But," Kes continued, "right now... I think we're better off with Jerry's deal."

"I'm on the road in Utah, It's 4 a.m. I'll be there when I get there, if my wheels hold out, if not, I'll call to have someone come and get me." Hud disconnected the call.

The long drive stretched ahead of him, desperate for something—anything—to break the monotony, he constantly fiddled with the radio. But with no scan feature and only religious sermons and country music filling the airwaves, he gave up, letting the static hum in the background. Right now, nothing mattered more than getting to Salish, Montana and he was not sure why.

By the time he crossed into Montana, almost seven hours later and the sun was low on the horizon, casting long shadows over the road. It was nearly 7 p.m. when he finally pulled Shorty's van into the gravel parking lot of the Nighty-Night Motel—the only lodging for miles in any direction.

Hud checked in the Motel first, resisting the temptation to drive straight to the Bandero ranch. He needed a shower, and a reset. In the tiny room he stood in the shower just long enough to rinse off the road dust, he then pulled on some sweats, threw himself onto the sagging mattress, and dialed Kenny Garrett. The pick-up was instantaneous.

"Hud! This is Kenny Garrett—where are you?"

"At the Nighty-Night. Can you stop by?"

"Damn, you're hard to keep track of. Sure, you're not too wiped out?"

"I'm good." Hud rubbed a hand over his face. "How's Kestrel?"

Kenny hesitated. "He's… worried. Sylvia promised to call Kes when her flight landed in Burbank, but as of yet, she still hasn't checked in with him. Her plane landed in Burbank over an hour ago."

"That's not like her. She seems responsible," Hud said.

"Yeah. But Kes says she is careless about calling, so he's been trying to track her down through her friends."

Hud scratched is head his head. "Well, I'm here because I had to get out of LA. I was being followed—dangerous types. And Jerry Varene? He won't let up on me either."

"You sound pretty wrecked, Hud," Kenny replied.

"Yeah, well…"

Kenny's tone shifted. "Kestrel and I are flying out to all seven reservations to collect mail-in ballots. Butch wants to make sure every single one gets in and counted."

Hud frowned. "So… you're a contract postal carrier now?"

Kenny laughed. "Thanks to Senator Roberts! I have got an official USPS authorization letter allowing me to pick up pouches of mail—including ballots—from remote sites around the state."

Kenny continued, "Roberts is nervous—he and Butch are too close in the polls. And now his supporters—big ranchers—are doing everything they can to pull him ahead. He's got them rounding up their wranglers and giving them mail-in ballots to fill out. But Most of those cowboys aren't permanent Montana residents, so... who knows. But ballots almost never get checked for fraud here."

"But doesn't Roberts realize how much work Kes and Sylvia put into the reservation vote?" Hud asked.

"I didn't tell him. I will be making official Postal-pickups at the reservations for Roberts," Ken said. "I'm pretty sure Roberts would not approve."

Hud glanced at his watch. "When are you leaving?"

"As soon as I finish this call," Kenny replied.

Hud exhaled. "Looks like I'll miss you, then."

"You will," Kenny confirmed.

"Alright," Hud said, sitting up. "I'll drive to the ranch and see if Butch has anything for me to do."

Kenny's flights with Kestrel, hopping from reservation to reservation, consumed most of the day. Montana was massive, and each stop added hours to their route.

In between, Kenny also made a few detours to ranches, following Senator Roberts' request to round up every possible ballot. But as the day wore on, it became clear—the ranch ballots were sparse, while the reservation mail pouches were heavy.

By the time the sun began to dip behind the mountain ridges, Kenny guided the plane toward a small private airstrip in Helena, one he knew well. He landed smoothly, taxiing toward the lot where his pick-up truck sat waiting.

He and Kestrel climbed out, mail pouches in hand, and made their way toward one of the state office buildings—the place where ballots would be tallied.

Inside, in the presence of election monitors, Kenny unfolded his official authorization papers and presented the ballots to the election officials.

One of the monitors, a tired-looking man with glasses sliding down his nose, peered over the documents. "Roberts going to win again?"

Kenny's expression never wavered. "One can only hope."

Nearby, another election official—a short, round man wearing a bolo tie—grinned broadly and winked at Kenny.

"I know you," the man said. "You're one of Roberts' men." His grin widened. "So, what's the plan? Another last-minute miracle with these ranch ballots?"

Kenny tapped the pouches. "These," he said smoothly, "are also reservation ballots."

Chapter 50

Sylvia stepped into the Burbank Airport ladies' room, setting her bag down on the counter. She took a moment to study herself in the mirror and liked what she saw.

The cornrows were gone, replaced by a curly crochet style she considered an improvement. Her black cashmere cardigan draped effortlessly over her favorite little black dress, paired with sheer black tights. But what made her smile was the contrast—with her new white Nike running shoes.

Power and comfort. The perfect mix.

Still brimming with self-assurance, Sylvia exited the restroom and stopped a passing flight attendant.

"Where's the best spot for ground transportation?"

The woman motioned toward the nearby Uber stand.

Sylvia thanked her and headed in the direction indicated.

She had barely set foot in the designated area when a black Mercedes with tinted windows pulled up.

The driver's side window was cracked just enough to make out a figure behind the wheel.

"You my Uber?" she asked.

The driver nodded.

Without hesitation, she hopped in the backseat but before she could even register click of the car door lock, strong arms clamped around her, and rough hands shoved her face-first into the carpeted floor.

A heavy foot pressed down hard against the back of her head, grinding her cheek further into the thick carpet.

Sylvia did not even have a chance to scream. She struggled against her captors, trying to turn her head, but she could see only a pair of black wingtips. Then—a sharp jolt of pain as another shoe dug into the back of her neck, and one moor pressed into her spine.

Her legs had been bent backward at an unnatural angle, crossed over each other, and pinned beneath the weight of yet another foot, she could not move or cry out, and didn't try. It was all she could do to pull small gasps of air through dirty carpet fibers.

A voice drifted from the front seat. "Hey, dogs—remember, boss said bring her in alive. If she dies on the way back, you two are next." The accent was Southern.

A second voice—soaked in whiskey—scoffed. "Aw, shove it, man, She's fine, aren't you, gal?"

The pressure let up slightly, but not enough for Sylvia to move or respond. The drive was long and for the first forty minutes or so, the car moved smoothly, the sound of heavy traffic filtering in through the windows, then she felt the pavement shift to the slow curve of an off-ramp. Brief stops followed. Traffic lights?

Then, the pavement changed from smooth and straight to, twisted, as if climbing a winding hill. Finally, the Mercedes rolled onto a softer surface, Sylvia heard the crunch of gravel as the car came to a complete stop.

Sylvia braced herself for whatever might come next.

Whiskey Voice spoke again, "Should we blindfold her before dragging her inside?"

She heard a wheezy voice—the one belonging to the man pinning her legs back at that cruel angle— his foot had been the worst, pressing down hard on the small of her back, sending and searing pulses of fire up and down her spine. Thankfully now, her legs had gone completely numb. She felt nothing below the waist— except for the burning agony that still shot from her lower back straight into her skull.

The wheezy voice sneered and responded through his smoker's rasp. "No sense in a blindfold," he snickered. "She ain't never leaving."

"Pull her sweater over her head anyway before she gets out so she doesn't see nothing." the driver ordered; his tone cruel. "Boss is calling the shots, not you."

A rear car door swung open. Whiskey Voice climbed out first, keeping one heavy hand on the back of Sylvia's head, still pressing her face into the carpet.

Then, with his other hand, he yanked her sweater up over her head, gripping both the fabric and a fistful of her hair.

Sylvia sucked fresh air into her lungs for the first time since her capture at the airport, but her ribs were still aching from the vice-like grasp that held her. Before she could react, she felt hands—rough and eager—pawing over her body.

Her stomach turned, still the moment she was dragged out of the car, she was able to let out one wild desperate scream.

"Shut her up, Zeke!" the driver ordered. "Boss has visitors."

Zeke's groping hands suddenly shot up to cover her mouth, however his thumb slipped into her mouth. Sylvia didn't think but bit down—hard. Her molars clamped shut with a sickening crunch, as Zeke's scream tore through the hills.

"Shush! You two," the whiskey voice of Pete and the driver hissed together, both men panicking. "You damn fools are going to have the whole house out here! The boss will tear all our heads off."

But Sylvia was not letting go, she could not have if she tried. Her jaw was locked tight like a steel trap. Zeke was sobbing now, trying to smother his own cries, while pounding his fist against the side of Sylvia's head trying to release his thumb. Her skull throbbed with each blow, but she could not loosen her teeth, holding on like grim death of their own volition.

One last desperate punch and the hand came free from Sylvia's jaws.

"Whoa! Zeke, do not do that," the driver yelled. "Boss said to bring her back in one piece, that punch could have killed her. If that had happened, Boss might have told Gunther to kill all of us."

Pete grabbed Zeke's gun hand and pinned it behind him, pulling the weapon from Zeke's fingers as he did so. Meanwhile, Sylvia could feel bones crunching in her mouth and the taste of blood.

Zeke was long and lean, with large features—nose, ears, lips, hands, and feet. A lifetime smoker, he was no match for the burly Pete, whose bowling-ball head and bulging biceps betrayed excessive steroid and barbell use.

Pete pulled the weeping Zeke to the ground and examined his mangled hand. Blood gushed everywhere.

"Jeezus," Pete whistled. "His thumbs gone!"

Turning to the driver, he ordered, "Hubert, give me something to stuff in the bitch's mouth. Then get Zeke inside to the doctor."

Once she was tightly gagged, Pete expertly ripped off part of Sylvia's dress and tied her hands behind her back with it, "Now isn't that a pretty package to show the boss," he chuckled.

Pete tossed Sylvia over his shoulder in a fireman's carry, entered the house through a side door, and immediately climbed the stairs to the second level.

Walking down a long hallway lined with rooms, Pete entered an empty chamber and closed the door behind him. Crossing the room, he opened a closet and tossed Sylvia inside like a sack of laundry and then closed the door.

Just then, the door behind him creaked open. Pete turned to see old Mr. Stanley, accompanied by Hubert.

"Took you long enough," the old man rasped. "I hear she gave you quite a tussle."

"She's a panther, that one," Pete laughed. "Have you seen Zeke?"

"No, he just went in with the doc," Stanley chortled. "Where is she? Let me see her."

Pete gestured toward the closet.

The old man walked to the closet and opened the door, leering inside for several minutes.

"Whoowee, what I could do with that if I were forty years younger," he said after he was through gawking.

Just then, Zeke entered with blood on his clothes and a heavily bandaged hand.

"Well now, Zeke boy," old Stanley said, "I hear tell you had a run-in with a buzz-saw."

"I'm gonna kill her nice and slow, boss," Zeke's voice was thin and shaky. "Just as soon as you're through with her."

"Well, that remains to be seen," old Stanley said. "What we are after is my stolen documents. If those boys play nice, and there is no other way to get my goods, we may have to trade her. However, if there ain't a fair trade, then I suppose you can have her."

"She likes biting," Zeke muttered. "I'm going to give her to my dog Max, one bite at a time for a couple of hours."

"You're a sadistic bastard," old Stanley cackled. Then, patting Zeke on his slumping shoulders, he winked and said, "If you do get her, have Pete take some nice videos of her and the dog for me," he grinned with cracked lips. "In the meantime, you and Pete go out and bring in them two scoundrels that stole my property, if they still have it. If not, Gunther will make them get it."

Chapter 51

Early Monday morning, Hud and Kestrel headed south out of Montana, making their way toward Los Angeles. They crossed into Cowley, Wyoming, and six hours later, they arrived in Little America, near the Utah-Wyoming border.

They bought a big bag of pretzels and a six-pack of ginger ale before checking into the only hotel. The television news came on, but there were no reports on the national elections yet.

By five a.m., both men were wide awake and hungry. There was a 24-hour truck stop, so they decided Kes would go inside and grab two carry-out breakfasts, while Hud gassed up the van.

Kes ate first while Hud drove, then they switched, with Kestrel taking the wheel.

Hud checked his map app and told Kes, "Still 800 miles to Los Angeles." As they settled in for the long haul.

A little over an hour later, they drove out of the Wyoming mountains and into Utah.

As they neared Salt Lake City, Hud noticed connectivity returning to his phone and immediately began searching for election results from Montana.

"Big news! Bandero Beats Roberts!" he read aloud from a CNN post.

Hearing the news, Kestrel slammed his hands against the steering wheel and leaned on the horn.

"We did it! By God, we did it!" he whooped, over and over.

Hud kept reading. The article explained that there had been a lower-than-expected turnout from Roberts' supporters, while Bandero saw a windfall from the Indian Reservations.

Butch had won by fewer than 2,000 votes, but in a state with less than half a million voters, the margin was considered significant.

The report confirmed that Senator Roberts had conceded without filing for a recount. "Holy shit! I wish I was back at the ranch right now," Kestrel yipped. "Buffy and I would be celebrating in oh so many ways."

Just then, Hudson's phone rang, it was Jerry.

"I hope you're on the way back," he warned.

"We'll be in by Thursday morning—don't get so huffy," Hud said. "And we'll have the package you want so badly."

Jerry's tone softened.

"It's not for me, Hud, you know that. Our movement needs money more than anything right now."

Hud changed the subject. "Did you hear about Butch's victory?"

"I did, I did," Jerry sounded genuinely pleased. "I've already called and congratulated him."

Then, after a pause, "Don't worry, Hud. With Butch in the Senate and us having the money to spend on reform, we'll have everyone driving electric cars in no time."

"Let's hope so," Hud responded before ending the call.

PART X:
END GAME

Chapter 52

Lillian Blake had an appointment to meet Bruno Stach at LJ's house that very evening. She did not show up alone. With her was a petite attractive young lady. Her soft platinum blonde hair, just covering her ears, was highlighted with streaks of mint green. Lillian introduced her as Sheela Stanley. "It's green because I am," the girl said with a coy giggle, lightly fingering the strands around her ears.

"Well, my green eyes match your hair," Lillian retorted fluttering dark lashes, her smile revealing sparkling green eyes and very white teeth. It was obvious to Bruno and LJ that the two were flirting with each other if body language had anything to say about it.

"You know Sheela," Lillian spoke to Lady Jane. "She has been to several of our meetings."

"Of course," LJ spoke, "how are you dear?"

"What you don't know," Lillian interrupted, "Is that Sheela is the granddaughter of the owner of the Stanley Energy Company, owned by Bueford Stanley. What you also do not know," she said looking at Bruno, "is that she witnessed the death of the man with the suitcase."

Bruno's eyebrows lifted noticeable. "Do tell," he said.

"Well . . ." Lillian began.

"No, let Sheela tell it," Bruno said. "Take a seat here at the table young lady and tell us what it was you observed."

"I don't know exactly," Sheela began in a thin voice. "You see, I had been sleeping in the back of grandfather's big limo. When I awoke, I started to sit up and I saw through a window a man standing holding a suitcase or briefcase. It was made of shiny metal. Other men were walking slowly toward the man with the case as if to block him from escaping." Sheela paused reflecting for a moment.

Clearing her throat she continued; "Just behind the man with the case was an airplane with its propeller spinning. The airplane turned a little," Sheela sobbed, her fingers clutching the arms of her chair. "And then the propeller hit the man in the back of the head." Her sobbing continued quietly as she stared with red eyes at Bruno. "That's what I saw."

Brumo listened without emotion. "Where did you see this and when?" Bruno asked.

"I don't know where I was, it was starting to get dark, I had been sleeping. But there was still enough light left for me to see."

Bruno's hand lightly stroked his jaw. "So, this was here in California?"

"Oh, no sir, I'm sorry, this was in West Virginia or maybe Virginia." Her voice still quavered. "I attend college in Virginia but I live in grandfather's big house in Bluefield, West Virginia when I am back east, but I don't like it there much. I like living here in California."

"Why do you think you might have been in Virginia?"

"Well, the two states, West Virginia and Virginia are very close, and we had been driving for some time so it could have been either state, I'm not sure which, I had been sleeping and it was pretty dark."

"Okay, please continue" Bruno said, settling into his chair.

Sheela cleared her throat and sat more upright, hands clasped tightly in her lap, "Grandfather was driving me home from a production of *The Lion King* in Washington, D.C. Both of us always liked driving trips better than flying trips. One of grandfather's chauffeurs was driving the car. I am not sure which one it was, we use different drivers, I think it was Hubert. Anyway, I was in the way-back, I liked to sleep back there. I woke up when I heard a buzzing sound like the one a small airplane propeller makes. I know the sound because my grandfather sometime flies a small airplane."

She hesitated, "That kind of woke me up, the car was stopped. I thought maybe we were coming to grandad's house already."

"What happened then?" Bruno said, "and relax. You are in no trouble here."

Sheela glanced nervously at Lillian who simply smiled and nodded for her to continue.

"That was when I saw the man get hit by the propeller!" She said clasping one hand over her mouth as the horror of the moment came back and tears again flooded her eyes. Sheela began speaking rapidly, as if letting her words escape quickly would remove the awful moment from her mind forever. "He had been holding a shiny case but when the propeller hit the man's head, the case went flying way up in the air, glinting in the moon light. Blood went flying from his head too and he toppled over."

Her eyes were wide, as if watching the scene play out in front of her. "I lay right back down, really scared." The fear she was describing filled her voice. "I saw men moving toward the car, I thought they meant to come and kill me too so I crawled back on the floor of the limo and hid under a thick comforter we keep there for when it's cold."

"Were you at an airport or landing area?"

It was at a clearing in a wood. There were shadows. That was all I saw."

"So" Bruno asked, "what time was it when you left Washington; was it early?"

Lillian reached out and dabbed at Sheela's eyes with a tissue. "She's really had enough for now don't you think?" she said giving a stern stare in Bruno's direction.

"Yes," he replied, "but we are finished with the most difficult part, let her continue, it won't take much longer." Then returning his attention to Sheela. "Please continue at your own pace."

"Cook made us a picnic lunch and we ate it on the mall, just a little while before attending the play." Those present could tell Sheela was in a more pleasant place now. "After a couple of hours driving on the way home, grandfather and I had dinner at a restaurant. He began teasing, calling me 'sweet little Sheela,' words from a song he would sing that made me happy. He wanted me to drink my milk because I needed it to take my sleep medicine and he knows I do not like milk."

She was much calmer now almost enjoying the spotlight. "Can I have some water?"

LJ immediately produced a water bottle and Sheela began sipping while she spoke.

"Grandfather got up to go to the men's room so I poured out most of it, I don't much care for milk, and the sleep medicine gives me bad dreams. When we got back in the car and started driving, I began to feel sleepy so after a while I crawled into my nest of blankets in the way-back and fell asleep. That is all I remember happening," She shrugged and smiled at Lillian, "Did I do okay?"

Lillian nodded, and then turned toward Bruno. "Is that all, Mr. Stach?"

"Just a couple of more questions. "When did this incident occur?"

"At least a couple of years ago, I'm not sure of the exact date but you could find out by looking up when *The Lion King* was playing in D.C. about that far back."

Bruno scribbled briefly in his notepad before continuing.

"Was it you, Sheela, who telephoned a Mr. Bandero in Montana and informed him of what you saw regarding the case the man was carrying?"

She pondered this question for a moment. "I remember at a CCC meeting Hubert dropped me off early. My eyes had been itching, allergies you know? There are more things I am allergic to in California."

She glanced briefly at Lillian who returned an encouraging smile. "Anyway, I went to the bathroom to put drops in my eyes but Jerry was in it freshening up for the meeting. He said I could use the bathroom upstairs. When I got up there, I saw a business card on the counter of the upstairs bathroom. On one side it read Butch Bandero, environmental law. On the back was written in ink, 'Butch can solve everything!' I put the card in my pocket, I was not sure why at the time."

Sheela began sobbing again. "Everyone was working so hard for the animals, and forests at CCC, I loved the group, and I loved Jerry and most of all Lillian until she started bringing a boyfriend to the meetings with her."

Encouraged by the attention, Sheela continued. "I wanted to do something – to help. People at the meeting had been talking about a shiny suitcase or briefcase and about my grandfather's energy company. That was when I remembered the shiny case I saw go flying when the propeller hit the man in the head. I had to tell someone what I saw; I was sick inside."

Tears were running down her cheeks once more. With red eyes she looked at Lillian. "That's when I called the man on the card," her lips were trembling.

Lillian was distressed. "Alright that's enough," she stood up, "leave her alone, can't you see how upset she is?"

"Almost finished," Bruno said calmly looking only at Sheela.

"Did you use your own phone to make the call?

"Yes, but I get my phones from grandpa. He says they are secure. He worries a lot about kidnappers and things like that."

"Did Jerry know your grandfather?"

"Yes, but they were on opposite sides, I was on Jerry's side. I watched 'Nature' on TV and all the wildlife shows. My favorites were the ones about the oceans and climate change. I told grandfather I wanted to help save the oceans, the sea turtles, and the kelp forests."

The recollection brought her smile once more, "Grandfather said he understood. He called Jerry and made a donation to the Coast Conservation Corps. That is how it all started." Sheela concluded wiping her eyes.

"Grandfather said it was okay if I called Jerry and that I could attend his meetings and maybe even join the CCC. But neither Jerry nor I were to tell anyone who my grandfather was. Grandfather was very protective of me. Like I said, he was afraid I could get hurt or kidnapped."

"How old are you, Sheela?" Bruno asked.

"I'm 20 years old, almost 21, my full name is Sheela Stanley."

"Why are you living in California? Does your grandfather have a house here?"

"Oh yes! My favorite one. Our house is in the hills above Malibu. Grandfather says it is my house. Ever since I was a little girl I wanted to live in California, it looked so beautiful, the beaches and palm trees on all the TV shows and movies. It was too cold and damp for me in West Virginia, I got pneumonia three times, I almost died."

"Where are your parents?"

"They were both killed somewhere in Spain when I was very young, a car crash. Grandfather raised me mostly. We were best of friends. He built the house for me in Malibu so I could always be warm. I spent all my winters in Malibu, home schooled by my nurse Kathy. But when we found out how cool it could get by the beach, grandfather had big fire places built in every room. I loved the warm fires, and I never got sick anymore after that."

A cell phone went off with a distinctive chime. That's me Lillian said rummaging through her purse, "Hello? Oh, Hudson."

She put a finger to her lips signaling for silence. "Are you back yet? Jerry and Mr. Stanley are ready to meet with you tomorrow morning, do you have their package?"

There was an extended pause, "Okay it all sounds good then." A male voice could be heard commenting in background of Lillian's phone. "That is true no one wants to see you and Kestrel get into any trouble." Lillian said, "I will let Jerry know that it's all set."

Lillian turned to LJ and Bruno, "Jerry and I are to meet Mr. Stanley at his private residence in Malibu, the one he calls Sheela's house. I will be texting you the directions. Hud must be at the Malibu house at nine a.m., no later. He must bring everything that was removed from the suitcase. There will be settlement papers to sign, and papers negating the deal. If it is found that documents are missing or that reproductions were made. Violation of the agreement would mean serious legal consequences for Hud and Kestrel." Lillian affirmed.

"It sounds great if Hud shows up," LJ cautioned. "You know, Lillian, he has been anything but reliable."

Chapter 53

For the first time in a long time, Bruno was at a loss as how to proceed. He had learned from the morning news that Roberts had been defeated in Montana, so the whole Senate investigation would probably be on hold until the new committee members sorted things out. His letter of authority to investigate might already be rescinded. Maybe he would be allowed to clear up odds and ends with the FBI about Reddy, but even that could be considered outside of his purview. Too many maybes, he needed to get back to D.C. and find out his current status.

Also, being anywhere near the suitcase might put him in harm's way, because he was now aware of, and had a witness to, the murder of Jim Reddy.

Death by propeller did not seem like a good way to end what may well be his final investigation. Still, he wanted one more shot at finding the suitcase and knowing its contents. At last, he said, "I guess I'm through here, thank all of you for your contributions."

"What happens now?" Lady Jane asked.

"I'm going to return to D.C. and find out," Bruno answered. "Now that we will have new players in the Senate, I need to know how much has changed regarding the investigation Roberts' committee was conducting."

Bruno said good bye to LJ and that he would be returning to his hotel, but he knew differently. The investigation was coming together, he could feel it. Unless Hudson and Kestrel had made up a fantastic lie, important evidence might be soon available if for no other purpose than to shed further light on the demise of former FBI Agent James Reddy. Either way he was going to do his best to find out before returning to D.C..

Out in the car Bruno found the address for Hudson Halle and put it in his map-app so the little lady inside the phone could give him directions. Luck was with him, a 24-hour Starbucks appeared near his location, just ahead on Ventura Boulevard. Walking out with two large dark-roast coffees and a couple of cranberry scones he knew might needed for an all-night stakeout.

Bruno pulled the rental SUV across the street from the address his phone told him was Hudson's. He sat sipping his coffee, slouched down in the seat, ready for however long he needed to wait. Dozing off and on, while keeping track of the time, Bruno suddenly had the unsettling feeling that something was amiss. A dog yipped somewhere in the night, and Bruno heard a soft sound coming from the other side of the street. Instinct put him on full alert. It sounded like digging.

Silently he left the car and crossed the street. It was the sound of digging alright, coming from the side yard of Hudson's house. Peering around the corner he saw a man removing something from the earth. Bruno turned on his phone flashlight and shone it directly into the man's face. "Hey Hudson, what's new?" he said.

Hud lifted the shovel and advanced squinting into the source of the beam. The blade of the shovel extended forward. "It's ours," he said "Kestrel's and mine, we're turning it over to the Senate committee, no one else."

"Well, that would be me then," Bruno smiled. "I'm the Investigator for the Senate committee and if you will permit me, we can go inside and I will show you my badge and letter of authority."

Hud dropped the shovel and picked up the package he had just removed from the ground. "If that's true," he sighed in partial disbelief, "you don't know how relieved I will be."

The two men walked around the back of the house and into the kitchen where Hudson flipped on the light, "I can make coffee," he said.

"I already have some coffee in the car, Starbucks," Bruno said. "I'll go get it, if you have a microwave, we can warm it up."

Bruno came back with the coffee at the same time Kestrel came into the room, still rubbing sleep from his eyes. Hud had rousted him from the couch and explained the presence of the Investigator. Hud had three coffee mugs sitting on the table hot out of the microwave. What was left of Bruno's coffee filled each cup about half full.

A minute later the three men sat around the kitchen table while Hud and Kestrel read the letter of authority and examined Bruno's badge. "Butch told us about you," Kestrel said nodding over the badge.

"Let's have a look at the document package," Bruno said.

Hud shook the dirt off the outer plastic bag of the bundle from the kitchen counter, "I've never been so glad to get rid of anything in my life," he sighed, and Bruno could see that both Hudson and Kestrel were showing deep feelings of relief.

Carefully unwrapping the bundle, Bruno came to something just inside the package. He recognized it immediately, an official FBI evidence seal, only to be removed in the presence of an authorized official. "That would be me," Bruno whispered in such a low tone that only he heard it.

There was something else, the seal had been stamped C-1/3. Bruno sat up in his chair and then proceeded to read it again. He excitedly sifted through the package, filled with documents, thumb drives and video tapes. Then back to the seal, he stared for another long moment, his throat went dry, his palms slightly damp.

Had anyone else noticed? Of course not! But if in the one in a million chance any one had, they would not have been able to do anything about it. Only one person in the world could do that. Suddenly he laughed, "O-M-G," he said, and then repeated it over and over. "O-M-G, O-M-G!"

Hud and Kestrel were puzzled. It was not the reaction either had expected. "What? What is it? Tell us."

Bruno carefully put the package back together in its original condition, but kept the seal from inside the package before pushing it back across the table to Hud, before folding the seal and putting it in his jacket pocket. "It's my understanding you boys are in trouble if you don't deliver this to your friend Jerry Varene this morning," he said.

"We're not afraid," Kestrel snarled rising to his feet. "We've decided we're going to put this in the proper hands come hell or high water, and that means you."

"Okay, okay, calm down Bruno smiled, "I am the proper hands and I'm telling you to deliver it to Mr. Varene and stay out of trouble."

"I don't get it," Hud wore a puzzled frown. "Isn't it any good?"

"Oh, it's good all right," Bruno laughed shaking his head still in disbelief. "It's better than good, it's fabulous. You guys did great, your country, and the whole world owes you a reward that you will probably never receive. I do not know how you pulled it off, what may turn out to be the heist of the century. I can't tell you any more than that now, but this morning deliver the package to Jerry Varene."

Still shaking his head in disbelief, "You don't want any more trouble than you've already had," Bruno said standing. He drained the coffee cup in one big gulp and departed out the back door. His face was serious when he turned back, "Great job," he said and then he was gone.

Chapter 54

Hudson and Kestrel sat and stared at each other in a state of bewilderment. How could something a Senate Investigator called fabulous be turned over to the worst crooks in the world? It made no sense. "You know," Hud said, "maybe this Bruno Stach guy was really working for Roberts all along."

Kes thought about it, "Hud let's do one more thing with this crazy package. We both trust Butch and after being sworn in he will be a U.S. Senator! Let's drive up to Montana now, give it to him and be done with it forever."

"That's great idea," Hud agreed, "Neither of us will be able to ever sleep again if we simply give it back to the Stanley's so Jerry can get his big settlement. A man died trying to deliver this package to someone, and something else I just remembered. There was some kind of paper inside this bundle and that guy Stach removed it and never put it back."

Both men raced through the house grabbing anything they might need for the long drive to Montana once again. Tossing in several armloads of clothes and gear and then piling into the old Chevy Van from Smitty's, they were once again on the road. The sun was now up and another warm fall day was in the offing.

Six blocks from the house Hud noticed a large black car behind them. He made a couple of unneeded turns, but the tail stayed with them.

"What is it?" Kes asked.

"We're being followed," Hud replied thru gritted teeth.

"Then let's pull over and have at it," Kes snorted, "I've been itching for a fight with somebody."

"No, Kestrel," Hud replied, "not here, not now. I told you about the last time I was followed, these guys are mean dudes, they carry guns, and the least they will do is steal the package from us, the worst is shoot us and then steal the package."

Continuing to drive, Hud took Topanga Canyon Boulevard south and then slung out onto Mullholland Drive. "I'm going to try to make it to a place I set up several miles from here, Kestrel. If it works, we may be rid of these hoods once and for all."

Hud stepped hard on the accelerator. The old engine whined in protest but the tail car kept an even pace behind, not trying to overtake them but not losing them either. "Maybe they think we're on our way to Malibu to turn the evidence package over to Jerry," Hud wondered. When he approached the light at Malibu Canyon there was no traffic in sight. Hud tromped on the gas and twisted the wheel left, tires screeching in agony as the old vehicle plowed through the red light at the intersection without slowing down. The car behind did the same.

"Up ahead there's a tunnel Kestrel," Hud said. "Just on the other side of it I am going to pull over hard on to the shoulder. Then we're going to run into the trees, I'll go first because I marked the trail. Stay close. If they follow us keep running, after maybe a hundred yards or so you will see me leap out from the rocks. There's deep water below, but it's about 50 or 60 feet to the water so be prepared, take a deep breath after you jump and leap out forward as far as you can, you don't want to land in shallow water."

"What about our package?" Kestrel asked, "What if they don't come after us and instead search the van?"

"I don't think so," Hud said shaking his head. "We are the only ones who know where the package is, they know that, they won't let us get away on the chance that what they want might not be with us."

Kes laughed, "Okay brother, let's get these guys in the drink and then see how tough they are."

Once through the narrow tunnel, Hud pulled over to the shoulder and braked hard, "Let's go," he cried jumping from the vehicle as it shuddered in a cloud of dust before coming to a complete stop. The beer cans were still right where Hud had placed them, he was running full speed now right past the cans and could hear Kestrels pounding feet and heavy breathing right behind him."

Kestrel heard something else, a deep snarling growl. Glancing over his shoulder, not thirty yards behind and closing fast was a sleek Doberman, fangs barred and dripping with foam. Still further back he caught a glimpse of two men running, each with a gun in hand. It spurred him, on. Kestrel could have run faster but he couldn't get past the slower Hud even if he wanted to, the trail was too narrow.

Just ahead he saw Hud leap out over a protruding boulder and disappear, a moment later he felt the Doberman's jaws clamp into the flesh of his left forearm. The sudden stab of pain was excruciating. He fought hard to remain on his feet and keep moving forward but the weight of the dog was slowing him down considerably. Looking back, he could see the men would be upon him in seconds, close enough for a shot he thought but they didn't want to hit their precious dog.

Stumbling forward, Kestrel forced his legs up to the boulder and with his last ounce of strength hurled himself over the precipice remembering to fill his lungs with as much air as possible. Upon hitting the water, he realized he had not been able to get far enough out. When he went down, he felt his left foot hit something hard below the surface before both feet gently reached the bottom of the pool.

The water was no more than eight feet deep. Looking up he could see the dog's legs swimming above in the clear reservoir water. "I can't fight you on land," he thought, "so let's end it here."

Swimming up and under a hind leg he pulled the Doberman below the surface. In doing so he managed to catch one quick breath of air before diving back under and swimming toward the bottom still clutching the dog's leg firmly with one hand. Through the crystal liquid he caught sight of a length of re-bar protruding from a large broken chunk of concrete. With one motion he switched his hold from the Doberman's leg to its choke chain collar and hooked the chain under the re-bar, then he swam once again to the surface.

Looking around cautiously and ready to dive again if he heard a shot, however, Kes saw only Hud standing in the shallows and beckoning to Kes from the opposite shore. Kes approached with a breast stroke. "There were at least two men with guns behind me," he said. "Any sign of them?"

Hud pointed toward something dark floating in the water. "That's one," he replied. "I had already come up for air when I saw his fatal mistake. He got to the edge and tried frantically to stop but momentum carried him over. He bounced on the rocks once before splash down."

"There's at least one more," Kes said, "I saw two for sure, both had guns."

"Well, that's the only one that came over. I did see you fighting that dog, you look like you landed a little short. Are you alright?"

"My right foot's numb, maybe broken. I'm not feeling pain right now though, probably because of the cold water."

Hud helped Kestrel clamber up the shore. Moving furtively until locating a place among the boulders and brush that was hidden from view, Hud examined, Kes' damaged foot. "It's pretty bad Kes, you're going to have to remain here for a while. I'm going to climb back up. I left my cell phone in the van, if it's still there I'll call 911 to come and find you. If not, I can drive to Malibu and call from there, it's only ten minutes away. If the van's not there I will flag down the first car that drives by."

"Don't worry about me, Hud, be careful and watch out for the other guy."

Hud was scrambling up a steep side of the canyon about 30 feet from the crest when he came around a tree. There sat a man with a large nose and big ears, and one hand heavily bandaged, not four feet in front of him. The guy was holding a gun that was pointing it straight toward Hud's guts, no expression crossed the man's face. Hud froze, he looked around but there was no escape route, so this was how it was going to end. He closed his eyes, "So go ahead and shoot," he said, "I can't stop you," and waited for the fatal bullet.

Several seconds passed and Hud thought, "Perhaps they want me alive, that must be it, he wants to take me in and make me tell where the package is." These thoughts lifted his spirts just a bit. Maybe another chance to escape would present itself.

When he opened his eyes, the man had still not moved but was still staring directly at Hud. Moreover, a wasp had alit on the end of the man's nose, but he made no move to brush it away. "Are you going to shoot me or take me in?" Hud asked.

"Then the man's lips moved, "paralyzed," he gurgled, Hud could barely make out the word.

"Paralyzed?" Hud repeated. He looked at the man and then at the cliff above and it began to dawn on him what must have occurred. The second man had been running behind the first. When the first man bounced into the drink, the second saw the error and swerved off one side of the trail only to fall off a twenty-five-foot embankment where he now squatted at the base.

"Broken neck?" Hud asked feeling a twinge of pity.

"Think so," gurgled the voice.

"You won't be needing this then," Hud said, removing the gun from a very cold hand. "I'll be calling 911 for my friend when I get to the top," he said, "Hopefully, they'll locate you too."

Pushing the gun under his belt, Hud climbed the rest of the way out of the canyon. Looking towards the place where he had hurdled from the moving vehicle, he saw the van he had been driving and the black Mercedes that had followed them, parked one behind the other. A driver, complete with chauffer's jacket and cap, was leaning against the Mercedes staring at the highway and smoking a cigarette. Hud crept up behind him and pushed the gun into the man's ribs. The man jumped and let out a squeal.

"Don't make a sound if you want to live," Hud growled, open the rear door, and put your hat and jacket inside.

"I'm only a Chauffer for the old man," the driver moaned,

" Please don't hurt me."

"If you don't do exactly as I say you're going to be a dead Chauffer."

The man quickly removed the jacket and hat and tossed them in the back seat. "Now pop the trunk," Hud ordered.

"Now just a minute," the driver whined backing away and trying to sound brave. "I'm not getting into that trunk."

"Suit yourself," Hud hissed, pressing the gun into the man's cheek, "but you're going in, dead or alive."

"Wait listen," the man squealed again, "It weren't me that nabbed your gal; it was the other two who done it. I was only the driver for the old man. I had to go."

"You nabbed what girl?"

"The nigra gal, the old man told us to bring her in alive. He wants to trade her for something he thinks you stole. We done it too. She's alive at the compound right now."

"Where in the compound?"

"Upstairs bedroom at the end of the hall, locked in a closet. She is alive though, was the last I saw her anyway."

Hud pondered for a moment and then opened a rear door of the car. "Okay," he said. "You drive to the compound; I am going to be right behind you low in the back seat. Is there a guard at the gate?"

"No, I open the gate with a Blue-Tooth beep."

"Listen, pal," Hud said. "I think my chances of getting into the compound and out again with the woman are less than 50-50. However, if I get in trouble your chances of staying alive are zero, because this gun is always going to be pointed three feet from your spinal cord and I never miss from three feet. I am dead serious, if you don't believe me, I can take you back down into that canyon and you can ask your two buddies. But they won't hear you. They are never going to hear anyone again; do you get the picture?

The driver, sweat pouring down his face, nodded.

"Ok," Hud said now get in the trunk while I get some things from the van."

Defeated, the driver popped the trunk and climbed in. "Don't leave me to die in here," he pleaded.

Slamming the trunk, Hud walked back to the van and retrieved his cell phone and wallet along with the package from the metal briefcase. Using the button on the car key he popped the trunk and led the driver back to the driver's seat. He then climbed into the backseat and ordered the Chauffer to drive to the house where Sylvia was taken.

About a mile further down the road he dialed 911. "There is a badly injured man near the pool at the bottom of Rindge Dam," he said into a recording device. "He needs immediate medical attention."

A green light began blinking on the dash with a button just below it. The driver pushed the button. "Car 3 this is home – do you read me?" said a voice.

"Yes sir," the chauffer replied.

"Do you have everything?" the intercom spoke again. The Chauffer glanced over at Hud. Hud nodded.

"Yes," the driver answered.

"Remember not to garage your vehicle, the place will blow at two p.m. exactly, the car you are driving will be taking out VIPs, do you copy?"

"Roger that," the Chauffer replied, but there was no need to respond. The green light had stopped blinking and all was silent.

Hud ordered the Chauffer to pull over to the side of the road. He needed time to think. What did it mean the 'the place will blow at two p.m.?' He remembered the business card that Investigator Stach had given him, he retrieved it from his wallet and punched in the number.

The pick-up came after one ring. "This is Bruno."

"Investigator Stach, this is Hudson Halle, remember me?" Hud then proceeded to explain as much as he could in a couple of minutes, and about the message received over the intercom. 'The place is going to blow at two p.m.' A long pause followed.

Finally, Bruno said, "Send me a text with the directions of the compound in Malibu. This does not sound good. I am going to contact the California Highway Patrol." There was another pause. "Hudson, don't go in there whatever you do, Let the CHP handle it."

Stach listened but there was no reply. Hud had ended the call. "Shit," Bruno said.

The call to Bruno Stach, had given Hud time to think. Jerry had said Lillian was going to the Malibu house to sign papers and to ensure delivery of the packet he and Kestrel had brought back from West Virginia. Hud realized he had to get there to make sure that all other CCC members were out of the house and safe and now he had found out that Sylvia was at the house too, locked away in an upstairs room.

Several minutes later Hud spotted a turnoff from the canyon road onto a gated entrance way, the driver paused for several seconds while the gate swung open. He then drove the car through the gate, stopping about fifty yards further down a driveway lined on both sides with massive palm trees. Hud put on the chauffer's coat and hat and ordered him to get in the trunk. "You better hope I make it back to let you out," he said slamming the lid.

Hud then drove off the driveway, over a manicured lawn and into a grove of trees where he brought the limo to a stop, killing the engine. The windows of the Mercedes were heavily tinted. Maybe no one would recognize him wearing the chauffer's hat Hud hoped, as he slipped thru groomed shrubbery toward the large mansion just ahead. Carrying the packet from the back seat, he held it for a minute and then dropped it into some bushes a few yards away from the car. Gun in hand he crept up to the house until he found a side door with a window next to it. He tried the knob but the door was locked.

Peering through the window he saw two women, one was the girl with the green hair, the other was Lillian! They appeared deep in conversation. Hud tapped lightly at the window and Lillian looked up, recognizing him she hurried to the door and opened it. "Hud," she said, "how are you-and why are you wearing that silly hat? We thought you would be coming in with the others."

Chapter 55

"Come," Hud urged. "You have to leave here now you're lives are in danger."

"Nonsense," Lillian snorted her voice taking on a combative tone as she shrunk back, she looked down and saw his clothes were soaking wet. "I hope you brought the material from the suitcase or Jerry will be furious. Not to mention you and Kestrel will be immediately arrested." Lillian warned.

"I brought it," Hud said, "now leave by this door and don't let anyone see you go." He motioned toward Sheela, "Take her with you."

"I'm not going anywhere; Jerry's in the other room preparing for you now. I'll go get him."

Hud struck her hard on the side of her face with the barrel of the gun raising a dark red welt. "You leave by this door now," he ordered. "And you run and keep on running because if you stop, I will be behind you and I will shoot both of you."

"Lillian's eyes were wide with tears and terror as an ugly lump was forming on the side of her face. "You are mad!" she whispered. "Come, Sheela, let's go," she said clutching the girl's arm and moving toward the door.

"I am your worst nightmare," Hud scowled. "I will be following not far behind you. Go into the woods and do not stop running or you are both dead and you better believe it." He watched them flee into the woods and then turned his attention to the small foyer where he was standing. The room was empty except for a flight of stairs leading up to another level.

He quietly climbed the carpeted stairs and walked down the long hallway the Chauffer had described. He opened doors of each room as he went searching for one with a closet in the back. He noted that each room was a bedroom with a large gas fire place next to two king size beds. "One last miracle," Hud breathed turning the fireplace gas all the way up in each bedroom as he moved silently down the hall.

When he came to the last room, he saw the closet in the corner he was looking for. He opened the door and there was Sylvia wearing only a torn slip and a pair of Nikes, badly bruised, she appeared to be asleep. Hud went over to one of the windows. It looked out onto a roof that sloped down until it was only about six or seven feet from the ground. He could see shrubs growing below the roof line.

Finding that the window slid open easily, he went back to where Sylvia lay and shook her gently, she woke with a start. Wild eyed, she did not appear to recognize him, and started scooting crabwise back toward the darkest corner of the closet where she sat whimpering through chattering teeth. Hud put his finger to his lips to silence her. "It's me, Hud," he whispered, "I have come to get you out of here. Kestrel is waiting for you."

He reached for her, and found she was trembling and cold to the touch. Picking her up in his arms he walked to the window.

"Can you hear me, Sylvia?" he asked. Her eyes appeared to be more focused now. "Can you hear me?" he repeated. She met his gaze for a long minute and then nodded. "There are others I must get out of this place, too," he said. "Lillian and Sheela just left. They went that way," he said pointing in the direction they had run. "Have you seen Jerry?"

Sylvia shook her head.

"Do you think you can scoot, down the roof? It's not too steep and there are shrubs below in case you slip. Once you are down though you cannot stop. I think this house is going to burn, or blow up, so you must get as far away from it as possible, do you understand?"

Sylvia hugged his neck fiercely for a long moment. Finally, she pulled back her head peered into his eyes and nodded solemnly. There were fresh tears on her cheeks as she slowly slid from his arms and he helped her over the sill. "Remember," he whispered, "move quickly." Pointing out the window in the direction Lillian and Sheela had fled. "Go that way," he said.

He watched her make her way painfully down the roof. At the edge, not looking back, she slipped silently into the shrubbery below, which rustled for a moment and then stillness. "God's speed," he said under his breath before turning on the fireplace gas jet in the room before making his way back through the long hallway and down the stairway, until he reached the side entry from which Lillian and Sheela had recently departed.

Finding herself laying in shrubbery, Sylvia felt like she had to sleep but recalled Hud admonishing her to keep moving at all cost. Crawling on her hands and knees through sticker bushes and mud, she was finding she could no longer catch her breath. She began coughing to clear her air passage, something was stuck in her throat. She coughed again and suddenly she could breathe freely once more. Looking down on the ground in front of her lay a bloody human thumb.

Recalling the horror of her ordeal, she scrambled to her feet and began to run in the direction Hud had pointed, ignoring the branches and brambles that tore at her. "Thank God they didn't take my Nikes!"

Chapter 56

Hud heard heavy footsteps and voices as he opened a door leading into a pantry and kitchen area. All that was left to do was to find Jerry and get the hell out. Turning in the direction of the sound he pointed the gun at someone creeping up behind him, just as something crunched hard on the back of his head. Slumping to the floor, he heard an old man's voice, "Don't kill him you fool until we have my documents back."

For how long he had been passing in and out of consciousness Hud could not tell. His head was throbbing with unbelievable lightning bolts. Opening his eyes to slits, it did not appear anyone else was nearby. His mind was raging. He must stop them! They were winning and he must not let them beat him.

He heard the old man's voice again, reprimanding someone. "Bring him to the living room we need to get him to tell us where the stuff is, it is not in the car he arrived in. And go find Gunther."

Strong hands dragged Hudson into a large room and flung him to the floor. A dozen men seated in upholstered furniture were gathered there, several holding drinks. In one corner, Hud saw Jerry Varene pale as a ghost. Old Stanley approached Jerry, "We're all leaving here at two except you," the old man screamed. "Our deal is over; you promised to have this man and his Indian here with the contents of my briefcase by nine-thirty. That did not happen!"

Stanley waved a document in Jerry's face and then tore it in half. "So much for your settlement money." He raged. "Furthermore, we're leaving you here with your friend when this place goes up in flames."

Jerry's face was ashen as he tried to rise from his seat but strong arms restrained him. "Shall we lock him in one of the closets, sir?" a voice from someone Hud could not see asked.

"Yes, take him away," the old man sneered. Then turning to Hud and stabbing him with the glossy pointed toe of a shoe said, "Gunther are you ready for this one?"

Hud felt himself being tossed into a chair, where a grinning dwarf stood in front of him. A large cooler filled with liquid was pushed to the chair where Hud now slouched. Next to the cooler, was a blow-torch, a pair of tongs and an ice pick. "These are the tools of my trade," said the dwarf in an accent unknown to Hud. "Please tell these gentlemen what they want to know. There is not a lot of time so please explain quickly."

Hudson stared at the liquid in the cooler in front of him. Was it water he wondered, or acid maybe? A line from a verse he recalled brought a tortured smile to his bruised lips. "No more water, the fire next time." He murmured.

"What's that he said?" screamed old Stanley working himself up into another fit of rage. "Get busy, Gunther."

Hud looked at the grinning freak in front of him and he began to sob, "I said no fire, please, please, no fire!"

Crooked yellow teeth grinned ominously and the little man picked up the blowtorch. Holding it just in front of Hud's eyes. "Now I'll demonstrate to you what will be happening to the rain forests of the world after you are gone tree-hugger," he cackled. Then he clicked on the torch.

Hud perceived flames erupting around him. It was as if he were in the cauldron of a volcano. He braced himself for the extreme agony he knew would come and prayed it would be brief. Strangely though, he felt nothing although he saw figures around him dancing and screaming among the blazing furnishings. Then he heard his name called.

"Hudson Halle," a woman's voice called through the inferno. Amidst the conflagration he observed something or someone dressed in gossamer with short dark hair, standing in a shimmering gown. "I remember you," Hud yelled. "You, said something. You said watch for me!" Turning toward him Hud realized instead of a reptile the face of Nicole. Slumping to the floor sobbing, "I thought you had forsaken me forever," he cried.

"It's alright," Nichole's voice was soothing as she reached out with transparent fingers to touch his shaking shoulders. "Nothing is forever."

Chapter 57

Bruno Stach had left his car by the open gate of the Malibu mansion and was trotting down the road toward it when he saw two hysterical and disheveled women running out of the trees next to the gate. One had a large swelling from her left ear to her jaw, the other tousled green hair.

"It's Hudson," Lillian was crying and grabbing Bruno's shirt. "He has gone insane. He has a gun. I am afraid he's going to kill us all."

"The blood is on the blade," Bruno repeated in a voice so low only he could hear it.

A split second before they heard the explosion the ground shook beneath their feet. The tremor was followed by such a loud blast Bruno had to steady himself to keep Lillian from falling. Next came white hot flames shooting fifty feet into the sky. Bruno turned his head and held Lillian's face into his chest to protect it from the intensity of the blast.

"What in the world was that?" Sheela called out pointing skyward. Bruno cupped his hand above his eyes and looked where she was pointing. Smoke, flames, and pieces of furnishings filled the sky.

"Blood, lots of blood," Bruno said.

Chapter 58

In Washington D.C. at the Department of Justice building, Bruno walked to the Forensic Laboratory and entered the door marked Evidence Storage. Badging a woman at the desk he produced the embossed seal he had removed from the documents bundle in Hudson Halle's kitchen and the key from the certified envelope obtained from Viola McCoy. "I'm Bruno Stach from the Environmental Protection Agency assigned to a Senate Investigation," he said showing the letter of authority signed by the Vice President of the United States. "I wish to retrieve some of our evidence."

The woman closely examined Bruno's credentials and authorization documents as well as the embossed label from the packet. She then went to a computer terminal and typed for several minutes. "This indicates," she pointed to the screen, "that we are storing three fully validated copies of evidence, have you come for all three? And I am sure you are aware you must have the key to the bin."

"That's correct," Bruno nodded producing the key, "You probably know by now Senator Roberts is a lame duck so the Senate is deciding what the next move will be as far as our investigation is concerned." He placed the key on the counter and pushed it in her direction.

"Come with me," she said, he followed her to a room containing storage bins of various sizes. She squinted at the key. "Bin 608," she repeated, "why do they make these numbers so small?"

"Because they're secret numbers," Bruno smiled.

She laughed and then inserted the key into a medium sized bin. Three triplicates, fully verified originals of the same package that Hudson and Kestrel had found were contained therein.

"This will require loading assistance," Bruno said to the woman from behind the desk, If I bring my car around to the dock will you have it ready for me?"

"It will be waiting for you. Be sure to have your badge and your letter of authority out when you come to pick up your evidence at the dock."

"Will do. Thank you."

After loading the packages into his trunk, Bruno drove his rental car directly to his house in Lower Marlboro and mounted the back stairs carrying a large cardboard box marked Senate Investigation. "Can you give me a hand with the door?" he said to the attractive woman just inside holding a cell phone in her hand.

While pushing open the screen, and restraining a puppy with one foot, the woman announced with delight, "I just got off the phone with Lillian and guess what?" LJ said prior to answering her own question and ushering Bruno inside. "Kes and Sylvia got married in a double ceremony out on the beach at Point Dume."

"And the other couple?" Bruno asked while setting the box down on the kitchen table. "And why would anyone get married at a place named Doom? It sounds like the marriage is headed for a grim and terrible fate from the get-go."

"No, D-U-M-E, not D-O-O-M, silly, a Spanish name I think." Lady Jane giggled, in her tinkling way. "It is a place in Malibu - out by Zuma Beach. The other couple was Lillian and Sheela!"

"Well, we're not getting married at any place named Point DOOM no matter how it's spelled," Bruno added dryly.

"Afterwards," LJ went on, "Sylvia climbed on the back of Kes's motorcycle and they headed up the PCH to Oregon. A town called Taft, according to Lillian. She said the newlyweds wedding present from she and Sheela, was a beach cottage overlooking a place called Siletz Bay, near where Kestrel grew up."

"Sheela and Lillian?" Bruno asked," Really, they have money enough to buy a couple a house for a wedding present?"

LJ, looked surprised. "You have not heard? Sheela is the sole heir to her grandfather's billions. Perhaps the wealthiest women in the world! As we speak, Lillian and Sheela are endowing the CCC to where it will soon be a worldwide conservation corporation."

In response Bruno just shook his head and grinned, "Guess I missed that one," he said.

Lady Jane appeared to notice the box that Bruno had placed on the table for the first time.

"What have we here?" she asked pointing toward the box.

"Everything." Bruno said.

He opened the box on the floor in the kitchen. A hand written note fell from between two of the individually wrapped packages. Bruno recognized Jim Reddy's shaky scrawl from the certified green card. "One for the international court in The Hague; one for the Senate Investigation; one for EOL." Reddy's note read. Bruno was fully aware of what "Exposed On Line" was. The name of a secretive organization that leaked documents over the internet to the public. It was alleged to be located in Norway now but nobody seemed to know exactly where.

"So, this is what all the killing was about?" Lady Jane said peering over his shoulder and shaking her head. "What a waste."

"I think we need to deliver these packages in accordance with a murdered FBI agents wishes," Bruno said softly. "Do you want to go to Norway with me?"

"Well, I'm Norwegian on my father's side," LJ smiled.

Then wondering, "Where in Norway?"

"Not sure, maybe that is my last investigation."

The End

About the Author

The author is a former Federal Investigator with over 30 years of experience. His investigations were conducted in Washington, D.C., Maryland, Virginia, and California, as well as various other locations throughout the world. He currently resides near the Central California Coast. He has a degree in political science and a masters of public administration. He also served honorably in the U.S. Air Force in the middle east.

This is a first novel. Although the historical information is factual, the content is fiction and none of the characters are based on actual people or events.